BEST OF THE STRAND MAGAZINE

EDITED BY

ANDREW F. GULLI & LAMIA J. GULLI

BEST OF THE STRAND MAGAZINE

25 YEARS OF TWISTS, TURNS, AND TALES FROM THE MODERN MASTERS OF MYSTERY AND FICTION

BLACKSTONE PUBLISHING

Published in 2025 by Blackstone Publishing
Cover and book design by Larissa Ezell
Illustrated endpapers by Jeffrey B. McKeever

Printed in the United States of America

First edition: 2025
ISBN 979-8-228-01724-5
Fiction / Mystery & Detective / Collections & Anthologies

Version 1

Blackstone Publishing
31 Mistletoe Rd.
Ashland, OR 97520

www.BlackstonePublishing.com

To our older brothers for indulging (and encouraging) our bibliomania from the beginning, and for so much else.

And to Buddy, the beautiful girl parrot, loyal employee of *The Strand*, who brought us so much love, laughter, and joy.

TABLE OF CONTENTS

FOREWORD

ALEXANDER MCCALL SMITH

There really is no mystery here: The mystery story, in any of its guises, is very clearly and unambiguously one of the most enduring and popular literary genres. In libraries, it's almost always at the top, or near the top, of the list of most borrowed titles. In bookstores, the mystery section is hard to miss as it often occupies more shelf space than any other. From time to time, other popular enthusiasms may claim the limelight—variants of fantasy, romance, or even fantasy-romance. However, these do not have quite the same staying power as mystery, and few examples better illustrate the permanence of its appeal than that pillar of the genre—*The Strand Magazine*.

The Strand is synonymous with the mystery short story. Fans of Sir Arthur Conan Doyle will not need to be reminded that it was in the pages of *The Strand* that *The Hound of the Baskervilles* first appeared. Many other Sherlock Holmes short stories were published there as well, along with the iconic illustrations by Sidney Paget that defined Holmes's appearance for generations of readers. Conan Doyle, of course, is not the only distinguished author to have been published by the magazine; over the years, the list of contributors to *The Strand* has included numerous writers who enjoyed a widespread reputation both within and beyond the genre. Graham Greene, Leo Tolstoy, D. H. Lawrence, Agatha

Christie, Dorothy L. Sayers, W. W. Jacobs, P. G. Wodehouse, Rudyard Kipling, and H. G. Wells have all been contributors. And if one looks at the list of authors whose work is featured in this volume, one sees that the editors have continued the tradition of casting a net wide enough to catch a rich variety of household names.

All of which gives rise to an important point: There is a regrettable tendency in some literary circles to look down the nose at the mystery genre and to treat it as an inferior branch of literary endeavour—one not quite deserving of serious attention. This view carries a distinct whiff of intellectual snobbery. Mystery fiction is a broad church, encompassing an exceptionally wide range of material. Yes, there is mystery fiction that is clearly ephemeral—firmly in the potboiler category—but there is also a great deal that can hold its head high in any literary company. These days, indeed, such is the competition for an audience that anything achieving mainstream publication almost certainly has to meet high standards. Many of the most successful mystery writers produce work of considerable depth and intellectual merit—fiction that, at its best, offers characterisation and insight equal to anything found in the so-called literary novel. Mystery authors often delve deeply into the human condition and the dilemmas we face in our moral lives—dilemmas that transcend culture and era, and speak to the universality of the human experience. I often think of the late Patricia Highsmith as an exemplar of this ability to combine entertainment with serious psychological observation. While Highsmith's forte was crime and the psychology of the sociopath, she used the form of the crime novel to explore the complexities of identity, morality, and the human psyche, compelling readers to question their own moral compasses—and in doing so, ensured her work resonated far beyond the confines of crime fiction. I might cite other examples, but none speak more clearly than the writers featured in this collection and the calibre of their work.

The Strand had been entertaining readers for six decades when it went—temporarily—out of print in 1950. There was admittedly a hiatus after that, but you can't keep a good magazine down, and to the delight of mystery readers everywhere, the title resurfaced in time for a new millennium—revived under the editorship of Andrew Gulli, Lamia Gulli, and the dedicated team at *The Strand* who are committed to preserving and expanding the magazine's rich literary tradition. Now an important anniversary is added to the history of this remarkable magazine. It is an anniversary that will be applauded by fans of the mystery story not only in the United States, where the magazine found its new home, but wherever mystery or crime fiction is enjoyed and celebrated. And that is effectively everywhere.

Of course, as we celebrate this milestone in the journey of the mystery short story, a familiar question inevitably arises. What explains the perennial appeal of the mystery? A great deal of ink has been spilled on this topic by various commentators and critics. A classic analysis, in my view, is an essay written by W. H. Auden in 1948 and published in *Harper's Magazine*. Auden was not only one of the greatest poets of the twentieth century—he was also a self-confessed addict of the mystery story. His particular fondness for the classic English variety is reflected in the title of his piece, *The Guilty Vicarage*. Yet what he has to say about the enduring appeal of the genre reaches far beyond village greens and vicarages; his insights apply across all corners of mystery fiction and remain as relevant today as when he first wrote them.

Auden's theory of mystery fiction—he uses the term "detective story"—places a philosophical or moral issue at its heart. A murder occurs that disturbs the state of innocence that prevailed prior to its occurrence. Then the mystery begins. Auden points out that in a Greek tragedy the audience knows the truth all along, whereas in the mystery, the reader usually does not know who is responsible (although there is a certain frisson in knowing that the guilty person knows that he or she is guilty). The intellectual puzzle then unfolds, as enjoyably as any other intellectual puzzle—such as a cryptic crossword. At the end, though, the moral structure becomes apparent. The case is solved; we find out who did it, and the perpetrator is brought to justice. Or used to be. It is possible that the guilty get away with it in the contemporary mystery story—Tom Ripley was never caught, remember—but in general the reader wants to see the scales of justice balanced. Auden makes much of that requirement.

Auden's emphasis on the moral structure of the mystery story remains important today. The world we live in is one that, at times, seems characterised by a lack of stability and order. Who among us does not feel anxiety in the face of the challenges to coherence that loom so large in our lives? The mystery story is, in many ways, an antidote to all that. The crime is the disruption—a challenge not only to order but to the very ideas of innocence and virtue. The resolution is the reassertion of right, of justice. We yearn for that resolution; we refuse to give up on the idea of justice. The mystery story satisfies our desire to see wrongdoing confronted and set right. Its message is that wrongdoing will eventually be uncovered and punished. Just as a piece of music must resolve, so too must stories.

Of course, in real life, it is not always so simple. Wrongdoing, in its various forms, may be emboldened. Evil may mock those whom it oppresses. The guilty may bestride their tawdry empires—and do so with shocking impunity. But we take comfort in this: The agents of justice may be girding their loins. We should never give up hope. The mystery story usually ends with justice on top, and whatever they say to the contrary, life often imitates art.

INTRODUCTION

ANDREW F. GULLI

Whoever claimed experience makes publishing easier never put out a magazine. Between issues that begin to take on a life of their own—unexpected themes suddenly emerging—late nights, last-minute crises, and the self-doubt that begins to creep in twelve hours before going to press, one thing becomes very clear: Experience is no guarantee of ease. Still, I've never wanted to do anything else. I have had the chance to meet and publish, and even befriend, many of my literary heroes. And the thrill of seeing a new issue just back from the printer never gets old. Choosing the stories for this collection brought back the same feeling I had over twenty-five years ago when I held our very first issue and reminded me again why I've kept at it all these years.

A lot of the discussions about these short stories occurred in restaurants in either New York City or Michigan. R. L. Stine and I discussed his idea for "A Sad Mistake," his horror story that first appeared in *The Strand* and now appears in this collection, while enjoying positively vulgar slices of banana cream pie in Midtown Manhattan. Jeff Deaver and I discussed his story while grabbing a beer at the bar of a restored 1850s stagecoach inn inside Greenfield Village in Dearborn, Michigan. And in the case of Alexander McCall Smith, we talked about his story while enjoying a leisurely dinner in downtown Ann Arbor while he and my sister, Lamia, mused that the word *scamorza* (which appeared on the menu) would make a perfect name for a character. Other conversations took place at conferences: At the Edgars one year, Jo Nesbø and I had a long discussion about another work that appears here—his short story "Animal Planet."

It's said you shouldn't meet your heroes, but in my experience, they've not only been great writers—they've also been great people. There have been so many wonderful instances that should probably fill a memoir someday, but I will share a few here. During a difficult period, when our mother was very ill, it was John Mortimer's Rumpole—with his irreverence for authority, snobbery, and self-importance, and his ability to take life's disappointments with wry humor and a lack of bitterness—who got me through. Meeting John Mortimer was one of the highlights of my career. He was kind, highly intelligent, and interested in everyone around him and what they had to say. Over lunch at his club in London, our conversation ranged from the latest gossip to philosophy, religion, and politics. At one point, after discovering that our server was from Morocco, John struck up a conversation with the waiter about his homeland, where John had once kept a home. He also reassured me between courses that he was putting the final touches on a story he was due to send us.

In fact, almost every story in this collection has its own backstory, and each writer a unique relationship with Lamia, with me, and with *The Strand*. The great Catherine Aird—whose story "Due Diligence" appears here—was an ardent admirer of art and cityscapes, and often advised us on the magazine's cover art. Over tea with Michael Bond (author of "Monsieur Pamplemousse and the Grey Diamonds," which also appears in this collection) and his wife, Sue, I admitted that I could no longer eat in a restaurant without wondering what Monsieur Pamplemousse and Pommes Frites would make of the place. Lamia and James Lee Burke used to exchange emails about politics, history, and the finer points of editing while she was preparing "Deportees" for publication in *The Strand*. And when we received H. G. Wells's manuscript for "The Haunted Ceiling," we were elated, awestruck, happily trying to decipher his handwriting while listening to the 1960 film version of *The Time Machine*—with its unforgettable soundtrack—playing on a loop in the background.

While many of the stories in this collection were first discussed over meals or drinks in restaurants and bars, the idea for the book itself came out of a Zoom call with Blackstone execs Rick Bleiweiss, Anthony Goff, and Greg Boguslawski. There would be no *Best of* The Strand Magazine without Rick and Anthony, and of course CEO Josh Stanton. It was Rick who first put the idea on the table, declaring bluntly, "Twenty-five years of *The Strand*? There has to be a collection of your best stories!" It was Anthony Goff—a visionary publisher with the strategic mind of a chess player—who gave the project shape and made it happen. And it was Josh Stanton's leadership at Blackstone that fostered the kind of environment where a book like this could be made.

Blackstone started out as an audiobook publisher. If ever there was proof that print books are still very much in vogue, it is Blackstone's evolution into a *book*-publishing powerhouse in the last ten years. And *how* we read stories does matter. There's unmatched joy in curling up with an actual book—or magazine. The art on the cover, the weight of the paper, the act of turning a page and suddenly finding yourself in the middle of a gritty New York City crime scene. Turn another and you're in Holmes and Watson's sitting room at 221B Baker Street. Turn yet another and you're in the German countryside with a forlorn doctor driven to madness after recklessly thinking he could create life.

Fiction will always brighten lives—in *The Strand*'s case, adding a delicious tinge of uncertainty and paranoia along the way. For us, there will be more late nights, more editorial debates, more existential threats to face in the world of publishing. Yet the challenges will always be outweighed by a subscriber's thank-you note or walking down a major avenue, spotting *The Strand* in a bookstore window, and wanting to tap a stranger's shoulder and say, "Hey, we did this!"

Some things never grow old: humanity's need to solve a mystery—and the occasional ego rush that comes with it.

INTRODUCTION

LAMIA J. GULLI

From the cold, stark Nordic noir of Jo Nesbø's "Animal Planet" to the smoldering sensuality of Tennessee Williams's "The Summer Woman"; from the gritty realism of Michael Connelly's Los Angeles in "Blue on Black" to a sunlit town square and corporate espionage in Mexico City in Jonathan Rabb's "Santa Muerte"; and from Ray Bradbury's Dust Bowl in the haunting "Sixty-Six" to the halls of the Old Bailey in John Mortimer's witty "Rumpole and the Old Familiar Faces"—these works, along with the other stories in this collection, have helped form the rich tapestry that has been *The Strand Magazine* for the last twenty-five years.

In these pages you will find many of the detectives you all know and love (and some new ones); gems we've uncovered by literary greats like Tennessee Williams, H. G. Wells, and Shirley Jackson; mysteries by bestselling authors; and equally intriguing tales by lesser-known writers. You'll find the haunting lyricism of James Lee Burke, the intricate plotting and pacing of Jeffery Deaver, the layered psychological nuance of Joyce Carol Oates, the understated wit of Alexander McCall Smith, and of course the humor and ingenuity of our very own modern-day Conan Doyle—John M. Floyd. What Conan Doyle was to H. Greenhough Smith and the old *Strand*, John is to Andrew and me and the new *Strand*. He has, for the last quarter century, consistently turned out inventive, tightly written tales—always with his signature wry twist at the end. He's a favorite among our readers and editors alike because he never fails to deliver a great story.

Running *The Strand* has brought us some exhilarating highs, too many late nights wondering why we chose this path, and the constant negotiation and fine-tuning required to keep pace with a rapidly changing world. Within a few years of our first issue came the dawn of the digital age. Invariably, there were those who believed it would mean the end of print publications. For the last twenty-plus years, each issue of our widely read and much-loved print magazine has been our resounding and consistent response to that prediction. If there is anything the last two decades have taught us, it is that there will always be a market for physical media—books, magazines, even vinyl records—tangible objects that visually evoke the atmosphere and character of the works they contain. It's what we do with each issue of *The Strand*—aided by a loyal team of editors, artists, and authors who are as devoted to the magazine's literary heritage as we are—and what Blackstone Publishing has honored with this beautifully constructed anniversary collection, bringing together twenty-nine of the finest stories from those years.

A magazine is only as good as the people who work for it, and since the very beginning, we have been incredibly fortunate in that regard, especially when it's come to our copy editors. *The Strand* has benefited from two of the best copy editors around: Anne Schluender for our first eight years, and Christian Lewis since 2008. Anne was unafraid to strike through even the most famous author's words if she thought it would better serve a story. Her loyalty was, first and foremost, to the written word, and she retained a healthy irreverence for whoever's name graced the byline of a story she was editing. Several of the stories in this collection were carefully copyedited by Anne during those early years.

Christian Lewis joined *The Strand* during a time of change for the magazine, just a few years before we began releasing previously unpublished works by literary legends like Dashiell Hammett,

Graham Greene, and Mark Twain. He brought to *The Strand* a deep well of literary and historical knowledge, as well as a remarkable ability to rework a passage without losing the author's voice. He's caught historical inconsistencies, clarified obscure references, and strengthened most of the stories you will read in these pages, namely those from the last seventeen years. He has never shied away from offering his frank opinions, challenging us or disagreeing when it's been in the interests of making *The Strand* a better magazine. With his quiet consistency, he has become an indispensable part of *The Strand* as well as a trusted adviser—and a very good friend.

Of course, we wouldn't be here without our readers. The support we've received over the years from our loyal fans is what makes this job so fulfilling. Even in my most exhausted moments—the night before an issue goes to press, looking over proofs, drunk on caffeine (and late-night chocolate-chip cookies), wondering, *Why am I doing this?*—a letter or email from a subscriber, telling us how much they look forward to each issue, never fails to make me stop and smile and think, *Ah. They know what I'm doing. They get it.* And that makes it all worth it.

Are these stories "the best" of *The Strand*? It is, after all, a subjective term. What we have done is try to put together the best of every kind: dark and light, serious and humorous, big city and small town, a dash of horror here and there, and stories set in a variety of locales and eras—postrevolutionary France, Sherlock Holmes's London, postwar Rome, modern-day America. Some of the stories are quirky, some weird; some will appeal to many, and some to only a few. Andrew and I each have our favorites. The result is a collection that largely reflects what we try to do in each issue of *The Strand*—give our readers a broad range of stories that will entertain, provoke, and echo beyond the pages. So it feels only fitting to close by paraphrasing here the words of *The Strand*'s esteemed managing editor—Andrew Gulli, my very own brother—at the end of each of his editorials: We hope you enjoy the book.

BLUE ON BLACK

MICHAEL CONNELLY

Bosch had left her alone in the room for almost an hour. It was time. He knocked once on the door and entered. Rachel Walling looked up from the table. She had the photos spread out across it so she could view them all at once.

He moved into the room and sat down across from her.

"It looks like you like the photos," he said.

"There isn't much else here," she said.

She waved her hand dismissively at the record of his work on the case. He nodded. She was right. He didn't have jack.

"You see anything? You said you could only give me an hour. I don't want to—"

"But you knew I would start to look at the photos and I'd get caught up in it. That's why you called me, Harry."

"No, I called you because I'm desperate. I know this is the guy. I can put him in close proximity to both women. He was following them. He's got the history and profile—the guy's an apex predator. But after that, I've got nothing. So what have you got, Rachel? Can you help me or not?"

She dropped her eyes from Bosch's without answering. She returned her focus to the photos. Denninger's prior mug shots and prison ID shots from the rape conviction. Denninger posing with a number of prize fish he'd caught in Santa Monica Bay. Denninger on his boat. On the Avalon Pier on Catalina. Photos of his home, inside and out.

"He likes to fish," she finally said.

"Yeah. That and poker. He told us those are his hobbies."

"Does he own this boat?"

"Uh-huh. He keeps it down in Marina del Rey on a trailer lot. We were thinking he probably used the boat to dump the bodies. Because we sure haven't found anything in his house or pickup. Nothing on land."

"And you searched the boat."

"Yeah, we searched it. And got nothing. We took it to the police garage and put it in the blackout room. Lumed the whole thing and it glowed like Christmas. Blood everywhere, but it was all fish blood. Not a drop of human blood, not even his own."

She nodded and picked up the photo taken off the ATM video that showed the first missing woman, Olivia Martz, making a withdrawal. It was taken through a fisheye lens, designed to capture the entire environment around the ATM. Denninger was behind her and to the right, probably never thinking he would be on the film.

"So," Walling said. "You have his prior record as a sexual predator and then the two videos. The parking garage video puts him in the Grove at the same time Allison Beaumont was there on the day she disappeared, and likewise you have the ATM video of Olivia Martz making a withdrawal that puts him right behind her at the Third Street Promenade. Together this got you probable cause for search warrants, and the searches turned up nothing."

Bosch nodded in defeat.

"That's about the size of it."

"Are you watching Denninger?"

"We have a loose tail on him for now. But that won't last forever. There's no overtime left in the budget. That's why I called you."

"You should have called Behavioral. You'd get the whole package from them."

"Yeah, in about six months. How many more girls might go missing by then? Look, Rachel, I know this isn't your beat anymore, but you're good at it and you're fast. That's why I called you. Now is there anything in all of that that can help me? Your lunch hour's over."

She glanced at her watch to confirm the time and picked up one of the photos. It was the one of Denninger on his boat, holding up a fish with both hands. The seas were choppy in the background and the spine of an island rose in the distance. Catalina, probably.

"When I was in Behavioral, a significant number of the predators we encountered had hobbies like hunting or fishing. The percentage was higher than the percentage in the general population. It wasn't anything we could really quantify, but it was there. It has to do with the personality—the tracking and baiting. And, of course, the killing. I noticed that of the two, the fishermen committed crimes that took more thinking, had more finesse. The hunters committed crimes of stalking and disorganized abduction. The fishermen were smarter, were more organized."

"Great, so what are you saying, this guy is too smart for us?"

"No, I'm just saying Denninger's smart. He prepared for the time that he would become the focus of law enforcement. He was ready."

"Smart enough not to leave any evidence, to drop the bodies over the side and sink 'em so we'd never find 'em."

"Look at all these photos of the fish he's caught."

She moved the photos around on the table, turning them so they would face Bosch.

"Yeah, we got them from him. He had them on a bulletin board in his kitchen. He was proud of them. He said we could have them."

"Really?"

"He said he had plenty more."

"He's touching them."

"What?"

"In every picture he is holding up the fish or at least touching it in some way."

Bosch leaned forward over the table. She was right. He hadn't noticed this—wasn't sure what it meant.

"Okay," he said.

"Trophies. He likes trophies. He likes to touch his trophies. To be close."

"That's what we were hoping, that he had kept something from the girls and we'd make the link that way. Driver's license, lock of hair . . . anything. But like I told you, we got nothing. His place is clean. His pickup is clean. His boat is clean. The garage where he works is clean. He's Mr. Clean."

"Sometimes the trophy isn't a lock of hair. It's the real thing."

"You're saying he kept the bodies? Impossible. We would have found them. We've put six hundred hours into this case so far. No bodies. He dumped them in the Pacific and we'll never find them again."

Walling nodded, seemingly in agreement.

"I worked more than one case where the bodies were buried and the killer would return to visit. I had another where the bodies were found and buried by their families. Each night of the week the killer would go to a different cemetery to visit his victims. That's where we caught him. It's a strong attraction to be with his conquests, his trophies. Maybe it's the same with water. Maybe he weighted them and they are exactly where he put them. He visits them on the water."

"Yeah, but how would he mark the locations? He'd have to—"

Bosch stopped as he realized the answer to his own question. Walling handed him the photo of Denninger smiling at the camera and holding up the fish with two hands.

"The console," she said.

Bosch studied the photograph. The photo had been taken from the stern by an unknown photographer. The boat was a twenty-eight-foot open fisher, with a center console and a T-top that offered partial shade from the sun. Denninger was standing by the starboard gunwale, holding up his shining trophy fish. Next to him was the console. Scattered across the top in the shelter behind the windshield was a variety of fishing equipment. Bosch saw pliers, thick rubber gloves, a knife, and a plastic tray filled with lures and leaders and hooks. There was also a small electronic device with an LED screen that Bosch had previously dismissed as Denninger's cell phone.

But now, as he looked at the photograph, Bosch saw that Denninger had his phone clipped to his belt. The device on the console was something else.

"GPS?" he said.

"Looks like it," Walling said. "Small, handheld, perfect for marking fishing spots."

"And the locations of bodies if you planned to come back to visit."

Walling nodded. Adrenaline started to pour into Bosch's bloodstream. Walling had led him right to a solid break.

"There was no GPS in the possessions we searched," he said.

"He hid it somewhere," she said. "He doesn't need trophies. He just needs his spots. So he can visit the girls."

Bosch stood up and started pacing in the small room.

"Where could it be?" he said, more to himself than Walling.

"Who took these photos?"

"We don't know."

"Well, he's got at least one fishing partner. I'd start there."

Bosch nodded.

"Rachel, this is a big help. Thank you."

"The FBI is always glad to help."

Bosch pulled out his phone and made a call. Jackson picked up immediately.

"Where is he?"

"He's home. He's gotta know that we're watching him. Did your agent pal come up with anything?"

"Yeah, we're looking for a handheld GPS device. It's in one of the pictures. He marked his fishing spots and he might have marked the spots where he put the girls. I didn't see it on any of the search inventories and I know it wasn't on the boat. You or Tim have any ideas?"

There was a long silence. Bosch heard muffled voices.

"Rick, you there?"

"Yeah, yeah, I'm here. I was just telling Tim. I think we know where it is."

Bosch's eyes darted to Rachel and he held back his first response, which was to ask why the hell the GPS device hadn't come up before if they had known about it.

"Tell me," he said instead.

"When we interviewed the guys Denninger plays poker with, a couple of them said they hadn't seen him since he lost a big pot a couple weeks ago and stormed off."

"Okay."

"Well, you know, we asked how much he lost and they told us he lost like six hundred dollars and all his numbers. I said what do you mean, numbers? And they said his fishing spots. They didn't say anything about a GPS device and it didn't occur to me that—"

"Who won the pot?"

"I don't know but we can find out. I'll start calling those guys back."

"Do it. We need those numbers. Call me as soon as you have a name."

Bosch closed the phone and looked at Walling.

"Time to go fishing."

Bosch felt queasy. The police dive boat was rocking on three-foot rollers. They had been out almost two hours on Santa Monica Bay and were on the seventh location. Denninger's GPS had twenty-two waypoints stored on it. And it was shaping up to be a long day on rough seas.

Harry studied the blue-black water and waited. The captain had said they were in thirty-two feet of water. After a while he looked back toward the coast and saw the bloom of smog that hovered above the city. He thought about having spent his whole life underneath it, and it only made him feel more ill.

He quickly crossed to the other side of the boat and leaned over the side. The captain had given him specific instructions. If he were to get sick, he had to lean over the port side. That way the current would take his vomit away from the dive zone. He heaved twice, two deep exorcisms from the gut. He watched the current take away what was left of his breakfast.

He felt his phone buzz in his pocket. He wiped his mouth with one hand and pulled the phone with the other.

"Bosch."

"Harry, are you all right?"

It was Walling.

"Yeah. Just a little seasick."

"Yes. I wanted to check in. You're still out there?"

"Unfortunately. We're on the seventh location. Nothing so far."

"You sound terrible. Maybe you should go in."

"No, I'm here till we find them. Or till we don't."

"They can look without you. You're not diving."

"If they find the girls, I need to be here." He said it in a tone that ended the debate.

"Okay, Harry. Let me know, all right?"

"I'll call you."

By the time they got to the eleventh location, the sun was high, the wind had died away, and both the seas and Bosch's stomach had calmed. The water had changed color too. It was a lighter blue in the sunlight. More inviting, less severe. Bosch sat on the stern and watched the air bubbles boil to the surface. There were four divers thirty-nine feet down in low-visibility water. The boat captain, the forensics guy, and two deck hands were inside the cabin. Ever since Bosch had gotten sick, they had left him by himself.

Bosch heard splashing and turned to look behind him, off the stern. Two of the divers had surfaced. Between them they were holding up a body wrapped in a plastic tarp and weighted with chains.

Bosch quickly turned back toward the cabin and waved to get the attention of the others. "Hey!"

He then moved to the gunwale door. Before he could open it, one of the deck hands did. Bosch stepped back and watched as the two divers made their grim delivery. The man from forensics followed their progress with a video camera.

The deck hands grabbed the package by the chains and pulled it aboard, sliding it across the deck. It was grim duty, and water slopped over their shoes.

Olivia or Allison? Bosch thought.

Just as the question ran through his mind, the other two divers surfaced off the stern. They too carried a package of plastic and chains and moved with it toward the gunwale door.

The first two divers backed away from the boat rather than attempt to climb aboard. That was when Bosch knew that Denninger had put more than two bodies into the water here. He went to the corner of the stern and called out to them.

"How many?"

One diver removed his respirator and called back, holding up an open hand.

"Five more coming up."

Bosch just nodded and pulled out his phone to start making calls.

Jackson answered right away.

"Where's Denninger?"

"In the house. You find the girls?"

"Looks like it. We've got seven bodies. We're going to be here awhile."

"Holy Christ!"

"We'll probably have to check all the other spots too."

"Should we take him down?"

Bosch thought for a moment. The location had come from the GPS device that Denninger had lost in a poker game. There were gaps in the evidence line, but it still strongly pointed the finger of guilt at Denninger. Even if the recovered bodies did not include those of Olivia Martz and Allison Beaumont, they would make a case against Denninger.

Another detective—or a prosecutor—might move more cautiously. Keep the surveillance on the suspect, recover all the bodies, and work the evidence until it tightly wrapped around their man. But Bosch couldn't see giving Denninger another minute of freedom.

"Yeah," he said. "Take the bastard down."

"You got it."

"Call me when you're five by five."

Bosch closed the phone and then reopened it. He needed to alert the medical examiner's office that he had a multiple-homicide case and that investigators would need to meet the police boat at the dock. But first he called Rachel Walling back. He needed to tell her that her read on the file and photos had led to the break that blew the case wide open. He needed to thank her again.

As he waited for her to answer, the sun went behind a cloud and the water turned dark again. It was a cold blue on black, and it would always remind Bosch of death.

WHERE THE EVIDENCE LIES

JEFFERY DEAVER

"Mayday, mayday. This is Horizonjet Eight-Five-Eight-Four on IFR from Miami to Rio de Janeiro. Do you read me, San Juan Center?"

"Go ahead, Five-Eight-Four. San Juan Center."

"I'm descending through nine thousand feet. Not sure where . . . Hell, losing power. I'm declaring an emergency."

"Roger, Five-Eight-Four. We have you. Do you want vectors to Muñoz Marín Airport?"

"Let me . . . I'll get this under control. Yes, vectors to airport."

"San Juan Center to Five-Eight-Four. We're holding arrivals and departures. We're vectoring now . . . What's the nature of your emergency?"

"Power loss. Fire, I think. There was a bang, it sounded like. Aft. I'm—I'm, okay, descending fast through seven thousand feet. I don't know."

"We have your position, Five-Eight-Four. We're vectoring you to—"

"Descending . . . I can't slow rate of descent. Through five thousand feet. Not responsive. How far am I from the airport?"

"You're twenty-two miles from the airport, Five-Eight-Four. Can you make it?"

"Negative."

"All right. We're alerting Coast Guard air-sea rescue. They're getting your position, Five-Eight-Four."

"Jesus. Descending through one thousand. Rate's too high. No power. I—"

"Five-Eight-Four? . . . Do you copy? . . . Do you copy? . . . Any traffic in area north of Marín airport, ten miles out, do you see any sign of an aircraft down?"

Eastern Dade Airport was a small facility near the Atlantic Ocean. It featured a runway, about 3,000 feet long, big enough for small jets, though the majority of the two-dozen planes parked on tarmac were one- and two-engine props.

There was definitely some Everglades ambiance in the area—mangroves, royal palm, cabbage palm, live oak, gumbo-limbo, and West Indian mahogany, as well as orchids, bromeliads, and ferns. Lincoln Rhyme, presently in this part of Florida to lecture to the county police about forensics, had even spotted an alligator.

"Look," he said to Amelia Sachs, his partner—in both the professional and personal senses. She'd leaned over his wheelchair in the accessible van and gazed at the shallow canal in which a bored-looking gator sat in the humid heat, seemingly too tired to even think about chomping down whatever bored-looking gators ate.

His caregiver, Thom Reston, drove the van in a slow circle around this part of the field and then paused, as directed by Rhyme.

Sachs said, "There's a rumor they have those in the sewers of New York, you know. Parents buy them for kids and then flush them down the toilet once the kids get bored with them."

"Really?" Rhyme said. The details of the flora and fauna of this part of the state grew less interesting; he was more intrigued about where they were headed presently. His eyes took in the airfield once more.

The three of them were en route to the airport because a detective with the local sheriff's department had approached Rhyme after one of his lectures in the county building and asked for some help. Paul Gillette was a trim 45-year-old with impressive posture, a hairstyle that an army major would have sported, and a face that seemed incapable of smiling.

Despite that quality, though, he'd revealed a droll sense of humor by asking Rhyme which he'd prefer as a thank you for the lecture: a coupon to the local Red Lobster or an incident report on a local businessman who'd just died in what might or might not be an accidental plane crash.

Rhyme had replied, "Hm. Murdered crustacean or murdered human. I'll pick the latter. You up for that, Sachs?"

"Sure. Nothing pressing back in New York."

The lecture at the Dade County East Sheriff's Office was finished anyway and so Rhyme agreed to stay for an extra day or two and help out on the Stephen Nash homicide investigation.

Why not?

He'd enjoyed the trip here and had for the first time tasted stone crabs. Quite the delicacy. And the rum in Florida seemed better than the rum anywhere else but the Bahamas.

At Rhyme's direction, Thom now piloted the accessible van into the airport itself and aimed for the unmarked police car at the far end of the field.

According to Gillette, it appeared possible that a bomb had exploded in Nash's plane before it took off from here, though a mechanical malfunction could have been the cause. As they were driving in, Rhyme noted that it was unlikely that a bomber could have breached the perimeter fence and not been spotted. Or injured—the fence was topped with razor wire. Rhyme also noted cameras—facing down and out. That meant if anybody did get in to plant the bomb it was most likely—not certain, but likely—an inside job.

They drove to the one hangar at the airport, on the far eastern edge. It was a small windowless structure, doorless at the rear, which backed up to the water, and open at the other end. Presumably so that the relentless wind from the Atlantic, not far away, wouldn't blast the aircraft and workers inside.

Thom parked near the squad car and he, Rhyme, and Sachs exited the van and met the detective on the tarmac. A fierce storm had descended upon the area yesterday; it had passed but the wind still buffeted the law enforcers and the aide. Rhyme brushed his dark hair from his eyes with his one working appendage—his right arm.

"Thanks again, Mr. Rhyme. Detective Sachs."

"'Lincoln' and 'Amelia' are fine. What was the aircraft?"

"One of those new ones, personal jets. Horizonjet, twin engine, mounted in the rear. Real small, seats four."

"Nobody else on board?"

"No. For those planes you don't need a co-pilot. The autopilot's so good they do most of the work."

He added that this secure area was owned by Southern Flight Services, a fixed-base operator—a company that provided ground services to upscale private pilots.

Rhyme was familiar with such operations from a prior case and noted that this was a shoestring FBO. There was only one jet and two twin engine prop planes parked here now. And they were covered with leaf-strewn tarps. It seemed they'd been there for a long time.

"So, Lincoln, we've kept the scene secure. What equipment do you need? I'll call forensics and get you whatever. We've got some pretty good stuff."

Rhyme was looking at the dim hangar. Good. Concrete floors, which would retain footprints. And it looked like the place hadn't been swept for a week. Any trace would still be there.

"Where exactly was the plane?"

Gillette pointed—to the middle of the rain-soaked tarmac.

"It wasn't in the hangar?" Sachs asked.

"No."

"At any time?"

"No, sir."

Lincoln Rhyme grimaced. The storm would have destroyed any evidence of anybody planting a bomb on the airplane—tread marks would have been the best source of information. But trace evidence too. The bomber—if there was a bomber—might have shed trace evidence.

The storm, which Rhyme remembered clearly, had not exactly been a hurricane but the winds had been close to sixty miles an hour and the rain had fallen for hours.

He gave a sour laugh. "I'm sorry, Detective. But there's nothing left. Weather is one of the worst contaminators of crime scenes. This storm now'd be enough to destroy all the trace. Yesterday's downpour? Nothing'd survive."

"Oh."

Sachs laughed. "Thought he was a miracle worker, hm?"

"Guess I kind of did. Your lectures were pretty damn impressive."

Still, Rhyme reflected, this was only a secondary crime scene. The more important one was the plane itself. However powerful the improvised explosive device had been, it would have left bits of trace on the wreckage of the plane that had been recovered. There would be fingerprints, possibly, chemical residue profiling, even a bomb maker's signature—a unique construction pattern that ties a bomb to its builder.

Rhyme explained this to Gilette.

"Ah, well, that's the problem, Mr. . . . That's the problem, Lincoln. The plane didn't break up. Whatever the explosion was, it didn't blow it up, just destroyed the flight controls. It hit the water but stayed intact and sank."

"Well, that's okay. Water won't necessarily destroy any evidence." He frowned. "Unless you don't know where it is."

"Oh, we do."

"Good."

"Not really. It's at the bottom of the Puerto Rican Trench."

"I don't know what that is."

"The deepest part of the Atlantic Ocean. About twenty-eight thousand feet under water. Twice as deep as the *Titanic*. We can't raise the plane. And there's no way to get to where the evidence lies."

That's the problem, Lincoln . . .

They had moved into the hangar to get out of the wind. The place was deserted at the moment. Thom waited nearby as Rhyme and Sachs spoke with Gillette.

"I'm not sure how I can help you, Detective. You're asking my advice on a case where there's no evidence. My expertise is forensics."

"I heard your lectures, Lincoln. You've got a mind that's, well, like nobody else. I was hoping you could just give us your insights. The NTSB—the Safety Board—they'll be here tomorrow. I was hoping we could have something to tell 'em."

Sachs was turning to Rhyme with a smile. "You like your challenges, Rhyme. Doesn't get any more challenging than this."

She had a point there.

And what could it hurt?

He shrugged, one of the few physical gestures he was capable of. "All right, we'll give it a shot. Now, any witnesses to the crash itself?"

"A container ship, not too far away. All they saw was the plane come in and crash land and go under before any doors opened. They changed course and steamed over to the spot. But there was nothing there—just a little oil."

"Ah, oil?" Then he frowned. "But they wouldn't have collected it. It's all gone now."

"I'd guess," Gillette said. "And the way the currents run, the Coast Guard was sure the plane was five miles down in about a half hour. They had search and rescue combing the area, but no sign of anything."

"Do you have the last transmission?"

"Sure. On my computer. I'll get it."

He went out to his car and returned a minute later. He called up an audio file of the exchange between Nash and air traffic control.

Those in the hangar remained silent as they listened to the tragedy unfolding. Gillette shut it off.

"Well, I think a preliminary question is: Why don't you think it was an accident? Nash didn't mention a bomb. He just said 'bang.'"

"Sure, it could've been a malfunction. But I'm suspicious by nature. And I looked into Nash's life last night. He had enemies."

Who doesn't? Rhyme thought.

"Now, there's an ex. Sally Nash. Divorced two years and under a restraining order. She's still *Nash*—kept her married name. Never let go."

Rhyme asked, "He had an affair? He dumped her?"

"Nope. The other way around. She cheated on him and when he found out he filed for divorce. Didn't ask for money or anything, but wanted out. Still, she was incensed that he'd wanted to split up. Go figure."

"Any threats?"

"From time to time. Never amounted to much. But he called us a few times to have the deputies go out there and remind her of the restraining order."

"Okay. An angry ex. Who else?"

"Nash was in a dispute with his business partner. After he found the man was talking to competitors. At least, those were the facts in court. It was for a few million dollars but I'm not sure that's worth killing somebody for."

"Angry ex–*business* partner."

"What was his business—Nash's?" Sachs asked.

Gillette chuckled. "I really couldn't tell you. He owned companies that made components that went into other components. Apparently, he was pretty good at coming up with parts like that. Components. Nothing sexy. But he made a ton of money."

"Any other suspects?" she asked.

"He'd had problems with a stalker. A woman he dated. Her story is she's sort of a gold digger—do you still say that nowadays? Anyway, he walked away, and she threatened him a few times. Attacked him once but it was more throwing a glass of wine in his face at a fancy restaurant than blowing him up."

"Bad choices with the ladies, it seems," Sachs offered.

Gillette continued, "And Nash was serving on a grand jury in Orlando and so we wondered if that exposed him to threats. But they were pretty mundane cases. Mugging, some drug cases. Lot of them. But low level. Real low. Getting a bomb into a plane? I looked at the indictments and it just didn't fit—taking a measure that extreme."

"No obvious motive," Sachs said. "And stalkers and exes—ex-wives, that is—don't really have much access to IED makers. But you can find just about anything on the internet nowadays. Maybe the most likely explanation *is* mechanical failure."

"Should say we're exploring that with the manufacturer. They're going to run some simulations. They weren't optimistic about finding anything, not without the plane. I checked all of those folks out—the ex-wife and the others—and nobody was in town yesterday."

Rhyme then asked, "Assuming there was an IED, why do you think it was planted here?"

"Security in Orlando's a lot tighter than here. That's where Nash keeps the plane. Even the private aviation areas are swept with dogs and explosives detectors. Here—well, like I said, deputies make the rounds occasionally and that's it."

"Let's go through the details of how somebody could've gotten an IED on board."

He wheeled to the front of the hangar and looked out over the tarmac, the chain link fence, the buildings on the other side of the highway.

Gillette explained. In the short time Nash's jet had been parked here, there had been only four people inside the fenced area, with access to it. Three employees of the FBO and the deputy making his semi-daily security check, though the man checked the buildings and gates only, not the aircraft. Besides, Gillette knew him personally and could vouch for him.

"That video?" Rhyme said, nodding at a camera on a tall pole in front of the hangar. Another was nearby. "We may have some forensics after all."

But no such luck. The detective reported the cameras were trained only on the taxiway and the road approaches to this portion of the field, not the tarmac itself. The cameras were aimed at the area in front of the FBO; the plane was not in view. They knew no one had entered through the gate or jumped over the chain link but not if anyone actually approached the aircraft.

"What was the exact timing?" Sachs asked.

"The employees arrived between seven and eight. Nash landed at 8:10. He came into view on the camera at the gate about 8:30, met a cab. He met with his lawyer. We checked out the cabbie—and he's legit. Anyway, the video showed he didn't get out of the taxi. Then the deputy making the rounds for security arrived at the FBO about 9:10 and was seen walking away around 9:30. Nash returned at 10:30, and the plane took off a half hour later. Cabbie stayed inside his car again the whole time and nobody got out with Nash."

"How hard would it be to turn a video camera on the tarmac, hm?" Sachs said wryly. She added, "The good news, I guess, is that at least we can limit the number of suspects to the three employees."

"Tell me about them," Rhyme said. He laughed ruefully. "Since that's the only so-called 'evidence' we have to work with."

The detective pulled out a notebook. "Same staff here today was here yesterday. The manager of the FBO is Anita Sanchez. Forty-two, married. Joey Wilson runs the refueling truck. Twenty-eight. Single. Busted twice for pot. No biggie. And Mark Clinton is the mechanic. He's fifty, divorced. Iraq veteran. There're other mechanics but they weren't working this week. Been a slow time, apparently. Aside from the grass, none of them have any convics. None of them have any connection with Nash either. He lives in Orlando. Flies through here occasionally—to meet with his lawyer and banker, like he did yesterday. And as far as I can tell, Nash never had any disputes with anybody here at the field."

Rhyme said, "No, if any of them planted the IED, it was because they got paid to do it. Or extorted into it."

"And," Sachs added, "they'd all know airplanes and know exactly where to put in a bomb to do the most damage."

"They would, I'd imagine," Gillette agreed. "How do you want to proceed, Lincoln?"

"I'll talk to them. I'm going to treat them as witnesses. Put them at ease. We'll tell them we don't suspect them but I'll hint we're suspicious of the deputy who made the security rounds. What's his name?"

"Cable. Jim Cable."

"They'll get the idea that Cable's the main suspect. And we hope they can help us describe what they saw, if he went up to the plane. What they saw him do. If one of them's the guilty party, he—or she—will try to solidify the case against the cop or at least deflect attention from themselves. I'll try to catch them in a lie." Rhyme considered what he'd said. He laughed.

Gillette regarded him with a raised brow of curiosity.

"It's the opposite of what we normally do. I get a bit of evidence and try to find the truth. Now I'm trying to find the lie."

And smiled at the pun: *Where the evidence lies . . .*

Then his expression grew glum. A fierce downpour started once more. Gusts of wind. Then, insultingly, hail. "Goddammit, I think we've found a situation where Locard's principle doesn't apply, Sachs."

The French criminalist Locard posited that at every crime there was a transfer of evidence from criminal to scene of the crime or victim and vice versa. If one worked hard enough and was clever enough, a forensic cop could find that connection. Locard, apparently, did not have to deal with a Florida fence-raising storm.

"I need some facts before I start the interview, Detective," Rhyme said. "What was the orientation of the plane?"

"The nose was there." He was pointing. "Tail there."

The plane had been parked parallel to the hangar, about thirty feet away. The nose was to the left, tail right.

The detective continued, "So you'll tell them you suspect Cable slipped around to the far side of the plane, planted the IED, and then kept on his rounds?"

"I'll *hint* at it." A flash of light caught his eye. Rhyme looked through the rain and mist across the street.

"Sachs, while I talk to the witnesses, you go check out those buildings." He'd noted some glass-façade structures, an office complex. "A Burger King too. And a diner. See if there were any witnesses there when the plane was parked on the tarmac—or better yet, video cameras."

"Okay. I'll go see." Sachs jogged through the rain and climbed into the van. The vehicle rocked over the tarmac, buffeted by the wind, toward the exit.

"Where can I talk to them?"

"There? The corner of the hangar?"

Rhyme wheeled back into a small, windowless office in the back of the hangar.

His reaction to handling an evidence-free case had at first been dismay, then amusement, but now something within him was eager to try policing skills he hadn't used for a long, long time.

Detective Gillette went to summon the first witness.

Then, reminding himself he was about to become an interrogator, Lincoln Rhyme decided he better come up with a few questions.

Anita Sanchez was a businesslike woman in her forties. She had short dark hair, a dark complexion, and wore bright red lipstick. Her suit was conservative, navy blue, over a white blouse. On the lapel was a silver pin of eagle wings.

She sat across from Rhyme at a desk and seemed uneasy but no more uneasy than you'd expect under these circumstances—especially considering Rhyme's condition. The wheelchair, a complex motorized model, was an attention-getter. She wanted to look at it but didn't want to seem impolite.

Rhyme asked some neutral questions, then: "Did you notice if Deputy Cable went toward the rear of the airplane at any time on his rounds?"

"Deputy Cable?"

"That's right."

"He seems like such a nice guy. Do you suspect him?" She looked down at the digital recorder.

"We're just getting facts." He repeated: "Did you see him around the wings or engines of the airplane at any time?"

"I'm sorry, officer . . . Mr. Rhyme. I was in my office the whole time and you can't see the tarmac from where I was."

"The *whole* time?" He asked this because it seemed she'd emphasized the word.

Sanchez added quickly, as if Rhyme had known the truth, "Now that I think about it, I did go outside once. But I went to my car in the lot. That's the other direction from the jet. It was behind me so, even if the deputy was there, I didn't see him."

He asked other questions about Cable and if she'd seen anyone else on the property, other than the two other employees, even if the cameras showed no one else entered the FBO's area. The responses were short—she didn't ramble or volunteer information.

Rhyme had a friend, Kathryn Dance, who was an agent with the California Bureau of Investigation. She specialized in using kinesics—body language analysis—in interrogating suspects and witnesses, and he'd formed a grudging respect for the art by watching her in action. One thing he'd learned was when suspects rambled and offered details it was more likely that they were nervous, which meant they *might* be deceptive.

His take on Sanchez was that she was probably telling the truth and her demeanor didn't suggest guilt.

After she left, Detective Gillette brought Mark Clinton into the hangar. In blue jeans and a dusty gray work shirt, the lean man, beard slightly yellow from chewing tobacco, looked everywhere but at Rhyme as he sat down.

Rhyme began with some preliminaries. Had he known Nash? Did he know anybody who wanted to harm him?

He answered negative to all of those. He swallowed frequently and his fingers were twitchy, not necessarily signs of being deceptive, simply nervous. But, once again, that could be clues to lying.

Finally, Rhyme steered the question around to Cable. Had he seen the deputy near the airplane? Especially the back.

"When would that have been?"

"Around 9:30 yesterday."

"Oh, I was working in here then, but I didn't see anything. I mean, I couldn't. There was too much glare from the sun if you looked out of the hangar door."

He asked more questions, but Clinton kept referring to his hampered vision.

Rhyme had to admit that blindness—whatever the cause—was a pretty good out for a witness, or a suspect.

Using his good arm, Rhyme reached forward and paused the recorder. "All right. Thanks."

The mechanic stood, wiped his hands on his jeans, and followed the officer out of the hangar. Gillette returned a few minutes later with a heavyset man in brown overalls and a baseball cap, under which sprouted masses of curly brown hair, flecked with gray.

More preliminary questions, which Joey Wilson responded to with an attitude of being helpful.

Then Rhyme asked if he'd seen Cable near the airplane.

"Uhm, I think I did."

"Where?"

"I don't recall. I was headed to the lunchroom. For some breakfast. Ha. 'Lunch' room for breakfast. That's funny."

"You didn't see him while you were refueling?"

"Oh, I didn't tank him up."

"You didn't refuel the plane?"

Wilson looked up from the floor. "No, see, he wasn't scheduled for it. That jet of his can go two thousand miles on a tank. The more you carry, the more gas, I mean, the heavier it is and the worse the mileage. Best to fly with as little juice as you can. Mr. Nash'd refuel in Brazil. I remember one guy one time was flying a Cessna Citation—now, that is a fine airplane. You ever been in one? No, well, it's a superb piece of aviation machinery and he lands and has about a hundred gallons left, you believe it? He was trying to save the money on fuel! He's flying a two-million-dollar aircraft and scrimping on the Shell."

"Just to confirm, you saw Deputy Cable near the plane."

"I'm pretty sure. Couldn't swear to it. Say, seventy percent sure. No, fifty-five."

"Thanks for your cooperation."

The man gave another look at the wheelchair and then headed off.

Rhyme and Gillette were about to go over the man's performance when Sachs returned. "Got some finds, Rhyme."

"A picture of somebody with a moustache and black top hat filling a bowling ball bomb with gunpowder and sticking a fuse in it?"

"Not quite so good, but close."

"And?"

"Some video. From one of the office buildings."

"You got it that fast?" Rhyme asked.

"I was persuasive," Sachs said.

"Want to review it?" Gillette asked.

"Please."

He loaded the card into his computer and began playing the video. As they watched, Rhyme told Sachs what he'd learned—a synopsis of the three suspects' stories.

The video didn't show the airplane, but it did give a good image of the office door of the Southern Flight Services company. There was motion. "Look."

The door of the FBO was opening and Anita Sanchez was walking outside.

She turned and disappeared off camera.

"Ha," Gillette said.

He and Rhyme looked at each other.

Anita Sanchez was walking to the left. Exactly the *opposite* of the way she'd said she turned.

Rhyme said, "So she was lying. She did walk toward the plane."

"Was she carrying anything?" Gillette asked.

It was hard to see, given the bad quality of the image. She might have been holding a purse. Or maybe a small package containing C4 explosive.

Ah, interesting. Rhyme was beginning to think this interrogation business had something to it.

Gillette said, "It's probably not enough to bring her in."

"But we could get a warrant to listen in to her conversations. Maybe poke around in her office."

"Sure, I'll put that together." He pulled out his cell phone.

Then Rhyme cocked his head. "Dammit."

"What, Rhyme?"

"G-nissap sert on."

"What?" Gillette asked, his phone-hand paused in midair.

Then Sachs was nodding. "Just caught it, Rhyme."

He told the detective, "Look at the upper-right-hand corner."

"That sign?"

"Right."

"What about—? Oh, it's backwards."

G N I S S A P S E R T O N
N O T R E S P A S S I N G

Gillette was chuckling.

Rhyme, though, was not amused. "*That's* why the image was so dim. It was a reflection."

Sachs said, "The camera must've been pointed at the window of one of the office buildings. The glass façade was like a mirror. It looked like Sanchez turned toward the plane. Actually, she turned *away* from it. Just like she said. She was telling the truth."

"Almost as bad as witnesses, goddamn videos. Hell." He actually felt betrayed by the one forensic clue they had.

"She's innocent," the detective said.

"Not innocent," Rhyme corrected. "We just didn't catch her up with *that* lie." He shrugged. "And there's nothing else in her interview to implicate her."

"What about the mechanic?" Sachs asked. "What's his name again?"

"Mark Clinton."

"Right."

"You can't catch somebody lying if they don't tell you anything. He was sun-blinded."

"Was it sunny?" Sachs asked. "There was that terrible storm yesterday."

Gillette said, "Clear blue skies until about ten. Then the storm came in. Yep, he's telling the truth too."

Rhyme, though, said, "Or maybe not." He was studying the hangar door.

"How do you mean, Lincoln?"

"The ocean's behind us?"

"That's right."

"East."

Gillette said, "Son of a gun. Right. The hangar opens to the west. At nine in the morning, nobody in here would see any sun at all. The light was coming from the opposite direction."

"Okay, so he *was* lying."

"But what's his motive for lying?" the detective asked. "He was just saying he didn't see anything."

"That's not important," Rhyme reminded. "All we need to do is find deception and then start wearing him down."

"So, should we get that warrant?" Gillette asked.

"I'd say . . ." Rhyme's voice fell silent. He was looking out on the tarmac. "I'd say wait a minute. Get him back in here."

"Clinton?"

Rhyme's taut smile said, Who else?

A few minutes later, the man was in the hangar once more. Rhyme looked him over with a curious expression. "We're just trying to figure out exactly where the plane was parked and hoped you could help us with that. I know there was glare, but you had a sense of the plane's position, right? Because the sun was bouncing off the windows."

"Not so much the windows, but the fuselage itself. It was silver, you know. Not white, like most of the private jets."

"Silver, hmm. Must've been some glare."

"Always happens when the pilots park that way, you know, parallel to the hangar. We oughta put a door in but, being Florida, it's not worth the expense. We'd use it twice a year. But where those chocks are, yeah, that was pretty much where the aircraft was."

"All right. Thanks."

After he'd gone, Rhyme gave a cynical laugh. "Another reflection issue. See why we can't trust our senses?"

"So he's innocent . . . Sorry, Lincoln. What I meant to say was he may be guilty as sin, but we didn't catch him there."

Rhyme grunted. The allure of interrogation was wearing off fast. He was reminded of why he believed evidence was the cornerstone of investigations.

"How about the last suspect?"

"The refueller. Joey Wilson."

Rhyme thought back to that interrogation. "He's the one that most seemed to be lying. Maybe it's just an impression, but that was the sense I had. He was rambling. He seemed evasive . . . Ah, but maybe there is something here. He said he thought he saw that deputy near the airplane, right?"

"Thought so. Couldn't swear to it."

"But Cable *wasn't* near the plane," Sachs pointed out.

"Nope. His rounds take him around the buildings and the gas pumps."

Rhyme was nodding. "And how did he know Nash was going to Brazil? If he didn't refuel the plane, there'd be no reason to know the flight plan."

"Let's get Wilson in here again, talk to him again. Put some more pressure on." It seemed like a futile idea, but Rhyme had no other ideas.

"I'll go get him," the detective said. And strode through the rain toward where Wilson was parking his fuel truck, which apparently he'd just replenished. Rhyme saw the man glance Gillette's way and then, pretending he hadn't seen the detective's wave, walk fast to a battered Honda Accord, jump in, and speed away.

"He's rabbiting," Sachs said. She instinctively glanced at the only wheels available to her here—the van. Sachs loved cars. She worked on them, rebuilt parts, and drove like lightening. But she wasn't going to be doing any high-speed chases in an accessible van.

Not that it mattered. Detective Gillette was pretty good at the wheel himself. He was in the driver's seat in five seconds and, with the lights and siren going, he sped the car forward. It skidded once, but he controlled the big Chrysler from careening into the fuel truck and spun around it. Then he blew through the gate and disappeared onto the main highway.

Ten minutes later, Detective Gillette led a handcuffed Joey Wilson into the hangar.

He directed the refueling man into an orange fiberglass chair and helped him sit. None too gently, Rhyme observed, thinking it must have been a harrowing, if short, chase.

"What's the story?" Rhyme asked.

"I don't know what you mean."

Please. "Why'd you run?"

"I wasn't running. I just wanted to get home and close up my windows. Because of the storm. I forgot about them."

Rhyme said, "So you were lying to us. You *did* go out to the plane."

"Maybe I did."

"When?"

"Maybe 8:30, a little later."

"To plant a bomb in Nash's plane."

"No!"

"But you didn't refuel the plane. We can check the logs."

The man grumbled, "I told you no."

"Perhaps an attitude is not what we need now. What did you go out to the plane for?"

But just that moment the answer came via a phone call. Gillette spoke for a few minutes and then hung up. He grinned as he looked over Wilson. "The crime scene people just went over your car."

"Oh, hell."

"And guess what they found?"

"I don't know."

"A ki of dope."

"I don't know anything about that!"

"Not even how it ended up in your spare tire."

Wilson closed his eyes.

Rhyme said, "That's why you were out at the plane, Joey, right? You didn't plant any bombs; you were getting a delivery."

"I swear—I didn't kill him. But I lied about going to the airplane. I did, sure."

"Because you've got a network of people who work on planes, right? They smuggle some drugs on board in equipment holds or wheel wells. That's how you knew his flight plan."

The sigh said, Yep, that's right. He muttered, "It's not even very good shit. All this trouble and it's lousy pot."

"Was Nash involved?"

"Naw, none of the people who fly the private planes know. That's what makes the plan work so well. See, they don't get nervous talking to Customs."

This was undoubtedly true—using businessmen beyond suspicion made sense.

Rhyme continued, "Where were the drugs?"

"Port side. Left. An access compartment to the hydraulic system under the engine."

Gillette said, "Opposite of the bomb."

Rhyme wasn't pleased. Had the drugs been sitting next to the bomb, there might have been a transfer if the two items had touched. But, no, this case was simply not going to be a forensic one.

"And you didn't see anything else?" Rhyme asked.

"No, sir."

Gillette escorted him to his feet. Several other officers from the Dade County East Sheriff's Department took him away.

Sachs said, "Well, at least it's clear he didn't plant the bomb. We can believe him there."

Gillette nodded. "No, he's not going to kill his golden goose. He needs people like Nash to smuggle in his drugs."

"Well, on the surface, seems that those three suspects aren't suspects after all. We'll have to see what the NTSB says but my conclusion, from these facts, is that it was an accident." Rhyme gazed out over the tarmac. The planes seemed fragile in the wind and rain, as if the smallest of disruptions, let alone a bomb, could bring them down.

"Can they bring up the plane eventually?" Sachs asked.

"Five miles down?" Gillette said. "Maybe, for a few million bucks. But no police department in the world's got that kind of money. Well, I thank you both, Lincoln and Amelia. Especially for coming out to help us on one of our oh-so-pleasant Florida days."

Rhyme extended his good hand and the men shook. Sachs too gripped Gillette's palm.

Rhyme said, "Let's check in with New York, Sachs. Find out if there's anything that needs our attention. And I wouldn't mind a few more of those stone crabs."

But the case was not quite as closed as it seemed.

The next morning, Gillette, Sachs, and Rhyme were reassembled on the tarmac once more, at Rhyme's request. Thom was nearby. He'd occasionally wipe sweat from Rhyme's forehead. Today was much clearer, sunny and bright, and not a breath of wind, but the temperature was already soaring.

Sachs was explaining to Gillette, "When I was canvassing yesterday at those buildings and the restaurants, where I got the video tape?"

"Remember."

"I gave my number to all the businesses there, told them if anybody remembered seeing anybody next to a jet parked on the tarmac by the Southern Flight Services' office, to let me know. I got a call this morning. Seems a tourist and his family were sitting at that Burger King, outside around the time Nash's plane was there." She pointed. "They heard the story of the investigation on the news last night and got my number. The father has some pictures."

Rhyme squinted as he studied the fast-food place. "He'd have had a perfect view of the engine."

Gillette asked, "Tourist? Where is he, still in the area?"

"Blue Heron Inn."

"Sure, I know it. Five miles from here. Let's go talk to him. You want to follow me?"

"Will do," said Thom.

"I'll call dispatch on the way. Have a forensic team meet us there—with those programs they have to enhance photos."

"Forensic," Rhyme said, drawing a satisfied breath. "If I believed in clichés, I'd say, the fish is back in the water."

Dade County East Patrolman Jim Cable pulled off the highway and nosed his car—his personal Buick—into a stand of magnolia. Pulling on latex gloves, he reached into the glove box and removed a cold gun, a .38 special Smittie. He'd taken it off Billy or Rodrigo or Juan sometime, someplace over the past six months.

And he'd told the kid to get lost. Because a collar for a little coke and firearms possession wasn't as good as getting a gun that couldn't be traced to Cable. A gun that could be used in a situation like this.

Blond and beefy, Cable loaded it with bullets fresh from the box—rounds were always untraceable, if you touched them only with gloves.

And then he slipped into the marshy field behind the Blue Heron Inn and made his way toward cabin 43, which is where the tourist was staying, the tourist who'd videoed Nash's private jet the other day—and had very possibly gotten an image of him slipping the bomb into the right engine hydraulic access compartment.

At 32, Cable was too old to be a patrolman, looking through airport restrooms for illegals and chasing Billys and Rodrigos and Juans for little bags of drugs and big pistols. But he had a mouth on him and a temper and a problem with the bottle, so he hadn't moved up the way he should have, the way he deserved to.

But he wasn't going to have to worry about that anymore. He'd just made a cool hundred thousand bucks by slipping a little package into the side of Nash's plane, timed to blow up when the plane was over the deepest part of the Atlantic. Cable knew ordnance—he'd been a combat soldier until the fucking dishonorable—and had set up the device just right.

Things had seemed to go smoothly enough. But now the job had turned messy. This tourist and maybe his family would have to be killed. Still, the gun would be traced to the streets of Miami and Cable would scatter enough coke around the room to make it look like a drug-related robbery and homicide.

He hoped the tourist was in the room alone. On the other hand, if the guy was reluctant to tell him where the camera was, pointing a gun at his kid's head would make him talk real fast.

He didn't want to kill anybody else. But you did what you had to.

One hundred thousand . . .

Boat or mortgage?

Tough call.

No, it's not. Boat.

Then he was at the door of the bungalow where the Johnson family, from Nyack, New York, wherever the hell that was, was staying.

He looked around. Nobody. This cabin was the last in a row

near the field he'd just come through. Pulling back the hammer on the gun until it clicked, he leaned forward and put his head close to the door, listening. The TV was on. Cartoons. They were probably just finishing room service breakfast, before heading to the beach.

So the kids were in the room. He grimaced.

The good news, at least, was that if he wasn't going to leave any witnesses, he didn't need to wear the ski mask. It itched like hell and the day was already close to 90 degrees.

Thom parked the van beside Gillette's unmarked car in the front parking lot of the Blue Heron Inn. The place was what Rhyme expected of a near-the-beach resort in this part of Florida. The rear-facing rooms got a view of trees and power lines, the front got the highway and strip mall. An anemic pool, sandy parking lot, breakfast room with plate glass two days past a half-hearted Windexing.

Eggs Anyway
Ask about Our specials.

Rhyme thought about commenting to Sachs that the pronoun carried a certain theological connotation but refrained. Together they walked and wheeled toward the tourists' cabin.

"There's nobody here from the department yet," Sachs said.

Gillette looked around. There were no other police cars in view. "I'll give 'em a call. Funny they're not here by now. Well, let's go talk to the folks inside."

They approached the front door of the cabin and Gillette knocked. "Dade County East Sheriff's Office."

The door opened, though no one appeared at first. Gillette stepped in, saying, "Hello?"

It was at that moment that a pistol, held by someone inside, appeared from out of nowhere, and the muzzle touched the side of the detective's head.

Archie Crenshaw, the chief sheriff of Dade County East, read Paul Gillette his rights.

The massive fellow, tanned and sweating through his beige uniform, had nearly deferred to Lincoln Rhyme for this task, so impressed was he that the New Yorker had broken the Nash homicide case.

Rhyme pointed out, though, that he was no longer an official law enforcer. Amelia Sachs *was* active duty, of course, but not of this jurisdiction.

The same was true for the third member of the Big Apple team: Ron Pulaski, the young, blond NYPD Patrol officer.

Pulaski and Sachs and several local deputies were inside with Gillette's partner in crime—Jim Cable, the deputy who'd actually planted the bomb in Nash's aircraft. Rhyme was enduring the heat outside with Crenshaw, a handcuffed Detective Gillette, and a half-dozen other officers from the sheriff's department.

Now Sachs and Pulaski emerged from the cabin, followed by Cable, also in cuffs, his arms gripped by two grim-faced deputies. He was led off to the back of an unmarked car.

The two New Yorkers joined Rhyme, Crenshaw, and Gillette.

Sachs nodded in the direction of Cable. "Gave us everything we needed."

"Good," Rhyme said. "Won't have to do any more interrogations." A grin.

"What?" Gillette raged. "He gave me up?"

Crenshaw clicked his teeth and said, "You going to cooperate too, Paul? I'll put in a good word with the DA."

Gillette debated. His lips drew together tightly. Then he muttered, "Well, tell me. You!" A glare at Rhyme. "How'd you know?"

Rhyme, always pleased to explain—and to show off his

reasoning—was happy to oblige. "What was the key to this case? Deception. Remember? I didn't *have* any evidence, so I had to work with witnesses." He said the word as if it left the taste of tainted food in his mouth. "Finding out who lied."

"Yeah, yeah. I lied about vouching for Cable."

"You did, yes, but I didn't pick up on that. You were both law enforcers and you'd asked me to help. Why wouldn't I believe that? Naïve of me, obviously, but sometimes we have to take things at face value, don't we?"

Now it was Crenshaw who persisted. "So, how'd you figure it out, Lincoln?"

"I was thinking too narrowly. That was my mistake. I assumed that if somebody told a lie, they'd be guilty. But we saw how that isn't necessarily the case. The reflections, remember? The lie could turn out to be a mistake. And even if it was truly a lie, that might not mean the liar was guilty of the crime you were investigating—Joey Wilson, the refueller at the fixed-base operator, for instance. He was lying, but because of drugs, not bombs.

"Then it occurred to me that guilt can also be revealed by telling the truth."

"What truth?" Crenshaw asked. Another tooth click.

To Gillette, Rhyme said, "You mentioned which side of the plane the bomb was on. But there was no reference in the transcript of where the explosion was. How did you know it was on the right side?" He corrected: "Starboard."

Gillette began to speak then fell silent.

Yesterday, after Rhyme had become suspicious that Gillette mentioned that the bomb was in the right side of the aircraft, he'd discussed his thoughts with Sachs. Then they'd called Pulaski and had him fly down to Miami, check into the Blue Heron Inn, and play the role of a tourist who'd shot pictures at Burger King and possibly captured images of the bomb being planted.

This morning, Rhyme had Amelia tell Gillette about the witness and waited to see what would happen. The detective had told them he'd call the sheriff's office and have a forensic team sent out to the Blue Heron Inn.

But he hadn't. Rhyme had called NYPD headquarters and had an officer from the crime scene unit call the Dade County East forensic team and he'd learned that they knew nothing about an operation at the Blue Heron.

Rhyme had asked to be patched through to the sheriff himself and explained to Crenshaw what he believed was going on. Crenshaw sent deputies to back up Pulaski in the hotel and when Cable showed up, thinking he was going to steal the photo disk and kill the tourist and his family, he was immediately arrested.

The officers went back into position inside the cabin for the takedown of Gillette.

A perfect operation. Not a single gunshot fired, no injuries, sure, but more important, for Lincoln Rhyme, he had a case with trace evidence and tool marks and bank records and fingerprints. And all of it on the surface, not in Davy Jones's locker.

Rhyme then looked the blustering man over. "But I don't understand, Paul. Why did you ask me to help?"

"Because you're famous," Gillette muttered. "I knew if I had you saying the plane crash was an accident—which I thought you'd do—everybody'd believe it."

"So. You going to help us, Paul?"

Gillette glanced toward Cable, still sitting in the back of the unmarked car. He muttered, "Prick, selling me out . . . Yeah, I'll give you a statement."

"It'll have to include who hired you."

"What can you give me?"

Crenshaw clicked his teeth. He made a call and came back a moment later. "You give up whoever hired you and the state'll waive capital murder."

Gillette was considering this.

"Or you call a lawyer and take your chances."

"All right, all right."

A half hour later, Gillette signed the handwritten statement.

The ultimate perp was Nash's business partner. *Former* business partner, that is. The one Nash was in litigation with. There was a provision in the partnership agreement that if he died before a certain date, the partner could buy out the shares at a very discounted rate.

Money. The dullest of motives.

Though certainly one of the most common.

The partner, Gillette explained, knew Cable from the army and had raised the subject, knowing that Cable had been discharged for some shady business dealings. Cable suggested both he and Gillette—who together had carried out various criminal activities in the Miami area—would take care of Nash for $200,000.

"You did the right thing, talking to us," Crenshaw said, pocketing the statement. "Come on. Let's get you to the station."

As they walked past the squad car where Cable sat, Gillette glared at him.

But the younger deputy looked up and said, "Don't worry. We'll beat 'em."

Gillette stopped, frowning.

"Just don't say a word and we'll be okay. They don't have anything. No evidence, remember?"

Gillette blurted, "But didn't you . . . ? You gave me up!"

"Hell, no. I didn't say a word! What're you talking about?"

Gillette spun around and glared at Sachs. "You said he gave you everything you needed."

She replied, "He did. His address, phone number, and social. That was all we wanted at this point." She blinked in curiosity. "What did you think I meant?"

"You lied, bitch."

Rhyme said icily, “It was hardly a lie. You misinterpreted what she said.”

Crenshaw nodded toward the two officers beside Gillette. “Get ’em both downtown.”

The sheriff thanked Rhyme and Sachs and walked back to his own car, then Sachs and Rhyme returned to the van, where Thom was getting the accessible ramp ready. She said, “So what did you think, Rhyme? How was your first evidence-free case?”

“No question, Sachs: Between dealing with witnesses, on the one hand, and a crime scene five miles underwater, on the other: I’ll take Davy Jones’s locker any day. People . . . they’re way too much trouble. Say, Thom, is it cocktail hour yet?”

DEPORTEES

JAMES LEE BURKE

People think the Dust Bowl ended with the 1930s. It didn't in Yoakum, Texas. I remember how cold and brittle and sharp the air was at eight in the morning six days after Pearl Harbor when my mother and I arrived at Grandfather's paintless, pitiful home in our old coupe with the hand-crank windshield, but I remember even more the way the dust was piled as smooth as cinnamon against the smokehouse and barn and windmill tank, and how the sun was a dull silver disk and the sky an ink wash and the pecan trees bare and black like they'd been scorched in a fire.

The first thing Mother did when we entered the house was sit down at Grandfather's piano, which he had bought from a saloon in San Antonio, and play *Clair de Lune*. She was a beautiful woman, and had a regal manner, but she was also crazy and had undergone electroshock treatments and had been placed in the asylum in Wichita Falls. The edges of the wood grips on Grandfather's revolver were cut with nine notches he had tried to sand out of existence with a nail file. It worked about as well as the electroshock treatments did on my mother.

"How you doin', Buster Brown?" he said.

"That's not my name, Grandfather," I said.

"That's right, stand up for yourself, Aaron," he said. "But you ought to get you a little dog named Tige."

You didn't win with Grandfather. Even in old age he still stood six-foot-six. When he was a Texas Ranger he knocked John Wesley Hardin out of his saddle and kicked him in the face, and for good measure nailed chains on him in the bed of a wagon and threw him in the county jail and poured a slop bucket on his head.

He was sitting by the fireplace, his face warm and yellow as a candle in the light. "Y'all come to he'p me put up the Christmas tree?"

"Yes, sir."

He knew better. My father had disappeared again. My mother kept playing *Clair de Lune*, an expression on her face like the shadows rain makes running down a window.

Grandfather got up and went into the kitchen and lifted a tin sheet of biscuits off the woodstove. The biscuits were brown and crusty and oozing with melting butter. The sky was dark, dirty with smoke, and I could see flashes in the clouds and hear the rumble of thunder that gave no rain. I thought I saw people rush past the barn, gripping their belongings against their chests, their clothes streaming in the wind, their faces pinched as though raindrops were stinging their skin, although I knew there was neither rain nor hail inside the wind, only dust.

"There's Mexicans running across the lot, Grandfather," I said.

"They're wets. Don't pay them no mind."

He smiled when he said it. But I knew he didn't mean anything mean or racial. In hard times you don't share your secrets and you sure don't borrow trouble.

"A woman was nursing a baby and running at the same time, Grandfather."

He scraped the biscuits into a galvanized bucket, then slid a sliced-up ham onto the biscuits and draped a checkered napkin over the top and hefted the bucket by the bail. “Let’s go, Buster Brown.”

We didn’t need books to learn about the history of our state. It was always at the ends of our fingertips. It was even in the eyes of my crazy mother, who often seemed to take flight and travel back in time, for good or bad, mostly for bad. How about this? In 1914 an old woman outside Yoakum told my mother this story. When the old woman was a girl, two dozen mounted men with weapons tied to their saddles rode into the yard and asked if they could have breakfast. The girl and her parents started a fire under a Dutch oven and boiled coffee and cooked meat for the riders, all of whom spoke little. Their leader was a lantern-jawed man with soulful brown eyes and oiled, thick hair that hung on his cheeks. After a while he rested his knife and fork over his plate. “Why are you looking at us in such a peculiar way, little girl?” he asked.

“We don’t often see people who wear animal hides instead of clothes,” she replied.

“Back in Tennessee buckskin is considered right smart fashion. You and your folks have been mighty kind. One day you can tell your grandchildren you fixed breakfast for Davy Crockett and his Tennessee volunteers on their way to San Antonio de Bexar to give ol’ Santa Anna the fight of his life.”

I loved my mother. She stuck up for poor-whites and people of color, and was generous to a fault with the little money we had. But I avoided looking into her eyes and the memories from her own life that were buried there. The same with my father. He was an educated and genteel man from South Louisiana who went over the top five times in what he called the Great War. He was an extremely intelligent and perceptive man, and consequently doomed to a life of emotional and intellectual loneliness. Mother's depression and frigidity did not help, and I thought it no wonder my father's most loyal companions had become his beer at the ice house and the whiskey he hid in the garage.

"What are you studying on?" Grandfather said.

"Why do you call the Mexicans 'wets?'"

"Good question. You could walk across the Rio Grande on your hands. We're going outside. Find you a hat in the hall. That wind has no mercy."

He was right. It was dry and full of grit and as cold and mean and ugly as a witch's broom. We ran for the barn. There must have been eight or nine Mexicans sitting in the straw, and maybe more back in the darkness. The chickens were trying to hide in the loft. I don't think I ever saw people as hungry or lean. The baby I saw sucking at its mother's breast looked made of sticks and a hank of skin and hair. Grandfather passed out the ham and biscuits and went out to the windmill and unhitched the chain and used a clean syrup can to catch the water under the pipe that fed the stock tank.

When he returned, he passed the syrup can among the Mexicans and told them he would get them more water when the can was done. The wind was puffing under the roof, straining the tin roof against the beams and storm latches. From outside I could hear the sound of a car engine and metal rattling and bouncing. Grandfather put his eye to a crack in the door. He spoke without taking his eye from the crack. "Aaron," he said.

"Yes, sir?" I replied, aware of the change in his voice and the fact he had used my christened name.

"Keep these people inside. Don't open the door. Not for any reason."

"What's wrong, Grandfather?"

He slipped a shovel loose from a barrel of tools. "I try to avoid confrontations with white trash, but sometimes they don't give you no selection."

He pushed open the door and stepped out into the cold. I felt a solitary raindrop strike my eyeball, as bright and hard as a chip of glass. Then Grandfather shut the door. I squinted through the crack and saw him approach a Model T Ford in the middle of a dry streambed that led down to the river. A tall man as thin as a lizard stepped out on the ground, his tie lifting in the wind, his suit flattening against his body. He had a long, unshaved face and tubular nose, shadowed by a John B. Stetson hat. He had to shout to be heard. "Fixing to take a shit in the woods, Mr. Holland?"

"I don't abide profanity on my property, Mr. Watts."

"I'm here out of respect. I'm also here to avoid trouble."

"I have no idea what you're talking about, Mr. Watts. I'm sure the failing is mine."

The man named Watts looked at Mother's car and at the dust on the running boards and the swaths of it on the windshield. The wind flapped his coat back, exposing the brass star on his belt and the holster and sidearm on his hip. "Miss Wynona is visiting?"

"What's the nature of your visit, Mr. Watts?"

"We think there's infiltrators coming up from the border."

"Infiltrators?"

"To be specific, Japs."

"The Japs are fixing to bomb Yoakum, Texas?" Grandfather said. "That's what you're saying?"

Mr. Watts's face made me think of soil erosion. His eyes were as flat and black as watermelon seeds under his hat brim. "I never spoke badly of you, Mr. Holland. I know what whiskey can do. There's a seat in our church anytime you want it."

"I know your preacher well. I saw him at a cross-burning once. He was setting fire to the cross. I was writing down license numbers."

"Jesus didn't choose to be born a colored man. There wasn't any on the Ark, either."

"I got a theory on some of that," Grandfather said. "Know why God made certain kinds of white people?"

"No, and I'm not interested. I been sent out here by federal authorities."

"He was sending a message to the nigras about the superiority of white intelligence."

The wind gusted, rattling the blades on the windmill. Mr. Watts gazed at the barn door. "You calving early this year?"

"My cows were gone in '31. My grandson and I were gathering up some eggs."

"You wouldn't go upside my head with that shovel if I looked inside your barn, would you?"

"No, sir. But I'd file charges against you if you did it without a warrant."

"I see. Tell your daughter hello for me," Mr. Watts said. He turned his face so it caught the light. He winked, a grin at the corner of his mouth.

I saw Grandfather's right hand twitch, as though stung by a bee. "Come back here," he said.

Mr. Watts drove back down the streambed, the tires of his Model T rolling over fat, white rocks that were webbed with algae and that crackled loudly when they were heavily pressed one against the other.

We fed the Mexicans and went back in the house. It had a second story and dormers, but it was a tinderbox and creaked with the wind and had bat and squirrel pellets all over the attic. At one time Grandfather had owned five farms and ranches, one of them on the green waters of the Guadalupe River outside Victoria. But his love of cards and liquor and outlaw women created numerous graves that had no marker and children who had no father.

He never got religion, at least not in the ordinary sense. I also doubted if he dwelled long on the men he shot, since most of them were killers and not worth the dirt it took to bury them. The children he had abandoned were another matter. He could not ignore the despair in my mother's face when the afternoon sun began to slip below the horizon and evening shadows dropped like wild animals from the trees and crept across the yard in order to devour her heart. In those moments there was no way to shake the terror from her face.

She found a substitute for her father when she was seventeen, but no one was ever sure who. There were many soldiers in town, and also traveling salesmen. Some said her lover died in the Meuse-Argonne offensive. Whoever he was, he disappeared from her life and she quit high school and went to Houston. Three months later she returned and picked cotton with the darkies, and later went to night-school and learned shorthand. For the rest of her life the one subject she would never discuss was abortion and would leave a room if anyone alluded to it.

After Mr. Watts had gone and Grandfather and I came back into the house, Mother kept staring at the barn and the trail of white rocks in the gulley that used to be a streambed. Her skin was still clear and youthful, her amber hair thick and full of lights, piled on her head like a 1920s woman would wear it. Her dress was paper-thin, printed with tiny red roses, and washed almost colorless. "What's going to become of the Mexicans?" she said.

"I know a man in Victoria who's hiring," Grandfather said. "He can pick them up tonight."

"There's an enormous hypocrisy about all this," she said.

"In what way?" he said.

"In good times we bring them in by the truckload. When there's drought, the Mexicans are the devil's creation."

He watched her eyes and the way they followed the streambed through the trees down to the river. "Was it Watts?"

She turned her glare upon him. "I have no dealings with Mr. Watts. I suggest you don't either."

"If it was him, Wynona, I need to know."

She sat down at the piano and began to play *Malagueña* by Ernesto Lecuona. She played and played and played, hitting the keys harder and harder, until Grandfather stuffed his fingers in his ears and walked out of the room. Then she stopped and stared at me. “Get your coat,” she said.

“Where we going?”

“To town.”

“To the matinee?” I said.

“We’re going to buy some milk.”

We walked past Grandfather in the kitchen. He was at the window, his back to us, framed in the gray light, his right hand opening and closing at his side, as though he were squeezing a rubber ball, the knuckles ridging.

Mother and I drove down a dirt road into the county seat and parked at a grocery store on a side street, next to an ice house and a cinderblock building where chickens were butchered. It was Saturday and both the grocery store and the ice house were crowded. She pressed a nickel into my palm. “Go get you a Grapette, Aaron, but drink it in the car,” she said.

“Yes, ma’am. Are we breaking the law?”

“Who told you such a thing?”

I picked at my hands. “It’s the way we’re acting.”

I said “we” instead of “you.” She kissed me on the head. “You’re a good boy. Don’t be speaking bad of yourself or me, either.”

I went inside the ice house and pulled a Grapette from the cold box and paid at the counter. Through the side windows I could see the rear lot of the slaughter house and a sloping rivulet of feathers and chicken guts that had merged and congealed with the runoff from the ice-maker.

The men around me were bundled up and drinking beer and smoking or chewing tobacco, their clothes sour with the odor that sweat makes when it’s trapped inside wool. They were talking about the American sailors who had been drowned inside the *Arizona*, a subdued anger as thick as spit in their throats.

"What you doin' in here, little fellow?" said a voice behind me.

I looked up at the silhouette of Mr. Watts. "Drinking a Grapette," I said. "But I'm supposed to drink it in the car."

"Where's your mama at?"

"The grocery store," I said. "Across the street," I added, not knowing why.

"Getting y'all a mess of eats, is she?"

"Not really," I replied. "Grandfather gets by on the preserves he puts up in the fall."

"Bet she's buying milk. Right or wrong?"

I knew somehow he had bested me and caused me to give up a secret, but I wasn't sure how or what. He smiled down at me and stuck a long, thin cigar in his mouth, then took a kitchen match from his shirt pocket and scratched it on the butt of his revolver. He puffed on the cigar, his eyes hazy, and fitted his hand like a starfish on my head and worked his palm and fingers in my hair. "You don't like that? If so, just say. Don't be giving adults mean looks."

I went back across the street with my Grapette and climbed in my mother's car. I felt dirty all over. She came out of the store with a big grocery bag clutched against her chest. She set it on the seat between us. Inside it were three sweaty bottles of milk and two cartons of Cream of Wheat.

"What's wrong, Aaron?"

"Nothing."

She hadn't started the car. She twisted around and looked through the rear window. Mr. Watts was crossing the street, his Stetson slanted sideways, his cigar poked back in his jaw. "Did that man say something or do something to you?" she said.

"He put his hand on my head, like he was wiping it on me."

She looked straight ahead, her face tight. She started to turn the ignition, her hand shaking on the keys. The keys fell to the floor. She reached under the seat and pulled out a leather quirt. "Stay in the car."

She opened the door and stepped outside, her hair blowing, her profile cut out of tin.

"You haven't changed," Mr. Watts said, tipping his hat. "As fresh as the dew, no matter the season."

"You touched my son?"

"I don't know rightly what you mean by 'touched.'"

"Don't you put on airs with me," she said.

"I thought we were friends."

She slashed the quirt across his face and laid open his cheek.

"Lord, woman, you flat cut loose, don't you?" he said. He pressed the back of his wrist against the cut and looked at the smear of blood on his skin. "Warn me next time and I'll stay out of your way."

She began to thrash him, raining blows down on his head and shoulders, weeping at her own rage and impotence and shame while two men grabbed her by the arms and dragged her back on the sidewalk, easing the quirt out of her hand.

"It's all right, everybody," Mr. Watts said to the onlookers. "Miss Wynona is distraught. She didn't mean no harm."

People patted him on the back and shook his hand and told him what a kind and Christian man he was. I ran to my mother and hugged her around the waist, as though we were the only two people on Earth.

The man from Victoria who was supposed to pick up the Mexicans never arrived. Mother fed the Mexicans and Grandfather cussed out the man from Victoria on the phone. "You're going to he'p the war effort by not hiring wets?" he said. "I got a better way for you to serve your country. Shoot yourself."

The sun went down and so did the glow of lights from town that sometimes reflected on the bottoms of the clouds. In the general store at the crossroads the radio with the tiny yellow dial broadcast stories about the Japanese dropping parachutes loaded with incendiary devices into our forests and grasslands. There were also reports of pamphlets that floated out of the sky and burst into flame when children picked them up. Street mobs were attacking Japanese businesses in Los Angeles.

Grandfather put on his canvas coat and tied on his wide-brimmed hat with a scarf and walked his fences with a lantern, not out of fear of the Japanese but the evil potential of Mr. Watts, or maybe in bitter recognition that his era had passed and the injury he had done to his family could not be undone and the moral failure that characterized his life had poisoned everything he touched and saw.

That night I helped Mother and Grandfather in the barn with the Mexicans. She gave her greatest care to the woman breast-feeding her infant and held it in her arms while the mother used the outhouse. The Mexicans were a sad lot, their skin as gray as the fields, their faces like mud-masks, their clothes and hair sprinkled with bits of hay that had turned yellow.

Back in the kitchen Grandfather told me the Mexicans had crossed the Rio Grande far south of us, then had been betrayed by an illegal contractor who was supposed to drive them to San Antonio.

"He took their money and left them with the clothes on their backs," he said.

"What's going to happen to them?" I asked.

"They'll get caught and sent back. The government calls them 'deportees.'"

"That little baby is mighty thin," I said.

"Your mother worries me."

"Sir?"

"I let her down," he said. "She blames herself for something that wasn't her fault."

"She never speaks bad of you, Grandfather. Not ever."

"Past is past. Wait here." He went into the living room and picked up a deep cardboard box from behind the couch and carried it back into the kitchen. I heard scraping sounds inside the cardboard.

"I got this from a lady-friend of mine. Take a peek."

The pup could have walked right off a Buster Brown promotion in a shoe store window—chunky as a fireplug, his brown eyes as round and big as quarters, his stub of a tail swishing against the box.

I picked him up and breathed his clean puppy smell and felt his tongue on my face. "He looks just like Tige."

"I declare, you and him make quite a pair."

Two weeks went by, then Wake Island fell and supposedly a Japanese submarine fired artillery shells into a California oil field. Some of the Mexicans went away on their own, single men who hopped a freight or women without children looking for work as cooks and cleaning maids. A half dozen stayed with us, including the woman with the infant. Her name was Maria; her child's was Jesus. Her husband had died of a snake bite in Coahuila, just before they crossed the river into Texas.

As we entered the new year, Grandfather incrementally gave jobs to the remaining Mexicans so their visibility would grow a little each day, until a passerby might think they had always been with us, patching the barn roof, washing clothes on the porch, burning tumble weeds in the ditches, harrowing a field for the spring. I don't know what he paid them. I'm sure it wasn't much, if anything, for he had very little money. But the Mexicans didn't seem to mind. My mother bought baby clothes for Jesus and started teaching Maria English. Toward the end of January Mother received a postcard from my father. He said he was returning to Houston and hoped she and I would rejoin him in our little ivy-covered brick bungalow on Hawthorne Street.

"We're going home, aren't we, Mother?" I said.

"I suspect," she said. "Directly, anyway."

"What's 'directly' mean?"

"It means 'directly.'"

She twisted her fingers idly in my hair, her gaze just this side of madness.

Two days later we drove to town with Grandfather. He had never learned to drive a car, and always looked upon a ride in a car as a treat. We parked at the open market by the train depot and got out. I had forgotten my bad experience with Mr. Watts, as though it were a bad dream that fell apart in the daylight. A locomotive with a caboose and only two passenger cars on it had pulled into the station, the engine hissing steam. Mother was browsing through some open-air clothes racks, and Grandfather was buying a piece of cactus candy from a booth when we saw Mr. Watts ten feet away, eating caramel corn from a paper sack while he watched us.

"Good morning," he said. He was wearing a black suit with a silver shirt and a vest and a string tie. "A friend of yours on the train would like to say hello."

"Tell him to get off the train and do it," Grandfather replied.

"Maybe him and some others don't want to draw attention."

The shades were drawn on all the passenger windows in the train. "They're celebrities?" Grandfather said.

"Maybe one of them was there when Bonnie Parker and Clyde Barrow got it," Mr. Watts said. "Know who that might be?"

"You're talking about Frank Hamer?"

"He didn't give his name. He just said he knowed you."

"Which car is he in?"

"The second behind the engine."

Grandfather took me by the hand and we walked past the caboose to the first passenger car. It was the dark green of an olive.

"Let's see what's going on, Buster Brown." He swung me up on the steel steps.

The passenger seats had been removed from the car and replaced with benches, a pickle barrel, and a table that had smoked fish and several half-empty bottles of Hires root beer on it. There was a potbelly stove in one corner. Five men in suits and slouch or cowboy hats were sitting on the benches. Two of them wore mustaches. All of them were unshaved and looked like they had slept in their clothes. All of them were armed.

"One of you wanted to see me?" Grandfather said.

A tall man stood up. His mustache was jet-black and drooped to his collar. "I always wanted to meet you. I heard you slept with the girlfriend of the Sundance Kid." He grinned.

"You must have me mixed up with somebody else," Grandfather said. "Number two, I got my grandson with me."

"Excuse me," the man said.

"Y'all Pinkertons?" Grandfather said.

"Friends of the railroad."

"One of y'all saw Bonnie and Clyde get it?"

"*I* did," said the same man.

Grandfather studied his face. "No, you didn't," he said. "I know every man who was there."

"I got pictures. But I won't argue."

"What do you fellows want?"

"We think there's some Chinamen coming through here with the wetbacks. Except they're not Chinamen."

"They're Japs?" Grandfather said. My hand was still inside his. It felt hard and moist and callused and yet gentle.

"Would that surprise you?" the tall man said.

"Stay clear of me. That includes my family and workers."

"We don't call the shots. The railroad is going to be carrying a lot of soldiers through here."

"I understand that and I don't need to hear any more," Grandfather said. "You got my message."

"You really knew the Sundance Kid?"

"Yes, I did. He was a moron who breathed through his mouth a lot. Are y'all going to make trouble for me?"

"That's up to you, Mr. Holland."

"Son, you don't know what trouble is," Grandfather said.

One of the other men set his Hires root beer on the table. In the silence the sound made my face jerk.

I was too little to understand adult cruelty. Like most children, I thought adults possessed all the power they needed and hence had no reason to be cruel. So I was not equipped to comprehend the events that happened three days later when Mr. Watts's Model T drove up the dry streambed, followed by a big khaki-colored truck with a canvas top on the back.

Mr. Watts and the man with the mustache got out by the barn. The truck made a circle into the field behind the windmill and herded three Mexican men toward the house. No, I didn't say that right. The men hung their heads and walked with the docility of animals going up a slaughter chute. Maria was squeezing out the wash with a hand-crank roller on the back porch, her baby in a bassinet made from an orange crate. Three of the men from the train car jumped off the back of the truck, rifles in their hands. Mother came out the screen door wearing a man's suitcoat, her face disjointed, the way it did before one of her spells came on.

"What do you think you're doing?" she said.

"The Mexican woman and the child are illegals," a man with a chin beard said.

"You have no proof of that."

"We don't need it, lady."

"Don't you dare put your hand on her," Mother said. "Did you hear me?"

"Ma'am, don't mix in it or we'll have to take you, too."

"That's what you think," she said.

"Step back, please," the man said.

"Hold on there, Ed," Mr. Watts called, walking toward us. "I'll handle this."

"You will handle nothing," Mother said.

"Get your father out here," Mr. Watts said.

"He's in town," she said. "If he was here, you'd be dead."

"Well, we'll have to do our job without him, won't we, Wynona?"

"You will not address me by my first name."

Mr. Watts turned to the other men. "Load them up, the female and the baby first. Search the barn and the loft. Look in the outhouse as well, and then in the main house."

"You don't have the authority to do this," Mother said.

"I'm head constable," Mr. Watts said. "These men are contract law officers working for the government. Now you stand aside or I'll arrest you myself."

"Like hell you will," she said.

Mr. Watts looked at the windmill spinning and the dust blowing out of the fields. His eyes were bright and small under the brim of his hat. He bit the corner of his lip. "Cuff her and keep her here till we're gone," he said.

And that's what they did, with her arms pulled behind her, her throat corded with veins. The child began crying in the orange crate, his little chest and fists shaking with the effort. Minutes later Maria looked back at us from under the canvas top on the truck, her body rocking with the movement of the bed, her face small and frightened inside the scarf tied on her head.

Mr. Watts started toward his Model T, then returned to the porch. "Stop yelling," he said to my mother. "Don't you tell lies to your father about me, either. Goddamn it, shut up! They're just deportees."

That night Mother sat in her room upstairs by herself, while in the kitchen I told Grandfather what had happened. He was quiet a long time. The wind was up, the sky black, and through the window I could see sparks twisting from the ventilation pipe on the smokehouse.

"Did she strike Mr. Watts?" he said.

"No, sir."

"You're sure?"

"Yes, sir."

"Did they put their hands on Miss Maria?"

"One man held her while another man carried the crate to the truck."

"The man with the mustache from the train, the one who was talking about the Sundance Kid, what was his part in all this?"

"He told me he was sorry. He said to tell you that. He acted afraid."

"Ask your mother to come down here, please."

"What for, Grandfather?" I rarely questioned what Grandfather said. But this time I was truly scared. For all of us.

"I need her to drive me to town. You'll have to come with us. I don't want you here by yourself."

"What are we doing, Grandfather?"

"That's up to other people."

I got my mother from upstairs. Grandfather had already put on his canvas coat. His revolver and gun belt and holster were on the table, the belt wrapped around the holster, the leather loops stuffed with brass cartridges.

"Don't do this, Daddy," Mother said.

"He's the man who caused you all that pain, Wynona," Grandfather said. "Now he's doing it again."

"I do not think about him anymore," she said. "He has nothing to do with my life."

"Will you drive me to town? I can saddle Blue. But it's fixing to rain."

"It might rain in your prayers, but that's the only place you're going to see it," she said.

"Either he'p me or I'll get my slicker."

We climbed into the car and drove to town. I could see flickers of light on the horizon, like a string of firecrackers popping on the rim of the earth.

The saloon was a leftover from the nineteenth century, the ceiling plated with stamped tin, the bar outfitted with a brass foot rail and cuspidors. Not far away some of the pens that marked the exact inception spot of the Chisholm Trail were still standing. Mother parked at an angle to the elevated concrete sidewalk and cut the engine. The window of the saloon was gray with dust, a solitary bulb burning inside. Through the windshield I could see men tipping tin cups in a bucket of beer and playing poker dice at the bar.

"We'll wait here," Mother said.

Grandfather got out on the passenger side, his gun belt looped on his shoulder, the revolver hanging under his armpit. "I want Aaron to see this," he said.

"See what?" my mother asked.

"That our family doesn't tolerate abuse."

She half-opened the driver's door and stood partially in the street and looked across the car roof at him. She wasn't wearing a coat, and her flesh was prickled with cold, her amber hair wild and beautiful. "I made my choices. Now, leave well enough alone, Daddy."

Grandfather looked down at me. "We do it our way, don't we, Buster Brown? Come along now and don't pay your mother no mind. She knows I'm right."

I put my hand in his and walked with him into the saloon. I thought I smelled rain. I was sure I did. The way it smells in the spring. Like a great gold-green world full of pure oxygen and mist and sunshine and new beginnings. The bell rang above the door. A half dozen men turned and stared at us. Mr. Watts shook the dice in a leather cup and slung the dice along the bar. "Wrong address, Mr. Holland," he said.

"What'd y'all do with Maria and her baby and the rest of my Mexicans?" Grandfather said.

"They're your property, are they?" Mr. Watts said.

Mother came inside and closed the door behind her, the bell tinkling again. The smell of rain went away and the air became close and laced with a masculine odor and a burnt stench from the woodstove. A man in a mackinaw bent over and spat a stream of tobacco juice in a cuspidor. Grandfather let go of my hand and approached Mr. Watts. "Say you're sorry."

"To who?" Mr. Watts said.

"My daughter."

"For what?"

"What you did."

"I have nothing to apologize for." Mr. Watts reached around for his tin cup and accidentally knocked it over. "Give me a towel over here," he said to the bartender.

"Forget the towel," Grandfather said. "Look at me."

"I will not do anything you say." Mr. Watts pointed his chin in the air, like a prideful child.

The man with the drooping, jet-black mustache was three feet from Mr. Watts. "We ain't part of this, Captain Holland."

"Then stand aside," Grandfather said.

"You're not really gonna do this, are you?" said the man with the mustache. "You're a smarter man than that, right?"

Grandfather picked me up and put me in Mother's arms. "Go sit by the stove, Wynona."

"Please, Daddy," she said.

"Do as I ask."

She walked with me to the rear of the saloon and sat down in a rocking chair. She kept me on her lap, her arms folded across my chest. I could feel her heart beating against my back, her breath on my neck.

Mr. Watts was staring at Grandfather, his hands by his sides, as though he didn't know where to put them. "This needs to stop. We're all white men here. We're all on the same side. There's a war on."

"Apologize and we'll be gone."

Mr. Watts looked sick. The contract lawmen around him moved slowly away from the bar.

"You cain't walk in here and shoot a constable," Mr. Watts said.

"Give me your word you'll bring Maria and her baby back to our house."

"They're already on their way to a processing station in Laredo," Mr. Watts said.

"Then you'd better go get them," Grandfather said.

Mr. Watts's bottom lip was trembling, as though he were about to cry. With time I would learn that his desperation was even greater than I thought. He had reached that moment of fear and humiliation when a man is willing to take whatever measure is necessary to avoid the shame and self-loathing that follows a public display of cowardice.

"You were a drunkard back then, Mr. Holland," he said. "Half the time you were in a blackout. That's why they took your badge. It wasn't me caused the problem with your daughter."

"What?"

"Ask her. I brought her home from the movies. A week later she told me what you did. You were drunk and you put the blocks to her."

He could hardly get the last sentence out. Grandfather shook his gun belt from his arm and curled his hand around the handle of the revolver as the belt and cartridges struck the floor. He cocked the hammer.

"Tell him, Wynona," Mr. Watts said.

"He's lying, Daddy," she said.

"Bring a Bible out here," Mr. Watts said. "I'll put my hand on it."

"Is he telling the truth, Wynona?" Grandfather said.

"How many times were you so drunk you couldn't remember

what planet you were on?" Mr. Watts said. "Down in Mexico in 1916. You didn't do that with Pancho Villa's *señoritas*?"

"You close your mouth, you vile man," Mother said.

Grandfather's eyes were pale-blue, lidless, empty of feeling or thought, as though his soul had taken flight. I saw him swallow, then he eased down the hammer on the revolver and picked up his gun belt and replaced the revolver in its holster. "We're leaving now," he said. "Come on, Aaron."

"He's a liar, Daddy."

"I don't know what I did back then. I never will. I killed people in Mexico who have no faces. There's a whole year I cain't remember."

We went out the door and into the night. The wind was howling, the clouds huge and crawling with electricity. I sat in the front seat of the car with my mother. Grandfather was hunched in the back, like a caged animal, his eyes tunnels of sorrow.

Grandfather finalized our defeat that night when he went into the barn with a lantern and returned with a bottle that had a cork in it and no label. He carried the bottle into his bedroom and sat on the side of the bed and pulled the cork and tilted the bottle to his mouth. My mother took me upstairs and told me to put on my pajamas and lie down. Then she put Tige in bed with me and sat down beside me and looked into my face. "Pay no attention to what you saw or heard in the saloon, Aaron," she said. "Grandfather is a good man and would never intentionally do harm to his family."

"What was Mr. Watts saying?"

"Never listen to people like Mr. Watts. Their words are like locusts in the wind. I have to run an errand in town now. Don't worry if Grandfather gets drunk. He'll be all right in the morning."

"What kind of errand?"

"I know someone who might be able to help Maria and Jesus," she said. "He's a federal judge."

I looked at her eyes. They were clear. "It's too late to go to town," I said.

She stroked my hair, then clicked off the light and went down the stairs and out the front door. Through the window I could see the beams of her headlights bouncing on the fence posts and fields along our road.

I woke to sunlight and the sound of rain ticking on the dormers and people's voices downstairs. I got up and put on my blue jeans and went to the head of the stairs. I could see Grandfather talking to the sheriff and a deputy and a man in a suit with a stethoscope hanging from his neck. I did not see my mother. I walked down the stairs, Tige running in front of me, his nails clicking on the wood, his rump waddling on each step.

"We need to look at it, Hack," the sheriff said. "Hackberry" was Grandfather's first name.

"Big waste of time, if you ask me," Grandfather said.

"You know the position I'm in, Hack," the sheriff said. He wore a white beard and was almost as big as Grandfather. "Just bring it out here, will you?"

"Whatever you want," Grandfather said.

He went into the hallway and returned holding his holstered revolver, the belt wrapped around it. The sheriff took it from him and he slipped the revolver from the holster and half-cocked the hammer, then opened the loading gate and rotated the cylinder. "Smells and looks like you just cleaned and oiled it."

"A couple of days ago, I did."

"When did you start loading with six rounds instead of leaving an empty chamber?"

"Since I stopped toting it," Grandfather said.

"I'll keep this for a while, if you don't mind."

"You're going to run ballistics on it?"

"I ain't got any ballistics to run. The rounds never slowed down and are probably halfway to San Antonio."

The sheriff shucked the rounds from the cylinder one by one and dropped them in his coat pocket and stuck the pistol back in the holster and handed it to his deputy. The only sound in the room was the creak of the wind.

"So we're done here?" Grandfather said.

"It was the way he went out that bothers me," the sheriff said.

"A bullet is a bullet," Grandfather said.

"Watts got one through the mouth and one that took off most of his penis," the sheriff said. "What kind of shooter is apt to do that, Hack?"

"I guess somebody who was a bad shot or pretty mad."

"Let me restate that," the sheriff said. "Which gender is inclined to do that?"

"It's a mystery to me," Grandfather said.

My mother walked from the kitchen into the hallway. "The coffee is ready if you gentlemen care to sit down," she said.

The sheriff looked at his deputy and the man with the stethoscope and at Grandfather. "I think that would be fine, Miss Wynona," he said. "Are you feeling okay today?"

"Why wouldn't I be?" she said.

"I know what you mean," the sheriff said.

In April of 1942 Jimmy Doolittle bombed Tokyo and crash-landed his B-25s on the Chinese mainland. In reprisal for the help given to his crews by Chinese peasants, the Japanese murdered two hundred and fifty thousand civilians. Maria and Jesus were brought back to Grandfather's place and Mother and Tige and I rejoined my father in our little brick home on Hawthorne Street in Houston. That summer, after the Battle of the Coral Sea, the war turned around at Midway, and we knew that in all probability the light of civilization had been saved. It was a grand time to be around. Anyone who says otherwise doesn't know what he's talking about.

THE CHRISTMAS PARTY

ALEXANDER MCCALL SMITH

This happened on the island of Grand Cayman. It is probably true to say that comparatively little happens on Grand Cayman, at least compared with more eventful places in the area, such as Miami and Havana, but this particular thing certainly did happen. And even places that are remote and tucked away have their dramas. Passions run as high in such places as they do elsewhere, and human nature is no different. People are as misguided, do the same bizarre things, wherever one goes in this world.

Some years ago, a wealthy Canadian, the heir of a substantial chemical fortune, decided to abandon Toronto, where he lived, and move lock, stock, and barrel to Georgetown, the capital and indeed the only town of any size on the Caymans. Ted Forester had two passions in life: one was art, and the other was rare books. When record prices were paid at Sotheby's or Christie's book and manuscript auctions, it was either a well-endowed university library making the bid, or one of a handful of serious collectors, of which

Ted was the doyen. He had first editions of all Ian Fleming's Bond books, a complete collection of Hemingway's firsts, and several thousand other works of equal significance.

Ted's decision to leave Canada for the Caymans was not lightly taken. He was something of a patriot and hated leaving his homeland. But the cold northern winters eventually wore him down, and he decided that he had to leave for a warmer climate. He acquired permission to live in the Caymans—not an issue if you are wealthy enough—and established himself and his wife in a house in an expensive part of Georgetown. This house had a costly hurricane-shutter system and a marble-floored patio that projected out over the shore below. The marble had glass panel insets within it so that one might look down into the sea and watch the fish come for feeding at night. Ted's building contractor, a likeable Jamaican affectionately known as Builder-Man, had rigged up an ingenious system whereby lights shone down into the water and an automatic dispenser released fish pellets. All sorts of exotic fish swam in for feeding. Ted joked to his friends, "Fish are very quick to get on welfare, you know." This was typical of his humour, which was on the dry side, and much appreciated among the island's expatriate community. "Really amusing things happen to Ted," one friend said. "He somehow seems to attract them, rather like a magnet. Very funny."

Ted was married to a woman with whom he had nothing in common, and it was generally agreed that he had married her for the most shallow and most dangerous of reasons—physical attraction. Elaine was the daughter of an English-speaking Montreal lawyer. This lawyer, a widower, had made heroic efforts to educate her, and had only conceded failure when she had lasted barely more than one semester at an expensive private college in Ohio. After that, he accepted the fact that she was destined to concentrate most of her talents on the finding of a husband—an old-fashioned view that most daughters would have angrily rejected, but not Elaine. She confessed to her father that this was exactly what she had always wanted to do.

"I'm not saying education isn't a great idea," she said. "Don't get me wrong on that, Dad. It's just that it's not necessarily right for *everybody.*"

"Oh well," said her father. "As they say, one can't make a silk purse . . ."

"Yes," said Elaine. "Whatever. Besides, how much would I earn as a teacher? Put that next to how much I'd have if I had a husband who had a bit of money. Work it out."

Her father nodded. "Still, it would have been nice for you to know things like Shakespeare was *not* a Canadian author."

"Wasn't he?" Elaine said, and they both laughed.

Elaine, though, was in deadly earnest, and shortly after met Ted Forester at a dance. After hearing that he was fabulously wealthy, she began a process to ensure that he would eventually feel as if he could not live without her. For a young man who grew up thinking that girls would never find him attractive, he could not resist her advances, and she knew how to manipulate the situation: "Ted, you do know that I have been saving myself for somebody really special. And you're the one. I've waited for you my whole life . . ."

The marriage was greeted with dismay by his friends.

"Ted's married a dumb blonde," one of them remarked. "The real thing."

"Poor guy," said another. "But what does he see in her? Does she have any interests?"

"Elvis," came the reply.

In spite of having nothing in common, the marriage seemed to survive. There were no children, which was a sadness for both of them, but apart from that things went smoothly enough. Ted used part of his inheritance to invest in companies, and most of these did rather well. He acquired a controlling interest in a small chain of local newspapers and radio stations, and he also became the owner of a business that built high-performance yachts. These new interests prospered, and he became wealthier, a fact that was particularly appreciated by Elaine, who had expensive tastes. These tastes were held in check by Ted, who, at times, refused to pay for the insanely expensive watches that she ordered, or for the double-strand diamond necklaces that she found in costly jewellers when they were passing through Miami to get to the Caymans after visiting relatives in Canada.

"All right," he said. "We've got money—or rather, *I've* got money. That's no excuse to throw it around."

"So what do we do with it?" challenged Elaine. "Sit on it? Frame it and hang it on the wall?"

"We use it responsibly," said Ted.

"You buy those books of yours," she said sullenly. "You spend thousands of dollars on them, and they're not even new. They're used, and you pay those prices. Crazy."

"Books are items of real value," he said.

"So are diamonds."

He shook his head. "Not really. They have a value that is created by scarcity and the manipulation of markets. There are plenty of diamonds in the system—enough to make sure that everybody got some, if they wanted them. But if that happened, nobody would want them."

Elaine had not entirely followed this argument. "Everybody wants them," she said. "That's the whole point."

But he was still fond of her—perhaps even loved her, in an odd sort of way—and inevitably he gave in to her demands. Thus the necklaces were eventually bought, as were the designer dresses and all the other items that Elaine felt she needed. Some of these purchases were sent away soon after being acquired, as Elaine had always intended, to her sister, whose husband's lack of business sense had led to bankruptcy.

"Ted would like you to have this stuff," said Elaine, as she sent it on. "It's just that he doesn't really talk about these things. You know how men are."

Ted, of course, would not have wanted Elaine's sister to have any of it. He did not like her, and her vulgar, grasping ways. When they came to see them in the Caymans, on a ticket bought by Elaine, he found himself avoiding their company, making excuses to go out to non-existent meetings just to get out of the house.

"What do you talk about to people like that?" said a friend, to whom he described his predicament.

"The price of gas," said Ted, smiling at the thought. "They love talking about the price of gas. That, and Elvis."

The friend guffawed. "Elvis? What on earth is there to say about Elvis?"

"More than you'd think," said Ted. "Some of these people think that Elvis is actually alive."

"How strange," said the friend. "Some of these show-business types won't lie down, will they?"

The lives led by Ted and Elaine followed a very different pattern. They had breakfast together, sitting out on the terrace above the sea. Ted read the previous day's copy of the Toronto *Globe and Mail*, while Elaine paged through one of the many interior decorating or fashion magazines to which she subscribed. She also received copies of a glossy British publication devoted to the lives of celebrities. She enjoyed the features on people's houses, in which the cameras were invited to photograph the subjects sitting on their sofas or cavorting in their swimming pools.

"Our house is every bit as nice as these," she said. "Look at this one here. Look at the wallpaper. They could send their photographer round here and get a much better shot."

"We aren't celebrities," said Ted. "Nobody would be interested."

She did not reply. She harbored a vague sense of resentment directed towards her husband that for all his wealth he had not brought any glamour to her life. If Ted would only try to cultivate people who moved in more exotic circles, then she could attend the sort of parties featured in the magazines. She had never had her picture—*never*—in any magazine. And they were rich enough to be there, she thought bitterly. If only he would spend some of his money: he had enough of it, after all. It's just that he refused to spend it on entertaining and getting them entertained in return.

The thought crossed her mind one day when she watched Ted swimming in the small cove near the house: *What if he were to get a cramp and drown?* The water around the island was warm and a cramp was unlikely, but there were all sorts of things that could happen to somebody swimming by himself. Last year one of their neighbors, a retired accountant who liked to swim right out to the reef and back, had a heart attack and went down. It took them two days to find him, and the fish had already started to take an interest. She shuddered. It must be terrible to be eaten by fish, although one would never know anything about it, of course. Still, it was a terrible thought.

After breakfast, Ted went for a swim while Elaine took the dogs for a walk. That done, she drove over to the tennis club and played doubles with her friends before it became too hot. They lunched together—the same four of them—and then went home to rest through the afternoon hours. At six o'clock, friends came round for drinks on the terrace, or they went to the houses of friends.

Ted spent his day in his study, which was in the coolest part of the house. He perused the catalogues of book dealers throughout the world and placed orders by telephone. Every day, or almost every day, parcels of books were brought by couriers to the house and he filed them away in his air-conditioned library, placing them in plastic sleeves that would protect them from what humidity managed to make its way through the system. This kept him busy all day.

After they had lived in the Caymans for three years, Elaine started an affair with her tennis coach. He was Australian, having come to the Caymans shortly after graduating from the University of Melbourne. He was sixteen years her junior, but he seemed to think nothing of this age gap. He was bored, and vaguely flattered by the attentions of an attractive older woman. He would not be there forever, he thought, and Elaine would help to pass the time.

She imagined that he was in love with her, and certainly he told her that. A more perceptive woman, perhaps, would have noticed that when he confessed his feelings for her, the slightest of smiles, almost undetectable, played about his lips. It was a look that should have warned her that he did not take what he was saying seriously. She, however, was deadly serious when she told him that he had changed her life, that he had brought something into it that she had never experienced before. *What exactly was that?* he asked. She searched for words to describe what it was that she felt, but could not find them. Love, she thought, maybe it was love; but that somehow did not capture the intensity of her feelings.

Her friends were aware of the affair, having seen how she behaved in the presence of the coach. They talked about it among themselves.

"Why is she so crazy about him?" one of them asked.

"Can't you tell?" said another. "It's glaringly obvious. He looks like Elvis, doesn't he? A complete double. And you know how Elaine feels about Elvis."

They were right. The coach looked remarkably like the young Elvis. He did not have to work on it—as some Elvis look-alikes do—it came to him perfectly naturally. At school, in fact, that had been his nickname—Elvis—and he had taken it in good stead. He had no interest in the real Elvis. That was for the vacuous, he thought.

That year, Ted announced that they would hold a Christmas party, on Christmas Eve, he said, when everybody would be in the mood.

They had not had one the previous year, and there were a number of invitations to repay. "We can have a dance band," he said to Elaine. "You'd like that, wouldn't you?"

She nodded. She was already going over the guest list in her mind. "And I'll arrange the band," she said. "Leave that to me. You organize the drinks."

They began their preparations in good time. Elaine spoke to somebody at the tennis club who knew a bandleader in West Bay.

"I'd like them to play some Elvis numbers," said Elaine. "Could they do that?"

She was told that not only could they do that, but that the leader knew of a very impressive Elvis impersonator. Would she like to engage him to come to the party . . .

When Christmas Eve came, the house was a riot of colour. There were exotic and expensive flower arrangements in every room, and a team of white-jacketed waiters hovering about, waiting to attend to the guests' glasses at the slightest sign of their needing to be refreshed. There were large plates of cold salmon and assorted savories. There were large silver bowls, chilled on ice, filled to the brim with caviar. And in the background, there was the band, now established in the small marquee on the lawn. A photographer stood discreetly on the sidelines, ready to snap the local celebrities as they arrived. Even the Governor was coming, and a parking place for his limousine had been kept at the very front of the house, so that everybody else would see it when they arrived. That was Elaine's touch.

Ted was strangely quiet during these final preparations. The reason for his taciturnity was that he had just been told by Builder-Man, who was helping with the bar, that his wife was having an affair with somebody at the tennis club.

"I just got to tell you, Mr. Forester," said Builder-Man. "Your wife is carrying on. A man should know that sort of thing."

Ted thanked Builder-Man. "I'm glad you told me," he said. "Who is this man?"

"I don't know his name," said Builder-Man. "All I know is that he looks mighty like Elvis."

"I see," said Ted. He felt calm, as a man might feel calm when he has been given some awful piece of news and is determined to remain in control of himself.

"And I think he's coming to the party," added Builder-Man, shaking his head. "She invited him. That's bad, Mr. Forester. A man taking another man's wife is not entitled to come to his house and drink his alcohol and all that. That's not right."

Ted was silent. Then he asked, "What would they do in Jamaica in such a situation, Builder-Man?"

Builder-Man had no hesitation in answering. "They'd kill him. Simple as that, they'd kill him."

Ted nodded. "Understandable," he said.

"You want some help?" asked Builder-Man.

Ted thought for a moment. He had had enough of being indecisive. He had had enough of being meek and accepting. For once he would assert himself; he would act.

"Thank you," he said to Builder-Man. "Come with me. We must talk somewhere more private."

The Elvis impersonator arrived by motorbike. He parked by the side of the road, as the driveway was full of visitors' cars, including the Governor's limousine, with its Union Jack pennant. He combed his hair carefully, slicking it back as Elvis did, and then he checked his appearance in the bike's mirror.

"You're the King," he said to himself. Then he made his way up the drive, to be met halfway by Builder-Man.

"Somebody was looking for you," said Builder-Man. "Could you come this way?"

The Elvis impersonator did as he was asked, and followed Builder-Man into one of the large garages beside the house. It was dark inside.

"Happy Christmas," said Ted, as he struck Elvis over the head with a large piece of wood.

"Yes, and a Successful New Year," muttered Builder-Man, as he aimed a kick at the falling figure of the victim.

Then somebody turned on the lights. It was the Governor's police driver, who had left the car and was looking for a washroom in the garage. He stared at Elvis and then looked up at Ted and Builder-Man.

"What's going on here?" he asked.

Ted gestured to the groaning figure of Elvis, seated on the floor now, holding his head in his hands.

"Tried to attack me," he said.

"Yes," said Builder-Man. "I came to Mr. Forester's rescue. Attacked in his own house! On Christmas Eve, by this Elvis scum!"

The police driver took his cell phone out of his pocket. "I'll call for some constables to come and take this man away," he said. "Are you all right, Mr. Forester?"

The Elvis impersonator was charged with assault and was convicted. As a first offender, he received a suspended sentence and a large fine. Two weeks later, Elaine went for a swim in the sea in front of the house and did not return. Ted explained that he took his boat out to look for her, but could see no sign of her. A child, who had been playing on the rocks at the edge of the sea, gave a slightly distant account of events, and told the police that he had seen the boat go out at the same time as the swimmer did. But this inconsistency was put down to a confused recollection of events on the child's part and was not followed up.

Ted adjusted remarkably well to being on his own, people said. He took a new interest in a number of things and eventually contacted the tennis club with a view to taking lessons. The club secretary recommended a young Australian coach, who would be prepared to take him on and who should improve his game quickly enough.

Ted went for his first lesson a few days later, and met the coach. He stared at him intently, and throughout the lesson watched him carefully. At the end, he said, "I enjoyed that. Would you like to come fishing some day with me and my friend, Builder-Man?"

The coach smiled. "I'd love that. I've never been deep-sea fishing before."

"Good," said Ted. And he thought of the sea, and how deep it was, and how lonely.

FOREVERGLOW

JOHN M. FLOYD

Sam Keaton was in love.

It was a new experience for him even though he'd just turned twenty-three and had been on his own for four years. Simply stated, Sam had never known anyone quite like Virginia Fairweather. Even her name sounded mystical and glamorous.

They'd met three weeks earlier in a downtown café called Nelligan's. Sam had stopped in for supper after driving across town to pick up a new battery for a 2014 Ford Explorer, and Virginia ("Call me Gin") was there for a snack after getting off work. He was wolfing down a bacon-burger in a corner booth when she asked if she could join him. Somehow he avoided choking, mumbled "Sure, I guess," and that was that. They hit it off immediately. Like Sam, Gin was in her early twenties, undereducated, single, with no close relatives, and working at a job she endured rather than loved. In her case, it was a position as a salesclerk in the cosmetics section of the department store across the street from the café; in his case, auto mechanic gig at a garage on the west edge of town.

His collar that night wasn't blue, but it should've been. And she was fine with that.

Almost every day since, they'd met at Nelligan's to eat before heading off for a movie or a walk in the park or a cramped romantic adventure in the cab of Sam's ten-year-old Chevy pickup. It was a complicated relationship, but both of them worked six days a week, and Gin had a roommate and Sam had a nosy landlady, so neither had invited the other one home, but their long talks occasionally edged into wistful long-term planning. Still, no commitments were made. Both were well aware of their stations in life: her nails were painted purple and his had grease underneath. They had grown up poor and would probably die that way. That was just the way it was.

And then Gin got an idea.

"What's a riverglow diamond?" Sam asked.

They were at their usual table, eating what had become their usual fare: BLTs, fries, and iced tea.

"Foreverglow," she corrected. "It's a line of diamond jewelry—rings, bracelets, watches, earrings, necklaces. The store got 'em in last week, the fanciest stuff anybody around here ever saw." She shot a glance at the other customers in the café. "And keep your voice down."

"Do many people buy it?"

"Don't matter if they do or not, Sam. What matters is that it's sitting there in plain sight in the store all day, on a sales counter twenty feet from where I work."

"I thought you sold perfume and fingernail polish."

"I do, but whoever maps these places out always puts the fragrance and cosmetics area right next to the jewelry area." She grinned. "See, you learned something today."

"I learn something every day," he said. "It's because I don't know much to start with."

"Don't say that—you know plenty about fixing motors and such. It's just stuff like this you don't know about . . ." Her voice trailed off and her smile was gone.

He took a bite of his sandwich and stared across the table at her.

She leaned forward over the tabletop. "They're worth thousands and thousands of dollars, Sam."

He shrugged. "So?"

"This could be our chance. Our ticket out of here."

He finally got her drift. "Like I said, Gin, I don't know about a lot, but I know I'm not a thief. I never stole anything before."

"Well, me neither. But that didn't stop me from doing some checking. The jewelry section of that store has sales of close to half a million bucks a year. That's almost a quarter million in profit. And you know what they pay me? Sixteen grand. For fifty hours a week, half-hour lunches, and pitiful benefits."

Sam started to say that was way more than he made but decided not to. The only thing he knew for sure was that Virginia Fairweather was a lot smarter than he was. If she thought this was a good idea, thief or no thief, he wouldn't stand in the way.

Three diners at a nearby table finished their meals and left. Gin took another look around and said, "Here's the deal. The Foreverglow collection is in two flat leather cases just alike, each about the size of a hardcover book. When the tops are latched they look like big fat iPads. One of these cases stays locked away in the safe, but the salesladies keep the other one open and out on the counter all the time, so that the customers can see the jewelry. You with me so far?"

"No," he said, chewing. "Aren't they afraid somebody'll steal something out of the case?"

"They would be—but every piece of that collection's attached to a little thingy called an R.F.I.D. anti-theft tag. If the item goes anywhere near one of the exits, the tag sends out a radio-frequency signal that says something's being stolen and identifies what it is.

And the security system's been programmed to watch especially for the jewelry in that Foreverglow group. Anybody tries to leave the building with any part of it, that's all she wrote."

"Wouldn't a thief be able to take off the tag?"

"Nope. It's locked on with one of those clip things and stuck inside this rubbery shell—silicone, I think. Only way to take it off is with a detacher at the point of sale."

He sat back and stared at her. "How do you know all this?"

"I got a friend in the security department. Randall MacLaurin. He knows all that stuff, backward and forward."

"So you're saying the salesladies don't have to bother to watch the case too close."

"They barely look at it," Gin said. "That's why I'll be able to snatch it."

For a moment Sam didn't answer. He had stopped eating and was looking at her face, which had reddened a bit with excitement. Her eyes sparkled. *She really thinks she can do this*, he said to himself.

"Remember I said the jewelry case is about the size of a big flat book? Well, whenever we decide to do this, I'll arrange to work late—it needs to be at night—and I'll be watching the case from across the way, at my beauty-products counter. Meanwhile, my friend MacLaurin will be standing by, in the little restroom alcove behind the customer-service area. When I see the time's right and the salesclerks are otherwise occupied, I'll call Mac on my cellphone and tell him to pull the fire alarm on the wall in the alcove."

"What?"

Gin nodded. "He'll activate the alarm and everything'll go crazy. I saw it happen once a couple years ago, just after I started at the store—it's total chaos. And in the middle of all that, while everybody's running around doing the funky chicken, I'll stroll over to the jewelry counter, close and latch the case, slip it under my jacket, and head for the door."

Sam frowned at her a moment, trying to take all this in. "I thought you said the jewels can't be taken through the exits. They'd set off the alarm."

"You're right, they can't," she said. "But that's only through the doors."

"Huh?"

"That's where you come in."

The operation worked like a dream. Two days after she'd revealed her plan to him at the café, Gin swiped the jewelry case exactly as scripted. As the fire alarm blared and she hurried toward the exits with everyone else, she broke off long enough to swing by one of the display areas behind the floor-to-ceiling windows at the side of the building. That particular display window had somehow been cracked weeks ago in its lower left corner, and the space behind it inside the store was carpeted loosely with greenish felt to make it look like grass. Standing on the felt were—for the joy of the viewing public—golf bags, volleyball nets, tennis rackets, and other sporting equipment.

Moving fast, Gin leaned into the display area, slid the case of jewelry underneath the green floor-covering, and positioned it carefully a foot or so from the spiderweb crack at the base of the window. Then she dashed back to join the throng headed for the doors.

She made sure to stop once she was outside on the sidewalk. She wanted to remain in full view of her colleagues and bosses, at least until the security folks got around to discovering that the jewelry was missing and searched the employees who were on duty. In the next few hours everyone would be a suspect, and she wanted the record to show that she was as clean as Kleenex.

Sam Keaton, who'd been idling in the shadows outside the building, heard the shrieking of the fire alarm, waited the agreed-upon three minutes, and wandered over to a spot beside the correct window. One glance confirmed the book-sized lump underneath the green carpeting just inside the cracked glass. All he had to do was tap the bottom left corner with a hammer. The already weakened window broke easily, and as soon as he had a cantaloupe-sized hole he reached in with a gloved hand and pulled the case out from under the felt. He knew from what Gin had told him that a broken-window alert was now blinking on the police station's monitors a mile away, but no burglar alarm was heard here; at the moment, it was being overridden by the nerve-grating noise of the fire alarm. Sam tucked the jewelry case into his coat, checked again to make sure the coast was still clear, tossed a brick in through the hole he'd made in the window, and left in a hurry.

The deed was done.

The next day they both reported to their jobs, spent an ordinary but jittery day dealing with mostly old customers and mostly old vehicles, and met that night at Nelligan's Café. For a moment neither of them spoke. They just sat down and looked at each other across the table. Gin was the first to break into a grin and Sam followed suit.

"You have it with you?" she asked.

"Right here." He nodded to a paper grocery sack on the seat beside him. "What happened at work?"

"They're going nuts. During and after the fire alarm, the security guys watched the people who left to make sure nothing was taken from the store—and there wasn't a single hiccup from any of the anti-theft tags. A while after that they found out it was a false fire alarm, and that the case of jewels had been stolen. They searched and questioned the employees just as a precaution—that's standard procedure—and then, since they knew the stolen merchandise had to still be on the premises, they searched the store, top to bottom. All they found was a display window smashed by a brick on the first floor, but all the broken glass was on the inside and the hole was too small to let anybody in anyhow. They're still hashing it over." She grinned. "We're free and clear."

"So what now?"

She shrugged. "We take off. My car's packed and ready, and I saw your truck outside. We can follow each other and drive all night. Atlanta's closest, but there are plenty of places in New Orleans or Birmingham or Tampa or Miami that'd be happy to take the diamonds off our hands."

"I vote for New Orleans," Sam said.

"Suits me. I figure we'll get eighty or ninety thousand. Not a fortune, but enough for us to make a good start, together." She reached across the table and squeezed his hand. "Together," she repeated. "We did it, Sam."

"It was a good plan," he said.

A passing waitress looked at Sam and raised an eyebrow. He shook his head. Tonight this was just a place to meet, not to eat.

When he looked again at Gin, he saw her eyes straying to the paper sack.

Sam smiled. "You want to see 'em, don't you?"

She blinked and looked embarrassed. "No—that'd be stupid. It's too crowded in here." Still, she glanced again at the sack holding their treasure trove.

"What are you thinking?" he asked.

She gave him a tiny smile and touched her throat. "It's silly. There's a necklace in there along with all the rings and earrings. It's probably ten grand if it's a dime. I just wondered, you know, what it would look like . . ."

Sam studied her face. "There's a mirror in the ladies' room, right?"

"There's always a mirror in the ladies' room."

He opened the sack and took out the heavy leather case. After a careful look around, he passed it to her underneath the table. "Keep it latched tight, for now, and put it under your coat. Does the restroom have a lock on the door?"

"Yes."

He smiled again. "Go try it on."

She beamed at him, rose from her seat, and bent down to kiss him on the cheek. "You're a sweetheart. I'll be back in five minutes."

He watched her leave, then looked up at the clock on the wall. When thirty seconds had passed, he stood and walked back to the restrooms and knocked on the door to the ladies' room. "Anybody in there?"

No answer. He stepped inside, saw an empty room, and peeked under each of the stall doors to make sure. After coming out, he didn't bother to see if there was a rear entrance to the café. He already knew there was.

He went back up front and out the door. He paused a moment on the sidewalk, breathing in the air of a new life and wondering if Gin would stop on her way out of town to pick up this Randall MacLaurin she'd been talking about. He suspected she would. Then he imagined the looks on both their faces when they got around to opening the empty leather case.

Sam smiled to himself. He wasn't smart; he knew that. He also knew he wasn't in love anymore. But he was rich.

He walked to his truck, checked his glove compartment to make sure the diamonds were there, and headed south.

He'd always wanted to see Miami.

FINAL INTERVIEW

JOYCE CAROL OATES

1.

You have arrived alone at the Purple Onion Café. Not long after noon judging by the position of the sun in the sky.

No idea why, why here. Why heavy hiking boots which would make running difficult if you had to run. And this *ticking* in the air close about you like the quivering of insects' wings, so small the human eye can't detect them.

Seated in a table near the rear of the (busy, bustling) terrace.

Where the *ticking* has followed you. Louder.

No idea why, but has to be here. And why now?—after so many postponements, has to be *now.*

Waitress approaches to take your order. Young. Shimmering-blond hair. Bare legs. Bare feet in sandals. Eyes slide onto you with an expression of surprise. Female disdain. That look you've seen so many times in your life it's almost reassuring—*You are in the right place. This is the right time.*

2.

"D'you mind if I record our conversation?"—X fidgets with his iPhone.

Why the hell would I mind. "Of course not. That's fine."

"Did you say—*why?*"

"What? No. I said *fine.*"

Making an effort to disguise your irritation. Making an effort to appear courteous.

(Fatuous question, an interviewer asking if an interviewee minds their conversation being recorded!)

"Some people do mind," X says defensively, as if you've spoken aloud, "—they object to being *recorded.*"

You let this remark pass. Seething anger, quick as a spurting artery. But *no.* An error to reveal your emotions to a professional journalist.

"In any case," X persists, with that wide wet smile like a disinfectant swab across your raw brain, "I am not in the habit of misquoting those with whom I speak, whether I 'record' or take notes the old-fashioned way."

X speaks English as if translating from another language. The German-inflected accent is particularly grating since you know that X was born in the United States.

Again, you say nothing. Noting that it is (already) 12:34 p.m. Four minutes into the scheduled interview. You know that X was informed by your publisher that he could have only one hour for the interview, the excuse being that you have another appointment shortly afterward, and so must end your conversation with him promptly at 1:30 p.m.

This way you will not be considered rude. Just a busy man, practical-minded, expedient. Despite your reputation as a reclusive individual of "poetic" erudite texts.

But now, X has thought of a new way of annoying you. A small mean light glimmers in his rodent eyes.

"I'd meant to ask you—is this the café where a suicide bombing took place?"

"'Suicide bombing'! No."

It's a quick retort, reflexive as a sneeze. Almost, you feel the instinct to reach into a pocket, rummage for a tissue to wad against your eyes.

"No? Really? It was an outdoor café, I think. Here in Santa Luce. With a name like . . . 'Purple Onion' . . ."

Does this terrible person mean to torment you? As if there could be another restaurant in Santa Luce with a name *like* Purple Onion!

Since his (several-minutes-late) arrival X has been glancing about the bustling café terrace. As if, the fool, he might be in actual danger in such a banal place. (Most of the luncheon patrons are women. A tribe of well-to-do, very fit, streaked-blond "youthful" women whose laughter hurts your brain like the sound of crystal being shattered in manic repetition.)

Can't determine if X is serious about this concern or merely being comical. X's face—which is unusually long and droll, with a high dome of a forehead and thick tufts of eyebrows—is markedly expressive, like a mime's. Fatuous behavior can sometimes conceal genuine anxiety, as you know as a "keen observer" of human psychology, so you make an effort to be patient with X.

You acknowledge that, yes, you'd heard that there were bomb threats made against the restaurant, some time ago. The proprietor, Nadia, the cheerful *zaftig* woman with the untidy horse's mane trailing down her back, who'd just shown X to the table, has been an activist in liberal causes for years—protesting, picketing, marching. Gay/lesbian rights, immigration rights, No Nukes, Clean Water. Possibly there'd been an attempted bombing at the Purple Onion, but—so far as you know—no actual bomb was detonated . . .

"Hmm! Are you sure? Because I—"

Tersely, calmly, you say with a clenched set of jaws: "I live here, and I would know."

"Ah! I see. Of course."

X, who has traveled thousands of miles to interview you, does not wish to antagonize you. (At least until the interview is over.) Very easily X could consult his iPhone to determine who is correct, you or he, but he says only, in a conciliatory voice, that he'd heard "something vague" about a high school dropout in this part of California, near San Francisco, who'd assembled a bomb following directions he'd gotten on the internet from an ISIS site . . . But whether it was actually detonated, X doesn't know.

"This sort of 'terrorist' news is usually exaggerated"—you laugh softly, a sort of hissing-laugh, the laughter of contempt and indifference, finality.

At the time of the (alleged) bombing you'd been in residence at the American Academy in Rome. Or maybe it was the American Academy in Berlin. Focused on your work, no time for news of bombings, school shootings, mass murders in the United States that seemed to be a near-daily occurrence.

Overhead, a high droning sound like a dentist's drill, but you refrain from glancing skyward.

At last, a waitress approaches your table, takes your orders gravely, departs. X pushes the iPhone gently toward you. Bares his big teeth in a smile that appears lewd but might be only conspiratorial and says, with a wink: "Cut to the jugular, friend. Tell me what you've never told any other interviewer."

3.

Precisely 12:19 p.m. when you arrive at the Purple Onion Café for your interview with X, which is scheduled to begin at 12:30 p.m.

For it is *your way* to arrive early for appointments. Particularly those appointments you dread.

X, the internationally renowned interviewer, is known to be a disagreeable person. X will flatter you in conversation, then eviscerate you in prose. You know, though you must pretend otherwise.

X has a name, but you decline to supply the name. In fact, you will never address X by his name.

You were away in Europe when the Purple Onion was closed for repairs for nine months. Just recently reopened, much fanfare in local media. You see that the exterior of the restaurant has been repainted—the shingled roof looks new—a new flagstone terrace, new tables and chairs. You have no interest in going inside the restaurant. You suffer from a mild claustrophobia and recall that the interior of the Purple Onion is crowded with tables, and loud. And close quarters, in the company of X, would be disagreeable.

Today you are greeted by the proprietor/owner of the Purple Onion with her brave smile, ankle-length peasant skirt, knitted vest, and Navajo jewelry, gray-white hair falling loose past her shoulders like torn silk. Nadia is a stout, hearty, big-boned girl of fifty with skin that glows like an incandescent light except for the net of fine white scars across her forehead. One of those well-intentioned locals who murmurs slyly in your ear, *I have read all your books!* Also, *It's an honor, sir. Thank you, sir.* Air of excited embarrassment that makes you wince.

Nadia seats you at the table you've requested, which is your usual at the Purple Onion—farthest corner on the terrace, beside a wall of wisteria just beginning to bloom. You will take some small solace from the fragrance of the wisteria. Often in this (late) phase of your life your eyes glance skyward, astonished at the heartbreaking beauty of clouds that look sculpted in white marble, sometimes a faint daytime moon, blue sky beyond like washed glass. That beauty that is (literally) *out of your reach.*

You are not a person who is comfortable *being seen;* it is your strategy to be the individual who *sees.* Not to be the center of attention is, to you, the goal of your relationships with others, for you are not unlike a thief, a thief who steals whenever he can, and from whom he can, often randomly, with no plan, as a matter of survival. Yet, you are acclaimed as a "master" of some sort: the criminal hiding in plain sight.

From your strategic table you can peruse the terrace as it fills up with a chattering lunchtime crowd of mostly women. (Some of these women you know socially but would be pressed to say their names.) You can observe, through charmingly gnarled wisteria vines, figures approaching the café entrance on the walkway; if you make the effort you can even see a corner of the parking lot.

Is there something unreal about the scene? You feel uneasy, unsettled.

A prematurely warm April day. But—which year?

As in dreams we often have no idea how old we are, and what exactly we look like, so you are thinking that this place has become strange to you, though in all (evident) respects it is (dully) familiar to you.

The sky has become overcast, the hue of watery skim milk. Weather at this time of year can be mercurial in northern California near the coast. Sudden wind from the Pacific Ocean twenty miles to the west, darkening sky, within minutes a violent thunderstorm. Or, wind from the east, dry-desert wind, the sky bursts into pieces of sunshine like shards of broken glass raining down onto your head.

Laughter at nearby tables. Evidence suggests that humankind seems to have decided it is wiser to laugh than to cry.

4.

Waiting for X to appear. Reluctant to admit, you are fearful of X. Fearful that X can peer into your very soul as it has been (ludicrously) claimed of X by previous interview subjects whom you respect—Rushdie, McEwan, Oz, Ondaatje.

Glancing nervously at your watch. Already 12:26 p.m. You feel a pang of loss as the minutes pass.

Almost, you can hear time *ticking.*

The (notorious) interviewer, based in Berlin, was scheduled to fly to San Francisco via Chicago; from San Francisco, to be driven by hired car to Santa Luce, twenty miles to the east and south, where you have lived an (inexplicable) suburban existence for more than three decades.

X will surely comment upon that fact. *Withdrawn, reclusive, near-anonymous, innocuous. A bourgeois existence—shameful?*

In bed this morning you felt oppressed as by a heavy object, a body, lying upon you—hot-skinned demonic face pressed against yours. Bulging eyes pressed against yours.

An effort to open your eyes, force yourself out of bed.

Wanting badly that X disappear. Midair?

You have acquired a reputation for being cantankerous, unpredictable. Though to anyone who knows you well you are totally predictable.

"Just one hour with *Der Spiegel.* Is that too much to ask? What can go wrong?"—your editor in New York City pleaded.

Your publisher is eager for the interview to take place. Publicity for your books, which enjoy a degree of critical acclaim but which have never been commercial. The interview will appear in *Der Spiegel* on the occasion of your receiving a distinguished international literary prize, to be presented in Berlin later in the year but until that time, confidential.

This new award is a source of pride to you, and unease. *Lifetime achievement.* Will you then become posthumous?

Idly you think, the interview will be published as an obituary.

Unless X doesn't appear? Then, all remains unaltered.

Often in recent years, most markedly this past year, you find yourself hoping that whoever you are waiting for will fail to appear. Even appointments which are crucial to your well-being, like medical appointments—secretly you hope they will be canceled.

Waking early this morning, hours ago, with a jolt. Unwilling to open your eyes—*God, let today be canceled.*

But now your eyes lift, startled: you are in a bustling public place and a tall lanky man looms above you. Tight-fitting suede jacket, black T-shirt, jeans. Big-buckled leather belt. Ridiculous!—X, a citizen of Berlin, has costumed himself for the American West like a character in a film by Werner Herzog.

Somehow, this person managed to slip past your scrutiny. Identified himself to the proprietor of the Purple Onion who led him at once, proud as the prow of a Viking ship, to your table. Bursting your precious solitude as a balloon might be burst between big-knuckled hairy-backed hands.

"Hel-*lo*! Sorry I'm late."

5.

Alone and breathless on the outdoor terrace at the Purple Onion Café. Never came to such a place before by yourself. Everyone here is an adult—*old*.

Just the place your mom might be. Drinking wine with her women-friends. Last person she'd expect to see here—*How-ie? What on earth?*

That look in the woman's eyes. Sick, sinking. For though she couldn't possibly know, she would *know*. The pupils of her eyes would shrink to pinpricks and her mouth contort to a perfect O of a scream.

But no, you don't see your mom. Anyway not yet. Blindly making your way onto the terrace without waiting for the hostess to seat you because (let's face it) you don't know any better, or have forgotten that's how it is done in restaurants like the Purple Onion where the clientele is adult and has money.

Stumbling to an empty table in the farther corner. Weeks,

months of fantasizing the scene yet somehow you'd failed to factor in the presence of other people. The possibility there would be no empty tables and you'd be turned away, ticking tote bag and all.

Panting, sweating. Though also shivering inside the hoodie. Christ!—just to get here, twenty-minute walk from your home on Cargot Street, exhausting like climbing a rocky landscape uphill.

The hostess is a broad-hipped woman your mother's age with long hippie-hair, jangling Navajo jewelry, frowning mouth. She isn't happy with a pimply kid like you in a khaki hoodie, baseball cap, mud-crusted hiking boots daring to take a seat by himself on the terrace café, but signals it's OK, she'll send a waitress over.

Doesn't recognize you as your mom's son, evidently. No reason why she should. Yet. Relief.

It is 1:11 p.m. when a waitress approaches your table with a menu.

You calculate: should you order something to eat, or will that be a waste of money? There isn't much time. The detonation is set for 1:30 p.m. Still, you have not eaten since the previous night. You'd meant to eat this morning but were distracted. And even the night before, you'd choked and gagged on whatever it was your mom had prepared, locked upstairs in the bathroom.

The waitress is a young blonde your age. Panic grips your heart that possibly she knows you, went to school with you, but no—evidently not.

Though eyeing you as if she knows exactly who you are.

Hot bitch, the guys would call this one. Not your friends, you don't have friends, but it's exactly what they'd call her, your guy-friends. If you had them.

In high school, you had a friend. At least one friend. For a while.

Fag. Fags not wanted.

Fuck fags.

Inside your caved-in chest there's something beating and fluttering like a bat. You'd read online, lots of bats are rabid right now.

Or, bats are dying from a weird kind of lice. Fungus?

How nature fucks itself up. Almost, you'd think it was on purpose.

Warm day, yet you're wearing your khaki hoodie. Need to hide your bumpy shaved head that looks like shit, grimy Giants cap you've had since middle school pulled down tight over your forehead. Pinching your ears flat.

Hiking boots laced tight: paramilitary. Thick soles, rubber treads. Proper hiking socks, wool. (Stiff with dirt. Why a pair of soiled hiking socks were in your sock drawer you have no idea.) In another lifetime you'd have been a hiker, mountain climber. Rock-face climber. That mountain in Yosemite—El Capitan. If your dad hadn't left your mom and you. If your dad had taught you to climb. But then, your dad wouldn't have been *your dad* if he had.

Carrying your mom's farmers' market tote bag, which you set beneath the table at your feet. What's inside is *dense.* Covered with a sheet of crumpled newspaper.

Sweat like cold oil oozes from your face drawn tight as a plaster of Paris mask. You brush away those tiny insects—gnats—you can't see but can hear. *Ticking.*

6.

You tell Nadia that the "new" Purple Onion is looking very good.

Noticing that the exterior has been renovated, repainted—dull weatherworn blue replaced by pale cream, covered in purple vines and tendrils in an intricate feverish pattern that undulates up onto the roof.

Wisteria just beginning to bloom, red geraniums in clay pots, petunias in hanging baskets—glass-topped tables, woven-hemp chairs on a flagstone terrace that looks unusually clean.

Possibly, this flagstone is synthetic—not "stone" at all. The old flagstone was discolored, cracked.

Many customers. Midday din! Almost all the terrace tables are filled. A poor idea to have insisted upon meeting X here.

You'd wanted to sit outdoors. You'd wanted a place with no liquor license. You'd wanted a place not far from your residence on Cargot Street.

It's true, you have become (increasingly) eccentric in late middle age. And now, you are beyond late middle age. An individual of certain fixed habits, routines. At first, you'd experimented with making demands of others, then you saw how they capitulated to you, how easily it was accomplished. Your shyer self was abashed, that a bully could elbow him aside so readily; that a bully could be mistaken for you.

And now, you are boxed in by your habits. Can't remember your life before your habits. Can't remember *you.*

Compulsive checking of time. As you await X. It is 12:32 p.m. A minute before, 12:31 p.m.

A minute later, 12:32 p.m.

(Has no one realized this, before you? Your eyes stare glazed, hypnotized.)

You are reasoning that, if X has been eager to interview you for months, he should have made it a point to arrive earlier than you did, out of politeness.

Accident, plane crash . . . Never arrived at the airport.

Blasted out of the sky, all passengers and crew perished.

Midair, thirty thousand feet, utterly vanished . . .

You smile. You shudder. It can happen that quickly, you suppose—annihilation.

Tick tick ticking. Blood-pulse in your inner ear.

7.

Cut to the jugular, friend. Tell me what you've never told any other interviewer.

Indeed, this is a challenge. Your mind has gone blank like power-washed pavement.

Seeing that he has surprised you, X continues, almost self-effacingly, like a young pedant advancing a theory: "My definition of a serious artist is a 'buoyant imagination' attached to an individual, as a balloon might be attached to an individual, floating above him, string tied around a finger.' Yes?"

Vaguely you indicate *yes*. But your manner is noncommittal.

"In the true artist the imagination is always stronger than the individual. That's to say, the individual's personal life. The imagination is, in a sense, impersonal. It is transcendent, it is all-consuming. If in a duel with the personal life, the imagination wins."

You suppose this is so. But you don't give the interviewer the satisfaction of agreeing. Instead you merely smile in that way observers have described as *inscrutable, enigmatic.*

"So, the challenge for the interviewer is to penetrate the 'personal self'—the *persona*—in order to speak with the artist's deepest and truest self which has nothing to do, as we know, with the outer being."

Outer being. You are thinking, what a curious phrase.

Outer being. You feel the impulse to scratch at your arms, the backs of your hands—to see if you can bleed.

Fortunately a waitress comes to your table to take your orders. Cursing under his breath, X fumbles to *pause* the iPhone.

Self-consciously and gravely, like a schoolgirl reciting poetry, the waitress recites the specials of the day. X is amused by her solemnity, cocking his head in a pretense of attention, and when she has finished her litany of odd, quixotic dishes, X asks her please to repeat.

You don't like the way X engages the waitress in supercilious banter while he is undressing her with his eyes. Unless you are imagining it, X glances at you as if inviting complicity, as men sometimes do with other men, in the presence of a sexually attractive female in a subordinate position.

You ignore X, of course. Indeed, you have hardly looked at him since the start of the interview.

What an awkward ritual this is, like sharing a meal with your executioner!

No choice but to examine the Purple Onion menu, which is absurdly elaborate, several pages stapled to a purple woven-hemp board. In flowing script a fixed set of terms recur—*vegetarian, vegan, organic, locally-grown, dairy-free, gluten-free*. Fodder for the malicious journalist to note in his snarky prose provoking readers to laugh in derision at you, a pretentious *avant-garde* American writer.

You are not hungry in the slightest. You resent the very fact of having to order food in the presence of the disagreeable X. Yet, you tell the waitress you will have the *soup de jour—ginger-orange carrot*. And X tells her, with a wink—*eh bien, moi aussi!*

X is in an ironic mood having discovered that the café has no liquor license. No wine, not even beer. A very strange sort of American café!

No meat on the menu either, not even seafood. Not even oysters. And X has come so far.

At least, X concedes the bread is decent. *Eleven grain, non-gluten, baked on the premises.* He jams a sizable piece into his mouth and chews lustily. Restarts the iPhone and turns belligerently to you.

"All yours, my friend."

8.

You know, I am not your friend.

Explaining to X, or to someone resembling X, as you have explained countless times: You were not in Santa Luce at the time. You were not married to that woman at the time.

You were not an *absent dad*. You insist, you have never been anyone's *dad*.

Whoever wishes to blame you, take a good look in the mirror.

As Jesus said, he who casts the first stone had better be without sin.

Yes it's curious, why you chose to live in Santa Luce. Why, when you might have lived in any of the great cities of the world, you came to Santa Luce where nothing happens, repeatedly.

When you can't prevail, retreat. Eventually the world will come to *you*.

In Santa Luce there is "local news"—but not "news" that will travel more than a few miles beyond the perimeter of Santa Luce. The police department here is comprised of less than a dozen officers. The department is housed in a single-story municipal building that also contains the public library and the township office. At the time of the (alleged) *Purple Onion bombing*, which was also known as the (alleged) *suicide bombing*, there were only four full-time officers on duty. The police chief Dave Ruggles, fifty-eight, a thirty-year veteran in law enforcement, was slated for early retirement in another month.

No one was more surprised than the residents of the upscale community. No one was more shocked. You knew (of course) of "suicide bombers"—Islamic fanatics who dwelled in faraway places with unpronounceable names. You were filled with pity seeing smoking rubble, carnage, lifeless bodies on your flat-screen TVs.

You hesitated to switch channels for you knew that you should bear witness to the world's suffering. But such suffering soon becomes repetitious on flat-screen TVs.

You were not in Santa Luce at the time. You are certain.

Not clear that such an act of violence could occur *here*. The midday terrace of the Purple Onion is the most innocuous of privileged places.

What was the motive for the (alleged) bombing? The delusional bomber himself hadn't known.

Posted in his Facebook account—*I am not politicle, I did this for mysef*

Inexpert, fumbling-fingered, the *suicide bomber* blew himself up with his (partial) bomb. Three other persons died in the blast, it was claimed. Seven persons injured including the café proprietor who was seen helping the wounded though she was herself bleeding badly from a head wound.

Parts of bodies, hair, food mixed as in a crude low-speed blender. Shattered glass, metal fragments, teeth, toes. Pieces of skull, brain. Remains of a wild staring eyeball. Fingers, no nails. Brain matter, pulpy and suety, laced with shreds of kale flung across bloodstained flagstones.

Most lurid photos not shown in local media but, within minutes, widely disseminated online and in weeks, months, years to come.

Santa Luce Police Chief Ruggles collapsed at the bloody scene. Near-fatal cardiac episode. Treated by EMTs at the site with other casualties.

Chaos, pandemonium. Sirens. Emergency vehicles, barricaded streets. Police helicopters from adjoining townships.

The (alleged) *suicide bomber* was nineteen years old, a dropout from Santa Luce High School two years before. Son of a single divorced woman who lived less than a mile away from the Purple Onion on (coincidentally: for this is your street too) Cargot Street.

While still in high school the (alleged) *suicide bomber* had been suspected of having made prank calls to local schools, libraries, theaters, and other public places threatening bombs, shootings. Online he'd posted mysterious references to ARMAGEDDON.

Possibly, he'd managed to assemble a bomb following directions he'd discovered on a terrorist website, but was apprehended by police officers before he could detonate it in public . . . Or, acting on a tip, police officers discovered, in the boy's home, materials for making bombs, as well as a "small arsenal" of guns.

Much was made in the media of the fact that the boy's mother had long been a gun control activist who'd (evidently) failed to notice that her son was hoarding rifles, ammunition, and explosive materials beneath her very roof.

Rarely do you watch TV. Yet you recall having seen the distraught mother of the (alleged) *suicide bomber* interviewed on local TV: ravaged face, bloodshot eyes, flesh beneath her eyes drooping like oysters, defending herself in a hoarse voice—*If you have a nineteen-year-old son who dropped out of high school without graduating, unemployed, living at home, locks himself in his room, won't let you in his room, won't talk to you when he sees you, won't look you in the face, you wouldn't need to ask these questions, you would understand.*

Bursting into tears. Painful to watch. Quickly you switched channels.

Yet, you admired the woman's courage even as you pitied her. Baring her tattered soul on TV. Every pore of her aging skin, every burst capillary in her eyes, every crease and dent in her face—exposed to the ravenous eyes of strangers. If you had half such courage, such audacity, such heedlessness, you would not have required the circuitous route of *artist* to confront the world but would have confronted it without subterfuge, head-on.

You consider confessing this to X—but no. Better not. Such a sincere remark would only return to haunt you.

". . . an artist is one who detaches himself from his surroundings. If indeed the artist perceives his surroundings it is as *material*. Not as *surroundings*."

Damned voice is overloud in your ear. Or, X is leaning closer to you than you would wish.

In panic you think—*Is this someone who knows me? Someone I should know?*

You have always feared interviews. Often you fear that an interviewer is someone who knew you in another lifetime, whom you fail now to recognize.

Someone who knew you when you were not yet yourself, but rather *no one*. And no one who has been *no one* is ever *not–no one* in the memory of those who knew him at that time.

". . . like a dirigible, your imagination—your soul; floating and roaming the sky while your body, and these other bodies, are left behind here below."

To this, you can think of no reply that is not in some way incriminating. Even to laugh, to share a laugh, to nudge X in the ribs in a brotherly manner—these would be mistakes.

Finally you say, dredging up the words like one shoveling black muck, yes there is some truth to that observation; but you have always been a practical person, as well as an artist. You tell X that it's a common mistake, to over-emphasize the "romance" of the artist. In truth, most artists are bourgeois individuals who care about their comfort, their routines, their safety, the next meal, social status, finances . . .

X has been frowning at his iPhone. Peering at the little screen. Fussing. You feel a flash of despair, rage as X mutters, "Sorry! Excuse me, I think something is seriously fucked up here . . ."

He insists, please would you repeat what you've been saying, in the identical words if you can.

Identical words! You've totally forgotten what you were saying. Your emotions show on your face like grease smears on a platter.

"Man, I am sorry! I can see that you're annoyed as hell. I don't blame you in the slightest. You are a famous person, and a very busy person, and this interview with me is a terrible imposition . . ."

X is vehement, contrite. Forcing you to protest—No. Not at all. You are not annoyed, at all.

But this is impossible! The wily intruder has forced you to sound as if, perversely, you are begging for the interview.

No escape. The mistake was agreeing to meet X at all. From that blunder, others follow.

X is saying: "We all know people who *fantasize.* It's a child's first strategy of defense. In the artist, *fantasizing* is compulsive. It might seem voluntary to the artist, but in fact it's involuntary.

It's a retreat, but an aggressive retreat. People engage with you, you appear to be engaging with them, but you are not involved in the slightest—are you?"

X laughs offensively. Though you are annoyed as hell you insist yes, of course you are involved.

"Well, you are here. With me. But we both know that you are not—really—*here.*"

Again, you insist. *Of course I am—here.*

Of course you are engaging with X. Even as X peers impudently at you, leaning forward on his elbows to the point that, to your additional annoyance, the glass-topped table tilts.

The more you smile, the more you insist, the more reasonable and amicable you are, the less you are here, with X.

Observing the two of you from an aerial perspective. Twelve feet above the Purple Onion terrace. Your head is inclined forward, you give every sign of listening to your companion who is also leaning forward, shoulders hunched.

From above, the two heads are scarcely distinguishable. On both, hair thinning at the crown, dark streaked with gray. Almost, your heads could be brought forcibly together, joined at the forehead.

And then, abruptly the scene fades. Bursts to white. A deafening flash and yet—soundless.

9.

Where is your mind?—no one has ever thought to ask.

Already in the cradle. In the crib. In the mommy's arms. At the mommy's breasts. In the arms of the daddy.

Drifting, detached. Resisting capture.

In school, in a row of desks. In church, in a hardwood pew.

Leaping ahead to the solution of the problem. Impatient with "steps." As others spoke slowly, enunciating each syllable of each word like a tightrope walker buffeted by wind.

Though you sat very still at your desk with your hands clasped, and beneath the desk your feet side by side like roots secure in the earth.

But your brain was buzzing. In flight.

Blizzard. Swirling, spiraling wet-white-blossom snow.

You have slipped away. Sleek and sinuous as an eel forcing your way to freedom.

In fact, you are yourself, but a child. That old-young child. Making your way along a road. An unpaved road, in a forest. The trail splits in two, each equally faint, trampled grass and damp earth. You take the left trail but then, when the trail splits again, this time you take the right trail. Is there any reason? Any reason of which you know?

Something tugging me forward. A kind of gravity.

10.

Dyslexic was the label. The way your eyes scramble letters front to back, upside-down. Fuck *words*!

Your mind turns off, detaches. Whoever is speaking you hardly listen to, though it's your "self."

Might be a stranger or might be *you*.

If you blow yourself up, which you don't think (seriously!) you will do, it will be an experiment to see how many brain neurons retain the memory of who you are, what the fuck you thought you were doing, and what your guy-friends will think of it when they see the footage online, on their iPhones. Any scene in your life, plucked out of your memory, you only see yourself at a distance of about five, six feet. Was that who I was? No.

Not that you hate yourself. Not that you love yourself. Mostly, you stare at whoever he is, a brain inside a skull inside a head with "hair" on top and "face" at the front and you marvel at how such a creature came into existence.

Not just you, it's the *human* part of it that is so—bizarre.

You wonder if you have already died and some part of you has remained behind, like vapor. Or a strong rotted-rancid smell.

Making your way along a path cut jaggedly through underbrush. Many paths through the underbrush but this is your path. You glance down—you are wearing hiking boots. The kind that protect your ankles when you're climbing in a rocky terrain.

You'd tried, alone. Not much fun alone. Not good to be alone in a remote rocky place.

You never planned to grow up to be the (alleged) *suicide bomber.* You never planned to grow up at all.

11.

For the record: you weren't in Santa Luce at the time of the (alleged) bombing. You weren't in California. You weren't in North America. You are not sure of the details, even if it took place, or what it was that took place. And it isn't clear that it did take place. For what an extraordinary act of courage, if it had! *You* doubt that you are capable of it.

Though you are beginning to see, the Purple Onion has been repainted. Rebuilt. Can't remember what color the walls used to be but the cream color is new. Flagstones also look new, synthetic.

But the wisteria vines are mature, gnarled. The wisteria vines are not new.

If there was a detonation it looks as if only a part of the terrace was destroyed. A corner of the restaurant. (You seem to have read this somewhere. Or heard it somewhere—a rumor?) You were not here in Santa Luce at the time and you are not an individual who scrolls through the internet in pursuit of the most stomach-churning news.

You didn't know the (alleged) *suicide bomber.* You didn't know his (alleged) father who'd moved away from Santa Luce years ago, a research biologist. Yes, you knew the mother. You know the mother.

You are not the father. *You* are not to blame.

Single mother, divorcée. Grim bright brave *civic-minded, activist.*

The kind who takes Pilates classes. Yoga. She's a vegetarian, she believes passionately in organic foods. Shelf of vitamin pills—A (anise seed) to Z (zinc). One of the smaller houses on Cargot Street. You've passed that house countless times without knowing who lives there. The (alleged) *suicide bomber* had an ordinary name—Howard, Howie. He'd been a child like any other child. Baby like any other baby. Soft-boned head like any infant's. Years were required to shape him into the (alleged) *suicide bomber.* Pimply face, pimply back. On his back, reddened pimples like boils. Topology of pimples, pustules, boils. Scratches with his nails. Draws blood. Homely face, eyes too small. Nose too long. *Homely* rhymes with *lonely.* You'd heard them quarreling all your young life. Behind shut doors, drone of adult voices. *Why'd you marry me then, if you hate me? Why'd we have a child? Now—it's too late.*

Your dad moved out. You were just a kid. Ten, eleven. Scrawny little guy. Trying to figure—How's it your fault? Knew it was your fault. Cried and cried.

Learned young that crying will bring you nothing except a runny nose, headache, sick sensation in the guts. So badly you wanted your dad to return you'd remained upstairs hiding when he did return for a visit. *Howie, come down—your father is here . . .* Your mom calling up the stairs excited, drunk-sounding.

Fuck you, Dad. Thanks and fuck you.

Love you son, you know that don't you?

Yes I know that Dad, fuck you very much.

Fuck you too, son.

Fuck you Dad!

Laughing. From inside the room you'd barricaded the door.

Angry at you, like hell your dad is going to climb the stairs and knock on your door. Goddamned spoiled kid.

Years later, you still hear these words through the floorboards.

Years later, no one would dare knock on your door for you've posted warning signs: NO ENTRY. NO TRESPASSING. VERBOTEN.

A smaller sign, female figure, X drawn through it in black.

You were never a Nazi. Whatever they said of you, assholes got it wrong at school. Sure, you'd inked stuff on your arms. One of the tattoos meant to be a four-leaf clover but the swastika is tricky. Hammer and sickle? You wore long sleeves. You picked at the scabs. Some of the cuts became infected. Fuck!—a hurtful kind of pleasure scratching and *scratching.*

Disappointment you saw in adult faces. Teachers, your mom.

(Your dad too for sure. Except you never saw your dad any longer.)

Think that I am a disappointment? I will give you something to be disappointed about.

Mesmerized by the internet. Hours, nights. Years. Age thirteen to whatever you are now—nineteen. Waking with an aching neck, head on your desk like it'd fallen off your shoulders. Cheek on the desktop. Eyeball pressed flat. Faint hum of the internet like your own fetid breath. Had the idea for years. Researching for years. For months actively working on The Device.

Never thought of it as a bomb. Technical term—*explosive device.*

Not a fucking terrorist. Middle East, towelhead ISIS. Not an asshole Nazi either.

Thing is, you are unique. You are not a herd animal. ISIS, Nazis are herd animals.

To yourself, you call it The Device. (Not once do you utter the word *bomb.*) Shave your head like a monk.

Howie? Honey? Why on earth did you shave your—

Shamefaced you'd yanked the cap down over your ears. Tight over your forehead. Stiff-backed, walked away from your mom. None of your business Mom, fuck you.

Beginning to lose your hair, like your dad. Male pattern baldness. Already combing your hair, hairs came out in the comb. Fucking shit, only nineteen.

Trying to decide, *where*. The Device is only as effective as its location.

First target you'd planned was Santa Luce High. Assholes who'd made your life miserable, those years. But fact is, they've all graduated. They are all gone. Away at fucking college and would not even remember you.

Who? Him? That loser?

The café with the weird name—Purple Onion. Yes.

Crazy coincidence if your mom is there. No doubt, some of your mom's friends will be.

Preparing The Device requires months. The most painstaking work of your life, nobody to observe and admire. You'd flunked junior year chemistry. If Mr. Alonso could see you now he'd be goddamned impressed.

Your first time in the Purple Onion Café. Though you've passed the place many times. Kind of run down, back terrace with tables and hanging plants. Painted a dull blue, starting to peel. Kind of place old hippies used to hang out at, now more upscale.

Carefully choosing clothes. Khaki hoodie, T-shirt. Jeans, hiking boots, Giants cap. Dark glasses. Farmers' market tote bag belonging to your mom, hanging from a doorknob with a half-dozen other useless tote bags. Newspaper pages on top hiding The Device.

The sort of precision device you set beforehand. Not the kind of device you trigger at the site and not a belt you strap around your middle.

Many hours are required to calibrate The Device, attached to a clock. Old wind-up clock you'd found in the house but it's working. Reliable. Loud-ticking.

Sweating as you calculate: if you set the detonation for 1:20 does this leave enough time? But you don't want an excess of time, either. Your fingers are icy, numb. You are disbelieving—*Is this really happening?* Laughing at yourself, what kind of bullshit is this, you fuck up everything you do, flunked out of chemistry, never showed up for exams, some kind of joke you'd actually *build a bomb.* Wild!

At the Purple Onion, making your way to the back terrace, trying not to be distracted by so many people, women's voices, laughter like breaking glass. In your imagination the scene has been silent, dreamlike. Not so many other people and these were filmy, imprecise. Trying not to panic, you sight an empty table. Make your way to the empty table gripping the tote bag tight with sweaty hands. All you can see is what's ahead of you, so sharp-focused it hurts. Your peripheral vision seems to be gone.

Realizing belatedly you'd forgotten to wait for the hostess. That's the way it's done in a restaurant like this—you wait for the hostess. Wait to *be seated.*

Anyway, you're sitting down. Buzzing in your head like locusts. It seems to be OK, nobody is asking you to leave. Can't see very well. Eyeballs feel dry. Interior of mouth very dry. Busy café, servers carrying trays, shimmering-blond waitress approaches you as if she's hesitant to give you a menu. You fumble taking it from her, your dry lips mutter *Thanks.*

Staring at the menu. Can't make out the words. Some of the menu is handwritten in purple ink.

Ticking sensation inside your head. Clock-ticking beneath the table.

Really you don't believe that anything will happen. That *it will happen.*

Your mind just bypasses it like water rushing around a rock. Could be an old boot tossed in a stream, the water rushes around it indifferently. Though you are sweating pretty badly, and your heart is beating like crazed wings inside your ribcage, and there's a two-inch scared smile on your face. In a movie, light breaking onto your face like wonder.

Glancing about, curious to see who is close by, who will die with you in—how many minutes? Twenty-two? No, twelve.

Of course, you can leave the tote bag beneath the table. You can walk away. No one is stopping you. No one knows where you are. No one is waiting for you. You have no "associates": you are a "lone wolf." Act as if you're going into the café to use the restroom, instead keep going out onto the street. At the street, walk fast. Don't run, walk fast. A block away when The Device detonates, nobody will know it's you. No trace, you are sure.

But your legs are leaden. Feet are heavy as hooves in the hiking boots. Heartbeat so hard, blood is draining from your head and there's the risk you might faint if you tried to stand up. So better sit still. You are here, you are not leaving. Why'd you go to such an effort if you leave now? You are making a profound statement. First project you've actually finished since seventh grade. You are rejecting the rejectors. You are sneering at the sneerers. Your mouth is dry as sand, it's like a convulsion the way you are swallowing. Imagining breaking news on CNN. Santa Luce, the place where nothing happens. Rarely on TV. Bond issues, school board elections, sewer repair, library referendum, but now, this evening—*breaking news. Santa Luce, California, rocked by ingenious explosive device . . .*

Draw a deep breath, you are actually becoming calmer. You'd remembered to take three of your mom's "nerve" pills. To your left, a table of chattering women. To your right, a table occupied by just two men.

One of the men seems to be interviewing the other. Fake foreign accent, annoying as hell. iPhone on the table.

In a sudden rage you think—*Who the fuck cares about what either of you think? What any of you think?*

That's when you realize—*It will happen!* You feel a rush of relief as if a burden is being lifted from your shoulders. Time ticking away means time running out and time running out means all choices running out.

Peering at your watch inside the khaki sleeve—1:19 p.m.

SANTA MUERTE

JONATHAN RABB

The first note came in the form of a poem, or perhaps a haiku, which of course is a poem, but Saunders didn't realize that because he'd never studied Japanese. The message, though, was clear enough:

> *If you continue*
> *You will be dead, my dear friend*
> *And that will be that.*

It seemed an odd pairing, "dear friend" and "dead," but it added a kind of charm to the scrawled penmanship that, if Saunders had been looking a bit more carefully, he might have recognized. But he never bothered to take the time and instead shoved the note into the pocket of his blazer before heading out the door of his hotel room.

The blazer was more of an affectation than anything else. Mexico City in the summer was a place for short sleeves and linen pants. It was linen pants everywhere these days. No doubt the locals thought it lent them a touch of class or refinement. It was an unfair assessment—Saunders was known for his unfair assessments—and were he capable of pulling off linen pants himself, he might have felt differently. But he wasn't and he didn't.

He stepped out into the square and checked his watch. It was ten minutes before he was meant to meet her at La Tranquilidad. The café served some of the worst coffee in the city—no tea to speak of—so Saunders always brought a little tin of his own. He knew he could look forward to the glance of disdain from the waiter, but better that than the coffee.

If pressed, Saunders would have admitted he hated the heat. He had spent the first years of his relatively young life in the dank of English seaside towns, followed by three unremarkable years up at Cambridge, after which it had been more of the same in and about London. He was not one of those at the firm who secretly wished for short pants and climbing boots, pith helmets and empire. His paste white skin liked a desk and a window and a gray sky hovering drearily beyond it. It made his assignment to Mexico something of a catastrophe—personally, not professionally—but he spoke a perfect Spanish, knew the ins and outs of pharmaceuticals, and had enough Russian and German to make his way through the clutter of corporate espionage. Plus, he hated Canadians, which was always a good thing when dealing with Mexicans.

He had met Pilar his second day in the city. She was young, though not too young, and much earthier than any of the girls he had worked with in London. She smoked beautifully—smoking was still something to be admired in Mexico—with a delicacy in her lips as they reached around the cigarette before inhaling, and Saunders had felt an immediate sexual interest in her. She spoke with the same kind of daring.

"Your Spanish is good, Señor Saunders."

"Yes."

"And you're here to make my husband richer than he is."

"I believe so, yes."

"Good."

She had approached him at their first meeting not at the scheduled rendezvous but just outside it, and a few minutes early. Saunders liked that she had taken the initiative, even more so that she was punctual. So many people in his line thought there was something bold in making others wait. Saunders himself had let the clock tick on occasionally back in London—a gesture of machismo or aggression—but Pilar's devotion to accurate time had cured him of that. He checked his watch again and picked up his pace.

She was there, standing in front of the café, in dark glasses, calf-length dress, and a broad white hat that drooped down as if pointing to the small but perfect breasts he had asked about on more than one occasion. Even when lying naked next to her, he had felt the need to discuss them, such was his particular fascination.

She saw him and at once darted across the street to meet him. It was not her usual way. Never breathless, she said, "He's dead."

"What?"

"Raul. Raul is dead."

"Raul?"

She took hold of his arm and started to walk with him through the crowd. At just over six-foot-three, Saunders was convinced he was the tallest man in Mexico.

"How? When?" he said. They stared straight ahead as they moved with an unwarranted purpose.

"This morning, last night," she said. "I don't know. They found him."

"Who? The police?"

"Why would the police . . . ? No. Sergei and the man from Munich. In his office. They say it was his heart."

"I'm—" For perhaps only the third time in his life, Saunders struggled to find the right words. "I'm sorry."

"Are you?"

"Yes, of course I am."

"Even though you were screwing his wife. They think you were involved."

It was unheard of for Saunders to be at a complete loss twice in one minute, but here it was. Had he not been personally involved, he might have made a note of it.

Finally, he said, "That's absurd."

"That's what I told them. They're not convinced."

"But no one knows about us except you . . . and me."

"Obviously."

"Obviously."

"Well," she said, with too much relief, "there it is, isn't it?" She pulled him toward the Starbucks half a block from the Zocalo and together they stepped inside. It was, after all, the only decent cup of coffee in the city.

Two hours later, Saunders sat on a loveseat, nursing a very large whiskey, in the court just outside his third-floor hotel room door. The court came equipped with a small aviary so that the sound of peeping birds worked in nice counterpoint to the popping of the ice in his glass. It was like this on every floor, cages and fronds, and the distinct odor of human decay.

Pilar had gone to the coroner's, where Sergei and the man from Munich no doubt had met her. She had decided it was best for Saunders to wait for a telephone call. None had come.

All the while, the word "absurd" kept running through his head. Absurd that Raul's heart had given out. The man was a fantastically fit fifty-five. Why Pilar had found the need for comfort in the arms of a slightly pudgy Englishman remained a thing of mystery—happy mystery, but still. Absurd that Sergei and the German had been there to discover him. Absurd that he, Saunders, was sitting in a tiled and arched atrium that even the likes of Philby, Burgess, and Maclean would have found *outré*, while waiting for a call destined to condemn him. And most absurd that he'd completely missed the sound of the footsteps from the detective who was just now coming up the stairs behind him.

"Señor Saunders?" The voice was the crackle of well-worn phlegm.

Saunders turned and saw the thick face, broad mustache, and gentle eyes of Inspector Ruiz. The cigarette seemed a permanent appendage on his lower lip.

"I'm Saunders."

"Yes, Señor, I know."

"I imagine you're here about the Alvarez business."

"It would seem so."

Ruiz moved around to a long couch and sat. He squeezed his lips, inhaled, and let out a long strain of smoke through his nose.

"You worked for him?" said Ruiz. He offered a cigarette and Saunders took it.

"*With* Raul," Saunders corrected and lit up. "I'm at Nebo. Nebo Scientific. UK. We do cancer pills."

"It's good work you do then."

"Let's hope."

The two men nodded for no reason.

Ruiz said, "Alvarez Chemical was working with Nebo?"

"Nebo and Alvarez. Yes. About two years now."

"And you—"

"Two months. I've been here two months."

"That's a long time to be in a hotel room."

"I haven't been spending all of it in the room."

"So I've heard."

"Yes, I'm guessing you have."

Saunders took a long pull and brought his glass to his lips. He took a drink and exhaled. He felt Ruiz staring at him.

Ruiz said, "So we can get right to it then. You were sleeping with the wife, you wanted Alvarez out of the way, and you poisoned him."

"It was poison, was it?"

"Chemicals are your business. It would make sense."

"Excellent sense." Saunders tossed back the last of his whiskey and set the glass on the table. "I didn't do it, of course."

"No?"

"I'm leaving Mexico in two days. I don't think Señora Alvarez will be with me."

"And she knew that?"

Saunders allowed himself a nervous smile. He was also beginning to feel the booze. "I'll be forgotten before the plane lifts off. Yes—she knew."

Ruiz finished his cigarette, lit up another, and placed the fresh one on his lip. Saunders wondered if the man was even aware he had done it.

Ruiz said, "But everything points to you."

Saunders had to agree and remembered the note in his pocket. He pulled it out and placed it on the table. "The icing on the cake," he said.

Ruiz sat forward. He was careful not to touch the paper and used the back of his pen to turn it so he could read.

Saunders said, "The fingerprints will be mine and Alvarez's. It's his scrawl, I think, now that I actually look at it."

Ruiz removed a small plastic bag from his pocket and gingerly maneuvered the paper inside.

"You come prepared," said Saunders.

"You didn't kill Alvarez," Ruiz said. "The wife did. It's quite clear, but there's really nothing I can do given the way things have gone." He sealed the bag and placed it back in his pocket. "I'm in something of a bind."

"*You're* in something of a bind," Saunders said. He took the glass and lapped at the last few drops that had settled at the bottom.

"You've got no leverage," Ruiz said. "Nothing but the truth, and that's never much help."

"How are the prisons in Mexico these days?"

"Not good."

Saunders finished his cigarette and crushed it out. Two months' work was about to be tossed away, but what could he do?

He said, "And what if I do have some leverage?"

Ruiz measured him and then said, "The world would be a very different place."

"You have no idea what this is about, do you?"

"Probably not."

Saunders stood. "Tonight. At the Terrazo. Eight-thirty. Bring a few men and I'll show you my leverage."

The patter of car horns and engines, and the muted sound of a trumpet, wafted up from the Zocalo and settled just beyond the awnings of the rooftop restaurant. The food wasn't terribly good, but it was the best view of the city and Saunders imagined he wouldn't be seeing it again any time soon. He had always liked the bold line of red canopies along the stone windows of the National Palace across the way, and the colossus of the Mexican flag billowing from some unseen wind. The cathedral up on the left—dual bell towers and a cupola at the back—looked to Saunders always in need of a good wash, its grottiness prompting him to make only one foray inside during his stay. He had found it something of a pleasant surprise, its dankness reminding him of distant summer holidays, but its sense of corruption he had thought was uniquely its own. Wooden saints with chipped fingers and half-painted robes hung high above endless steps of votive candles, all ablaze as if in some unintended *auto de fé*. Printed descriptions came in the form of yellowed pages retrieved from wearily constructed wooden holds. He had been amused by the stories of Our Lady of This, Our Lady of That, no less drawn to the sellers of pagan-inspired artifacts who swarmed the area just beyond the cathedral gates. He had even bought a little Santa Muerte—Saint of Death—for himself, unaware that he might be tempting fate. In fact, it had been at the very moment of the purchase that Saunders decided to cuckold Alvarez. Seediness and spiritual duplicity seemed to his mind the perfect impetus for an affair of the heart.

Pilar, Sergei, and the man from Munich all arrived at nine. Ruiz was at a table by the door to the terrace, his men scattered about. There was no need for small talk. It was clear to them all why they were here.

"I had no idea you wanted your husband dead," Saunders began. "I thought you were happy."

"Happier now," she said.

"I couldn't convince you to admit to that more publicly, could I?"

"You killed my husband. It's a terrible thing."

"Yes, I didn't think there was much of a chance you'd do me the favor." He looked past her and nodded once toward Ruiz. Ruiz stood and made his way over. Saunders waited until Ruiz was with them before saying, "Hello, Inspector."

Pilar gave Ruiz only a passing glance. "You're going to turn yourself in," she said. "That seems the right thing to do."

"No," said Saunders, "I thought I might tell the inspector about RA-871. It's a chemoprevention agent. The señora paid me to steal it."

This was, of course, entirely untrue. Saunders had stolen the pill all on his own with the intention of selling it either to Pfessler or Granular Bragg when he got back to the UK. These days it wasn't enough simply finding the file and the formula. You had to have the hard copy, as it were. But telling Ruiz that Pilar had motives of her own—far more lucrative motives for framing him for her husband's murder—would paint things in an entirely different light. He'd have to produce the pill, of course, and that would mean no sale back home, but he imagined it was a fair price for having indulged a bit on the side. There would probably be a fine, which Nebo would pay thinking he'd stolen it for them. Next time, he'd remind himself to be more careful.

Pilar's expression was wonderfully alive—first bemused, then pained, then severe to the point of color in her cheeks.

"That's a complete lie," she said, with remarkable self-restraint.

"Then how would I have the pill," Saunders asked, "if you hadn't told me where and when I could get my hands on it?" He looked at Ruiz. "It's been kept hidden away. They brought it in on a train from one of the labs near Pueblo—ostensibly, a university research facility. She told me which train and gave me a placebo replica. I did it because I love her."

Saunders thought he might have pressed too far with this last bit, but Ruiz seemed convinced.

Ruiz said, "That would certainly be leverage, Señor Saunders. You can produce this pill?"

Saunders reached into his blazer pocket and returned with a small key. He set it on the table.

"There's a cold box under the second set of votives in the cathedral. On the left-hand side. The key opens the box and there's a storage unit for the pill inside, along with the file and the formula. You can send one of your men."

"The cathedral," said Ruiz. "Of course."

Ruiz looked at Pilar, and Saunders caught a moment in the eyes that tripped a tiny buzzing in his own ears.

The second note arrived over Saunders's shoulder just as he was about to speak. It was in the same penmanship. All it said was: *Turn around*. But it was no less poetic.

There is a moment when a man learns to take the world seriously and this was that moment for Saunders. The gun, aimed at him casually, extended out from Raul Alvarez's hand set just below his finely trimmed abdominal region.

So here it was, thought Saunders. No Inspector Ruiz, no Pilar, not even a Sergei or a man from Munich. There was—there had always only been—Alvarez.

"Such are the things we do," said Alvarez, "to keep the things that are our own."

Saunders heard a voice from down in the Zocalo, a shriek like the cry of Santa Muerte, and knew it was his time to die.

PEEPHOLE

ANDREW CROWLEY

Aren didn't remember her dream. Always, she was left with the feelings, an affective imprint she called the dream signature. But the shifting stuff of the dream—the *what*s and *where*s and *who*s—was lost. Some nights she awoke feeling euphoric, some bemused, others frightened or sad or agitated. Tonight was dread.

The time, projected fuzzily onto the ceiling by her novelty clock, read 2:13 (or maybe 2:15 or 2:23) when her eyelids cracked open. Since moving out on her own, Aren had developed an antagonistic relationship with the night. It was her dark tormentor, the depriver of all things—like light and sound and bustle—that made her not afraid. So she turned all the lights on, even the closet lights, and banged pots and cleared her throat loudly and hummed whatever upbeat pablum the radio had played at work that day. But still she was alone.

The late night talk shows, with their levity and currency, were ideal substitutes for real company, but she usually woke too late and would settle for 24-hour news or Turner Classics. Old movies had the benefit of displacing her, making her nostalgic for times she never knew, and something about the monochrome settled her bones.

It was 3:27 when she looked up from the television at the oven clock. She'd have to head back to bed soon if she hoped to be asleep by four. It was an unnatural hour—too late for night and too early to be morning—the Hour of the Wolf, her grandmother called it. If she reached it awake, her chances of getting back to sleep dropped steeply. Then she would be a prisoner of her thoughts, a captive audience to the phantasmagoria of fears and failures projected on the walls of her mind.

Ten more minutes, she allowed herself. *Well, thirteen makes it round.*

She kept her phone in the pocket of her robe, and there was the compulsion, always resisted, to call home. She would be comforted by her mother's voice, but she knew the assault would follow, some passive-aggressive warning shots, and then the frontal attack: *A girl your age shouldn't live alone; it's no wonder you have nightmares; you never should have left us.* What she wanted were the old assurances: *Mommy's right here, sweetheart; no one's going to hurt you; there's no such thing as monsters.* These weren't intentionally withheld, of course, but Aren was a grown woman, practically, and there's no use telling a grown woman what she already knows is true. Or what she knows isn't.

The Corn Is Green finished at 3:42, leaving little time for Aren to settle into a sleep state. And deadlines being inconducive to a relaxed mind, she resigned herself to three hours and eighteen minutes of waking hell on her back, and then nine more on her feet at work.

She stopped at the threshold of her bedroom. It was a sepulchral accommodation, her landlord having converted the small studio into its current, technically-one-bedroom format with some drywall and a rapacious business sense. *It looked bigger online*, she thought. Though a tenement would have compared favorably with her old bedroom on Washer Street—six inches of plaster between her and her brother's room. But at least she had slept there. Aren pulled the fitted sheet tight and contemplated her pillow and blanket options, convincing herself that a careful adjustment of linens would induce sleep. She went with a single down pillow and her grandmother's quilt, folded over to fit her twin bed. 3:48.

All right, no more fooling around. It's late and you need your sleep. Her father provided the voice of these thoughts, strong and calming, like the voice of God amid the cacophony of ghouls unleashed by her amygdala to keep her conscious. *Isn't it enough to torture me in my sleep?* She sat slowly down on the edge of the bed, not to ruffle the sheets or stir the ghouls, and reached into the drawer of her nightstand for the bottle of prescription sleeping pills procured during her last serious bout with insomnia. She had only taken one, which had the advertised effect of knocking her out and the unadvertised one of giving her night terrors. *Maybe a half-dose.* She snapped the pill in two and in careful sequence placed it on her tongue, took a sip of water, pulled the quilt up to her chin, and closed her eyes. 3:51.

The noise she heard at 3:53 could have been anything. She didn't open her eyes, for that would be fatal, but instead breathed deeply through her nose, and felt her weight on the mattress, and wiggled her toes. *Okay—be still now.*

The old building was a place of strange noises. The original pine floor had been covered with a subfloor laid over with linoleum tiles in the fifties, which gave way to hardwood at some point before being carpeted over in the eighties, for a total of four creaky layers. This combined with the din of two heating systems, as well as loose siding and shingles, poor insulation, and thin walls. These varied elements made for orchestral combinations on any night, but this sound, which continued into 3:54, was different: the grinding could have been a blender down the hall; the hissing, maybe hot air from a vent; but there was more. These were guttural sounds infused with breath. Something alive was making them. And close by.

Before she could subdue it, Aren's mind had made a list of possible sources for the noise, such that she could not ignore it. She gently folded the quilt back and, lifting her legs, rocked out of bed onto the floor. She slipped her robe back on and moved to the foyer, where a scatter of shoes gave the door swing minimal clearance. The sound was clearer here. She pressed her ear to the door first and listened. It was breathing, all right—gasping, asthmatic inhalations followed by staggered, forced releases.

Aren kept a hand in her pocket and ran her fingers over the buttons on her phone. She wondered if the breather, with his, her, or its present difficulties, could hear her heart slamming against her chest wall.

There was only one thing to do. She aligned her closed right eye with the peephole and, taking a breath, opened it. It was hard to make out anything in the distorted fisheye reality of the hallway. Her apartment was at the far end, giving her a deep perspective, and the ceiling lights shone with exaggerated intensity, like little supernovas. She watched for movement.

Something outside her neighbors' door might have been a big dog, but she knew their habit of leaving coats and shoes in the hall, and there was no movement timed to the breathing. She dwelled instead on the short jog to the stairs that received no light. Her surveillance grew difficult as the strain on her eyes blurred her vision. Her glasses would help, but they were all the way on her nightstand, and as scared as she was to look out, breaking the vigil was scarier for the same reason the dark is scarier than the light.

She made a run for it, sprinting on her tiptoes into the bedroom, snatching her glasses, and sprinting back. She cleaned them on her robe, wrapped them around her ears, and peered once again into the hall. She saw the man and looked away reflexively before her brain could process the image. She bit her lip and looked out again, another reflex.

He lay flat with his belly to the floor, crawling like infantry under barbed wire, and closing the gap between them. Was he hurt, or trying not to be seen? And why was he crawling her way? It was a dead end. He must have heard her run for the glasses. *These floors, these creaky piece-of-shit floors.*

He kept his head down as he advanced. She wanted to get a look at his face—something to tell 911—but when the man was just a few feet away, she stepped back and instinctively turned off the lights. She realized instantly that she'd given herself away, if she hadn't before. She backed up against the wall and slid down to the floor with the phone pressed so tightly between her hands that she worried it would break.

The sound was now unmistakably a man breathing, and more pointedly, a man breathing outside her door. It was so loud, it gave her hope that the fat man down the hall who listened only to Roy Orbison records, or the very old lady who talked to her dead husband, would hear it and come out and make a citizen's arrest. This man was trespassing, after all.

She was surprised not to be crying. Her mouth dried up completely, and she scraped a thick slimy layer off her tongue with her teeth. Her mind occupied itself by tallying her physiological responses and decrying nature's wholly inadequate selection. *Dry mouth, for Christ's sake?* Invisibility, laser vision—these were advantages.

Suddenly, a break in the breathing. She heard the man shifting around, straightening himself out. Her door moved. He was leaning against it.

"Is someone there?" he asked. His voice was softer, younger

than she had expected. She had expected the Devil. "I know you're there. I could see your shadow under the door."

She knew a silent 911 call would bring help, but she lost the dexterity to dial.

"I think I'm dying."

She wished he would.

"People are chasing me," he said. "Please, don't let them have me."

Her bogeyman had his own. She tasted saliva again.

"Who?" she blurted. "Who's chasing you?"

"The men who keep me. The ones who do things to me."

He knew she was there. She lost nothing by calling the police, but she didn't move, didn't speak. Her father's voice: *Step into the living room, Aren, and quietly call the police.*

The breather's refrain: "I think I'm dying."

"I'll call you an ambulance. They'll help you."

She dialed before the words crossed her lips.

"Please don't. They'll take me back."

He's lost his mind. He needs a doctor.

"They'll kill me."

"Who?" She crouched to speak at his level and placed an empathetic hand flat against the door.

"I was in jail but they took me away and did things to me—experiments."

"They don't do that sort of thing anymore."

He didn't respond. She could hear the 911 operator, who had asked twice already: "What's your emergency?"

Aren put the phone to her ear. It was the only sensible thing.

"I'll show you," he said tremulously. "You can see what they did."

As she heard the man struggle to his feet, she recalled peeking through her father's fingers at the scary parts of movies. There was none of that exhilaration now. He stood and blocked the light from the peephole.

"Just look."

She stood back from the door and slowly closed in on the lens. She could make out a human shape immediately. From a few inches back, she confirmed the basic lineaments—a nose, two eyes, and a mouth. By the time she felt the cold brass ring against her cheek, she beheld a monster. He didn't have a face so much as the markers of where one should be. His eyes were eight ball–hemorrhaged and black like a shark's. His pulpy cheeks looked like raw poultry, and his mostly bald scalp was one festering sore. It gave a putrid appearance, and she imagined a smell to go with it.

He licked his cracked, swollen lips, and his fat tongue became an eel in her mind, and other phallic images. She ran for the bathroom, but vomited in the hall. She held both hands over her mouth to muffle her screams, which she could not otherwise contain. She couldn't put his face out of her mind, and when she closed her eyes, it shone against the black like a light bulb.

She thought about trips to the video store when she was a little girl. Her brother would try to scare her in the horror section, where the distributors, in the peddling tradition of pulp and porn magazines, featured images on the covers more shocking than anything in the movie itself. These mangled, mutated fiends peered out from their clamshell cases at her, portending harm. Later, when she tried to sleep, the faces of the monsters would commingle in her mind, combine and swap features. Perhaps she was doing the same now. Maybe she was misremembering the man at the door, filling in gaps with the clamshell demons.

She heard his voice, but was too far away to make out his agonized whispers. She sat and listened, but moved no closer. She thought she heard him say "Daniel" and reasoned that it was his name. That meant someone had named him, and with this humanizing detail she tried to lift her thoughts out of the lower realm of her brain, up from the reptilian pits and into the higher chamber where reason happened. Daniel was a person and needed her help.

She thought of Roger, the border collie who had been her best friend. At their cottage, when she was nine, Roger came across some coyotes and they did a number on him. Her father managed to pluck him from the fray alive, but he lived only an hour at the vet's office. Her mother kept repeating when they let her in to say goodbye: *Don't be scared, Aren. It's still Roger.*

The blood-matted mess was still Roger, and the monster in the hall was someone's Daniel. She picked herself up, and wiping throw up from her chin, moved to the door.

"What do you want me to do?"

"They'll find me out here," he said, "and take me back and hurt me."

She straightened herself, fixed her hair, and adopted her mother's taking-care-of-business voice—the one she reserved for rude waiters and telemarketers.

"I can't let you in here, Daniel. I'm alone in here. It's out of the question."

"There are lights."

She hadn't noticed the flashing blue and red. She ran to the window and saw the police car come to a stop in front of her building. A lone officer emerged and strode to the front door. This stalwart was answering her muted call for help; he was here to slay her dragon. She ran back to the door.

"Daniel, the police are here."

He wouldn't even need to buzz in. The front door lock hadn't worked for weeks. She had thought about calling the landlord, but left it to someone else, and her laziness had let Daniel in, and now the stalwart. He would be at her door in thirty seconds.

Daniel offered nothing. She combed her brain for guidance, macheteing the jungle of moral complexity to get at the simple truth, the glimmering aphorism of a long-ago bedtime. But which fairy tale informed her predicament? Was Daniel the beast with the soul of a prince, or the huffer and puffer and eater of the pigs? As it often did, Aren's conscience ran interference for her instincts, reducing the background noise of intuition and petty self-assuring rationalizations, and tuning her in to the clean signal. That no one would begrudge her the wrong decision made it no less wrong.

She slid the chain back on its track, disengaged the dead bolt, and helped Daniel inside. She marveled at the bulk of him, the breadth of his shoulders. He pulled himself around the corner, and she closed the door and looked through the peephole again. The officer appeared in the hallway a moment later.

"Just keep quiet now," she told him, her mother ringing through her ears. "Go into the kitchen and breathe into a towel."

She watched as the policeman went about protocol in the hallway, checking his corners, observing his surroundings. His clean, handsome face occupied the space Daniel's had, just minutes before. She wanted more than anything in the world to invite this man inside, with his gun and his law. *It's still Roger, Aren.*

He tapped on the door with the butt of his flashlight, and she shuffled around to give the impression of surprise. When she opened the door, he was looking past her into the apartment.

"Ma'am, we received a 911 call from this residence. Is everything all right?"

"From here? Are you sure?"

He consulted his notes. "This is 832 Gerry Street, Apartment 205. You're Aren Donaldson?"

"I'm sorry, I had the phone in my pocket. I have emergency preprogrammed, and I must have pressed it by accident."

"You're up awfully late, Aren." He spoke in her father's voice. She thought that was strange.

"I couldn't sleep."

He looked past her again. "You know, Aren, most people are

startled when a cop knocks on the door in the middle of the night. Nine out of ten times, they ask what's wrong before we can get a word out. You looked like you were expecting me."

"I saw you pull up outside."

"I don't want you to be alarmed, but we're tracking a man who escaped from prison this evening, and we think he's still in the area."

"But there's no prison around here."

"He was being held at St. Luke's. It's Daniel Morgan Navens." He said the name like she should know it. *Daniel Morgan Navens.*

"There's blood at the other end of this hall, and more just outside your door here. You're not even looking at it."

She looked down at the carpet.

"I'm sorry, I'm really just overtired. I don't know how it got there. Really."

He leaned in close enough that she hoped he couldn't smell the throw up. "If you're in danger, just step into the hall."

He rested his hand on his holster. Every part of her wanted to stand aside. Daniel Morgan Navens was a convict, he admitted that much, and she was harboring him. This handsome, strapping man, Officer Clark according to his badge, couldn't possibly do Daniel any harm. His eyes shone with a purity of soul. *Or is that vacancy?*

But she knew better than that. Officer Clark was just a cog in a mechanism that would deliver a tortured man back to his torturers because a lot of paper said that he must.

"Well, Officer, I certainly won't be getting any sleep now."

He smiled reassuringly. "Don't you worry. We won't stop until we have him."

"I'm sorry about the call. Won't happen again."

"Sorry I disturbed you. Take 911 off your speed dial; we get five of these a night. And get some sleep now."

She closed the door and watched him leave through the peephole. At the end of the hall, he seemed a mile away. She heard him talk into his radio: "That was a misdial on the 911 at Gerry

Street. I think I spooked the girl. Hell, I think I'm spooked. You know what they call this guy, don't you?"

There was a muffled response Aren couldn't make out.

"Yeah, you know why they call him that?"

Officer Clark disappeared into the stairwell. Aren tried to imagine what cruel name had been coined to match Daniel's disfigurement. *Bastards.*

She turned back into her apartment. She could hear Daniel in the kitchen and went to him. He was sitting on the floor, resting his head against the wall like it was too swollen and heavy to hold up. She turned off the overhead light, which revealed all the details of his countenance, and left only the range hood light on. She poured a tall glass of water and handed it to him. He threw it all back and let some of it drip down his chin. She felt the knot in her stomach tighten, but got the poor man another glass.

The hydration woke him, alerting his mind to his surroundings. He saw a pretty, frightened girl filling a glass with water. *Who is she? Where am I?*

"You can't stay here, Daniel—not for long, I mean."

The hall. I crawled into the hall and talked to her through the door. Why? How did I get here?

"Are you hungry?"

The hospital. I was at the hospital. That's where they did this to me . . .

His thoughts flowed through: ". . . did this to me."

"What? I don't understand."

I ran away and I found this girl and she helped me . . .

". . . she helped me."

"Who helped you, Daniel? I want to help you."

She took an apple from the counter and reached for a knife to cut it. She saw lights in her periphery and heard Officer Clark ride away, probably still chuckling with the dispatcher, she thought, laughing about . . . *the Wolf.*

Daniel Morgan Navens is called the Wolf.

He stared at her now with his dead eyes. *The pretty girl is scared. She wanted to help me, but now she sees my face and she hates me . . .*

Why do they call him the Wolf? Because of the old lady, his grandmother. They call him the Wolf because he ate her, like the wolf in the story. The Wolf eats old ladies—but not just old ladies, maybe.

Daniel felt for something under the towel.

. . . she brought me into her apartment, but now she hates me. How many men has she brought here? She's a slut.

His hand closed around the object, which Aren could now identify as the knife missing from the counter.

Daniel Morgan Navens is the Wolf. The Wolf kills and eats people but doesn't remember it. They put him in jail, but they had to move him to a hospital, to St. Luke's, and the PTA was angry about it. They didn't want the Wolf in their neighborhood . . .

Why am I here?

Aren watched him watching her. He was between her and the door, and she knew if she ran, he could stop her. It flooded back: . . . *The Wolf blacks out and forgets what he did, but when he remembers, he hurts himself. The Wolf is a self-mutilator, and he kills and eats women, and the PTA doesn't want him here. I tried not to know this. I skipped all the articles and changed all the channels not to know this. So I could sleep.*

But she knew it all.

The pretty slut hates me because of my face and won't ever love me—like someone else. Someone else wouldn't love me and I . . .

They talked about the Wolf on television. Smart men talked about the Wolf and tried to explain him so the news wouldn't call him a monster. The Wolf was unloved and punished others for not loving him, and he hated himself, and he punished himself for what he did when they didn't.

Aren sat at the kitchen table, a few feet from where the Wolf sat.

I asked him if he was hungry. Jesus Christ, that's funny. Where will he start on me? I should be more scared, but this is so familiar. It's not scary now. Will they cut me from his belly? Will I step out whole and be reborn, like the story? Will I wake from a dream and say, "You were there. And you, and you, and you were there"?

. . . It was the old lady. She never loved me, so I made her.

There was a gasp and then light followed from blackness.

I remember.

MONSIEUR PAMPLEMOUSSE AND THE GREY DIAMONDS

MICHAEL BOND

"Sadly," said Monsieur Pamplemousse, "I never did get to dine at Picot while the *patron* was at the height of his powers. The one and only time I went there was because of something highly untoward in the cold meat store. That, in turn, led to Pommes Frites's nose being mistaken for a truffle when he rested it on a lady's knee . . . although it has to be said the latter encounter did have a satisfactory outcome. It was one of his finest moments."

His pause for effect at that point received its due reward. The mere mention in the same breath of two such legendary figures—Pommes Frites, bloodhound *extraordinaire*, late of the Paris Sûreté, and Henri Picot, until recently chef-patron of one of France's premier Three Stock Pot restaurants—was sufficient to bring all other conversation in the room to a halt.

Pommes Frites gave a deep sigh. He had been toying with the idea of taking a late night stroll through the shrubbery, but from past experience he knew that once his master got going with a story there was no knowing when it would end.

Concealing his disappointment as pointedly as possible, he lowered himself onto the carpet and closed his eyes. As an afterthought, he added a snore for emphasis—though one ear remained cocked, lest he miss something important.

The occasion was the annual staff party given by Monsieur Henri Leclercq, Director of *Le Guide*, France's oldest and most respected gastronomic bible.

The venue was, as usual, Monsieur and Madame Leclercq's summer residence in Normandy. It was well past midnight and the host and hostess, pleading urgent business the following morning, had retired to their rooms. Those remaining, however, understood that July 15 marked the start of the flat racing season in nearby Deauville, and the Director, normally the most gracious of hosts, would be keen to make an early start.

One by one the office staff drifted away. The food had been beyond reproach and the wine had flowed freely; a little too freely as far as some were concerned, for Monsieur Leclercq was not one to stint his guests. Even Madame Grante, Head of Accounts and not usually given to lowering her guard, had joined in the singing of the *Marseillaise* as the last coach headed up the driveway to begin the long journey back to Paris.

It was left to the Inspectors, accustomed as they were to serious eating and drinking, to wind up the evening with a final glass or two from a bottle of *Roullet Très Rare Hors d'Âge* Cognac left out for them, before they, too, made tracks for home. It was one of the few times in the year when they were able to hold a get-together and they intended to make the most of it.

The tail lights of the coach had hardly disappeared from view when someone told a story about a Frenchman, an Englishman, a German, and an American who found themselves shipwrecked on a desert island. The Frenchman was the only one who lived to tell the tale but, as he put it, "the gravy had been particularly good!"

After the laughter died down, that led to a discussion on the essential differences between the various nations.

Bernard made the point that had France been populated by *les Anglais*, restaurants would have been staffed by foreign waiters, for the English do not take kindly to serving others. They consider it beneath their dignity and either resort to using funny voices or acting as though they are infinitely superior to their guests, often to the extent of ignoring them altogether.

Allard was of the opinion that had France been run by Americans, Paris *restaurateurs* would no longer get away with removing the ashtray from one small table near the door to the toilet and designating it the "No smoking" area.

Glandier had a theory that with the Germans in charge it would have been dumplings all the way.

However, it was generally agreed that these very differences made life more interesting. As Duval pointed out, it is the people who mould a nation, a fact which gave France a head start, *naturellement*.

As the night wore on, conversation turned to the problems of running a restaurant, particularly the few—currently some eighteen in number—enjoying the accolade of three Stock Pots in *Le Guide.* The annual wages bill for staff alone in such establishments could run into millions of euros. As for the cost of sourcing ingredients of the highest quality, you needed a degree in higher mathematics to cope with it all.

Along with caviar, truffles were a prime example. During their comparatively short season even a modest basketful cost a small fortune. It was a chicken and egg situation; one in which Mother Nature held all the cards. Despite his best attempts, man had yet to find a successful means of producing them artificially. But then, as someone remarked, if it were that easy the market would become flooded and in no time at all they would lose their cachet and the price would plummet.

For some reason, that triggered off a discussion about the current trend of certain well known chefs to embrace the cuisine of the Far East and the rise of what had become known as "fusion" cookery: Vongerichten in New York was one of the first, and there had been a time when even Paul Bocuse had spent much of his time flitting to and fro between his restaurant in Collonges-au-Mont-d'Or and Tokyo.

The name Picot came up because in recent years he had acquired a reputation for flirting with that most dangerous of Eastern fish, the fugu. If wrongly prepared, one bite of that delicacy was capable of causing death from tetrodotoxin poisoning within moments, for there is no known antidote.

That, of course, led on to the subject of crime, which was when Monsieur Pamplemousse held forth, and in so doing managed to encapsulate each and every one of the subjects under discussion.

"You may remember," he began, "that unfortunate business last year when there was talk of awarding Picot a golden lid to his Stock Pot."

A murmur of assent went round the room. The top awards in *Le Guide* had remained unchanged for many years, but recently there had been talk of introducing an extra accolade in the form of a Golden Stock Lid for the very best in the top echelon—a kind of holy grail to which others might aspire.

Picot had been nominated, but at the very last moment not only did his restaurant *not* make the grade, it failed to gather even so much as a Bar Stool, the symbol for a venue where it was possible to obtain a good snack.

At the time people had talked of nothing else. To lose one Stock Pot was bad enough; to lose all three in one go was literally unheard of.

It had also caused a major crisis in the offices of *Le Guide* itself. If the name Picot was to be expunged from its pages not only did they have to move quickly, they had to be absolutely sure of their facts.

"So what really happened?" asked Glandier. "Give us the dirt."

Glancing up at the ceiling to make sure there were no discreetly placed cameras or microphones—the Director was very security minded and in these high-tech days one couldn't be sure of anything—Monsieur Pamplemousse began his story.

"It started with the Chief," he said, lowering his voice. "Early one morning, on the very eve of *Le Guide* going off to the printers, I received an urgent message requesting Pommes Frites and myself to join him for *petit déjeuner*; not at headquarters, but in a small café in rue Jean-Nicot, not far from Poujauran, who just for the record actually supply their *croissants*."

"It's all right for some," said Bernard. "Are they as good as everyone says they are?"

"You will have to ask Pommes Frites," said Monsieur Pamplemousse sadly. "I hardly tasted mine. He managed to down three in quick succession and lay there licking his lips during the rest of our visit.

"Monsieur Leclercq was already there when we arrived and he looked as though he hadn't slept a wink all night. There were dark shadows under his eyes and he had a plaster on his chin where he had cut himself shaving.

"I tell you, he was in such a state he hardly knew where to begin and for a moment or two we just sat there, leaving our *petit déjeuner* untouched. The Madame behind the counter was clearly restive. Such a thing had probably never happened to her before. She kept exchanging uneasy glances with her underlings."

Having set the scene, Monsieur Pamplemousse closed his eyes in order to transport both himself and his audience back in time . . .

"Monsieur Leclercq spoke first. 'Tell me, Aristide,' he said, 'how would you describe Picot's restaurant?'" (Monsieur Pamplemousse captured the Director's booming voice to perfection. Indeed, it was so realistic Pommes Frites's other ear twitched nervously in his sleep.)

"'I visualise it being the equivalent of a piece of exquisitely crafted machinery,' I replied. 'A musical box perhaps, or a rare example of the watchmaker's art—each separate part perfect in itself, yet when the many items are assembled it becomes something else again.

"'I see subdued lighting and waiters seemingly endowed with extra-sensory perception as they materialise out of the shadows, anticipating each and every customer's slightest whim.

"'I see Ministers dining together, some immersed in matters of state, others perhaps discussing affairs of the heart; here and there a captain of industry, possibly celebrating the successful conclusion of some multi-national deal or other. I see a scattering of gnomes from Zurich. Film producers accompanied by starlets . . .'

"I was just getting into my stride when Monsieur Leclercq interrupted me. 'I agree, Pamplemousse, that is how one would normally picture the scene. Unfortunately, it is far removed from what actually transpired yesterday evening when I took my wife there to celebrate her birthday.

"'Madame Picot, who is usually present to greet the guests, was nowhere to be seen.

"'That being so, as we entered, Chantal automatically turned her back on a minion so that she might be relieved of her coat; one which I might add cost a small fortune when she had it made—over one hundred wild Russian mink went into the design. It only sees the light of day on special occasions.

"'Then, as she walked away, all eyes turned in her direction. You will never guess what had happened!'

"Seeing that something was clearly expected of me," said Monsieur Pamplemousse, "I made a hasty stab at a possible answer. 'Madame Leclercq was so excited she had forgotten to put on a dress?'

"The Director clucked impatiently. 'Something even more unthinkable,' he said. 'Without so much as a second glance, the waiter let go of the garment, allowing it to fall to the floor while he drifted aimlessly away to empty an ashtray.'

"'He retrieved it for her, of course?' I said.

"'No, Pamplemousse,' said Monsieur Leclercq, 'he did not. By the time Chantal realised what had happened he was nowhere to be seen. I had to retrieve it myself.'"

Once again chuckles went round the room as Monsieur Pamplemousse captured the Director's indignant snort to a tee.

"'Perhaps, Monsieur, he was a member of Animal Rights,' I suggested. 'A lover of mink in their natural habitat.'

"'I think not, Aristide,' said the Director grimly. 'There was worse to come. Can you guess what the maître d's words were as he led us to our table?'

"Conscious that my success rating could do with a boost," said Monsieur Pamplemousse, "I decided to play it safe and suggested a *bon appetit* might not come amiss.

"'Far from it,' said the Director. 'They were, and I quote his words verbatim, for they are indelibly imprinted on my mind: *Ah, Monsieur,* he said. *The third time this week!*'

"I couldn't resist picking up the Director on that," said Monsieur Pamplemousse.

"'To dine *Chez Picot* once is beyond most people's wildest dreams,' I opined. 'But three times in one week . . . There are those who would say you are very fortunate.'

"'Unhappily, Pamplemousse,' replied Monsieur Leclercq, 'Chantal is not one of them. I had spent the earlier part of the evening telling her how much I was looking forward to the occasion, since it was many moons since my last visit. To say conversation was minimal from that point onwards is to put it mildly.

"'I tried to make amends by ordering the truffle menu. Frankly, it was little short of a disaster. The scallops were overdone and the *foie gras* left a great deal to be desired. The *poulet* when it eventually arrived resembled a backyard bird of the very worst kind—which it may well have been. And even making allowances for the fact that it wasn't the season for truffles, so they must have been preserved in some way, they tasted of absolutely nothing.

"'As for the behaviour of the *sommelier* . . . I had ordered a bottle of *Latour* '85, but before I had a chance to taste it, the wretched man grew impatient and began pouring it. His hand was shaking so much most of the wine went down the outside of the glass. That in itself would have been bad enough, but he actually had the temerity to cover the stain on the cloth with a butter dish as though it was an everyday occurrence.

"'The final indignity came at the end of the meal with the arrival of a cake I had ordered specially for the occasion. The candles turned out to be those dreadful ones that are impossible to extinguish. Chantal was not only rendered breathless, she was mortified, for it gave those at nearby tables ample opportunity to count them. She blamed me, of course, for getting the number wrong, but I swear I told them fifty, not seventy.

"'I tell you, Aristide, it was not a happy evening. Little wonder Picot spent his time skulking in the kitchen rather than brave the dining-room.

"'To compound the injury, as we were leaving, the maître d' asked after the health of my wife, adding that he hadn't seen her for a long time.

"'I am paying dearly for his crass behaviour. Chantal informs me she is visiting Dior with a shopping list this morning.'

"At that point," said Monsieur Pamplemousse, "I must admit I couldn't help feeling that all things considered the Director was getting off comparatively lightly, but before I had time to say anything he dropped his bombshell.

"'On their showing yesterday evening,' he said, 'Picot doesn't deserve one Stock Pot in *Le Guide*, let alone three. As for the award of a Golden Lid, that is clearly out of the question.

"'Somehow or other we must contrive to get behind the scenes while preserving our anonymity.'

"'That will be no easy task, Monsieur,' I said. 'Picot is reputed to have a very short temper. He is not renowned for welcoming visitors to his domain when the service is in full swing. It will need someone skilled in the art of subterfuge; perhaps making use of an accomplice to create some kind of diversion while the other makes notes.'

"'*Exactement*, Pamplemousse,' said Monsieur Leclercq. 'You have hit the nail on the proverbial head. That is why I suggested this meeting. Your time spent with the Paris Sûreté fits you admirably for the task. I can think of no-one better. I suggest when you go there this evening you take with you not only Pommes Frites—I would value his opinion on the *foie gras*—but your dear lady wife, Madame Pamplemousse. At an appropriate moment she can ask to see around the kitchens.

"'I want you to note down all that transpires and report back to me as quickly as possible. Something untoward is going on and we must take immediate action. I cannot hold the presses for long. People will start to talk.'

"I considered the matter," said Monsieur Pamplemousse. "Monsieur Leclercq was right to be worried. His disastrous meal apart, discretion has always been one of the restaurant's hallmarks. Over the years the waiting staff must have been privy to more state secrets than the whole of successive French cabinets put together. The fact that nothing has ever been revealed was, I suspect, one of the chief reasons why Picot received *La Légion d'honneur*.

"'But, Monsieur,' I said, clutching at straws, 'will I be able to get a table? The waiting time is normally many months for those who are not regulars.'

"'Rest assured, Pamplemousse,' said Monsieur Leclercq, 'there will have been cancellations. Word travels swiftly in the higher gastronomic circles of Paris. Bad news spreads like wildfire, and I was not the only dissatisfied customer that night. They will greet you with open arms.'

"I must confess I felt dubious. 'Doucette will not be happy, Monsieur,' I said. 'She hates going to places where the guest menu is unpriced. As for suggesting she visit the kitchen . . . She will undoubtedly say she has nothing to wear.'

"'Tell her to take an apron,' said the Director crossly. 'Buy her a new dress. Two if necessary. I will authorise your expense account with Madame Grante.'

"'Suspicions will be aroused, Monsieur,' I warned. 'She is funny that way.'

"'In that case,' said the Director, 'you must arrange for someone else to act as a partner. There must be others you can call on.'

"'If you are suggesting I call on the services of an escort agency,' I said, 'that, too, might have unhappy repercussions. Especially if I arrive home late.'

"'Don't be difficult, Pamplemousse,' said Monsieur Leclercq testily. 'You know very well what I mean.'

"He fell silent for a moment or two, then the merest hint of a smile spread over his face. 'Leave it to me, Aristide,' he said, 'I think I know the very person.'"

Monsieur Pamplemousse chose that moment to break off his story. Sensing the appetite of his colleagues had been well and truly whetted, he allowed the others time to recharge their glasses before continuing.

"Our arrival at the restaurant that evening went smoothly enough," he said, when quiet was restored. "Pommes Frites received a gracious welcome from Madame Picot; although having said that, I thought I detected signs that she had recently been crying. Despite skilfully applied make-up there was a slight puffiness about the eyes. The right one looked distinctly bloodshot, possibly as a result of mascara running into it.

"The Director was correct in his forecast. There were a number of empty tables, so I was able to decline the first we were offered in favour of one nearer the kitchen. As I'm sure you all know, Picot is one of those restaurants where the *brigade* can be seen at work behind a long, soundproof window and I wanted to be as near to it as possible.

"A place was laid for Pommes Frites under the table and while a waiter went to fetch a bowl of water, he made himself comfortable on a silk cushion, doubtless with the intention of keeping an eye on things from his hidden vantage point.

"I sometimes wonder," mused Monsieur Pamplemousse, "what I would do without him."

He maintained a respectful silence while his audience contemplated the unthinkable.

"Meanwhile," he continued, "I began my usual routine of checking the system. Helping myself to an olive, I deposited the stone in the centre of a large Bernardaud plate discreetly initialled with the letter 'P' in gold leaf.

"The plate was promptly whisked away, only to be replaced seconds later with a clean one. It was the kind of attention to detail that might be construed by some as the ultimate in perfection and by the less charitable as an attempt to unnerve a new diner. Deciding it was the latter, I mentally deducted points because the letter 'P' was facing the wrong way on the replacement.

"Give the man his due, it didn't happen when I consumed a second olive and a third plate arrived.

"Glancing through the window to my left I saw the *patron* moving about amongst the kitchen staff. Not for the first time I was struck by the parallel that might be drawn with the world of ballet; each and every player carrying out their moves with ease and precision night after night, day in, day out.

"And yet . . . as I eyed the scene reflectively . . . was it simply my imagination, or was there something odd about the ballet master himself?

"Monsieur Picot was reputed to be a 'hands-on' chef, yet not once did he so much as dip his finger into a sauce or pick up a spoon to taste one of his creations. If anything he seemed to be acting like a fish out of water. Plates offered for inspection on their way to the dining-room received only a cursory glance; not a single one was commented on or sent back. Everything was distinctly low key.

"Having ordered an *aperitif*, I turned my attention to the *carte* while waiting for my unknown guest to arrive. Clearly, whomever the Director had in mind, their strong suit was not punctuality.

"A ripple of laughter came from a party of Japanese ladies occupying a large table on the far side of the room. They looked as though they had been on a shopping spree, probably paid for by their company as a reward for good work during the year. Hermès scarves abounded.

"And everywhere there were fresh flowers. Madame Picot is noted for her good taste and no expense is spared in expressing it.

"A waiter went past bearing a credit card validating machine on a silver platter. He crossed to a bureau near the reception area and placed it discreetly inside a drawer, sliding it gently shut lest the sound of the tiny printer disturb the other diners.

"I reached for the notepad I always carry in a hidden pocket of my trousers on such occasions. It was a bonus point, and I must confess for a moment or two I began to wonder if Monsieur Leclercq hadn't overstated matters.

"Seeing a waiter approaching with my *aperitif*, I was about to remove the menu to make room for the glass when he stumbled and almost dropped the glass in my lap.

"'Forgive me, Monsieur . . .' he said, looking over my shoulder, 'I . . .'

"Turning to follow the direction of the man's gaze, I have to confess my own heart missed a beat.

"You will never guess who I saw emerging through a service

door leading to the kitchen. Even from across the room I would have recognised the legs anywhere. As for her other accoutrements . . .

"Their owner was carrying a large Gucci bag and as she caught sight of me she waved and blew me a kiss.

"Elsie was the very last person I had expected to see and at first I wasn't sure whether to be pleased or not. But one thing was certain; I couldn't have wished for a better ally, or one I would have trusted more."

Monsieur Pamplemousse paused.

As ever, the mere mention of Elsie's name caused yet another stir amongst his audience, even among those who had never met her, for Nature had been more than generous in its manifold gifts to Elsie; a fact that hadn't escaped Madame Leclercq's notice, and she had lost no time in putting her foot down. Despite the fact that her cooking was out of this world, Elsie's stint at the Leclercqs' residence was short lived. But at the time she had left her mark on all who came into contact with her, and it was a case of once seen never forgotten.

Monsieur Pamplemousse waited patiently until the wolf whistles and obscene grunts had died down before returning to *Chez Picot* . . .

"'What on earth are you doing here?' I asked.

"'I got a call from on 'igh, didn't I?' she said. 'Made me an offer I couldn't refuse, so I came over this morning on Eurostar. First Class, all expenses paid.'

"Reaching into her bag she produced a clip-board. 'Ron's right. 'E maintains all you need to put the fear of God into a restaurant is to turn up armed with one of these and ask to see 'round the kitchen. It works best when they are at their busiest. Open a fridge door or two and peer inside, lift a few saucepan lids and do likewise, run your fingers along the work surfaces, making sucking noises through your teeth all the while. Jot a few things down while shaking your 'ead, and you've got them where you want them. Tell them 'ow sorry you are, but regulations is regulations, and others will be in touch once you've made your report.'

"'How is Ron, by the way?' I asked her, referring to her partner, who seems to spend most of his time behind bars.

"'All right,' said Elsie. 'Sends 'is regards. Only got another three months to do.'

"'And he is happy?'

"'Like a pig in you know what,' said Elsie. 'Ron's got it made where 'e is—all mod cons—telly, fax machine, e-mail on 'is computer, most of 'is pals around 'im. No aggro. Apart from that we see each other every weekend to catch up on you know what. 'E's going to feel the draught when 'e gets out.'

"I decided to change the subject," said Monsieur Pamplemousse.

"'So,' I asked. 'Having carried out your inspections, what are your conclusions?'

"'Well,' said Elsie mysteriously, 'if I was you I'd stick to the fish.'

"'Why do you say that?' I asked.

"'Because,' she said, lowering her voice. 'There's a dead body in the cold meat room . . .'

"'A dead body?' I repeated. 'You mean a stiff?'

"'They don't come any stiffer,' said Elsie. 'They tried to tell me it was a side of beef.'

"'Are you sure it wasn't?' I asked.

"'The top 'alf was all wrapped up in butter muslin,' said Elsie, 'but I could see 'is face poking through. 'E looked Chinese.'

"To prove her point she produced a mobile phone and punched up a picture.

"'Anyway,' she continued after I'd had a good look, 'sides of beef don't come wearing trousers. If you ask me, somebody dressed him in an 'urry; shoes on the wrong feet, fly's open. We women notice that kind of thing.'

"I had been thinking of ordering the truffle menu," said Monsieur

Pamplemousse, "but my mind was racing with other things. It was possible, of course, that a member of the staff had died on the job. As you well know, death in a restaurant during opening hours is always a problem. The arrival of morticians to dispose of the body tends to cast a gloom over the proceedings . . .

"Just then Elsie gave a squeak. 'Ooh!' she cried. 'You don't change, do you?'

"For a moment," said Monsieur Pamplemousse, "I thought she was talking to me, as did everyone else around. Then I realised she was addressing Pommes Frites. Having recognised her voice, he was making his presence felt by resting his chin on her knee.

"'Doesn't lose any time, does 'e?' said Elsie. 'Talk about 'aving a nose like a wet truffle . . . any more of that and I shan't give you your prezzy, but thanks for reminding me!'

"Reaching inside her bag, she produced a round black object about the size of a golf ball. 'Found it along with a pile of others in the deep freeze.'

"Pommes Frites emerged from under the table, gave the object a passing sniff, then dismissed it in favour of resting his head on Elsie's knee again."

"Can't say I blame him," said someone at the back of the room. "I'd have done the same. Truffles are all nobbly, whereas from what I remember of Elsie's knees . . ."

"Be that as it may," Monsieur Pamplemousse cut in. "As it happened, Elsie was thinking what I was thinking.

"'That's not like you, Pommes Frites,' she said. 'Saying no to a truffle. Don't tell me your nose is playing up. I thought you were supposed to 'ave won some kind of an award for it when you were in the police.'

"'The Armand Marcel "Sniffer Dog of the Year" award,' I reminded her.

"'On the other 'and, Monsieur Leclercq did say 'e found 'em tasteless when 'e dined here last night, so 'e 'as a point.'

"'I wonder,' I suggested, 'if we shouldn't dine somewhere else? There is a lot to talk about and we can come back here later when things are quieter.'

"'Some'ow,' said Elsie, 'I 'ad a feeling you might say that.'"

"A cunning move," broke in Glandier enviously.

"We went back to Picot later that night," said Monsieur Pamplemousse, ignoring the remark. "It was nearly midnight. There is nothing like catching people at the end of a long day when they are tired and all they want to do is get to bed.

"At first they tried to bluff their way out, denying all knowledge of a body. They all shut up like the proverbial clams. Chefs stick together. It is a kind of brotherhood. They even took us into the cold room to prove their point. They must have used the time to put the body elsewhere. No doubt it had been expertly dissected.

"But Elsie stuck to her guns and when she produced her photograph it didn't take long before everything came pouring out, helped on its way by a few choice warnings about everyone present being accessories after the fact.

"The story, as told by Madame Picot, is that the previous afternoon, between lunch and dinner, Monsieur Picot returned to his restaurant and found a gang waiting for him. Having read somewhere of the daily turnover—a figure that doubtless had been trebled or even quadrupled by the media—they had come to stake a claim. They reckoned without the fact that in a restaurant like Picot very little actual money changes hands. It is all done on account or by credit card.

"Despite all his protests, they refused to believe him—even when he showed them the contents of the safe—so they resorted to a particularly fiendish form of torture. They sat him on a hot plate and threatened to keep turning up the heat until he talked.

"As Elsie succinctly put it: 'I've 'eard of people putting things on the back boiler, but that's ridiculous!'

"Fortunately, before they could carry out their plan other

members of the staff came to his rescue. A fight broke out, and during the course of it, there being no shortage of knives, the ringleader was stabbed to death. Everyone denies seeing who was responsible, of course, but I strongly suspect Picot himself. In any event the rest of the gang fled and *Chez Picot* suddenly found itself near opening time with a dead body on its hands.

"Imagine the dilemma. Three visits in one week from the Director of *Le Guide*; it didn't need a mathematician to put two and two together to guess what was behind it. They were desperate. One breath of scandal and their chance of a Golden Stock Lid would be gone for another year."

"The Chief wouldn't be pleased if he knew he'd been recognised," broke in Glandier. "Imagine the fuss he would have made if it had been one of us."

"Monsieur Leclercq is like a great many people in a position of power," said Monsieur Pamplemousse. "They go to great lengths to avoid being recognised and then get upset when they aren't. At such moments he has an endearing habit of turning his profile to the audience.

"Anyway, by the time they had cleaned up and got rid of all the blood, the first of the evening guests were arriving. They did what seemed to be the best thing at the time—they put the body in the cold room."

"So it was there all the time the Chief and his wife were dining," said Bernard. "That explains why Picot kept out of the way."

"He not only kept out of the way," said Monsieur Pamplemousse. "He wasn't even there. He'd gone off to hospital to have his burns treated."

"Then who was it?" asked Glandier. "Don't tell us they found a look-alike at five minutes' notice."

"It wasn't necessary," said Monsieur Pamplemousse. "There was one already to hand. Picot has a twin brother.

"I tackled Madame Picot on that very point and in the end she showed me a family photograph. Picot's brother is an accountant with no interest whatsoever in food—he can't even boil an egg without burning the saucepan. He was brought in until things could be sorted out and they were safe for another year."

"They planned to carry on like that until after publication day?" exclaimed Allard. "No wonder the staff didn't know whether they were coming or going."

"At that point it was still panic stations," said Monsieur Pamplemousse. "Besides it wouldn't have been for very long. Once *Le Guide* goes to press there is no turning back. I doubt if anyone had thought it through. Picot, to coin a phrase, was 'going for gold' and nothing was allowed to stand in his way."

"What did Monsieur Leclercq have to say about it when you told him?" asked Guilot.

Monsieur Pamplemousse assumed his Director's voice. "'We are none of us perfect, Aristide, and chefs are only human. The heat plays havoc with their metabolism. I think we should err on the side of leniency and let artistry receive its just reward. Strings can be pulled. That is what they are there for. It just so happens that in a few days' time I shall be dining with the appropriate Minister . . .'"

"If that was the case," broke in Glandier, "why didn't Picot himself send for the police? Surely, with all his contacts it wouldn't have been too late."

"No court anywhere in the world would have found Picot guilty of murder," agreed Glandier. "Given a good lawyer, he could have pleaded self defence."

"He would have needed a good one," said Monsieur Pamplemousse. "Hiding the body in the cold room wouldn't have looked too good for a start. Disposing of it would have been something else again. Skilled in the art of butchery as they are, it wouldn't have been much of a problem to get rid of the bits and pieces. However, I agree, and I must admit I asked myself the same questions.

"Something kept bothering me about the way Madame Picot

told the story. Not once did she mention the nationality of the gang, and yet Elsie swore the body she saw had been that of a Chinese man and her picture seemed to confirm it.

"There was only one possible answer. Picot had something to hide. Which was where Pommes Frites came in. He didn't win the title 'Sniffer Dog of the Year' for nothing."

Reaching into his pocket, Monsieur Pamplemousse removed a small object wrapped in silver foil, carefully undid it, and held what was revealed for all to see.

"Exhibit 'A,'" he said. "Often known as the Black Diamond of French cuisine. Only in this case it happens to be 'grey' in colour. Elsie gave it to me as a souvenir. I carry it with me as a reminder of the standards we are all honour bound to uphold.

"It is not, as one might think at first sight, a *tuber melanosporum* from Périgord; smelling and tasting of the French earth from which it sprang. It is a Chinese truffle from the province of Szechwan, and on the wholesale market costs a third of the price.

"The truth is, for some time Picot had been passing them off as the real thing. If it hadn't been for Pommes Frites turning up his nose and revealing it for what it was, he might have carried on doing so. My guess is that the gang who paid him a visit had blackmail in mind; they were threatening to reveal all. That, on the eve of *Le Guide*'s publication, would have been a total disaster."

"But why would he do that?" asked Allard. "A man in his position who stood to lose everything."

Monsieur Pamplemousse shrugged as he slowly rewrapped his exhibit. "We shall probably never know. As we agreed earlier, running a Three Stock Pot restaurant these days is not all champagne and caviar; more and more it is a matter of balancing the books. Unfortunately, though, there can be no short cuts to perfection."

"So that's why the Chief dropped Picot," said Glandier.

"For Monsieur Leclercq," said Monsieur Pamplemousse, "publisher of the most prestigious food guide in France, there was no other choice. There is no greater crime in the world of *haute cuisine* than that of 'passing off.' To ignore it would have been tantamount to saying it was of no account. The perpetrator received his just punishment, but it was an ignominious end to a glittering career."

The room fell silent.

"Going back to our earlier conversation," said Bernard. "If Picot had been English, he would have sold his story to the tabloids and lived happily ever after."

"If he had been American," said Allard, "he would have done even better by writing a book, and ended up selling the film rights."

"I have no idea how a German might have reacted," said Glandier, "but if he'd been Japanese, he'd have issued a formal apology and disappeared into dignified retirement."

"How about a certain person?" Someone else broke the silence. "What do you think he thought of it all?"

"Perhaps," said Monsieur Pamplemousse, "you should ask him."

All eyes turned towards his friend and mentor. For a moment or two the answer remained elusive, then, Pommes Frites gave vent to a long drawn-out sigh as he stretched himself luxuriously on Monsieur Leclercq's favourite Caucasian rug.

To the uninitiated it might have sounded suspiciously like another snore, but those in the party who knew him better recognised it immediately as the canine equivalent of *c'est la vie*—it was all in a day's work.

ANIMAL PLANET

JO NESBØ

TRANSLATED FROM THE NORWEGIAN BY DON BARTLETT

They don't know what gravitation is. Or, to be more precise, they don't know *why* it is there, why this planet's mass causes dead sparrows to fall to the ground. Or the sun to go on its perfectly predictable orbit around the Earth. Or is it vice versa? Whatever. All they know is that there *is* gravity. A merciless law that just is, like a blind dictator who has forgotten what he wanted, which without any programme, morality, or discernible purpose determines our lives. And we are small planets and moons that go round and round in perfectly predictable orbits, held in check by the mass of the sun and gravity. Or is it vice versa? Shit! I look down at the rifle that has slid along the table and startled me as it hit the floor. I was on the verge of falling asleep again. I breathe in and out quickly, take air down into my lungs to get more oxygen to my brain while peering into the horizon with sore eyes, at the unbroken line of the expanse that surrounds me on all sides. No one. Nothing. Empty. Just heath, rock, moss, and a cleansed sky with a sun in a slow circuit. I bend down, pick up the rifle, put it on the table in front of me. It only took a couple seconds, yet I scan the new countryside, hunting for a movement, a change, a warning of what is to come. Because it is going to come. *They* are going to come. My eyes smart from staring at this expanse under a sun that never goes down, my skin is numb, anaesthetised by bites from blood-thirsty mosquitoes, and my body is screaming for sleep after endless passages of time just waiting, keeping watch, drinking coffee, smoking, and thinking. But after a while the brain stops obeying, the mind wanders, you begin to think about what happened. Why you are here: in a shack under the midnight sun in the middle of the Finnmark plateau. A weakened sun so near to the North Pole but which can still make the heat inside the shack quiver, which makes the boards and the tar stink and the sweat run into your eyes. And you are thinking about gravitation.

Outside, swarms of mosquitoes dance in the diagonal light. Again I check that the rifle's safety catch is off. As if I could be caught off-guard. But there is not a tree, not a mound of earth, not a rock to hide behind for four kilometres in any direction. And my no-man's land is floodlit day and night. I will see them long before they get here. I will be able to pick them off one by one. I have cupboards and shelves full of ammunition. But they are going to come anyway. Why? It is gravitation. It just *is*.

The sun was shining on the northern wall of the shack when I heard the bell twist sharply and saw that the reindeer buck had raised its head. The antlers were still, like a statue, silhouetted against the sky. I pointed the rifle at the animal. Aimed at the chest above the front legs where I imagine the heart is. I saw the reindeer for the first time last week. *Saw*, didn't hear. It is strange. You would think sound carried a long way over this open terrain, but that is not the case. Maybe it is because of all the mosquitoes; they are like a duvet. At any rate, I didn't hear the bell it wore around its neck until it was a couple hundred metres from the hut. Since then it has been grazing around here. Eating grass. Do you call it grazing when animals eat lichen? *Lichens?* Whatever.

It must be an outcast from a herd. Perhaps it has done something unforgivable. Succumbed to some temptation or other. Mated with one of the alpha male reindeer's heifers. It was unlikely to survive long on its own. There are wolves up here; they howl at the moon, just like the wolves on Animal Planet. In the summer, like now, the reindeer would outrun them, but when the snow comes its thin legs will sink down, while the wolves with their broad paws will have the necessary support, the necessary thrust. Animal Planet. It is inevitable. It is gravity.

I lowered the rifle. I had no intention of shooting it. Of course it was tempting. Just to shoot, to kill, to bring down the prey. It is natural. It is instinctive. But it was practical having an alert animal with a bell; it could act as a guard dog. And then there was the company. The mute animal cleared off as soon as I opened the door, but nevertheless. It was someone. Because I was so damned lonely. It was the worst part. The mozzies, the sun, the lack of sleep; I could cope with that. But the loneliness . . . And the sound of Amelie's death throes that woke me every time I closed my eyes for too long and was on the verge of sinking into deep sleep. The screams that at one point drove me to put the rifle in my mouth. To taste the salty metal and gun oil. To steal a march on them. But it was a long barrel and my finger had not been able to reach the trigger. I had wept for hours afterwards. I was not used to loneliness. And seeing the outcast reindeer out there, I knew why it was grazing here of all places. We were a flock. A flock of two.

Mikkel came. He was easily recognisable with his bowlegged, rolling gait. And the rest was like all the other Sami I had seen: small, thickset, black-haired with narrow eyes in a broad face that possessed two expressions: stony, and stony with a grin. I paid him to buy me food, tobacco, and booze in the village and bring it to me once a week. I had absolutely no doubt that he was cheating me; the receipt was always "gone" or he had "forgotten" it. He claimed the liquor he brought cost four hundred kroner a bottle, but I knew where it came from; I recognised the seal. He was a man of few words, but was hardly likely to keep his mouth shut if someone tossed a silver coin onto the table and asked if anyone knew where I was hiding. But what could I do? It wasn't as if I had a lot of people to choose from. My hope was that it would take them time to trace my movements to that dump of a village down in the hollow, because you would be hard put to find anywhere more off the beaten track.

I opened the window.

"Hot," said Mikkel, wiping the sweat from his brow and putting the rucksack down on the heath. "There's a wedding on Saturday. Coming?"

He spoke Norwegian with Sami intonation. That is, with stress and a high key on the first or second word and falling thereafter through the rest of the sentence, whatever the content. It made everything sound like a lament.

"I haven't been invited, man," I said, picking a strand of tobacco off my tongue and watching while he unpacked the plastic bags from the rucksack and placed them by the closed door.

"Cut the crap," Mikkel said. "No one needs an invite in K. Everyone comes. Nice women."

"Mm." I scanned the horizon. The shack was one room, three metres square with windows in all the walls. I assumed it had been built for herdsmen to keep an eye on the flock. Or hunters. If anyone was going to lead them here, it would be Mikkel. But not unseen. They would suffer casualties.

"Hot women," Mikkel said. "Moonshine." He swung on the empty rucksack, squinted at me with the eternal sun in his eyes, and mounted his second expression. The one with the grin. "You need a good screw, Odd."

I smiled. Not because of his reference to screwing, which was quite true, but because he used the name we both knew was false.

He turned his back on me and began to walk across the heath. "Twelve o'clock in the church!" he shouted.

The church was small and nestled in the centre of a clump of houses, which was K.

From where I was standing, some distance away, it looked as though the houses were clinging to the church, the way that animals sought the centre of the herd, where there was the most security.

Organ music wafted from inside. I had dug up the jacket and shirt I was wearing when I arrived here some time in June. And I had rinsed my hair in a stream on the way down from the plain. Which was a waste of time since it had started to rain straight afterwards, the first time in four weeks. I was soaked and already regretted setting out on the walk. I had convinced myself by saying I was only going to pop down to see. To recce. Stretch my legs. Check everything was as it should be. And—if it all seemed calm—perhaps poke my head round the church door and see if what Mikkel had said was true: that there were some nice-looking women there.

The hike had taken four hours. And I was freezing.

Then I went into the church.

I had stepped in regardless.

The church was half-full. Which is to say that the majority of K's inhabitants had turned out. I hadn't seen any good-looking women in the few hours I spent in the village when I first arrived, and I couldn't see any now. On the other hand, I was sitting at the back and no one had turned round when I entered. But none of them looked that great from the back. Not even that.

"The man we are burying today . . ." the priest intoned.

Burying? Wasn't this supposed to be a wedding?

". . . was not without blemish," the priest said, placing his hand on the white coffin where he was standing.

Yeah, well, these people drank and partied hard. And in my

experience death had never stopped the sex drive. More the opposite.

"He stole and coveted his neighbour's wife," the priest continued. "And while God forgives our sins, man is not always as forgiving. This is why he ended his life in this brutal and horrific manner."

I straightened up. I had been walking for four hours, so if the priest had a good story with "brutal" and "horrific" in it, I was a willing listener.

"The deceased worked as a truck driver for a boss who ran a profitable business. The company imported goods from outside the usual channels so that the products could be sold to ordinary folk for reasonable money instead of the exorbitant prices that were charged after the politicians had imposed their insane taxes."

"I'll drink to that!" shouted a candid soul in the congregation.

The priest smiled with indulgence. "The deceased cast his eyes on the boss's young wife. And she—in her youthful innocence—allowed herself to be seduced. Afterwards, he persuaded her that the two of them were meant for each other, and proposed—out of fear of reprisals—that they should flee together and settle in another country. But in order to acquire the funds to do so he stole a truck of imported goods and pocketed the income from the resulting sales. Then he drove the empty truck to Oslo to collect the young wife at an appointed place."

I was dreaming. This had to be a lack of sleep.

"But something happened," the priest continued. "The woman was not enough of a schemer to play her role. The boss became suspicious. And when he found the new passport in her bag he put two and two together."

I screwed my eyes shut and opened them again. High time I woke up.

"When the deceased did not find her where they had arranged

he rang her number. And got the boss on the line. And the boss let him listen as they killed her."

I heard a sob. Mine. Someone turned round. I quickly looked down, desperately trying to take in air.

"The boss swore his faithless employee would suffer the same fate as his wife. The deceased threw the telephone out of the window, started up the truck, and fled north. He drove day and night, not even stopping to eat or sleep. Finally he found a fjord deep enough to swallow up the truck without leaving a trace. He continued by bus and on foot. And eventually discovered a place where he thought he could hide."

I had to get out. But I had barely got to my feet before I sat back down. For two men had taken up position in front of the church door. Black suits, hands calmly folded. Blond and twice as tall as the Sami filling the pews.

The priest lowered his voice: "But darkness fell. And destiny caught up with him." He bent his head for the final words: "May peace be upon his memory."

The organ burst into life; a mighty tidal wave of notes washed through the narrow church. The priest nodded and five men jumped up from the front pew and lined up on either side of the white coffin. I leaned over to my neighbour and whispered: "What's the dead man's name?"

"I don't know," the man answered in the language of the lament. "But I think the priest said Daniel."

Daniel. I gulped. Closed my eyes. This was not happening. This simply was not happening.

"Odd!"

I heard this from far, far away.

"Odd!"

It was Mikkel's voice. He was here. He was standing outside a shack window trying to wake me. Relieved to relinquish the rest of the dream, I opened my eyes. I was still in the narrow church that stank of wood and body odour. Mikkel was one of the coffin-bearers and he was standing by the altar waving to me.

"We need one more strong man, Odd!"

I rose to my feet, staggered up the aisle, and took up the sixth and final post beside the coffin.

"Lift," the priest murmured.

I grabbed the handle on the side and lifted. I am five-feet-nine tall, so I knew I would be carrying the brunt. But the coffin was light. Too light. As light as a coffin without a body.

We carried it to the now open church door, and I felt the eyes of the congregation on me as I looked down at my feet to make sure I didn't trip.

Outside, the light on the plain wooden houses and the deserted, colourless countryside was grey. Autumn came early up here in the north. And it didn't last long. It could start to snow tomorrow if it felt like it.

The two blond giants each held a door open to the back of a black van. We pushed the coffin in. The doors were slammed shut. The two men climbed into the driver's cabin, started the engine, and slowly drove away.

"What's happening?" I asked Mikkel. "Isn't he going to be buried in the cemetery here?"

Mikkel shook his head. "We don't bury people here. In the winter the frozen ground forces the coffins back up. Cracked, and with the bodies perfectly intact."

I stared at him.

"But the gravestones?" I said, nodding towards the cemetery beside the church.

"Gravestones for us to visit," he said. "The bodies are buried down south, in soft ground."

The van had stopped in the car park. The ceremonial sending-off was finished. The two men stepped out of the van. Straightened their jackets.

"Who are—?" I began.

"Funeral parlour drivers from down south. They're taking the body tomorrow."

Could I have seen them before? Perhaps, who knows? Herr Schmidt's import company was not small.

I wake with a jerk to Amelie's screams. The light has gone. I rub my eyes. The rifle has slipped to the floor again. I pick it up, put it to my shoulder, scan the grey horizon through the sights. The sun has gone down for the first time in two months. It probably corresponds with a sunny day on some planet rotating a little more slowly than the Earth. But even there the day will end; it is predictable and it is inevitable. It is gravitation.

For the moment, I can't see anyone out there. My sights have stopped on the reindeer standing with its head stooped over the moss-grown rocks. The sun will be up again soon. But tomorrow the night will be a little longer and a little darker. I won't see them come.

I sniff the air. It is a smell I recognise. The smell of snow.

The reindeer suddenly raises its head. Stands there, tense, listening. Antlers against the night sky.

I take a deep breath.

Stealing a march on them.

I press the trigger with my index finger. Aim at the chest above the front legs where I imagine the heart is.

THE HAUNTED CEILING

H. G. WELLS

At first, when Meredith made the room his study—it was a year after he took the house—the ceiling was as commonplace as any ceiling could be: slightly discolored by smoke (for the chimney always smoked when the wind was westward, in spite of Meredith's experimental openness to patent cowls), and perhaps a shade paler near the centre. But that was all. After the inauguration of the study, the darkness of the ceiling grew apace for Meredith was always leaving his matches and turning up the lamp beyond its natural conditions in order to light his pipe. Besides which, about Christmas, one of the patent cowls got tired of always having its back in the wind or grew faint from overmuch rotation. Anyhow, it took to swallowing the air in spasmodic gulps, so that the study was filled with a haze of little dry tiny black tadpoles during the whole period of its aberration, and not only with black specks, but with some of the choicest language I have ever heard—even for Meredith. Early in January however, he got a new cowl that acted fairly well when it was not jammed, and thereby the nuisance was abated, almost as much as if he had had no cowl.

But this intemperate inhalation of particles of soot, coupled it may be with the influenza bacillus, made Meredith ill. He sat at his work with his cold growing worse with him, until at last early in February the cold, and a cough that followed, and that wretched sense of thick-headedness that was so distinctive of the influenza, drove him to bed. And there he fell back upon his favorite panacea of well-matured Scotch whiskey.

Now I don't think Meredith and his wife got on very well together. This is pure supposition on my part, for usually when I went to see him she was invisible. It may be I do her an injustice in saying she neglected him. Yet it seems to me that there must be something a little wrong when a man who is ill as he was is allowed to lie and sodden himself with whiskey as he did. However, his great secluded drink certainly ended in the cure of his cold.

When I went to see him early in March he was back in his study, but lying on a couch in a very shaky state, loose and trembling about the lip and red and shifty in the eye.

"Look at all that work," he said, pointing to a pile of books by his desk. "It's worrying me awful."

He sat up and filled his pipe. About as much tobacco fell on the floor.

"It's a beast of a job with me this time," he said, trying to set a light from a match that jerked and vibrated over his pipe. "My mind's got out of hand. Won't fall in. Won't march."

He sat and stared at the fire for a few minutes while I told him he would be better soon and worked delicately round to a warning against very much more whiskey. He bit the mouthpiece of his pipe.

"You're right enough," he said. "Perfectly right. *Delilium*—what is it? *Delilium* tremens—can't be nice. And I'm near it. I don't doubt I'm near it."

He passed his hand over his eyes. "I haven't got it. That wall-paper"—he pointed with his pipe—"ought to make faces at me. There ought to be beasts come and look at me round the legs of the table, and rats—green rats for each of these green dabs on the carpet. Really there's nothing of the sort."

He looked upward over his shoulders suddenly and then asked me for another match. His pipe had gone out. I got up and lit it for him. He looked at the smoke just in front of him and ran his fingers through it.

"No rats there," he said. "No delusions. You see I'm perfectly clear-headed.

"Now tell me," he continued after my assent, and fixing an inflamed eye upon me, "do you see anything remarkable about this room."

I looked round. "New?" I asked.

"In a way."

I turned to look behind me. He twisted himself at the same time so as to follow my eyes.

There was the same old sage green paper, the same tall book-case, the same table with periodicals and cuttings from the Cosmic Press Agency, the darker ceiling. Even the heap of unbound *Athenaeums*—the lower ones grey with sooty particles—was just as it had always been in the corner.

"Don't you see it?" he said.

"See what?"

"The—thing. The woman."

I shook my head and looked at him.

"All right then," he said abruptly. "Don't see it!" He turned back to the fire. "Out again!" he said, looking at his pipe. "Gimmy nother match."

I lit his pipe again. He puffed at it with the angry air of one who battles against human folly in vain. Then he took it out of his mouth and standing up—a little shakily—extended his hand and spoke aloud in a pleading tone.

"Look at that ceiling."

"It wants whitewashing."

"Can you see nothing but ceiling there?"

I looked. It was just as it always had been—save perhaps for a shade more richness in the colour. "A ceiling," I said, "just a dirty discreditable ceiling—ceiling of a literary man. It has a bit of radiating crack, and there are two beams faintly outlined in a lighter tint and a cleaner patch near the middle—"

"That's it," said Meredith.

"The devil it is!" I said.

"I don't believe you see it now," said Meredith.

"It's the shape?" I asked.

"Oh of course!" said Meredith haltingly and sitting down abruptly he began to feel for a match in his pocket. "All right! Put it down to—to *derilium*."

I looked. The outline of the patch seemed to me to be more like a map of Ireland than anything else. I turned to him. His hand was extended. "Match," he said.

When his pipe was alight again he made a final effort. "I know I'm shaky," he said, "and can't tackle—that word, but I'm sober enough all the same. Now just sit down on the sofa where I was and lean back on the pillow, like I was, and look up. Go on. I tell you I'm as sober as a judge. You do it."

I did as I was bid, still incredulous. No sooner had I assumed the assigned attitude than I saw what he meant.

I sprang to my feet with an exclamation and looked into Meredith's face.

"What a beastly thing!"

"No dil—*dilleryum* there?" said Meredith. "Eigh?"

I looked at the patch again. It was like those puzzle faces one has to hunt out of pen and ink sketches. Once discerned, it becomes impossible not to see it.

"Now," said Meredith, "perhaps you understand."

"I should whitewash the ceiling if I were you," said I.

"Nice thing to have jump at you. When you're shaky. Eigh?"

"I've seen patches and discolouration that took odd shapes before," said I, "but nothing so realistic as this. It's perfect. In the Sickert[1] style."

"I should think so," said Meredith, missing the point. "And we get to look at it day after day!"

"Wash it out," said I. "I am going down the village by Parry's. I'll tell him, if you like, to send up tomorrow. Your ceiling isn't a ghost morgue. If corpses with throats cut choose to photograph their heads and necks on your ceiling they do it at their own risk and peril. Perhaps Parry could send up today."

And when I called on Meredith the Friday after, there were splashes of white on the sage green wallpaper and dots of lime on the pier glass and the ceiling was immaculate and the mind of Meredith was at peace.

I heard nothing more of Meredith's ceiling for a year and a half. Indeed, I forgot all about it until he revived the memory.

Bordell, the man who got his F.R.S.[2] two years ago for his investigations upon the radiometer, was staying with me at the time, and we were playing chess in the summerhouse. He was meditating a move and I was thinking how much nicer Bordell would be if he did not profess such an objection to tobacco smoke, when Meredith came out of my home and bawling after me down the garden.

1. Walter Sickert (1860–1942) was an influential British painter known for, among other things, his provocative depictions of females and his fascination with the Jack the Ripper murders.

2. F.R.S., or Fellowship of Royal Society

"That woman!" he said as soon as he saw me. "I simply can't stand it!"

I thought for a moment he had quarreled with his wife.

"She's coming at me again. With her throat cut and everything. I'm hanged if I can stand it!"

He came into the summerhouse and simply disregarding my introduction to Bordell went on talking. "I shall begin to think I murdered her after a bit. She's worse than ever."

Bordell rested his chin under his hands and stared at Meredith in that complacent collected way he has. I asked Meredith what he meant. "The ceiling, man," said he. "Don't you remember that thing on the ceiling? Well, for the last few months it's been coming through again—more than ever. I've not said a word to anyone. Thought it was my fancy. But it's getting a bit too vivid.

"Just the same turn of the head—just the same glare in the eyes—just the same gash. It'll drive me mad."

"May I be permitted," began Bordell interrogatively.

"It's his ceiling," said I—"haunted."

Meredith swore. "But why is my home haunted? Always a most respectable home: Adamson had it before me and before him it was new. If it was the home he has now it would be different. There was an old woman murdered down *there*, an undiscovered murderer and all the rest of it. Just the place for a ghost."

"I don't understand," said Bordell. "I wish you would explain."

He put up his hands as if he was saying grace and watched us in a judicial manner with his chin on the point of his fingers while I told him about the marks on the ceiling. Meredith embroidered my account with conversational solecisms and fitful inquiries about what he should do now.

"It's a perfectly simple matter," said Bordell when I made an end to my story. "Perfectly simple."

"Cure it then," said Meredith.

"White patterns on ceilings have been described and discussed often enough. It's got something to do with the woodwork above. Poulton[3] described a dirty ceiling at Felixstowe that showed all the nails in the joists and there's a remarkable case at Woolwich[4]—I think it is—in a mess room there. Professor Lodge[5] thinks the reason why the deposit of soot upon plaster is affected by the overlying wood—"

"But this isn't woodwork! This is a woman with her throat cut!"

"All the same," began Bordell, "I hold—"

"Oh! You come and see it," said Meredith.

Bordell, confronted with the ceiling, retained his equanimity. "A remarkable simulacrum," he admitted, but refused to feel emotion. "It must be due to something lying above the plaster and immediately in contact with it. Cunningham—"

"Do you mean to say that there is a dead woman—"

"Certainly not," said Bordell. "A dead woman would have made the home impossible, in a few days. But something there certainly is, above there, a block of wood, a scrap of metal. The resemblance to a face is no doubt—"

"We can soon see that," said Meredith. "Precious soon." And went out of the room for some tools at once.

Bordell came upstairs with us into the room above the study—it was Meredith's bedroom—and kept multiplying instances of soot figures and suggested explanations, out of his special knowledge, while Meredith went to work upon a plank. "You will find—I can certainly prophecy—a curved object that made the contour of the cheek, a roundish body that gave the high light of the neck, and something with an uneven surface that caused the ripple in the

3. Sir Edward Bagnall Poulton (1856–1943), British evolutionary biologist
4. Royal Artillery Barracks at Woolwich, London
5. Sir Oliver Joseph Lodge (1851–1940), British physicist

hair. You see how simple the matter becomes—this ghost story of yours—in the daylight of science."

Meredith knelt where he had taken up the plank and put his arm down into the black space under the floor and felt about. Bordell beamed. "Well?" he said.

"There is something," said Meredith. "Several things."

"Ah!" said Bordell. "I am afraid your ghost is done for."

Then Meredith drew his arm out of the hole and displayed two gold brooches with ornamentation of worked hair.

"Treasure trove!" said Bordell. "I claim my share."

"Odd how they got there," said I.

"There's more yet," said Meredith, and dipping again drew out a very rusty old-fashioned purse made out of steel links through which a solitary guinea glittered. An old-fashioned gold watch and chain followed, that Bordell took from Meredith's hand with some light remark. "Wait a bit," said Meredith. And feeling once more under the boards, produced—holding it gingerly by the blade—a large bread knife, red and blackened with rust.

I thought of the figure we had seen on the ceiling of the room below. So, I think, did the others.

Meredith broke the silence. Imitating Bordell's manner, unconsciously or deliberately, he looked at him and said, "Well?"

We stared at the knife.

"Now I remember," said *this* Meredith slowly. "That old lady was Adamson's second cousin. She was supposed to have been murdered by tramps. I've heard Adamson was suspected at the time but nothing was proven against him. He was next of kin it seems. Now this was once Adamson's bedroom. He buried these little treasures of hers here to make it look like an ordinary robbery. It seems plain enough."

"But then," said I, "why should it be a young woman's face downstairs?"

"It was the woman's ghost you see," said Bordell.

Meredith was still sitting on the floor with his legs on either side of the hole. The watch, the purse, and the knife were spread out before him. He looked up at Bordell. "It may be all coincidence," he said, "but I'm thinking it'll be a confoundedly awkward coincidence for Master Adamson before this business is over."

CARNIVAL

LAURA BENEDICT

I'm still awake when the motion spotlight outside my bedroom window comes on at 3:36 a.m. When I'm alone in the house, I don't even try to sleep until I pass out.

Nerves, my husband Paul says.

At the foot of the bed, the big dog crate is empty. If our Labrador, Polly, were here, she would be standing up inside it, nosing at the crate's latch, knowing I'm afraid. She's a good dog that way.

From my bed, I can only see the spotlight's glow limning the narrow space between the drapes. I listen for the wind. Sometimes it shudders the limbs of the trees at the edge of the ravine, and the light turns on. Or at least that's what Paul has told me happens.

But there are mornings when I find the bird feeders ripped from their shepherd's hooks, empty, their lids torn off and cast into the weeds.

Goddamn raccoons, Paul says.

Or I find scat from some large animal. Scat whose smell makes Polly turn her head and slink away, growling deep in her throat. So

I get the shovel from the shed and chuck the stuff into the ravine where it belongs.

Last night, when the spotlight came on, I stayed in bed, waiting anxiously for it to go off. Tonight, I put on my robe, pick up my phone—quickly turning down the brightness to near nothing—and push aside the curtain a few inches. The weedy grass in the side yard is a silver moonscape in the artificial light. The ragged tree line along the top of the ravine looks two-dimensional, like a painted scrim on a stage. Nothing moves.

Why can't we open the windows at night? Paul says. *You think the bogeyman's going to get us?*

I wait for a stray dog or fox to jog by. Or maybe a coyote from the pack that lives in a low place across our country road. At this point I'd settle for some deer, which usually stay away because of Polly. But then I remember that deer don't feed this early in the morning. My breath fogs the window the slightest bit. Suddenly I hear a click and I jump. But it's the air conditioner coming to life and, for a moment, I feel ridiculous.

When the spotlight finally blinks off, I exhale my relief and let the curtain close. But before I can turn back to the bed, and my book, it blinks on again. Quickly, I open the curtain. A figure—maybe human, or is it animal?—moves within the black and silver scrim of leaves, and I find I can hardly breathe. Unlike the leaves and brush, it's a filmy white. I hold the phone up to the window to get a picture. Bright light flares against the glass, blinding me. I squeeze my eyes shut.

My coffee is tepid. Outside the kitchen window, a light rain falls, but the morning is sunny so the raindrops glint and sparkle in the air.

Devil's beating his wife. What a son-of-a-bitch, Paul says.

Three days ago, he texted to tell me that his buddy's Labrador outdid herself fetching geese from the fields and lake. *Wish I had you and Polly here hunting with me. Sure you don't want to come down and get your feet wet?* He ended with a winking emoji. Our little joke. I can shoot pretty well, but I can't swim, and prefer to get my meat from the grocery store.

I open the photos on my phone and—probably for the tenth time—pull up the picture I took six hours earlier. No matter how long I stare at it or how many times I enlarge parts of it, I can see nothing outside the window. There's only a blaze of white reflected on the glass, and—if I look very closely—a shadowy image of my own face twisted with fear.

At noon, after a shower and a lame attempt to repair my two-hours-of-sleep face with makeup, I drive to my sister's house to take my niece and her friend to the local Catholic school's big carnival. We're not Catholic. You might call us Presbyterian, if we were to pick a church. My sister fakes it sometimes, dropping her kids at Sunday school, then going grocery shopping.

Allyson and the friend, Kaylin, are twelve years old, so now they are too cool to run down the front walk to the car where I'm waiting. They stroll, both talking at once, trading looks at each other's phones. Kaylin's tiny denim shorts are embroidered with pink and lavender sequin flowers—expensive and a little trashy. Allyson wears jeans.

Allyson opens the passenger door, smiling brightly as she slides in, unselfconscious of her new braces. "Hey, Aunty Lo!"

"Hey," Kaylin echoes, getting in the back.

I wave to my sister standing on the porch and she blows me a kiss. After a few exchanges with the girls about the new school year (seventh grade!), and Polly's recovery from being hit by a car, Allyson, as usual these days, changes the radio station from talk to Top 40.

The sunny rain is long gone, leaving the mid-September day as hot as July. A carnival on a parking lot blacktop is going to be hell.

As soon as we arrive, the girls ask for rainbow slushy drinks that may or may not contain coffee and, of course, I oblige.

"I told you she's the cool aunt." Allyson leans her head against my shoulder, smirking at Kaylin. Then she looks up at me and asks what time we should meet to go home.

That's how it is. Flatter me and ditch me. Glancing around at the booths and the itinerate midway, I try to remember what it was like to be twelve and on my own at a carnival: cheesy thrill rides, sneaked cigarettes, frozen lemonade, Skee-Ball, and sweat plaguing the waistband of my shorts. My feet getting dirty in their sandals. Boys.

It's Kaylin who looks as though she's going to freak out if I don't let them get going. *Definitely boys for Kaylin.* Allyson hasn't caught the bug yet.

"An hour and a half?" I say, keeping my opening bid intentionally low.

Allyson smiles ingratiatingly. "Oh, come on, Aunty Lo, three hours. Please?"

"Hey, we can have my dad pick us up later, and you can leave if you want," Kaylin volunteers.

Not my first rodeo, cuties, I want to say. "I'll go two hours and fifteen minutes. Meet me back here at 3:00."

I buy myself a funnel cake I know I'll regret. The pastry is hot through the plate, the grease working its way through the cheap paper. Parking myself at a plastic folding table, I eat the whole thing. Powdered sugar coating my fingers, I feel like I could eat myself to sleep. The idea of another night lying awake is almost more than I can bear.

Looking down at the plate, I think about Polly. How she would love to lick it clean.

Dog's mouth is cleaner than a human's, Paul says.

Midway rides aren't for me, so I wander a while through the booths of homemade crafts, ecology displays, and insurance peddlers. In the school cafeteria are 20th century "antiques and curiosities," a clever committee person's euphemism for junk. In here, it's cool and bright, yet weariness overcomes me. I sit down at one of the picnic-style tables pushed against the wall. The room is nearly empty of people, and it occurs to me that it would feel nice to simply lie on my side and stretch out.

"Excuse me, Miss."

I open my eyes to a sideways view of two middle-aged women in matching red polos bearing the school's logo. They look concerned.

"You can't sleep here. This is private property."

"Private property," the second woman echoes. "Just because we're having a carnival doesn't mean you can come in here and sleep."

"I'm sorry." I rub my eyes. "I didn't mean to fall asleep."

I tell them that I need to find my niece, and then we'll leave. And I suddenly realize that they must think I'm some kind of criminal.

Outside, I start to text Allyson, but stop myself. It's been just shy of two hours, not long enough to avoid argument. Kaylin would pout all the way home, if I could even get her in the car.

Always willing to split the difference. That's my Lo, Paul says. *Probably should've been a lawyer, after all.*

I wonder how Polly is doing at the animal hospital. They told me she might get released today. If not, maybe the girls and I can visit.

Then I see something in the distance that I hadn't noticed before.

I make my way across the stream of people bound for the midway and head for the circus tent set up in a nearby field. Looking back over my shoulder, I see no one is headed the same direction. It's as though they don't even know it's there.

It's not until I reach the tent's grubby entrance that I see a sign that tells me what it's for.

A large chalkboard propped on a cart beside the entrance advertises *Mother Orlov's Flying Circus* in bold, hand-drawn letters. I imagine a portly Slavic woman with a heavy accent wearing all black as she puts her flying children through their paces. The next show is at 7:00 p.m.

I peek through the narrow opening between the tent's heavy flaps. The women back at the cafeteria would say I'm trespassing, but I can't help myself. Being impulsive is not something I'm terribly proud of, but sometimes it pays off. I push a flap aside to find that the tent's setup is the real thing, with four spotlights directed toward the ceiling, and three tightropes at various heights. The tightropes are empty, the trapeze swings are empty, and the platforms are empty. Nothing moves except me.

At least the place doesn't smell of dung, and there are no colorful pedestals for animal performances. Circuses with animals depress me.

Walking through the quiet, I'm drawn to the tallest pole, with its narrow platform, imagining myself bravely putting one foot out into the vast air. Then I might tip forward a bit. Perhaps let myself lose my balance. There's no sign of a net.

We all have to pay for our mistakes, Paul says.

Like you, Paul?

I feel a dizzy anticipation as I reach for the rope ladder hanging beside the pole. With my other hand, I slip off my shoes to better grip the slats with my bare feet. What I'm not ready for is the ladder's loose sway when I barely manage to get four feet off of the ground. It's like that arcade game where you have to climb across a rope ladder to ring a bell at the other end to win a prize. The ladder I'm on lurches wildly, swinging halfway around the pole, and I thud onto my back in the scuffed dirt.

I lie there with my eyes closed, feeling ridiculous, until I feel hot, fuggy dog breath on my face. The chest and long snout of a Doberman loom above my chin. In the distant glow of the spotlight I see a thick tear of drool forming on one of the dog's lips. I hold my breath, waiting for the dog to take a chunk out of my throat.

"Queenie." The man's voice is calm but commanding. The

Doberman turns its head, and the drool strings out and attaches itself to my throat. Still, I don't move. With a mournful glance back at me, it moves away toward the man's voice.

"You a jumper?" the voice asks. It's not a friendly question.

"Of course not," I groan.

Rolling onto my side, I get up as quickly as my bruised backside will let me. The owner of the voice is an old man with a wiry build, and a face whose wrinkles tell of way too many hours in the sun. The sagging skin draped over his still-taut biceps and forearm muscles is heavily tattooed. He must be over seventy, but his hair is jet black without a hint of gray.

"I was just curious," I say.

"Sure you were."

We both know he's right. In some universe I've already jumped off the platform and lie motionless on the ground. I mumble *sorry*, looking away from his face. The entrance to the tent is beyond him, yet I'm reluctant to pass by.

"Go on. Get out of here." The dog at his side lifts her snout in the direction he points. It's the opposite direction of the entrance behind him. I turn to see an identical pair of tent flaps with a glowing EXIT sign above them.

"But I came in a different way," I protest.

He doesn't even blink.

Anxious to get out of there, I head for the exit he indicates, feeling the hard gazes of both the man and his dog on my sore back.

Immediately outside the exit is the forest. The sounds of the carnival, which I couldn't hear inside the tent, come from my right, and I head that way. Why do I feel like I was in there a very long time? Did I pass out when I fell off the ladder? I dig my phone out of my purse to check it, but the sun's glare prevents me from reading the screen. Cursing, I think of Polly at the animal hospital and ache to be back at home with her.

As I round the curve of the tent, I see a group of seven or eight people sitting on logs or low camp chairs, circled around the cold remains of a bonfire. The smell of pot smoke lingers in the air. Only one person—a girl of maybe eighteen—stands, or leans rather, against the tent. She is costumed as a pierrette, in the classic female clown's black and white outfit. The leotard, stretched over her small breasts and painfully narrow ribcage, is covered in black and white diamonds, and her muscular legs are encased in white tights, blinding in the sunlight. Only her hair is out of costume. Dirty blonde and stiff, it sticks up around her head in sweat- or gel-stiffened clumps. But it's the face above the black and white ruff that commands my attention: it's also painted in black and pasty white, yet her clown's mouth is a bright red slash from ear to ear, like a vicious wound, broken only by the curve of her lips. She takes a long draw from a burning cigarette, then emits a series of perfect smoke rings. When she finishes, the slash of a mouth grins with pride. Then she notices me and the grin disappears.

One by one, the people around the dead fire turn to stare at me. They're mostly teenagers, and a lone man, perhaps in his thirties. Unimpressed with me, they all look away again—with the exception of Kaylin, who jumps up from a stringy teenage boy's lap. The pierrette barks a sharp, mirthless laugh.

Kaylin, her face reddening, lets a beer bottle drop to the ground. She hurries across the circle to Allyson, who sits alone on a short log. "Allyson, come on!" She tries to get Allyson to stand, but Allyson resists.

The pierrette stares at me, oblivious to Allyson and Kaylin. There's something about her eyes, glittering and small within the diamonds of thick black face paint, that makes her seem ancient and knowing. I feel emotionally naked under her gaze, and for a moment I worry she can see into my soul.

A flash of white among the trees.

The pierrette's hard eyes stay on me as I approach the group, calling Allyson's name. Allyson won't look at me.

"Let's go, honey." I gently take Allyson's arm. Now that I'm closer, it's clear that everyone's high except me. And maybe the pierrette.

"Aunty Lo," Allyson says, looking up. Her pretty eyes are blood-shot. "I'm *so* hot."

"I'm *so* hot! Oh, I'm *so* hot, Aunty!" one of the boys mimics in a prissy voice. Several of the boys laugh, shifting their eyes to each other for confirmation of their mutual brilliance.

In my most authoritative mother-like voice, I ask the group what the hell they think they're doing, getting two twelve-year-olds stoned and tipsy, but my priority is to get the girls away from this place, away from the pierrette, who is so obviously in charge. My imagination goes a little wild with thoughts of what might have happened if I hadn't found them here. Alcohol poisoning? Kidnapping? Rape?

Kaylin, already recovering from the surprise of my appearance, gives the stringy, unshaven blonde boy a mournful look.

"Let's go," I tell her. To her credit, she joins me as I walk Allyson slowly out of the shadow of the tent and onto the faint path of flattened grass leading to the midway. No one left behind says a word.

"So sorry, Aunty Lo. I'm so sorry," Allyson says. She doesn't smell of beer, at least. But it looks like she might be one of those people who feel too guilty to enjoy themselves when they get high. Or maybe she's just freaked out, afraid of what her parents will do. I'll have to fix it so she doesn't get in trouble.

I look behind to make sure Kaylin is still with us. She is, but I'm stunned to see that the pierrette is there also, maybe thirty feet away. She skips barefoot through the grass, her thick white legs carrying her in a zig-zag pattern, as though not intentionally catching up to us. When she sees me looking, she gives a jaunty wave, and exposes her teeth in a cheerless smile. Back by the tent, the group erupts in hooting and whistling and noisy laughter. They are laughing at her. At us. What does she want?

"Come on. Faster." I jerk Allyson along, and now she glances over her shoulder. When she turns back, her mouth wears a little smirk. "Allyson!"

"Sorry," she mumbles. But she doesn't sound it.

I hear footsteps rushing through the grass, and suddenly the pierrette runs past us, trailing a wave of sweat and cigarette smoke. Once she's in our path, she tumbles and cartwheels, her sturdy body embracing the air, shaping itself around it. Her toes bounce from the ground as though off a rubber mat. Her speed and dexterity are daunting. Almost frightening.

"What's she doing?" Kaylin is breathless. "I don't understand."

This show is for all of us, but I feel it's mostly directed at me. The pierrette and I have some kind of connection that I don't understand. I'm not someone who believes in the supernatural comfortably. But this, I think, is not supernatural. There's something decidedly *too natural* about the girl. Natural and disquieting.

Each time we move to evade the pierrette, she adjusts her path so she's once again ahead of us. Having had enough of this, I decide to keep going straight. We're approaching the backside of the midway, with its generators and thrumming motors and pistons that keep the rides in the air or spinning or dropping. There's nothing she can do to us. We are three against one.

Just when we are as near as five or six yards, she collapses on the ground, her flat chest heaving.

"Now," I say, speeding up. We can disappear into the midway crowd. Allyson nods, breathing as heavily as Kaylin.

The pierrette raises up on her elbows to watch us approach. Except she's not watching *us*. She's watching me. Sweat pours from her hairline, glistening on her painted brows and nose. Her tongue flicks briefly out to touch her lips as though searching for moisture. *Don't look at her eyes*, I tell myself. *Don't look*. But it's inevitable. I do. And those eyes are as hard and knowing as they were when I first saw her. The lips within the slash of red on her face part, as though she might speak. Still staring at me, she leans all of her weight to one side and gives me a thumbs-up with the opposite hand.

The girls are silent as we drive away from the carnival. I hand back a tin of wintergreen Altoids to Kaylin. Both girls appear to have been shocked back into a sober state of pre-teen chagrin, but breath mints never hurt anyone. I don't bother to lecture, mostly because I'm still freaked out by the pierrette. There's no rational reason to believe she knows anything about me, I tell myself over and over.

Kaylin doesn't bother to thank me for the trip to the carnival, but I can't blame her when I drop her off. I too wish I'd stayed home. "Later, Ally," she says. It's not until she's halfway up her walk that Allyson finally nods in response.

I should drop Allyson off, too. It's clear that I'm not the kind of person she should be hanging around with right now. But my sister will put me in niece-and-nephew time out for months if she finds out Allyson was smoking dope on my watch.

"Why don't we go to my house?" I suggest. "If you want, you can stay over. We haven't had a sleepover in months."

"Really?" Allyson looks directly at me for the first time since I bought her the rainbow slushy. With her rather childish straight brown bangs and freckles, she could be my sister twenty years ago. Tears tremble at the inner corners of her hazel eyes. "I feel so stupid."

"Wasn't what you thought it would be like?"

Shaking her head, she says seriously, "It was crap. And that clown lady was weird."

I laugh despite the chill that comes over me.

Five minutes later, while on the phone with my sister, the vet's office calls. Polly is ready to come home.

Lifting Polly from the back of the car, I set her gently on the grass beside the driveway. She's sixty pounds of chocolate Labrador retriever, with a liver and pink freckled nose, a cast on her leg, and a torso wrapped in bandages. Watching her creep over the grass, my heart fills with pity and I get angry all over again.

"Is she really going to be okay?" Allyson sounds worried. "I mean, it's sick. Who would hit a dog and just drive away like that?"

"The vet told me that a week from now I'll probably have to sit on Polly to keep her from running around too much." That part is true. Though I had to lie to everyone about the way she was hurt.

Polly urinates and, ignoring us, makes her careful way to the porch. I have to help her navigate the first two steps until she figures out how to handle the cast. Inside the house, she goes straight to her water bowl in the kitchen and drinks and drinks. When she lifts her dripping muzzle, I could swear she's smiling. Within minutes, she's crashed on her bed in front of the cold fireplace, the casted leg dangling awkwardly from the cushion.

What the hell was I thinking in that circus tent? I definitely wasn't myself. No matter what happens next, I could never abandon Polly that way. Perhaps my sister would take her if I were dead, but they already have Butch, a miniscule papillon who's a cranky thirteen. They don't need a four-year-old Lab with counter-surfing issues.

If I'd gotten hold of her as a puppy, she wouldn't have such bad manners, Paul says.

After a dinner of homemade mac and cheese and applesauce in front of the television, Allyson finally asks about her Uncle Paul.

"On the road," I say. "Business. You know what he's like."

Your sister's kids are all right, but they don't give a shit about me, Paul says.

"I thought Mom said he went hunting."

"He did. Then he came back and left for work. I took him to the airport. Want some devil's food cookies for dessert?"

By the time night falls, I can hardly keep my eyes open. It's been three nights of almost no sleep. Allyson is curled up on the small sofa across from my bed. Polly is in her crate but I've left the latch open—she deserves her freedom. Feeling grubby—physically and emotionally—I head for the master bathroom to shower. What I see in the mirror before I undress shocks me.

A streak of reddish dirt, or clay, runs along my right jawline, and the mascara I'd hurriedly applied that morning is smudged in amorphous half-circles beneath my eyes. There are white smudges, too, on either side of the V of my T-shirt. Surely they can't be from the funnel cake I'd eaten ten hours earlier! My shorts are in similar shape, the front and back streaked with whatever is on my face. My hair is only slightly less disreputable, but probably only because I redid my ponytail before dinner.

While my vanity is appalled, at least the pain from my fall in the tent has faded. How funny that Allyson never said anything about how I looked.

I would've told you, sweet pea. I wouldn't let you go around looking like five miles of bad road. Where've you been, anyway? Paul says.

I can feel him behind me even though I can't see him in the mirror. Will he always be there?

"Aunty Lo, wake up." Allyson is shaking me. Before I open my eyes, I know it's 3:36 a.m. Polly is growling and pacing the room with slow, uneven steps. Behind Allyson, the curtains are parted a couple of inches. Light from the activated spotlight fills the side yard and makes a pale rectangle on the rug. "I think there's something outside," Allyson whispers, excited. "Should we let Polly out?"

"God, no. She might be hurt."

"Come look out the window. Please?"

"What did you see?"

The twelve-gauge feels good, with a gravity all its own. Yesterday, I'd felt heavy inside, but strangely untethered. *This* feels like reality. Back in the house, Polly barks, but she might as well be miles away. Poor Allyson is worried. She doesn't understand why I have to be out here with the gun.

The security spotlight has blinked off, telling me that whatever triggered it has either moved on or is staying perfectly still. The pierrette is on my mind. But only an insane person would imagine that a clown, a stranger from a carnival five miles away, has been hanging around on her property in the middle of the night. If anything, the pierrette is in my head, her knowledge of me pushing me forward.

Blackberry vines catch at my nightclothes, tear at my arms and legs as I enter the ravine. There's plenty of poison ivy here, too. I'll pay for running outside so impulsively, for not first putting on pants and a long sleeve shirt. I'm far enough away from the house that I don't set off the security light—whatever is out there should not see me coming—but the beam of the tiny tactical flashlight I can blink on from time to time at least keeps me from falling over a log.

When I stop moving, I hear a moist snuffling and pawing somewhere below me. It tells me I've reached the ravine's shelf. Below me is the wide, barren area I'm searching for. A dozen more steps in the darkness and I would've fallen.

I turn and make my way farther down the slope, doing the best I can without using the flashlight. But when I'm close enough to see what's happening below the shelf, I slide several feet, and stupidly use the shotgun to try to catch myself. I feel a split second's fear that my finger is on the trigger, but it's not, and I get a solid hold on the butt. My eyes have adjusted to the dark, so I can see that the animal in front of me is some kind of canid. Light gray, best that I can tell, and much bigger than a coyote. A bone hung with a chunk of flesh dangles from its mouth. Its eyes shine a hellish red.

Paul, my hero husband, has saved me from this creature by sating its hunger with his own body. Paul, who returned from his goose-hunting trip without geese, but with a serious drunk on. Paul, who ran over our beloved Polly with his truck, and who grabbed a shotgun from inside it, determined to "put her out of her misery." Paul, whom I had loved, but who wouldn't listen when I told him she would be okay. Paul, who looked so shocked when I brought out my own gun.

You were right, Paul says.

Paul wasn't a bad man, but Polly is better.

I steady myself and snug the shotgun against my shoulder. I don't want to shoot the animal. It's my fault that I didn't bury Paul deep enough. But I can't have it using his grave as a midnight buffet and scattering his bones over our land.

Silently releasing my breath, I finger the trigger and aim at a spot in the trees somewhere south of the creature's back end. I pull the trigger, and the shotgun's blast carries through the ravine and pounds my eardrums. The animal drops the bone and springs onto the hillside in one giant leap, then launches itself onto the shelf. I duck in fear as—after the briefest of pauses—it springs again, in my direction, and sails over my head. In my panic, I'm not fast enough to turn and look after it. For a few brief seconds, I hear it crashing through the ravine's undergrowth.

In the morning I will make the hole deeper.

ADVENTURE ON A BAD NIGHT

SHIRLEY JACKSON

Before dinner was quite finished Vivien began wanting to get outdoors, into the air she hadn't seen since afternoon. In an hour or so the evening would have settled down, with George in his chair by the fire and someone maybe calling up about bridge. If she left right away she could stay out in the air for twenty minutes or so, before it turned into night outside, before she had to start thinking about reading a mystery, making George's hot chocolate, going to bed, before the night started being tomorrow morning, with breakfast and dusting and the telephone.

She sat through George's second glass of milk, watching him finally lift his napkin to wipe his mouth carefully under the moustache. "Think I'll run out for a few minutes," she said.

"For heaven's sake, what for?" George swung around in his chair to see the window. "On a night like this, for heaven's sake?"

"I want to get a few things. Cigarettes."

George picked up the empty cigarette package on the table

and looked at it disdainfully. "Ought to give it up," he said. "I feel a hundred percent better."

"I want to get some coffee for breakfast, too."

"Weighed myself in the gym today," George said as he left the dinette to get into the living room. "Gained three pounds since I gave up smoking."

"Good for you," Vivien said, stacking the coffee cups on top of the other dishes in the sink. She could do them when she came back and tonight, because she was going out for a few minutes, she would darn George's black socks. She stopped in the hall closet to pick up her coat, so that she could go into the living room with it on. "I'll be right back," she said, and crossed the room to kiss him.

He was already reading his paper, but he said, "You go ahead and smoke if you want to," fondly, without lifting his eyes. "Can't I go for you?" he asked as she opened the front door and started down the stairs.

When she got to the bottom and she had her hand on the outside door she waited for a minute, to see if he would call her back and check on whether she had her money with her. When she opened the door she lifted her face and looked into the fine rain. I hope it keeps on all night, she thought. Going down the street she wondered at how easy it was to tell it was early in the evening still; her grocery was still open and lighted and the people walking on the street were going slow, even on a rainy night, because they were in no hurry to reach wherever they were going before the fun started. Vivien stopped in the delicatessen where they overcharged you, and waited her turn at the counter.

"What'll it be, honey?" the clerk asked her finally.

Vivien wanted to say something funny and cutting, but the people waiting in line after her were already smiling, and she said quickly, "Pound of your special coffee, please, and a pint of milk." She gave the man her money and counted her change carefully, waiting at the counter while she did it.

"Don't trust me, do you, honey?" the clerk said, and Vivien solemnly stood there counting her change while the woman in back of her in line began to call an order over her head. When she took her package and went out she heard the clerk saying "She doesn't trust me," and the people laughing.

Of course I don't trust him, Vivien thought, he's a crook. I wish I could say it. I wish I didn't have to shop there and none of these other people did either. She usually responded to the clerk by a comforting revenge; she bought less than she had intended to, finishing out her shopping at another delicatessen.

She walked slowly up Seventh Avenue to the cigar store, feeling the rain on her face and resenting the thought of going home. There was no one in the cigar store except the clerk and a young woman, very pregnant. About eight months or so, Vivien thought right away, looking at her, not good for her to be out in this rain. The clerk was saying "—company store. What would they think if I just locked the door and went over to the phone?"

The woman stood, looking at the clerk patiently, while he waved his hands and spoke loudly and happily. "You think that I can just walk over to help out anyone who comes in?"

He doesn't have to keep on saying it, Vivien thought. I understand him perfectly and I should think she would, too.

The woman was watching the clerk as though she expected him to get his anger worked off and then help her do whatever she had asked him. When the clerk saw Vivien he said, "And suppose this young lady had come in and found the door locked and me taking telephone calls all night for anyone who came in? What would you think?" he asked Vivien.

Vivien was frightened; she wanted to agree with the woman, eight months pregnant, but the clerk was talking so loud, and she wanted to buy things from him. "I'd like to get some cigarettes, please," she said finally.

The woman, as though seeing her for the first time, turned

around and looked at her with the same patient watchfulness. "You can read?" the woman said.

Vivien was startled; she had not realized the woman was foreign, from the accent, Italian. Having her baby here and not even able to talk to the doctor, Vivien thought.

"Sure she can read," the clerk said. "What do you think she is? But she's not going to read for you. I can't have you jumping at anyone who comes in here to buy cigarettes. Remember this is a company—"

"I can read," Vivien said. The woman was young, about twenty, very pretty.

"Please to read for me?" the woman said.

"Certainly." Vivien took the envelope the woman held out. She began to read aloud. "Miss Tessie Antonio, 435 West 21st Street . . ."

The woman, who had been listening with a frown on her face, suddenly stepped forward and put her hand on Vivien's arm. "Not that," she said. "That part I know. Miss Tessie Antonio, 435 West 21st Street, that is me." She nodded reassuringly at Vivien. "Read at the top."

"The return address," Vivien said. She began to read carefully. "Corporal John—I can't make out the last name."

"As well as you can," the woman said.

"It seems to be Trevakos," Vivien said. The woman nodded again, and Vivien went on. "It's a company and an identification number," she said. She held the envelope out to the clerk. "Can you make it out?"

The clerk pushed it away in annoyance and the woman rescued it before it fell on the floor. "I got to wait on customers," the clerk said.

Vivien took the envelope again and tried to make out the numbers. The woman was pushing at her hand with a pencil. "You write?" she said.

Vivien took the pencil and turned the envelope over. She wrote down the name as well as she could make it out and then the numbers and handed the envelope to the woman, but she pushed it back. "Write more," she said. "Write what I say."

"She wants to send a telegram," the clerk interrupted. "To this guy. Tell her not to bother."

"He must send me the money," the woman said anxiously to Vivien. "Write that he must send me the money right away, I am in bad condition, and I will send him letter soon as he sends the money. He must send it tomorrow. And write I will tell him about it when I send him letter."

Vivien wrote: "Send money immediately. Condition very bad. Will write details later." She read it to the clerk. "Sound all right?" she asked.

"Put in he must send the money right away," the woman said.

"I don't know what she thinks she's going to get out of it," the clerk said.

The woman gave the clerk a dollar bill. "Change," she said. The clerk handed her the change and she gave it to Vivien. "You telephone for me?"

"Listen here," the clerk began, but Vivien said, "Of course I will." She went over to the phone and the woman followed her. With a handful of change in her lap and the envelope in her hand she put a nickel in and got the operator and asked for Western Union. When the voice answered she said, "I want to send a telegram." She felt very competent and smiled reassuringly at the woman. She gave the address and added to the Western Union operator: "I am not sure of the numbers, but I think the company is right. Will you make sure that it is marked important and that every effort is made to find the man and deliver it right away?"

I still sound like a good secretary, she thought, and the operator said stiffly, "Naturally we will make all attempts to deliver your message, Miss."

Vivien read off the telegram, while the woman kept opening the door of the telephone booth and saying "I must have the money right away. Tell them send it to me tomorrow."

Vivien told the girl the telegram was to be signed "Tessie," and gave them the woman's name and address. "Will you notify Miss Antonio at that address if there is any delay in delivering the telegram?" she added.

The operator said, "Certainly, Miss," and read the telegram back.

When Vivien hung up and stepped out of the phone booth the woman took her hand and said, "Thank you very much. You have been nice."

"I was glad to do it," Vivien said.

The clerk looked up at them. "Got the telegram off?" he asked. "I told her she was crazy to waste her money."

"I'm sure it will be all right," Vivien said.

"Now go on," the clerk said to the woman. "You got what you wanted done, now go on out of here."

"Wait," the woman said. "I want to give her something."

"What'll it be?" the clerk asked.

"Nothing, please," Vivien said. She wanted the woman to go away quickly without giving her anything.

"Cigarettes," the woman said. "She wanted cigarettes. Give her a pack any kind she wants."

"You kidding?" the clerk said.

"I'll pay," the woman said, holding out the change from the telegram. Helplessly, Vivien named one of the two or three brands set out on the counter and the clerk handed the package to her.

The woman paid him. "Now good night," she said to Vivien. "You have been nice."

"Thank you for the cigarettes," Vivien said, and kept saying "Thank you," as long as the woman took in getting out of the store.

"You shouldn't have done that," the clerk said. "I told her she was crazy."

"She would have gotten someone else to do it," Vivien said.

"But it wouldn't have been you or me," the clerk said. "How do you think she's going to feel when they never heard of the guy?"

Vivien shook her head.

"I know that kind," the clerk said. "You think they can't understand a word, but you say to them 'Sure I'll do it for you' and they understand right off. All I do is yell at them till they go away."

Vivien half turned away to look at the boxes of candy displayed on the counter. I wish he'd stop, she thought. I don't want to feel that this woman made a fool of me. "How much is this?"

"Ninety-eight," the clerk said. "You'll find those nice and fresh. Those people, they come in here one, two a night, asking me to do things for them. Lend them money, even. Nickel for a phone call or something."

"Most people are glad to do favors," Vivien said, trying to make it sound casual and meaningless.

But the clerk leaned forward over the counter and said confidentially, "Listen, a fellow in my job, seeing so many people all day, he gets to know right off about people. Some people, I know right off, it isn't any use doing anything for them, because it doesn't mean anything. See what I mean? That girl there, she wants to send a telegram to a guy that probably didn't even give her his right name. She thinks she's got a right to ask just anybody to do it. She wouldn't even say thanks for it."

"She bought me a fine pack of cigarettes," Vivien said defensively. She had put the candy back on the counter and gone towards the door. "She wanted to do something nice."

"You should've seen the look I gave her," the clerk said. "She was scared not to do something. She was so scared I could've charged her for the use of the phone."

Vivien opened the door and went out, holding the pack of cigarettes the woman had bought her. She went to the delicatessen two blocks away and bought more cigarettes, and some fruit juice.

When she started back the rain had nearly stopped and it looked like it might be a nice night yet.

When she crossed Seventh Avenue she passed three sailors standing on a corner and they watched her go by. They're going to whistle at me, she thought, or speak to me, only half a block from George in his chair reading the paper. She walked faster, and behind her the sailors were quiet; when she looked over her shoulder they were eyeing a girl going the other way. She ran up the stairs to her apartment and George looked up for a minute when she came in.

"Hello," she said, and he nodded, turning back to his paper.

She went out to the kitchen to put her packages away, and put the pack of cigarettes the woman had given her into her pocket. Then she went out into the hall and hung up her coat.

"I got my feet wet," she told George when she came into the living room on her way to the bedroom. She took off her dress and shoes and stockings and put on slippers and a warm flannel housecoat. She brushed her hair to get it dry and then came back into the living room to sit down across from George and pick up her mystery story from the end table. Holding the book on her lap she said, "George."

He looked up again from his paper.

"I had quite an adventure just now," she said. "I helped out a little foreign girl who had strayed off the path of virtue."

"You did?" George said, folding up his paper.

'TWAS THE SEASON

MARK MOWER

A few days before Christmas in the winter of 1887, I received a letter from a medical colleague I had worked with some years earlier, inviting me to meet up with him at the Criterion Restaurant in Piccadilly. Doctor Sven Larsson had proved to be a talented young surgeon and an affable clinician when we'd worked together at one of London's largest teaching hospitals. Unfortunately, despite my assurances, I had failed to stay in contact with the fellow, and in my embarrassment about this I lost no time responding to the invitation.

When we met at the Criterion, Larsson, as was typical of the man, was perfectly relaxed about the whole business and brushed aside my awkward attempt at an apology. Thereafter, we enjoyed a splendid meal, and later moved on to a gentleman's club in Knightsbridge to enjoy a few more seasonal beverages.

When he filled me in on the details of his life since we'd last met, he told me he had established a successful surgery in Belgravia with an enviable client list. In contrast, I felt that my own career had stalled, yet was reassured to hear the Norwegian say that he too had had a few bumps in the road before finally making a success of his practice. Throughout the evening, we swapped stories of our medical exploits—particularly those of a humorous or puzzling nature—before parting and agreeing that we would meet up again in the new year.

It was a crisp, cold evening, but wrapped up as I was in a thick overcoat, hat, scarf, and gloves, I felt impervious to the rapidly decreasing temperature. So much so, that I decided to walk back to Baker Street and enjoy the sights and sounds of the yuletide period.

Despite the lateness of the hour, the pavements around Piccadilly were teaming with good-natured revellers and street vendors of all kinds. There were stalls selling toffee apples, filled bread rolls, spiced cakes, and mulled wine. Small braziers offered jacket potatoes and roasted chestnuts, and there was a strong and welcome aroma of ground coffee in the air from one of the many Italian cafés that had sprung up in recent years. Shop windows were lit up and adorned with festive trees and decorations, and carol singers could be heard reciting seasonal favourites such as *Good King Wenceslas* and *Silent Night*. The whole experience was heart-warming, but as I made my way home, I reflected on one of the more unsettling medical cases that Larsson had recounted. Little did I realise that it was soon to be of keen interest to my close friend and colleague Mr. Sherlock Holmes.

Arriving back at 221B, I found that Mrs. Hudson had turned in for the night, while Holmes was in the upstairs study, enjoying a small cheroot before the open fire. His mood was ebullient: "Watson, it is a pleasure to see you both relaxed and full of Christmas spirit. It is clear that your roast goose supper at the Criterion was most enjoyable. It is equally evident that you and Dr. Larsson then went on to a club, where you treated him to a few whiskies and a single game of snooker. And yet, on your solitary walk back, I perceive that you have been mulling over something that Larsson left unsatisfied."

I had grown accustomed to Holmes's penetrating observational skills and unique deductive capabilities but was at a loss to know how he had managed to discern all of that in the few seconds it had taken me to ascend the seventeen steps to our apartment and enter the study. When I left 221B at a little after six o'clock that evening I had certainly not shared with him where I was heading or with whom I was meeting. My passing words were simply, "I'm meeting a medical colleague, and might be late back." My bewilderment at his pronouncement must have shown for he then sought to explain.

"There is no great mystery to all that I have posited," said Holmes. "Your departure this evening was unusual as, ordinarily, you share with me precise details about your comings and goings. That you chose not to, hinted at a liaison with a lady friend which you were embarrassed to acknowledge. And yet, I realise now that you were indeed meeting 'a medical colleague,' for the paper napkin protruding from the left pocket of your overcoat displays the name 'Dr. Larsson' in your handwriting. It is a name I have not heard you mention before, which leads me to believe that Larsson must be a colleague you worked with some time ago. That you have chosen to write down his name—and presumably his contact details on the bit of the napkin I cannot see—further supports this hypothesis."

I smiled, taking one of the cheroots he had offered me. "How did you know we went to the Criterion and I opted for the goose?"

"Straightforward enough, my dear fellow, the napkin testifies to the name of the eatery. And in the interests of variety, you frequently opt for any special dish that appears on the menu of a restaurant you visit on a regular basis. The Criterion has been advertising its special Christmas roast for some weeks now—goose with sage and onion stuffing, ham, potatoes, oysters, peas, and cabbage, if I'm not mistaken."

"Yes, and exceptionally good it was. Now, what about the reference to the club and our game of snooker?"

"Your uncharacteristic gait and laboured ascent of the stairs tells me that you have imbibed more alcohol than you might care to admit—one good reason you opted to walk home rather than hail a cab. And the smell of the strong single malt on your breath suggests that you have consumed more than one glass. Knowing that you would be reluctant to pay for the whisky at restaurant prices, I surmised that it was you who suggested moving on to a place where you would pay for the drinks. That you chose a club—which also gave you access to a snooker table—is evident from the blue chalk dust on your fingers and the cuff of your jacket. And calculating the length of time you most likely spent travelling to the restaurant, eating your meal, moving on to the club, and then walking home, I figured it unlikely that you would have had sufficient time to complete anything more than one frame of snooker."

"Astonishing!" was all that I could offer. "And on top of that, it appears you can read my mind as well."

Holmes smirked. "That was something of a longshot. I had chanced to look out of the window as you approached. The light from the lamppost illuminated your face enough for me to see that you were deep in thought with something of a troubled countenance. And yet, on entering the study, I see you are clearly in a cheerful and upbeat mood. I could conclude only that on your walk you were pondering something that was said or done this evening."

A short while later, as we enjoyed another of the cheroots before the dying embers of the fire, I recounted the tale which had absorbed my thoughts that night, with Holmes listening intently.

"Larsson told me that a week or so ago he was called to attend a new client, a wealthy shipping magnate who believed that someone had been attempting to poison him. He found the man to be bed-bound and in a very weakened state. The doctor's subsequent tests revealed the patient to be suffering from extensive liver and kidney damage, which gave some credence to the theory that poison had been administered. However, having taken samples, Larsson could find no traces of any obvious toxins within the man's bloodstream.

"Under Larsson's care, the patient began to improve rapidly. He was placed on a strict diet, and hour by hour his strength returned, so much so that within three days he could, with some assistance, get out of bed and walk a short distance.

"Larsson continued to be baffled by the man's condition and questioned him about the domestic arrangements within the house and whether anything had changed recently. He also quizzed him about his reasons for believing that someone had set out to poison him. In short, the only change that had occurred was in the kitchen, a month prior. The family had to that point been served by a middle-aged cook. But when she announced she was handing in her notice, they looked to find a suitable replacement. A business colleague said he knew of an excellent chef who was looking for work and could provide some short-term cover in the kitchen until a full-time replacement could be found.

"The man of the house felt this to be an excellent arrangement, which would leave his wife sufficient time to interview and choose the best cook. In the meantime, the chef fitted in well. Lodged in the house, he began to impress the family with the delicious, if extravagant, meals he prepared. Being of Austrian heritage, the shipping magnate was particularly partial to the patisserie of his homeland and was delighted to find that the new chef could turn his hand to a variety of pastries, from *Sachertorte* and *Apfelstrudel* to *Kaiserschmarrn* and *Linzer torte*. He took great delight in serving these to his new employer, and the kitchen took on all the aromas of fruits and spices.

"Yet while satisfied with the chef's work, the family had cause to question the man's integrity. Two weeks after his arrival, a sum of money was stolen from the parlour, and some of the other live-in staff began to complain that the chef was both foul-mouthed and lecherous. And as his own health began to deteriorate, the wealthy man considered that his new employee might be the cause. Sharing these concerns, he asked his trusted butler to keep a close eye on the man. It was not long before the butler observed the chef stealing some trinkets from a cupboard in the dining room. Of greater concern was his preparation of the pastries which the family so enjoyed. The butler had ascertained that the chef sometimes prepared two separate batches of anything he baked—one from which he served the mistress of the house and her three young sons, the other for her husband."

"That is certainly suggestive," said Holmes. "I'm guessing that on the strength of the butler's report, the chef was given his marching orders."

"Indeed. He was told to leave the house immediately, the reason for his dismissal being cited as his unprofessional conduct and the theft of the items from the lounge—accusations he strenuously denied."

My colleague took a moment to absorb this latest information before seeking some clarification. "Then nothing was said about the chef's baking?"

"That is correct. He left under a cloud but was unaware of the family's darker suspicions."

"And what was Dr. Larsson's view of the matter?"

"He thought it a possibility, particularly in light of the man's condition and in view of the liver and kidney damage, but he could see no reason why the chef would want to poison him. What did he stand to gain after all? And with the chef gone, and the man's recovery underway, Larsson considered that to be an end to the matter."

Holmes threw what remained of his cheroot into the hearth and poked at the fire for a final time with a wrought iron poker. "Let us hope that his assertion proves correct, for there certainly appears to have been some skullduggery involved. I noticed throughout your narrative that you refrained from mentioning the names of any of the principal characters involved. Was that to respect the confidentiality of Larsson's new client?"

I had to admit that was indeed the case: "In fact, Larsson mentioned only one name in outlining the case, that of the sacked chef. He was called Rory Eastman."

We talked for some moments more before setting the fire guard, extinguishing the gas lamps, and heading to bed. It had been a memorable night, and I felt pleased that I had been reacquainted with Dr. Larsson. Just how soon I was to see him again would come as a surprise.

The following morning was chilly, yet bright, and the pinkish tinge in the sky suggested we might be in for some snow in the days ahead.

I washed and dressed, and on entering the study was delighted to learn that Mrs. Hudson had cooked one of her marvellous breakfasts. Sitting beside my colleague, I began to eagerly partake of the thickly sliced bacon, fried egg, tomatoes, and kedgeree. In contrast, Holmes had contented himself with a single piece of toast and strong black coffee, and remained largely absorbed in the *Daily Telegraph*.

Suddenly he exclaimed, "Now, that is remarkable!"

I awaited further explanation, but none was forthcoming.

"What is?" I finally asked in annoyance.

Holmes seemed impervious to my agitation. "This private notice in the paper. I remain deeply suspicious of coincidence, but this is quite remarkable!"

He turned back to the table, picked up the newspaper, and passed it to me, pointing at the piece in question with the long stem of his churchwarden. The wording ran as follows:

NOTICE

LOWEST OFTEN LISTED. DRAFT ERROR. YEAST. MANHOOD WINK. EDIT SKILL. TIMED ON OWL.

I read it three times before looking back towards Holmes with an expression of some confusion. "I'll grant you that the wording is cryptic, but I can see no discernible statement or message. Why do you believe this to be 'remarkable'?"

He reached for his favourite ink pen and a sheet of foolscap paper and took the *Telegraph* back, laying it on the table once more and folding the broadsheet into a more manageable size. "I make it my job to scrutinise odd notices that appear in the London press. It is often the means by which the criminal fraternity broadcasts its intentions. This message has been deliberately concealed within what looks like a jumble of odd words." He began to write on the paper, rearranging the letters of the notice, before passing the sheet and newspaper back. "Is that any clearer?"

I looked again at the newspaper, and then at the sheet he had written on. All at once I could see the remarkable message he was referring to:

NOTICE

LOWESTOFT ENLISTED DR AFTER RORY EASTMAN HOODWINKED.

IT'S KILL TIME. DO NOW. L.

"How did you know how to look behind the original wording?" I asked, incredulously.

"I have trained myself to decipher seemingly nonsensical advertisements in order to see what is buried within. With my experience, uncovering this message was elementary. It seems we have discovered another thread which adds to our understanding of the tale which Dr. Larsson shared with you yesterday evening. And given the imminent threat posed by this missive, I would suggest we waste no further time in contacting the good doctor and gaining access to his client."

I voiced no objection, and having donned my overcoat, hat, and scarf, raced down the stairs after Holmes. Within minutes we had successfully secured a hansom for our journey and having retrieved the paper napkin from my outside pocket I was able to give the cabbie the address of Larsson's surgery in Belgravia.

Our destination was a white, three-story, stucco-fronted house in a quiet crescent. Larsson occupied the ground floor of the grand house, which testified to the success of his practice. On entering the surgery, we walked into a well-appointed reception area with comfortable seating and a marble-topped desk. Behind the latter sat an immaculately dressed receptionist with a pretty smile. She greeted us warmly and responded immediately when we explained the nature of our call.

We were shown into one of the larger consulting rooms in the practice. Dr. Larsson rose from his chair, removing his glasses as he did so, and looked across at us. His face lit up as he realised who had come to visit him.

"Watson! Great to see you again, so soon after our outing! And this must be the detective I have heard so much about. I'm pleased to make your acquaintance, Mr. Holmes."

"The pleasure is all mine, Dr. Larsson. Yet I fear we must save the pleasantries for another occasion as time is of the essence." He thrust his copy of the *Daily Telegraph* and the separate sheet of foolscap into the doctor's hands. "You will see from this coded message why we believe your patient is in some danger."

The impact on Larsson was immediate. The tall Norwegian handed the papers back to Holmes, turned swiftly, and retrieved his medical bag from a chair beside his desk.

"Then we should go at once," he intoned. "Fortunately, I have no appointments until this afternoon and had, in any case, planned to visit Mr. Lowestoft."

Some twenty minutes later, we were being shown into the parlour of a substantial property on Ebury Street. The room was bedecked with Christmas decorations of all kinds; paper chains and tinsel, hanging stars, ornate candles, and a large fir tree festooned with baubles. A young maid took our calling cards and said she would inform her mistress of our arrival. She flashed Dr. Larsson a smile before leaving the room.

Mrs. Liselotte Lowestoft was a slim, fair-haired woman in her early fifties. She wore a long, exquisitely tailored dress of blue silk which accentuated both her figure and elegance. Having seated herself on a sofa within the parlour, she invited us to sit and instructed the maid to fetch some tea. She then welcomed Dr. Larsson and asked if we had all come to check on her husband.

"Madam, you must forgive the intrusion. This is Dr. Watson, a close medical friend, and this is Mr. Sherlock Holmes, the eminent detective. We do not wish to alarm you, but have good reason to believe that your husband may be in danger . . ."

He did not have the chance to elaborate, for just then the door to the parlour swung open. Framed within the doorway was a solid looking man some years older than Mrs. Lowestoft, leaning precariously on two bamboo canes.

"Impressive, eh, Larsson? I can now do a full tour of the house with these walking sticks. I even managed some work in my study earlier. Now, what's this *danger* you speak of?"

It took a short while to explain the nature of our concerns, but the couple seemed extremely grateful for the intervention given the obvious threat. When the tea arrived, Holmes began to ask a few pertinent questions.

"I had understood you to be of Austrian descent, Mr. Lowestoft. So I am curious to know more about your surname."

The shipping magnate smiled as he sipped his tea. "Yes, my father moved the family to this country when I was seven years old. We settled in the east of England, where he bought into a successful fishing fleet. Our family name was Steiner, and it would be fair to say that our heritage did not endear us to the locals. My father therefore decided to choose a more English sounding surname and plumped for 'Lowestoft,' where the fishing fleet was located. Eventually, he took over the business and expanded the fleet, before investing in other forms of shipping. Since his death, I have continued to build the business alongside my colleague Dominic Linaker. The Lowestoft-Linaker Line is now recognised as one of the largest shipping firms in western Europe."

"I see," said Holmes, with keen interest. "Now, tell us a little more about Rory Eastman, and how he came to your attention."

It was Mrs. Lowestoft who now answered, placing her hand gently on the left leg of her husband who sat on the sofa beside her. "I blame myself for inviting that wretched man into our house, Mr. Holmes. Our former cook was like a member of the family, so it was a great loss to us when she decided to leave. We were desperate to find a replacement, so I asked Dominic Linaker if he knew of a good cook."

Holmes interjected, expressing some confusion. "I'm sorry to interrupt, but why did you think to ask Mr. Lowestoft's business partner such a question?"

She did not seem in any way offended. "Dominic manages all the financial and staffing affairs of the shipping business. The vessels regularly employ chefs, cooks, and galley staff, so I felt he would be ideally placed to suggest someone to us. Unfortunately, his recommendation proved disastrous."

Holmes turned to Edward Lowestoft: "Do you know of any reason why someone would wish to see you killed, sir?"

The man remained silent for some seconds before answering. "I honestly do not. It is some years since I faced any hostility as a foreigner. Few people would know that I am Austrian, for I have little by way of an accent. I have a limited social life, preferring to spend my time at home. In terms of the business, I leave much of the day to day running to Dominic, so have little contact with customers and suppliers. If anyone were to incur the wrath of a disgruntled worker, I would think it would be Dominic. I can only imagine that it is my perceived wealth that might make me a target, but I would have thought that holding me to ransom would be a more lucrative pursuit than murder."

"Indeed. And in relation to that, are you comfortable sharing with us what would happen to your estate in the event of your death?"

It was a direct and awkward question, but Lowestoft obliged easily. "In my will, I have made more than adequate provisions for my wife and children. Liselotte will take ownership of the house, while my other London properties and investment assets will be divided equally between the three boys. Given the sums of money involved, none of them will ever need to work, unless of course they choose to."

"And the business?"

"That is a different matter altogether. In expanding the shipping line as we have, I relied on Dominic to raise most of the money we required. While I have a controlling interest in the company at present, this will cease upon my death. The family will have no further claim on the assets of the company."

I was a little surprised to hear this, but Holmes merely replied, "I see."

As we finished what remained of our tea, Larsson said that he needed to give Mr. Lowestoft a full examination to ensure the man's recovery was proceeding as hoped. Holmes said that would give us time to examine the kitchen. While bemused by the statement, Mrs. Lowestoft asked the maidservant to lead us through to the room.

I was a little puzzled myself as to Holmes's thinking, but, knowing his methods, realised he would have good reason to investigate. The kitchen was a sizeable room with a long black cooking range. Above this, numerous copper pots were suspended by hooks from an airer and on either side were rows of labelled shelving with all manner of cooking ingredients. Holmes headed immediately towards two shelves labelled "Spices." There was little need for the labelling as the aromas around the various jars betrayed their contents—ginger, clove, nutmeg.

"Smells like a patisserie!" Holmes exclaimed. "Mr. Eastman invested heavily in these." He scanned the shelves and removed two specific jars to investigate their contents. "The unmistakable fragrance of cinnamon, which comes from its principal components, cinnamaldehyde and styrene, and other constituents such as clove oil. There are various cinnamons around the world, but this particular variety, *Cinnamomum cassia*, is imported from China. Most often, cooks will use *Cinnamomum verum*, which is harvested from the Ceylon cinnamon tree, a small evergreen species within the family *Lauraceae*."

I was not to be outdone. "Yes, and the spice can provide a measure of protection against a number of chronic health conditions."

"That is true. But in this case I suspect it was being used for more sinister purposes. Chinese cassia contains high quantities of the blood-thinning component coumarin. While a teaspoon a day can have health benefits—"

"Large concentrations can cause liver and kidney damage!"

"You have it, Watson! I believe Rory Eastman *was* discreetly trying to poison his employer. The quantity of cinnamon in these jars is way beyond anything that would be needed by a commercial baker, let alone a household cook."

We rejoined the others in the parlour after scouting out the back garden of the property. Larsson reported that his patient was continuing to make an excellent recovery. Holmes then shared his theory about the cinnamon poisoning before turning to the matter of protection for the family. "I strongly believe that the coded message will be acted upon very quickly. Those taking on the task will not know that we have wind of their attempt to poison Mr. Lowestoft. That is in our favour, for they will not expect any vigilance within the house. That said, the assassin may have been briefed by Rory Eastman on the home's security arrangements and any obvious points of access.

"It is now twelve o'clock. I would suggest that after lunch Mrs. Lowestoft take the maidservants and children into town for some impromptu Christmas shopping and an overnight stay in a hotel. I have some small matters to address but will return late in the afternoon. In the meantime, Dr. Watson will remain here alongside the butler to ensure that Mr. Lowestoft comes to no harm."

Dr. Larsson interjected. "I should also like to be of help, in whatever way I can. It will be easy enough for me to rearrange my medical appointments this afternoon. If I leave now, I can be back within the hour."

"Splendid," said Holmes, "we can share a cab."

With the arrangements made, Holmes and Larsson departed, leaving the rest of us to prepare for our lunch—a simple dish of shepherd's pie and peas cooked by one of the maidservants. By two o'clock, the womenfolk and children had gone off into town as planned and Edward Lowestoft, accompanied upstairs by the butler, had taken to his bed. Dr. Larsson returned as promised, and with his help I began to make a reconnaissance of the house. From my observations and the earlier walk around the garden, there was only one obvious way to get into the house unobserved. This would involve climbing over a sidewall in the back garden and using the cover of some bushes on the right-hand side to reach the door of the kitchen. With all the downstairs windows shuttered and bolted after dark, the door would be the most vulnerable point of access. Within the kitchen itself, a small pantry provided a perfect vantage point to await any such intrusion.

It was a little after five o'clock when Holmes returned to the house. In doing so he gave us quite a scare, for he had scaled the back wall into the garden and then proceeded to knock on the kitchen door. While it was dark outside, there was enough moonlight to illuminate his aquiline features and when I heard him whisper my name, I realised who it was and allowed Larsson to unlock the door. Holmes hastily explained that he feared the house was being watched from the front and did not want to alert any assailant to our presence. He brought with him a welcome gift—my old service revolver.

To give the impression that the house was still occupied by all the family, the butler had been instructed to light the lamps in most of the upstairs rooms. The rooms on the ground floor were now securely shuttered and Mr. Lowestoft was locked in his bedroom, with the butler making frequent trips up to the room to ensure that his needs were being met.

Holmes shared with us the progress he had made that afternoon, which included finding Rory Eastman. He had speculated the man would be trying to find a passage out of the country with the knowledge that the order to kill Lowestoft had been given, and once carried out might make him a suspect. Holmes further surmised that Eastman would be looking for a position as a ship's cook or chef, to enable him to secure a berth on one of the larger ocean-going vessels. He therefore focused his efforts on the Royal Victoria and Royal Albert Docks.

Posing as a ship's purser, he began asking if anyone knew of a capable ship's cook who could join the crew of a ship sailing to the United States that evening. One of the shipping clerks he spoke to recollected that a man called Eastman had been asking about just such a position. He remembered the man saying that he was lodged at a hotel adjacent to the Albert Dock.

Finding Eastman in the bar of the hotel, worse for drink, Holmes continued to maintain that he was a ship's purser and convinced Eastman to travel with him to Baker Street to sign all the relevant paperwork required for the sea crossing. While there, Holmes overcame the man and handcuffed him. Clearly fearful for his life, Eastman began to talk incessantly. It became clear that he believed Holmes to be the man who had arranged for him to take the chef's job in Belgravia, from which he could find a way to poison Mr.

Lowestoft. When Eastman then addressed him as "Mr. Linaker," Holmes knew that he had stumbled across a very vital piece of information.

"He had clearly never met Linaker," my colleague explained. "It transpired that he had been approached about the position by Reggie Thompson, a seasoned dock worker with a shady past, who owed him one or two favours. He explained that he was working for a Mr. Linaker who would pay good money for an experienced chef to "carry out a special task." Eastman was desperate for work and lured into the scheme because of the staggering sum of money on offer. He was paid a fair sum up front and promised the rest when he had completed the task. That day never came. When Eastman was fired, he went back to Thompson and explained what had happened. Thompson told him to keep a low profile as Mr. Linaker would not be best pleased. Earlier today, Thompson visited Eastman at the hotel and said that Linaker had placed a coded advertisement in a newspaper instructing Thompson to kill Lowestoft. He advised the chef to get out of the country as he was likely to be blamed for the killing."

"My word, these are dark waters!" I said. "But how did you leave Eastman?"

"I had Mrs. Hudson send a telegram to Inspector Bradstreet at Scotland Yard. When he arrived at Baker Street, I explained all that has happened. He arranged for Eastman to be placed in custody pending further investigations. I have convinced him to let us continue with our plans this evening, but he insisted on positioning two constables within close proximity of the house. They are currently hidden within the bushes at the back, with instructions to arrest Thompson as soon as he enters. Our job is to ensure that he gets no farther than the kitchen."

With our mission outlined, we gratefully accepted a plate of sandwiches from the butler and seated ourselves within the pantry. Dr. Larsson seemed to relish the adventure, saying he hadn't done anything so exciting in years. While we were fairly certain that Thompson would not appear until everyone had gone to bed, Holmes was taking no chances. The butler began extinguishing the gas lamps around seven o'clock to give the impression that the children were off to bed. By nine-thirty, the house was dark.

Left alone, the three of us conversed in hushed tones. A clear moonlit night made it easy to see. Thompson could not enter the house without passing within a couple feet of the pantry door, which was open sufficiently to enable us to watch for any movement. I already had my revolver to hand.

A little before eleven o'clock, we heard the distinct sound of the kitchen door being unlocked from the outside. Rory Eastman had clearly taken a key with him before leaving the house and passed this to Thompson. We then heard the doorknob turning and the light tread of the intruder as he stepped into the kitchen and closed the door behind him. We watched as our quarry took three or four paces beyond the pantry. I could see the glint of a stiletto blade in his right hand.

Holmes acted immediately, opening the pantry door silently and stepping into the room behind the intruder.

"Put the knife down, Mr. Thompson," Holmes said in a quiet but clear voice. "There are three of us and one of my colleagues is armed."

Thompson froze momentarily and then turned. His face betrayed a mixture of astonishment and anger. His eyes were fixed on Holmes, who stood ahead of Larsson and me. I raised the revolver and stepped forward. Realising that he could not take on all of us, Thompson let his arm fall and dropped the knife on the floor.

"Who are you?" he growled. "You're not the police!"

Before Holmes could respond, the two burly police constables crashed in through the door, their truncheons at the ready. Seeing that we had the offender under close guard, one of the officers stepped forward and promptly handcuffed the man.

"Neatly done!" said Holmes, as Thompson was manhandled out.

As the architect of the plan to kill Lowestoft, Dominic Linaker was arrested the same night, protesting that he knew nothing of the scheme. Eastman and Thompson had no compunction in naming him as the ringleader, although he maintained that he had never met them.

In the end, it was the dogged work of Inspector Bradstreet that provided the proof of Linaker's connivance. Reggie Thompson had only met Linaker on one occasion, some years before. Linaker had agreed to pay the docker to carry out tasks which required some muscle—usually collecting money owed to him. Instructions were always posted to Thompson, but when Rory Eastman was lodged in the home of Edward Lowestoft, Thompson received a final communique saying that future instructions would be given in coded messages placed within the *Daily Telegraph*. In this way, Linaker hoped that his links to the crime would be all but invisible. Unfortunately for him, Thompson had kept all the earlier missives revealing the links between them.

An audit of the accounts of the Lowestoft-Linaker Line revealed that Linaker had been defrauding the company of money for some months to fund several nefarious money-making schemes. As Edward Lowestoft had given him control of the finances, this was not difficult to achieve, but was difficult to hide. Linaker realised that with the year-end audit of the company due to take place after the 31st of December, he had to act fast. His plan was to find a way of killing Lowestoft so that he could assume complete control of the business. From that position he would maintain that Lowestoft had been the one defrauding the company and had already prepared a paper trail to demonstrate this. His plans were working well with Eastman installed as the Lowestofts' temporary cook. But when he heard that the chef had been sacked, Linaker became desperate and felt his only option was to have Reggie Thompson murder Lowestoft.

Holmes and I were generously rewarded for our work in bringing Linaker to justice. On Christmas Day, as we were seated at the table in our rooms enjoying a fine turkey roast with Mrs. Hudson, a letter was hand delivered to 221B. In it, Edward Lowestoft expressed his heartfelt appreciation for what we had done. Enclosed were two cheques, each for £5,000. Dr. Larsson, I later learned, had received the same.

Whether one distrusts coincidence or not, it was certainly a most singular affair. And in the years to come, even Holmes himself—despite his strict adherence to logic in all aspects of his life—would remark from time to time on the serendipity of the events which saved Lowestoft's life.

It most definitely was a Christmas the three of us would never forget.

TIN BADGES

LORENZO CARCATERRA

She was fourteen years old and weighed just shy of eighty pounds. She had on what looked to be a short white gown, miniature giraffes dotting the sides, a small tear under the left armpit. Her rail-thin body had been marred by burn scars and her thick black and soiled hair was matted to the sides of her thin, angular cheeks, the skin barely visible above the bones. Her skeletal legs were curled and braced against an exposed rib cage, held in place by the smallest hands I'd ever seen on a child.

She had been dead for twenty-four months minimum, thirty-six at the max, according to the tall man in the rimless shades walking the perimeter of what was now a crime scene. The call had come from a burner with a 718 area code, a heavily accented Hispanic male voice alerting the 911 dispatcher to the downtown end of the Henry Hudson Parkway, just a few miles shy of the Cloisters. It was there, deep in the shrubs and trees, buried under years of debris and old leaves and chipped branches, that they found the rusty white cooler resting on its side.

Two young uniforms were the first to respond, making their way down the narrow, sloping hillside, looking for the cooler, under a hot and heavy early morning sun. The one with the Marine buzz cut and chiseled arms and barrel chest said he got to it first, unlatched the locks, and stepped back with a jolt when he was hit with the heavy odor of decomposition and death.

I got the call even before the homicide detectives swerved off the parkway exit ramp. I picked it up on the second ring, the ID on my phone highlighting the name Shane Winston, my former partner. He skipped the small talk. "Got one for you, Tank. Get your shit together and meet me just past Grant's Tomb. There'll be a full crime unit there. You can't miss it."

"You just took a swing and guessed my day book was clear?" I asked, grabbing my jacket and heading for the front door of my two-bedroom SoHo loft.

"That and I checked downstairs with Connie," Winston said. "She said you were as free as free gets. See you in about twenty. I'll have a coffee waiting for you."

Just for the record, I'm no longer a cop. I had been a gold shield detective, pretty damn good at solving cases. Wasn't wounded on the job, didn't drink to excess, wasn't anywhere close to a burned-out badge. I just saw something I didn't like and since there was little, if anything, I could do about it short of going to the press, I decided it would be best to walk away. I wasn't part of the problem and could offer no solution so a walk was, to my mind at least, the best available option. No more complicated than that. That was the fall of 2009, closing in on six years now.

I had enough years in to qualify for a pension and at forty-two was still young enough to enjoy the second act of my life. I own my own place, bought it from an old neighborhood friend same year I joined the force. Back then, the neighborhood was closer to raunchy than trendy, and now it's worth a lot more than I could ever afford to pay, which pretty much means I'm there for the duration. There's a restaurant/jazz bar downstairs where I eat my meals and drink my wine when I'm in the mood and for the last two-plus years I've been in the mood more often than not. That has as much to do with Connie Rumore as it does with the Dixie Randolph Quartet that plays there every night. Connie runs and owns the place—Bella's, named after her mom. She's thirty-eight, New York tough, but with a smile that lights up a room, and is as beautiful as she is smart.

We hit it off from the get-go and make few demands on each other. Neither of us is looking for a family or marriage or a house in the country with a garage full of cars. We just want someone close enough to keep us warm on a cold night, to share a laugh with, a drink, a meal, and, best of all, the quiet moments.

It's a good life and the work the NYPD throws my way keeps me in the crime loop. The department has a discretionary fund they use to hire guys like me to work cases they are either too busy to take on or don't see much chance of solving. The pay's good and I can hire my own crew to help me piece the cases together.

And that's how the little girl in the cooler—Angela Maldonado—came to my attention.

I sipped the bitter coffee Winston had handed me when I got to the crime scene and looked down at the young girl's silent, cold, decomposed body. I figured her to be about fourteen years old when she died and that she knew nothing more than horror and darkness during that time. I'm not a religious man by any means. But if there's any chance at a heaven, this little girl had more than earned her place because she had already been to hell.

"She die in the cooler or before?" I asked Winston, who looked as shaken as I'd ever seen him.

"Won't know for sure until the M.E. does his end," Winston said. "But he's guessing by the position of the body she was probably alive when they put her in the cooler. How alive we probably will never know."

"And she's been here how long?"

Winston shook his head. "To look like that?" he asked, turning away and gazing up at the housing projects that butted the edge of the parkway. "Had to be closer to years than months." He turned to me. "You'll take the case?" His tone was hopeful, and I knew that this reminder of his own little girl, who'd died around the same age, was turning the knife in his heart. The reason they were pitching me the case had nothing to do with the department's caseload.

I nodded. "I'll walk the scene a bit once the lab guys are done," I said. "Meantime, see what you have on your end—phone calls, any unsolved with similar MOs, the works. Leave it with the desk sergeant and let him know I'll be coming by."

"I'm sorry to be handing off such an ugly one," Winston said, starting to make his way up the sloping hill toward his unmarked.

"They're all ugly," I said, my eyes still on the little girl.

I was on my second glass of Brunello, sitting at my usual back table at Bella's, poring over the batch of case files Winston had left for me at the stationhouse. It seemed only a teacher at the school had reported Angela missing. From all I had in front of me, Angela was of no interest to anyone else, not even her family.

"You didn't eat much of your dinner," Connie said, sliding into the chair across from me, strands of her light brown hair brushing against the sides of her face. "Want me to fire the chef?"

"I'll have one of the waiters keep it warm for me," I said. "Besides, you can't fire the chef. It would be a violation of his parole."

Connie sipped her wine and sat back, glancing at the folders spread out around me, curious, but not asking. "They always toss you the ones they don't want to touch," she said, matter-of-fact.

"Not this time," I said. "This one's personal to Winston, even more than it is to me."

"Why?"

"It's a dead girl," I said. "About the same age as his kid when she died. A homicide detective almost always has some skin in every case he or she catches. But this one just casts too large a shadow."

She smiled weakly, took another sip of her wine, and put it down, staring at the photos without seeing them.

"I tried calling you earlier but it went to voice mail and I didn't leave a message. Figured you were at the gym or maybe a movie. Besides, I thought it would be better to tell you in person."

I nodded that I was ready.

"Your brother . . ."

I looked up from a folder and across at Connie. I knew that look, had seen it too many times in too many other faces. "Okay," I said. "What's the bad news?"

"Your brother and sister-in-law are dead," Connie said, her emotions in check, relaying the details in as calm a manner as she could muster. "There was a car accident on the Pennsylvania Turnpike two nights back. Their car skidded off the road, hit a guardrail, and toppled over. The officer who called said they most likely died on impact."

I didn't say anything right away. Just nodded—slow, automatic.

Connie hesitated, then reached over and set a hand on the edge of the table. Not touching me—just there.

"How'd they get to you?"

"The restaurant's number was the only one the kid had," Connie said.

"What kid?"

"Their kid," Connie said. "Their son—Gabe. He gave the troopers the number he had for you. It seems you're his only remaining relative."

"Where's he now?"

"Funeral parlor," Connie said.

"They give you an address?" I asked, pushing my chair back and standing, the folders now cradled under my right arm.

Connie reached into the pocket of her black dress and handed me a folded slip of paper. "Take my car," she said. "It's parked out front, save you some time. If you don't get any traffic you should be there before the funeral parlor closes."

I never told Connie I had a brother, let alone a nephew. Point is, I never told anyone. Far as I was concerned I was on my own and so was he. We both had made good lives for ourselves, from what little I knew about him. He was an executive with a high-end accounting firm, pulling down a good salary, as happily married as anyone who claims to be. My brother and I had gone twenty years without crossing paths and it didn't bother me much and I would bet it bothered him even less. There's good reason for our distance, our silence, our lack of any form of family bond. Every family has its secrets and most of those are dark and best left barren of light. And our secret, the one that my younger brother David and I kept locked and stored as deep in the attic of our minds as we could possibly place it, was as dark as anyone could imagine.

Traffic crossing from New York into Westchester County moved at a fairly rapid pace and I made it to the small town my brother and his family had called home in less than an hour. It was more country than suburban and as far removed as you can get from where my brother and I had been raised. We each dealt with the family secrets in our own individual way. My brother chose to turn his back to it, as if he could erase its very existence. I faced it head-on, confronting it each day at my job. I'm not certain which approach is the correct one.

Gabe was sitting on a folding chair, alone in the viewing room, gazing up at the closed coffins of his parents. I phoned the funeral home on my drive up and asked if they would mind letting him wait until I arrived.

I walked over to the boy and sat two seats away from him, taking a minute to glance at the coffins, trying to imagine his sense of loss, his confusion, his anger, but most of all, the shock of knowing he would never see his mother and father again. He was alone in the world for the first time in his life and that's a hard blow for anyone to absorb, let alone a fourteen-year-old.

"I'm Tank," I said looking at the boy. He was tall for his age, a runner's body with thick dark hair and a handsome face. His eyes were coal black and he looked very much as my brother did at that same age. "I'm your . . ."

"Uncle," Gabe said. "I know who you are."

"Would have been nice to have met you in another way," I said. "I'm sorry about that end of it."

"My father never talked about you," Gabe said. "Not in front of me, anyways. But I read about you sometimes in the papers and saw you on TV after that big arrest you made."

"You hungry?" I asked. "Want to go and grab a bite somewhere?"

"You need to ask me something," Gabe said. "Might as well get it out of the way here and now."

I nodded. The kid might look like his father, but his bloodlines ran a lot deeper into the family springs. He was sharp, to the point, and nobody's fool. "Fair enough," I said. "Here's how I see it. You're an only child and you have to be under someone's supervision until you turn eighteen, which I'm guessing is still a few years away."

"Two months short of four," Gabe said.

"You can go into the system, foster homes," I said. "A few of them work out. My experience, most of them don't."

"Or?"

"What makes you think there's an 'or' to all this?"

"You wouldn't be here if there weren't," Gabe said.

This time I couldn't hide a smile. "Or you can come live with me," I said. "Hear me out first. I'm about as crazy about the idea as you probably are. You're in private school I'd wager and have a house with a pool, your own room with your own TV, and most likely have your eye on the car you'd be looking to score the minute you turn sixteen."

"All that's true," Gabe said.

"And all that's going to change if you come under my roof," I said. "You'll live in the city, go to public school, we share a TV, and there's no way you get a car at sixteen."

"You would rather I go to a foster home, is that it?" Gabe asked.

"For me, that would be the easiest choice," I said. "In your place, I would roll the dice in that direction. But I'm not you and I'm not going to even pretend I know you well enough to make that call. I put it out there and I wouldn't have done that if I didn't mean it. I'll treat you right and I'll treat you fair. I know it sucks being you right now and there's not a big platter of offers sitting in front of you. Just the foster homes or me. And it's your call to make."

"How soon do I need to decide?"

"I'm going outside for a walk," I said. "I spotted a pizza joint about half a block down on the north end of the street. You know it?"

Gabe nodded. "My dad would take me there after soccer practice."

"I'll be in there," I said. "Think it through and then come see me after you do."

I stood and started to make my way out the door of the viewing room. "I said my parents never mentioned you," Gabe said. "That wasn't completely true."

I turned and looked over at the boy, waiting.

"There was one time my dad did talk about you," he said. "We were driving back from a basketball game, saw the Knicks beat the Raptors at the Garden. He said he hadn't been to a game since he was a kid and that you were the one who took him. He said you always looked out for him, made sure no one picked on him or gave him any trouble. All that true?"

"Pretty much," I said.

"So what happened?" Gabe asked. "Why did you stop speaking to each other?"

I stared at the coffins for a few seconds and then looked back over at Gabe. "Come see me when you decide," I said.

Gabe moved in that night. I gave him the back bedroom, the one with the computer and which I occasionally used as an office. It had a foldout couch, a crammed bookcase, and stacks of DVDs and CDs. "Get some rest," I told him. "We'll pick up the rest of your stuff first chance we get, most likely right after the funeral tomorrow. If I can't stick around, Rocco from upstairs will take you to your house and you can pick out what you need."

"Who's Rocco?"

"To me, he's a friend of long standing," I said. "To you, he's the guy that will drive you to your house to pick up clothes and anything else you can fit in a duffle bag."

"Why can't you do it?"

"I caught a case earlier today which now seems like a month ago," I said. "I'll be working on that."

Gabe walked over to the bookcase and started to scan the titles. "I have a lot of these same books," he said. "Read all the John Douglas books and the ones by Ann Rule and Patricia Cornwell. I love her Scarpetta novels and the one she did on Jack the Ripper. You read that one?"

"Shouldn't you be working your way through Harry Potter or something?" I asked. "This other stuff seems a little heavy for your weight."

"It's what I like reading," Gabe said. "And I watch all the shows, too—*CSI*, *Criminal Minds*. I'm even in an online Vidocq Society Club for teens. Vidocq is the—"

"I know who he is," I said. "Your folks know about this particular hobby of yours?"

Gabe nodded. "As long as I got my school work done and kept my grades up, they had no problem with it. Dad thought I would study law and be a prosecutor. My mom worried that I might be . . ." He paused.

"Like me," I said.

"Yes."

"You mean a cop?" I asked. "She didn't want you to be a cop?"

"I don't think so," Gabe said. "But she watched the movies with me, even the ones I'm supposedly too young to see. She figured she couldn't stop it, not with a computer and Netflix, so she tried to monitor it. The only thing she really didn't like was when I read up on your cases . . . you know, the stuff that wasn't public yet."

I stared at him. He said it like hacking sealed files was something you did between algebra and gym class. "How were you able to do that?" I asked.

"We're pretty good with computers, me and my friends. If it's on a computer somewhere, we can find it," Gabe said, smiling for the first time since I'd met him.

For a moment, he'd stepped outside the nightmare. But I knew the next minute, the crash, the coffins, the silence would all come rushing back. And he'd remember again that his parents were dead.

"Good to know," I said. "You know that guy Mark Harmon plays on *NCIS*? The boss, the guy with all the rules?"

"Yes."

"I'm like him except I only have one rule," I said. "Don't hack on my computer. You want to look something up you shouldn't be reading, do it in the library. We clear?"

Gabe nodded.

"Get some sleep," I said. "You had a tough couple of days and tomorrow's going to be even tougher. But at least you won't be alone."

"What do I call you?" Gabe asked.

"Tank will do for now," I said.

I couldn't sleep. My mind in turmoil, I went to the gym instead. I couldn't shake the face of the little murdered girl and I had to come to terms with the fact that I was now taking care of a teenage boy who happened to be the only child of a brother I had turned my back on so long ago. I pounded on the treadmill as fast as I could, my mind racing between a three-year-old crime scene and the fourteen-year-old now living in my apartment—a boy as immersed in the study of crime as anyone I'd ever seen. Instead of zits, teenage angst, and loud hip-hop music, I was going to be dealing with "Young Sherlock Holmes" in my back bedroom.

I came back from the gym and stopped into Bella's to pick up some coffee for me and breakfast for Gabe. Instead, to my surprise, I caught a glimpse of Gabe sitting in a booth by the window across from Connie's father, Dominick. I went in, caught Connie's eye, and poured myself a coffee as she walked over.

"How'd he make his way down here?" I asked.

"I went up to check on you and I saw him sitting on your couch reading a book," Connie said. "One of those forensics books you keep on your shelf."

I looked over at Gabe and Dominick deep in conversation. Dominick was an old-school gangster, long since retired, but still not someone I would be eager to tangle with. In his day, he ran off plenty of high-end scores, ran a successful book-making operation, and had enough money earning him interest on the street that he could retire free of any worries. He had long ago made his peace with the fact that his one and only daughter happened to be in love with an ex-cop. And I had long ago come to understand that while Dominick had been a knock around guy, he had always dealt with equally ruthless men and had never hurt anyone who was innocent.

"He and your dad seem to be hitting it off," I said.

Connie glanced over at the table and nodded. "Figure by now, your nephew can tell you which horse to bet on in the third race at Saratoga and what the current neighborhood vig is on loans."

I smiled. "That's information any boy his age needs to know."

I leaned over and kissed Connie softly on the cheek. "You think the old man would mind keeping an eye on the kid for me later? We'll go to the funeral, but I need to start working my case. It's on the way back, so Rocco can drop me there after and then drive the kid back here."

"I can't think of better company for young Gabe than Rocco and my pop," Connie said, giving me a long, warm hug. "Have some bail money set aside, just in case."

After the funeral, I started working the streets of the housing projects along the Henry Hudson Parkway, doing what cops do best—knocking on the doors of strangers and asking questions none of them were eager to answer. I took a friend with me, Carl Rodgers. He's one of those street performers you see every day working a small space in a New York City park, in his case playing a blues guitar that made even the jaded stop, listen, and drop some change in his cigar box. Carl even caught a few legit jobs from time to time down in the better paying clubs in the Village. He was also good with people, got them to open up, tell him things they wouldn't normally tell a guy like me. I look and smell cop and these days in these poor neighborhoods that's not a plus. But Carl was my buffer. They knew he wasn't a badge and that made a difference.

After hours of revolving door conversations with people who either didn't know anything or claimed they didn't, we were walking down a side street that faced toward where Angela's body was found.

"This is it," I said to Carl. "If the paperwork's up to date, she's on the third floor."

"Who is?" Carl asked.

"Angela's mother," I said, starting up the tenement steps toward the broken front door.

"She the one who reported her missing?"

I turned to face Carl. He was in his late twenties, with a Meatloaf body and a ZZ-Top beard. "No," I said.

I walked into Bella's later that night and slumped into a chair in the back and waited for one of the waiters to bring me a glass of red wine and some water. I lowered my head and closed my eyes for a few moments.

The mother was a wash. She didn't even blink when talking about her daughter—a little girl found dead in a cooler less than a mile from her apartment. She never reported her missing. Said she figured the girl had run away, and with good cause.

Her name was Minerva and she couldn't give us the name of Angela's father since she didn't know it. She had a lot of men in her life back in the day and any one of them could have gotten her pregnant. At the time the girl disappeared, Minerva was living with a low-hanger named Truco. He'd been rough with the girl, said she needed to be kept in line. But Truco was in the wind and had been for a few years now.

"Any luck?"

I opened my eyes and saw Gabe and shook my head. "I might have a bite," I said, figuring he'd much rather talk about the case than the burials we'd watched that morning. Gabe had been stoic throughout, but I sensed there was anger just beneath the surface. "Boyfriend of the mother. Might lead somewhere. I'll have the detectives run his name through the system."

"I could do that for you," Gabe said. "If you want."

"Do what?"

"Get into VICAP and check out the boyfriend," Gabe said. "We'll get a last name if we're lucky or even his real one."

I stared at him for several moments and then nodded. "Connie's got a laptop in the back room. Bring it here and let's see if you're as good as you say you are."

Gabe smiled and went for the computer. Connie walked over and rested a bottle of wine on the table. "You think it's a good move to include him in this?" she asked.

"He's in my life now," I said. "And he's going to be living in our world. The sooner he gets to know it, the better."

"He's just a kid," Connie said. "A kid whose parents just died. He's hiding it pretty well. But he's got to feel lost."

"I know," I said. "That's why he also needs to feel he belongs. Needs to feel he hasn't lost everything. If we can give him that, it'll be easier for him to deal with the other stuff."

"That's how it worked for you?"

"To a point," I said. "You never get over it, Connie. You just live your life around it."

Gabe worked the computer for an hour, getting into sites I didn't even know existed, getting instant messages from friends across the country. Before long, I had a teenage squad working for me, trying to help me crack a case.

"Truco's rap sheet is longer than a Pat Conroy novel," I said. "But there's nothing in there that points to him hurting a kid."

Dominick and Rocco had joined us at the table. Dominick was average height with an old boxer's body, still ready for a tussle, his hair the color of silver. Rocco was tall and stocky with a thick head of white hair and hands that had handed out more than a fair share of beatings. He also had the warmest smile I had ever seen.

"Mamma didn't report Angela missing because she wasn't living at home," I said, scanning all the printed out information Gabe and his friends had managed to generate.

"You figuring she was on the street?" Dominick asked.

"Maybe," I said. "Or maybe living with someone else. There's always someone in those neighborhoods—guy usually—takes in runaways, plays the system, pretends to care, has room enough to keep six, maybe more in his place. Turns some of them out for more money. Whatever suits his needs. They're not kids to him—they're product."

"Sometimes, families give up their kids to guys like that and in return he forgives the money they owe to a street shark," Dominick said. "The kid is used to balance the books."

"And there's no paper trail," Rocco said. "Kid makes a run for it and goes in the wind, no one knows, no one sees."

"And if the kid gets out of line?" I asked. "Or maybe talks about it to somebody she shouldn't talk to?"

"Or maybe just wants to go back home," Connie says. "To be with a mother who never wanted her in the first place."

I looked at the faces around me and then at Gabe, listening intently. "Can you find me a name?" I asked him. "Somebody who might have had something like that going three years back?"

"I can try," Gabe said.

"Call me if you get anything," I said, pushing my chair back and walking away from the table.

"Where you heading?" Rocco asked.

"The kid can get the computer to talk," I said without looking back. "I can get the street to talk."

It took well into the night, the summer sun minutes away from warming the day, before I found who I was looking for. Frankie Robles was in his sixties, an overweight diabetic who reeked of Dewar's and lived in a railroad apartment he shared with four teens and six cats. The windows had long sleeves of wax paper hanging from them instead of curtains, and the place reeked of stale smoke and cat urine. It was on the top floor of the building and was just a quick walk to the roof, where Robles kept a small fridge packed with beer and a coop with only three pigeons in it. We stood there, both of us staring down at the park where only days earlier they'd found little Angela's body. I showed him her photo, rested it on the tar ledge.

"Think before you answer," I said.

"Well, everybody knows her face by now," he said. "Been in all the papers and all over the news. So, yeah, I know the face. So what?"

"I'm not asking if you know her now," I said. "I'm asking if you knew her three years ago."

"Hey, a lot of kids like her come through here," he said. "They turn to me when they got no place else to go. I'm like that place Boys Town. Only I take girls, too."

"Yeah, I could see that," I said. "Things are bad at home, some guy whaling on you, your mother strung out on drugs, why not come to a dump like this and live with a model citizen like yourself? Makes perfect sense."

"I do my best," Robles said. "Nobody puts a gun on them to come here. They just show up and I do what I can."

"Which is what, exactly?"

"Give them a boost, you know," he said. "A fresh start. A chance to earn their way, put some dollars in their pockets."

"And in yours, too."

"It's America, baby," Robles said. "It may be the land of the free, but there ain't nothin' out here that's free."

"I'm going to tell you what I am pretty sure happened," I said, staring at Robles. "And then I'm going to tell you what's going to happen."

"I'm all ears," he said. "I love to hear me a good story."

"You took Angela in, about three years ago—give or take. Looked after her just long enough to earn her trust. Made her think she'd finally found a home—dump that it was. You with me so far?"

"I can hear," Robles said.

"Then you did what guys like you always do," I said, my voice low. "You saw a scared kid with nowhere else to go—and tried to turn her into something you could profit from. You took her to the park, had a talk with her. See if you could convince her to start working the street for you. You smoked some weed with her, got her to relax, gave her a cold beer, maybe even two. Had a couple yourself. How am I doing so far?"

"You lost with the cold beers," he said. "It was too hot, holding four beers from here to the park, they be like warm water by the time we popped them open."

And then I was certain I was standing next to Angela's killer. "How did you know it was hot out?" I asked.

"Who goes walking in the park in the winter time?" Robles asked.

"Police haven't released a timeline for Angela's death," I said. "Not to the papers you say you read or to the TV news you say you watch. But you're right. It was summer time. And you know what's in that park in the summer time? Coolers filled with ice and beer. People keep them there for after work, to have a cold one under the shade of a tree after a long shift. It's a good place to stash your drink, cover it up with leaves and such. Stock it when it needs it."

Robles didn't say anything.

"My old man used to hide a cooler in the park, him and his friends," I said. "And me and my friends would go sneak some beers when we wanted something stronger than an ice pop."

"And you're saying I had me one of those coolers?"

"You got two of them down in your apartment," I said. "And there's one right here on the roof. Why wouldn't you keep one in the park? It's not like you buy them. You have the kids steal them for you. My father did it the same way."

"Just because I got a cooler don't make me a killer," Robles said.

"But you are a sex offender," I said. "Tried and convicted."

"I did my time," Robles said. "And I left that all behind me."

"That's not all you left behind," I said. "You also left DNA that's being checked now. We'll see if any part of you is on that girl's body. Once we have that, I got you."

"That girl's been dead a long time. You can't prove nothin'."

"I got a phone in one pocket and a gun in the other. When that phone rings, the voice on the other end is going to tell me all I need to know," I said.

"Then what?"

"Then it's up to you," I said. "Cuffs on the hands or a bullet to the head. I'm hoping you do something, anything, that makes me forget I have cuffs."

Robles stayed silent for several moments, sweat lining his forehead and marking large circles on his grey shirt. "She fell asleep, under one of the trees after . . ."

"You could have left her there," I said. "Let her sleep it off and then walk away from it. Instead, you popped open your cooler, emptied out the beer, picked up a sleeping drugged-out little girl, and dropped her in. You locked it and then dragged it where it wouldn't be seen by anyone. Hid it under brush or a bush that's not even there anymore. Tossed her away like an old can."

Robles hung his head and said nothing.

"You killed her," I said. "Let her die in a horrible way."

"How much time you think I'll get?" Robles asked.

"I'm thinking prison is too good for you," I said. "Which tells me the cuffs don't work for me. Which tells me I need a third option. And the gun, well, they can trace the bullets back to me in no time."

"Which leaves you where, tin badge?"

"You took the coward's way with Angela," I said. "So it's only fair you take the coward's way out for yourself."

"What does that mean?"

Robles turned and saw Rocco standing against the door leading down from the roof to the apartment. He looked back at me. "That means you go with him," I said. "And there's a bright spot in doing that. Angela's case will remain an unsolved. I won't report it to the police, so it won't impact your record. You'll just disappear. Just like she did. And trust me. Not only will no one ever find you, no one is ever going to miss you. After today, it'll be as if you never existed."

I looked at Rocco, nodded, and walked away.

It was Gabe's idea to have Angela buried in our family plot in Long Island. We all went to her funeral that day. A mass served in Latin by an old priest friend of mine. Dominick, Rocco, Connie, Carl, and Gabe all in attendance. Even my old partner Winston came to pay his respects.

"Thanks for your help," I said to Gabe as we walked from the gravesite toward the waiting cars.

"Thanks for letting me help," he said.

"You're good at this. Next case I catch, I'll be sure to include you."

"I'm already working on one," Gabe said.

"One what?" I asked.

"A case," he said.

I stopped walking and looked over at him. "What case?"

"My mom and dad," Gabe said, staring at me, his voice confident, his manner relaxed.

"That's not a case," I said. "That's a car accident."

Gabe took in a deep breath, looked around to make sure no one else was listening, then looked up into my eyes. "It wasn't an accident," he said to me. "It was a murder. And I'm going to prove it. We both are."

He then turned and walked toward Connie, waiting for him by her car.

Dominick came up next to me and patted me on the back. "That nephew of yours is something else," he said with a smile.

I looked at Gabe talking to Connie, now both of them smiling. "You have no idea."

SIXTY-SIX

RAY BRADBURY

I'm going to tell you a story and you're not going to believe it, but nevertheless I'm going to tell you. It's kind of a murder mystery. On the other hand, maybe it's a time travel story and, come to think of it, it's a story of vengeance, and then throw in a couple of ghosts and there you have it.

What I am is a motorcycle officer with the Oklahoma police on what used to be called Route 66, somewhere between Kansas and Oklahoma City.

During the last month a series of very strange discoveries have been made along the route from Kansas City to Oklahoma.

The bodies of a man, a woman, a younger man, and two children were discovered by me in fields along the way in early October. The bodies were widely distributed over a stretch of more than a hundred miles, and yet the way they were dressed indicated that somehow, I felt, they were all related, because the clothes they wore did not belong to this day, in this month, in this year.

Each of them appeared to have died from some sort of

strangulation, but that has not been completely ascertained. There were no marks on the bodies, but indeed all indications were that they had been slain and left by the side of the road.

When I speak of the costumes they wore, indeed they felt like costumes instead of the clothes you would buy at shops today. The man appeared to be a farmer who was dressed in work clothes: denims and a ragged shirt and battered hat. The woman resembled a timeworn scarecrow, starved by life. The younger man was dressed as a farmer also, but with clothes that looked like they had been through 500 miles in a dust storm. The two children, a boy and a girl around twelve, also looked as if they had wandered the roads in heavy rains and blistering sun and then fallen by the way.

When I mention dust bowl, memories come back which are not mine. My mother and father were born in the early twenties, and were alive during the Great Depression, which I heard about all my life. We people here in the center of America suffered that nightmare which we've all seen in motion pictures of dust blowing in great billowing gusts across the land, destroying the barns and leveling the crops.

I've heard the story and seen it portrayed so often that I feel I lived through it. That is why my finding the bodies of these people was so strange.

When I woke some nights ago at three in the morning I found that I had been crying and I didn't know why, but I sat up in bed and realized I'd been dreaming about these bodies found all along the road from Kansas City to beyond the Oklahoma border.

It was then that I got up and rifled through some old books left me by my parents and found pictures of the Okies; people who had gone west and who had been immortalized in Steinbeck's *Grapes of Wrath*. The more I looked at the pictures, the more I had an increasing tendency to weep. I had to put the books away and go back to bed, but I lay there for a long time with tears streaming down my face and only slept when the sun rose in the morning.

I've taken the long way to tell you about this because it has been so mysterious and so hurtful to my soul.

I found the body of the man in an empty cornfield, lying in a ditch, with his clothes burnt by the sun and parched as in a dry harvest, no signs of violence.

I called in the county coroner and moved on searching. I did not realize I was searching, but there was a sense in me that there were more bodies to be found. Why I should think this still remains an immense mystery to me.

I found the woman thirty miles further on, under a culvert, and she, in turn, bore no marks of violence, but seemed dead as a result of an invisible bolt of lightning having struck her by night.

Fifty miles further on lay the bodies of the children and the young man.

When they were all assembled, like a jigsaw puzzle, in the county coroner's office, we surveyed them with a terrible sense of loss, though we did not know these people. Somehow we felt we had seen them before and known them well and mourned their deaths.

The case went on for days, and then weeks, then several months, and would have remained a terrible mystery, if I hadn't been sitting in a barber shop one afternoon, waiting for a haircut. I dug through a pile of magazines on the barber shop table, came across an old issue, and leafed through to a page of photographs which caused me to jump up, throw the magazine against the wall, then pick it up, shouting to nobody, "Damn! Oh, Jesus! Damn!"

I clenched the magazine in my hand and asked the barber if I could take it and stormed out.

Because, my God, the pictures of the Okies in the magazine were of the people I'd found along the road!

But, looking closer, I read that these pictures had been taken a few weeks ago of folks in New York who had dressed up in old thirties outfits and were photographed to look like Okies.

The clothes they wore were new, but made to look full of dust.

If you wanted to buy them you could go to a store in New York and get these old clothes at new prices and think yourself back sixty years.

I don't know what happened next. I kind of went red-hot blood-shot blind. I heard someone yelling, and it was me. "Damn! Oh God!"

Crushing the magazine, I stared at my motorbike.

The night was autumn cold and somehow I knew I had to ride the bike somewhere. I had an appointment with someone, but I didn't know who and I didn't know why.

I rode the bike off in the autumn weather for a long while and stopped in between places. I didn't know where I was.

Now I'll tell you another thing that you won't believe, but when I'm done, maybe you will.

Have you ever been in a big wind storm? The kind of storm that came through Kansas and blew over Oklahoma in the years of the dust bowl? When you see the pictures and hear the name there is hardly a way for you to imagine the way it was when the people inside the great wind couldn't feel the horizon, didn't know what time it was. The wind blew so hard it flattened a lot of farms, tore off roofs, knocked over windmills. It razed a lot of really poor roads, which were nothing but red mud. Anyway, you're lost in the middle of a storm like that, when the dust burns your eyes and fills your ears, so you forget what day it is or what year and you wonder if something awful is going to happen and then maybe it's not awful, but it does happen and it's there.

This big wind roared up and I was on the road on my motorbike when it hit. I had to stop my bike I was so blind. I stood there with the sun going down beyond the storm and the wind howling and I was afraid for the first time. I didn't know what I was afraid of, but I waited with my motorbike and after a long while the wind sort of died and along Route 66 from the eastern horizon, going real slow, came an old jalopy—the kind of open car with bundles in the back and a water bag on the side, and steam coming out of the radiator and dirt crusted over the windshield so whoever was driving had to half-stand to look over it to see the road.

The car came puttering up and then sort of ran out of gas and stopped very close to me. The man behind the wheel looked out and I looked at him. He was a tall man, even sitting in his seat, and his face was bony and his hands were bony on the wheel. There was a crumpled hat on his head and he had a three-day beard. His eyes looked like he'd been in a night storm forever.

He waited for me to speak.

I walked over and all I could say was, "You lost?"

He looked at me with his steady grey eyes. His head didn't move, but his lips moved. "No, not now. Is this the dust bowl?"

I sort of pulled back and then I said, "I haven't heard those words since I was a kid. Yeah, this is it."

"And this is Route 66?"

I nodded.

"That's how I figured," he said. "Well, if I go straight on will I get where I want to go?"

"Where's that?"

He looked at my uniform and his shoulders sort of sagged. "I was looking for, I think, a police station."

"Why would you do that?" I said.

"Because," he said. "I think I want to give myself up."

"Well, maybe you can give yourself up to me. But why would you want to do that?"

"Because," he said, "I think I killed some folks."

I looked back down the road where the dust was settling. "Back there?" I said.

He looked over his shoulder very slowly and nodded. "Yup, back there."

The wind went high again and the dust was thick.

"How long ago?" I said.

He closed his eyes. "Sometime during the last couple weeks."

"Folks?" I said. "Killed? How many?"

He opened his eyes and his eyelashes quivered. "Four, no, five. Yeah, five people, dead now. Good riddance. Do I give myself up to you?"

I hesitated because there was something wrong. "This is too easy. You've got to say more."

"Well," he said, "I don't know how to tell you, but I've been driving along this road for a long time. Gotta be years."

Years, I thought. That's how it seemed to me too, that he'd been driving for years.

"And then what?" I said.

"These people sort of got in the way. One of them looked like my pa and another looked like my ma when she was very young and the third one looked like my brother, but he's long dead. I had another brother and sister; they were there too. It was so damned strange."

"Five people?" I said. And my mind went back to the five people found on the road between Kansas City and Oklahoma. "Five?"

He nodded. "That's it."

"Well," I said, "what had they done? Why did you want to kill them?"

"They was just on the road," he said. "I don't know how they got there, but the way they dressed and the way they looked, I knew something was wrong and I had to stop and fix each one. And when I say fix I mean make them disappear forever. I just had to do it." He looked at his hands on the steering wheel, which were clenched tight.

"Hitchhikers?" I said.

"Not exactly," he said. "Something worse. Hitchhikers are okay, they're going somewhere, but these folks, they were just poachers I guess. Claim-jumpers, stealers, robbers of some sort. It's hard to say." He looked back down the road again where the dust was beginning to stir up just a bit.

"Do you ever come out of church Sunday noon, feeling clean, like you had another chance for who knows what, and you stand there, reborn, with folks and grandfolks happy unto joy, as the preacher says, and then in the midst of noon folks from across town drive up in their dark suits and undertake you, I mean undertake your happiness with their demon smiles? And you stand there with your folks and feel the joy just melt away like a spring thaw and when they see they've undertook your joy they drive away in their own kind of sinful undertaking of happiness."

The driver stopped, added up the sums inside his eyelids, and at last let his breath out. "Ain't that a sort of, I don't know, kind of—"

He searched and found the word.

"Blasphemy?"

I waited, thought, and said, "That's the word."

"We weren't doing nothing, just standing there, fresh out of the revival, and they just came by and undertook us."

"Blasphemy," I said.

"I was only ten, but that was the first time in my life I wanted to grab a hoe and rake their smiles. You stand there, feeling naked. They've stolen your Sunday best. Don't you think I got a right to just say give back, hand over, I'll take that coat, shuck off those pants and the hat too, yeah, the hat."

"Five people," I said. "An older man, a woman, a younger man, and two kids. That sounds familiar."

"Then you know what I'm saying. They were wearing clothes. It's funny, the clothes they were wearing, it looked like they had been through the dust bowl, stayed there a long time, and maybe lived out in the open and slept at night with the wind blowing and their clothes getting full of dust and their faces sort of getting thin and I looked at each one and I said to the older man, 'You're not my pa.' And the old man couldn't answer. I looked at the woman and said, 'You're not my ma,' and she didn't answer either. And I looked at my brother and my other younger brother and sister and said, 'I don't know any of you. You look right, but you feel wrong. What are you doing on the road?' Well, they didn't say anything. They was kind of, I don't know, ashamed maybe, but they wouldn't get out of the way. They were standing in front of the car and I knew if I didn't do something they wouldn't let me continue on to Oklahoma City. So you know what I did?"

"Put a stop to them," I said.

"Stop is a good word. Yank off the clothes, I thought to myself. They don't deserve to have those clothes. Take away their skin, I thought, because they don't deserve to look like my mom and dad and brothers and sister. So I sort of edged the car forward, but they didn't move and they couldn't speak because they was ashamed and the wind came up and I started the car. As I rolled forward, they fell down in front of it and I drove straight on and when I looked back I hoped the bottom of the car had ripped their clothes off, but no, they were still full dressed, which they didn't deserve, and they were lying there on the road and if they was dead I wasn't sure, but I hoped they was. I got out and went back and one by one I picked them up, put them in the back of the car, and I took off down the road with the dust rising and I laid them out here and there and somewhere else and by that time they didn't look like any of my folks at all. That's a peculiar story, don't you figure?"

"It's peculiar," I said.

"Well then," he said, "that's it. I've told it all. You gonna take me in?"

I looked into his face and looked down the road and I thought of the bodies waiting at the coroner's office in Topeka City. "I'll think about it," I said.

"What do you mean?" he said. "I've told it all. I'm guilty. I did them in."

I waited. The wind and the dust were rising even more. I said, "No. Strange, but I don't think you're guilty. Don't know why, but I don't think you are."

"Well, it's getting late," he said. "You want to see my identification?"

"If you want to show it," I said.

He pulled a battered wallet out of his pocket and handed it over. There was no driver's license, just an old card with a name on it I couldn't quite read, but it looked familiar, like something out of the newspapers long before I was born. The back of my neck got real cold and I said, "Where you heading after this?"

"I don't know," he said. "But I'm feeling better than when I started the trip. What's ahead up there on the road?"

"Same as always," I said. "California, postcards, oranges, lemons, maybe government camps, bungalow courts." I handed him back his card and wallet. "There's a police station about ten miles ahead. By the time you get there, if you still feel you've gotta give yourself up, do it there, but I'm not your man."

"How come?" he said, his eyes quiet and grey and steady.

"All I know is sometimes some people don't deserve to wear the clothes that they wear or wear the faces that they got. Some people," I said at last, "get in the way."

"I drove real slow," he said.

"And they didn't move."

"Right," he said. "I just went right over them and that was it. Well, I better be gettin' on."

I stood back and let the car drift away. It went down the road, the driver hunched over the wheel, his hands on the steering wheel and the dust following him and he went away in the twilight.

I stood watching him for the next five minutes until he was gone. By that time the wind was rising and the dust was filling my eyes. I couldn't tell where I was or if I was crying. I went back to my motorbike, got on, hit the throttle, and turned around and went the other way.

PROVIDENCE AND THE BUTLER

P. G. WODEHOUSE

"His lordship wishes to see you, Mr. Keeling."

Keeling, butler to the Earl of Drexdale, rose slowly from the chair in which he had been enjoying his afternoon sleep, and toddled off down the passage. The footman who had brought the message watched him pass through the red-barge door which marked the boundary of the servants quarters.

"Jane," he said to one of the housemaids who had appeared from nowhere, "'ow old is old Keeling?"

"Blessed if I know," said Jane, "I've been here since I was a little bit of a slip of a thing, and he was just the same then."

"Poor old feller."

"Why poor old feller?"

"'Cos he's got to go see his lordship."

"Is his lordship in one of his moods, Tom?"

"His lordship," said Tom with emphasis, "is in about eighteen of 'em at once."

The guidebooks were wont to assert that the most interesting sight to be seen at Drexdale Castle was the thirteenth-century crypt. They were wrong. To the really thoughtful visitor the chief object of interest was Keeling. As a matter of fact Keeling looked a good deal older than the crypt. His air of antiquity and permanence was more marked. Nobody—not even James, the head gardener, who had been at the castle for twenty-five years—knew when he had first come to the place. When James was a sprightly young gardener's boy, Keeling had been exactly the same—so James asserted—as he was now. Keeling was not a mere butler. He was an heirloom, a part of the estate. It was believed that he knew more about the history of the Drexdale family than any man living. It was his hobby. He worshipped the Drexdale blood. He knew the family history back to the days of Edward the Confessor. He dated events by the length of time that had elapsed since the present earl had fallen downstairs and broken his ankle or the eleventh earl had fought furiously with his small brother in the stable loft over a disputed guinea-pig. The faithful old servant of the melodramas was a parvenu compared to Keeling. Footmen might come and footmen might go, but he went on forever.

Having negotiated the distance to his lordship's study at his best pace—for a summons to the presence in the afternoon meant that important matters were toward—Keeling tapped upon the door. A querulous bellow from within bade him enter.

John, twelfth earl of Drexdale, was seated in an armchair by the window. He was a short, red-faced man, inclined to stoutness. He wore a ragged grey beard. Those who knew Keeling's devotion to the proud name of the Drexdales often wondered what his opinion of the present earl might be. Both as regarded manners and appearance Lord Drexdale would have made an excellent bookkeeper or publican. In his youth his position and the blameless reputation of his father, a cabinet minister and famous philanthropist, had led society to welcome him with a friendly smile. The friendly smile had changed to a blank stare within the space of four years, and now the best the society papers could find to call him was "that well known sporting peer." Which was a polite way of intimating that his friends and associates today were the scum of the race course.

But whatever Keeling's views may have been, he confided them to none. A Drexdale, however far he might have fallen from the Drexdale standard, as a sacred subject, is immune to criticism.

"Come in, can't you? Shut the door. Don't stand there half in and half out, gaping at me like a fish. Ah!"

The last remark was elicited by a sudden twinge of pain in the foot which rested, swathed in bandages, on a pile of cushions, for his lordship was suffering from one of his frequent attacks of gout.

"Your lordship wished to see me?"

"Of course I wished to see you. For Heaven's sake, man, can't you close your mouth? Is it absolutely necessary for you to gape at me like that? That's better. Keeling, I want you to go up to London by the first train tomorrow."

"To London, your lordship?"

"Yes, London. You've heard of the place, I suppose? Here, read this letter. This will explain. Curse the young fool. I might have known he would be making an idiot of himself if I left him out of my sight. Read it. It's from Colonel Brant, who was here for the shooting last year."

Keeling took the letter, and fumbled in his pocket for his spectacles. Lord Drexdale was watching his maneuvers with growing impatience.

"Damn it, man," he broke out, "I can't wait all day. Give me the letter. I'll read it to you. It's about Lionel."

Keeling bowed. The Hon. Lionel, only son of the earl, was a pale, nervous young man who had been bullied through a sickly boyhood by his father and was now drifting aimlessly about London. Keeling, who had known him from his cradle, had an affection for him apart from the fact that he was a Drexdale. Lionel was quiet and diffident, and quiet and diffidence were a welcome change from the common run of manners at the castle.

"This is what it says," said Lord Drexdale, taking the letter. "I'll skip the inquiries after my gout. Here is the part I want you to hear. 'I think, if you feel well enough for the trip, I should run up to town for a day or two, if I were you. It might be just as well if you kept an eye on the hope of the Drexdales right now. Last night, after we had dined together at the club, Lionel, in a communicative mood, unbosomed himself to me. Not to break it gently, the young fool has fallen head over ears with a lady who, however attractive, is hardly in the rank of society, from which, I fancy, you would prefer the future Lady Drexdale to be drawn. To be exact, she is one of the performers in a sort of circus-spectacle which is now drawing the youth to the suburbs of Olympia. Lionel showed me her photograph. She seems to be deucedly good-looking, and I gather from Lionel that she rides magnificently. If these qualities are all you demand from your daughter-in-law, well and good. If not, you'd better come and stop the thing. I can't help you. I sail tomorrow for Egypt. That is how the matter stands. The next move is with you. I hope your gout . . .'—oh, never mind my gout. That's all. And about enough. I can't stir myself, with this infernal gout, and you're the only man I know I can trust to look after the interests of the family. You may be a fool—don't gape, man!—but I know you've got our interests at heart."

"If I might suggest, your lordship—"

"Well?"

"Perhaps a telegram, directing Master Lionel to return—?"

Lord Drexdale jerked his head toward the table.

"Do you imagine I didn't think of that? I wired the moment I got this letter. There's his answer. He says he is very sorry, but he is in bed with a severe attack of tonsillitis, and his doctor forbids him to move. Tonsillitis! Bah! I expect he's sitting in the six-penny gallery, cracking nuts and making sheeps-eyes at the girl as she jumps through paper hoops."

Keeling received this vivid piece of imagery in respectful silence.

"Catch the first train tomorrow, Keeling. Use your discretion, if you have any. Do what you think best. If the girl has to be bought off, buy her off. Never mind the figure. That's all. I shall dine up here."

Keeling bowed, and left the room.

The atmosphere at the castle was always a trifle electric when his lordship had one of his attacks of gout, but no one could recall a more exciting hour than that which followed breakfast on the third day after Keeling's departure. It was his lordship's custom to read his *Sporting Life* (he subscribed to the *Times* but he read his *Sporting Life* immediately after the meal). On this morning, Tom, the footman, removing the breakfast things, was surprised to hear a sort of combination roar and groan proceed from his lordship. Looking up, he saw that the latter's face was a rich purple, and that his eyes were bulging apoplectically. He was moving to offer assistance when the bulging eyes suddenly met his, and the earl, becoming aware of his presence, ordered him from the room with a stream of forceful words. Tom stood not upon the order of his going.

The paragraph which had disturbed his lordship so extremely was headed, "Interesting Wedding." And, in his lordship's opinion, that did not overstate the case. The paragraph ran as follows:

> *A wedding of great interest to lovers of sport was solemnized yesterday at St. Andrew's church, Walthamstow, when the Hon. Lionel Carr, only son of the earl of Drexdale, the well known sporting peer, was quietly married to Margaret, daughter of Nathaniel J. Trenton of Austinville, Texas, U.S.A. Mr. Keeling, a friend of the bridegroom, acted as best man. The bride was given away by her father. Both Mr. Trenton and the Hon. Mrs. Carr are members of Colonel Wilberforce's "Prairie Days" company, now performing at Olympia, where the bride's wonderful feats in the saddle have been attracting so much attention. After the ceremony the happy pair left in*

an automobile for Wales, where the honeymoon will be spent.

At eleven o'clock precisely Lord Drexdale made a coherent remark—his first. That remark was "When Keeling returns, send him to me."

In rehearsing scenes in our minds before they take place, we are apt to err chiefly as regards the attitude of the other party. We assign to him a certain deportment and allow our imaginations to run accordingly. Such scenes, as a rule, turn out otherwise than we had anticipated, owing to the other actor's treatment of his role. Lord Drexdale made this mistake. Even when he had a clear conscience, Keeling's demeanor was wont to be humble. With this frightful burden on his soul, Lord Drexdale expected him to cringe. And he did not cringe.

The Keeling who entered the room at five-thirty that evening was subtly different from the Keeling who had left the castle three days before. His back seemed straighter. There was a curious light in his mild eye. Almost the eye of battle. No good butler is ever perky. If he were perky, he would not be a good butler. But truth compels one to admit that Keeling, as he met the Basilisk stare in his lordship's protruding eyes, came as near to being perky as it is possible for a good butler to come.

"Well?" said Lord Drexdale in a calm-before-the-storm voice, which might have occasioned the boldest a tremor.

"Your lordship has read the announcement?"

Lord Drexdale's feelings burst their dam. He spoke his mind. Years of acquaintance with turf circles had given him the power of expressing himself with a certain generous strength.

"You old fool!" he shouted. "You moth-eaten monument of imbecility. You stand there and calmly—You mummy! You dodderer! You—!"

"If your lordship—"

"What did you get out of it? What did they pay you? Eh? No? They twisted you round their fingers. They—"

"Your lordship instructed me to use my discretion. Have I your lordship's permission to explain?"

Lord Drexdale tugged at his grey beard. The action seemed to afford him a temporary relief. He nodded.

"I delivered your lordship's wishes to Master Lionel immediately upon my arrival. Master Lionel declined to express an opinion. He took me to the place where the young lady was performing, and I am bound to say, your lordship, that I was greatly struck by her command of her horse. After the performance, Master Lionel did me the honor of presenting me to her. I can assure your lordship that this young lady is most satisfactory in every respect. I feel confident that your lordship will have no reason to complain of the manner in which she fits her position."

"Damn it, you talk as if you had been engaging a scullery-maid. Do you realize that this bounding, bronco-jumping female will be Lady Drexdale one day?"

"They are extremely fond of each other, your lordship. The young lady seems devoted to Master Lionel."

"Devoted!" A strand of the grey beard came away in Lord Drexdale's hand.

"She is an extremely sensible, good-hearted young lady, your lordship. She was opposed all the time to marrying Master Lionel without your lordship's consent. She had even persuaded Master Lionel on this point."

"But apparently they changed their minds."

"I induced them to do so, your lordship."

"What!"

"I induced them to do so."

"Then—then." His lordship stammered. "Then it was you—"

Keeling bowed gravely; and the storm broke out again. It was generally conceded at the castle that his lordship, when he started to deliver one of his militant harangues, did not leave out much. On this occasion he eclipsed himself. He rent Keeling. He savaged

Keeling. He tore Keeling to shreds. The butler waited patiently for him to finish.

"And you can get out of here tonight," concluded Lord Drexdale. "I don't care if you had been with us for half a century. Out you go. That's all. Shut the door after you."

"Am I to leave his lordship's service?"

"You left it a minute ago. Get out."

The light of battle shone in the butler's eyes. The years rolled away from him. His voice shook.

"Master Jack—"

Lord Drexdale started at the once familiar address. How many years had slipped by since Keeling had last called him Master Jack? And he looked just the same way now as he had looked then. Something—he could not say what—kept Lord Drexdale silent at that moment; and the butler went on, his voice growing stronger and fiercer as he spoke.

"Master Jack, listen to me. It's sixty years, just sixty years next October since I entered the service of the Drexdale's. I was a bit of a boy then, and I helped in the stables. And my father, he was butler to his lordship your grandfather, he used to keep telling me how the Drexdales were the greatest family in England and how, now I was in service at the castle, I must be a credit to them. He taught me to look up to the Drexdale name as if it was my own and be proud of their history and their future as if they belonged to me. And when he died, I took his place. His lordship your father was the earl then, Master Jack. He was a proper Drexdale! He'd ha' cut his right hand off, he would, for the sake of the name. Then he died, and you became master of the castle. You!" His voice rose higher. "You dragged the name down, Master Jack! You filled the castle with men who weren't fit to chop wood for its fires. Do you think I didn't feel it, seeing that scum sitting round the table and waiting on 'em? Waiting on 'em! Do you think I didn't feel it, reading of Lord Drexdale this and Lord Drexdale that in the papers and seeing the name dragged in the mud? And then, you marrying that cold, bloodless woman, caring for her no more than the name. And Master Lionel born, all delicate and all. And his lordship your father a man who could hunt all day and come in fresh as paint!" He stopped, shaking; then went on in a weaker voice. "When Master Lionel showed me this girl he's married, I says to myself 'You'll do!' I says it isn't rank the Drexdales want, nor is it money. It's health. Body and mind. Then maybe the next Drexdale will be a Drexdale. She's not one of your London society girls. She's a woman, she is. She's got blood in her, she has. She—"

His voice trailed away into a whisper. His hand went up to his throat. He turned half round, groping for the door, and fell with a crash.

Lord Drexdale, gouty foot and all, flew from his chair and tugged at the bell.

The concluding passage, the postscript as it were, to this episode in the history of the ancient family may be said to be dated at about five o'clock on a spring evening some eighteen months later, when Keeling, still butler to the Earl of Drexdale, might have been observed to toddle along the corridor and knock on the door of his lordship's study. He knocked again. There was no answer. He went in.

Lord Drexdale's back was turned to the door.

"Shall I remove Master John, your lordship?"

Lord Drexdale looked up.

"Can't you see he's got hold of my finger?" he said. "You're a perfect nuisance sometimes, Keeling."

The butler inspected the infant gravely.

"A fine boy, your lordship."

A sudden yell rent the air. The baby had taken a dislike to the pattern of the carpet. Keeling stooped and lifted the malcontent.

"Those," said Lord Drexdale complacently, eyeing the roaring bundle in the butler's arms, "are lungs. Keeling, you were right. The next Drexdale will be a Drexdale."

THE PROPERTY LADDER

RUTH WARE

The house was perfect—that's the first thing I thought when the email landed in my inbox. My heart started beating a little faster as I scrolled through the details. Two bedrooms . . . garden . . . beautiful family room overlooking the lawn—and holy crap, the price! Was it possible? We might actually be able to afford this one.

There must be a catch.

I clicked through to the website, looking to find a belching power station in the back garden, or a bone-rattling train line against the back wall of the house. But . . . nothing. Nothing visible to make me recoil. Yes, the decor was tired, and it could use a new kitchen. But it was nothing a bit of elbow grease couldn't sort.

I rang Mark. "Honey? I think I've found it."

When the estate agent's email came back, I forwarded it to Mark at work, and then before the email had even left my inbox, rang him to rant.

"Did he not understand when I said we'd like to book a viewing ASAP?"

"I think he understood," Mark said patiently. "That's why he's made the point that it's not up to him. It's not his fault if the vendor wants forty-eight hours' notice."

"But why? Are they playing games? Don't they *want* to sell?"

"Maybe there are tenants, or perhaps a rabid dog," Mark suggested. I hung up.

I spent the following two days jealously refreshing the estate agent's listing, watching like a hawk for the "under offer" flag to go up, showing that another buyer had got in there first. But hour after hour ticked by and still "for sale" showed reassuringly.

In the meantime, I brooded over the photographs. All the rooms were lovely, and I had already begun furnishing them in my imagination, talking with Mark about how our sofa would look in the bay window, and the exact shade of curtains that would go in the dining room. But there was one room in particular that already felt like mine. It was the second bedroom, the smaller of two upstairs, and I could imagine my desk by the window, nestled in dove grey wallpaper that I would put up.

Again and again, I found myself coming back to it in the little gallery, enlarging the pictures on the agent's website, trying to imagine it in different lights. The only odd thing about it was the books. There was a bookcase against one wall, but half a dozen books had been picked out, and were individually ranged along the windowsill, their covers facing into the room, separated into two groups. Somehow the little display seemed out of place, in comparison to the neatness of the rest of the house. The other rooms had almost no personal possessions on display, bar a few photos. Was it some kind of collection? A quirky child? They looked like children's books. One was

Heidi, I was sure of it. I had had the same edition as a child. The others, I couldn't recognise. The writing was too small to read.

When the day of the showing at last came round, I put on my best "responsible mortgageable adult" clothes, and wore socks in case the seller wanted us to take our shoes off indoors.

But he or she was out. The estate agent greeted us on the porch with a broad grin.

"Hi, I'm Phil. Nice to meet you guys. Sorry, you were a bit more prompt than I was expecting. I haven't opened up. Avert your eyes for a sec . . ."

We turned our heads away while he felt discreetly under a plant pot and removed a key.

Inside, Mark went around the house commenting on slip lintels and lead wiring. But I didn't care about any of that. This was our house. It *had* to be. After fifteen years in rentals, we were ready for a place of our own, and this already felt like the one. From the look of things, the current owner was an older man and the place hadn't been refreshed in years. I had a picture in my head of a man in middle age, children grown, maybe his wife had left him . . . now he was cashing in on the house and making a fresh start. Mark and I would give it the TLC it needed. It would be a first step up the ladder.

Phil and Mark were in the upstairs bathroom discussing whether the boiler needed renewing, when I went ahead of them into the second bedroom—*my* room.

There were wooden letters on the white-painted bedroom door. "E M . . . A"—with a flake of paint broken off where the final M must have fallen down. I pushed it open, almost holding my breath, and the room inside was just as I had imagined. The decor was tired, a girl's room of nearly twenty years ago, pink sprigged wallpaper, grubby with age. Posters from forgotten bands. An abandoned teddy bear leaning drunkenly on a shelf. But the slanting light through the windows, the polished boards, the view of the apple tree in the garden. All this was just as I had imagined it.

I was about to call Mark in when I noticed the books on the windowsill, the ones that had caught my eye in the photo. I paused. Would it be too weird to tidy them away? They just felt so out of place.

There were four grouped together on the left of the windowsill—*Heidi*, *Emil and the Detectives*, *Little Women*, and *Pippi Longstocking*. As in the photo, their covers faced into the room, their backs to the window and the world beyond. Similarly positioned on the right-hand side were *My Family and Other Animals* and *Emma*.

What was the logic? And why the display? They weren't particularly old or valuable editions, from what I could see. *Pippi Longstocking* looked like the oldest and seemed to be from the seventies. The others were the kind of paperbacks I remembered from my own childhood. The left-hand ones were more classically children's novels, I guessed. Was that why they had been grouped together?

The bookshelf beside the bed held others, rather dusty, their spines cracked from long reading. *The Wind in the Willows*. *Winnie the Pooh*. *The Farthest Shore*. *Tales of a Fourth Grade Nothing*.

I was still looking at the shelves when Mark and Phil entered the room and began discussing the state of the windows, and whether repairing the wood would be possible, or if a complete replacement was the only option. When they left, I trailed after them, down the stairs, half reluctant to leave *my* house, but I could tell that Mark didn't want to look too eager. He was making teeth-sucking remarks about the roof, and Phil was looking surreptitiously at his watch, evidently ready to wind up. But as we headed towards the front door, I realised something.

"So sorry," I said to Phil, rather breathlessly, looking in my handbag. "I think I might have dropped my keys in the upstairs room. Do you mind if I cut back?"

"Go for it," he said, though he glanced again at his watch. I guessed he had another appointment. "Do you see yourselves making an offer then?" he was saying to Mark, as I ran up the stairs, towards the back bedroom.

I looked again at the books, frowning, and sure enough, my memory had been right. My subconscious had been working on the puzzle even while Mark and I discussed storage and loft conversions, and it had supplied the answer almost too late—but not quite.

Heidi, Emil and the Detectives, Little Women, Pippi Longstocking

My Family and Other Animals, Emma

HELP ME

My heart was racing as I glanced down the stairs to where Mark and Phil were still discussing other properties. Was it a joke? Someone's idea of a bit of fun?

Quickly, I gathered up the books and put them all back on the shelf, except for *Heidi*. Then I picked up *Winnie the Pooh*, and scoured the shelves. There was one more book I needed.

"Liz, what are you doing up there?" Mark's voice floated up the stairwell. "Phil's got another appointment at twelve, and I need to get back to the office."

"They're not here. Just looking in the other room!" I called back, trying to keep my voice light and level.

There! *Oh, the Places You'll Go.* It was tucked away on the bottom shelf.

I arranged them on the windowsill.

Heidi; *Oh, the Places You'll Go*; *Winnie the Pooh.*

HOW?

I ran back down the stairs, my heart thumping, holding my keys up like an alibi.

"Sorry, got them. Thanks, Phil!"

"I think we should definitely put in an offer," Mark said in the car. "What do you think? Ten grand under asking?"

"No way," I said firmly. "Listen." And I told him about the books in the bedroom. Mark snorted, even before I'd finished talking.

"Liz, you're nuts. This is crazy, even for you."

"What do you mean, even for me? What's that supposed to mean?"

"Look, you know you're prone to let your imagination run away with you."

"Mark, you saw those books. They're in the photograph on the website, for God's sake. That's not my imagination."

"Secret messages through the medium of children's literature? Yeah. Right."

"The arrangement spells out 'Help me.' I can't see what's up for debate about that. Why would you do that if you had nothing to worry about?"

"It's a kid's room—they're kids' books. Probably some kid having a laugh."

"No one has lived in that room for fifteen years, Mark. Look at those band posters. Whoever the girl was who lived there, she'd be my age by now."

"So?"

"So this isn't some precocious nine-year-old."

"So what do you want to do about it?" he asked.

That was the question. *What did I want to do about it*? The book thing was weird—but not quite definite enough to call the police. I had a horrible feeling they'd laugh at me, just as Mark had.

And then, suddenly, I knew.

"I want a second viewing."

"Great news that you guys are interested!" Phil gushed as he let us into the property for the second time, two days later. The forty-eight-hour rule hadn't been relaxed and I'd had to wait two more agonizing days, listening to Mark talking about deposits and mortgages, when I couldn't think of anything except those books.

Inside the house, I could hardly bring myself to fake interest in the kitchen layout and the possibility of damp in the bay window. I had only one thing on my mind. But as we trailed around the rooms on the ground floor, I found myself noticing things that had escaped my attention the first time. The locks on the doors and windows. The sad series of pictures in the hallway, of a girl in a nineties school uniform looking wistfully out at the world. The pictures went up to when she was about fifteen—and then stopped. After that there were no more. No graduation photos. No wedding. No children.

At last, we had trailed around every room on the ground floor and I was free to race upstairs ahead of Mark and Phil to the second bedroom—*my* room. The first thing I noticed was the bars on the windows—nursery bars, I had thought before, but now they looked very different.

The second thing I saw was that the books had changed. There were only two there now.

Emma. And *Kidnapped*.

"And the books, this time they were *Emma*, and *Kidnapped*. I googled and it looks like an Emma Wright did go missing around the time the photographs stopped being updated—1998. The implication on the news stories is that she ran away—there was a supposed sighting of her in London a few weeks later. But what if she didn't? What if she's still in that house?"

There was a silence on the other end of the line and I could hear the police operator's scepticism even down the phone line.

"You don't believe me, do you?" I said.

"We'll investigate your allegations," the operator replied. But my heart sank.

I got a call back a few hours later.

"Just to reassure you, ma'am, you have the right house, but I've had a look at the original file and the investigators at the time were satisfied that Emma Wright did indeed run away. There were several sightings of her in London, and her bank card was used. She was sixteen at the time, and there was no evidence of anything other than a planned departure on her part."

"Then explain the books," I said angrily. "He could have used her bank cards, and there are always unconfirmed sightings, aren't there? Sixteen-year-old girls look a lot alike. I'm telling you, she's in there and she arranged those books!"

"Ma'am," the operator said wearily. "Don't you think it's a bit far-fetched that this woman can get out to rearrange these books, but not raise the alarm in any other way? And what's he doing with her during viewings?"

"It's not far-fetched!" I said. "He's keeping her somewhere in the house."

"Miss," said the policeman, but I hung up.

I called back the estate agent next.

"Phil?" I said as soon as he answered the phone. "It's Liz. I want to book another visit."

"Ah . . ." Phil said. His voice sounded regretful. "Sorry to tell you this, Liz, I've got some bad news on that front. The owner—Mr. Wright—he's taking the property off the market."

"What?"

"Yeah, sorry. Bit irritating for us too, truth be told. We'd had several expressions of interest. But it's my understanding he's gone away. Gone abroad, I think. I've got a house on Portland Way that might be of interest—"

I made my excuses and hung up.

All that day at work, I couldn't stop thinking about the house, about Emma. Her photo stared back at me from the newspaper report of her disappearance—young, pale, fair-haired—so much like the gawky, awkward teenager I had been myself, that I felt my heart hurting for her. What had happened to her? She must have tried to run away and been stopped—and she had been in that house, a prisoner, for almost twenty years.

The listing had been taken off the internet, but Phil had given us a printout that first time we visited, and now I found myself brooding over it, as if the answer lay there—in the photographs of the rooms and the arrangement of the furniture, but however long I stared I could see nothing—nothing out of the ordinary except those six, odd books. *HELP ME.* A message displayed on that website for all the world to see.

The locks on the internal doors, the bars on the windows—it all made sense. Emma, the long-lost daughter in those photographs, was still there. She was being kept prisoner somewhere in the house, allowed out only when no one was around. That explained the forty-eight hours' notice. To give her father time to get her out of the house and secure her somewhere else. But where?

The house was down the end of a long lane, but people would have noticed if a kidnapped woman had been ferried to and fro. It didn't look like the kind of neighbourhood where people came and went. The houses had the air of places lived in for decades—and the people who live in places like that have long memories. They'd remember a girl who went missing. They'd remember her face.

No, she must still be in the house.

It was when I flicked through the pictures for maybe the hundredth time that I noticed something.

The photographs of the rooms showed two windows facing the garden and the apple tree—one in the bathroom, and one in the second bedroom, the window where the books had been displayed.

But on the pictures of the exterior of the house, there were *three* windows on the second floor.

What had happened to the middle window?

I turned to the back of the details, where the floorplan was.

It showed the two rooms—the bathroom and the second bedroom—meeting at the end of the hallway, each of them with a little shallow alcove to take up the unused space. But there had been no alcove in either room. I had a clear memory of that—of looking at the blank, straight wall in the bedroom and wondering where I'd put a wardrobe.

And I had a clear memory too of climbing the stairs and remarking to Mark how dark it was without a window, and Phil saying that it would be easy enough to put frosted glass in the bathroom door.

Someone had blocked off the end of that corridor and the window that belonged to it, creating a space—maybe three foot by two. And I knew why.

I parked the car a little way up the lane and walked the rest of the way to the house, taking the opportunity to peer in at the neighbours, trying to assess what kind of people they were, but no one was around. When I got to the house, I knocked long and hard at the door. Phil had told me the owner was away, but I wasn't taking any chances. I waited as the sound echoed along the hallway, listening for any movement from within.

There was none. Nor was there a car in the driveway. It was just as Phil had said—he had gone away, abroad maybe. This was it. This was my chance.

My hands were shaking as I lifted up the plant pot by the front door, hardly daring to hope that the key would still be there. Was it possible . . . ?

It was.

I fumbled getting it into the lock, scraping the metal work, my fingers trembling with nerves, but at last I got it in, and it turned with an ease that felt almost too good to be true.

Inside, the house was completely quiet. Just the ticking of the clock on the kitchen wall disturbed the silence.

I ran up the stairs, past the photographs of Emma. Was it my imagination now, or was there something sad and a little wary in her expression as she looked back at the photographer? She seemed to be almost pleading with the viewer.

The landing was exactly as I remembered it—except that at the end of the hallway was something I had seen, but forgotten—something which now made a horrible kind of sense. It was a cupboard—built in, with a padlock on the door.

How—how had I missed this when we viewed the place? How had I thought it was normal for anyone living alone to padlock their hall cupboard? My heart was thumping so hard I felt almost sick with nerves—but I had come too far to give up now. As I got closer, I saw that it was not a padlock with a keyhole, but a combination lock, an alphabetical one, with four slots.

The possible combinations were endless, and I thought of the toolshed out the back, wondering if there was a crowbar or something I could use to break the lock—but even as I turned to run back down the stairs, a thought occurred to me, and I turned back.

The dials on the lock were small and almost unbearably fiddly, and I almost gave up halfway and went for the crowbar after all—but then the last letter clicked into place. E M M A.

It opened.

Before the door opened, I had felt scared. But at the sight of the boarded-up window and the rope ladder descending into the darkness I felt an overwhelming surge of something even more powerful, cancelling out my fears—triumph.

I had been right. In spite of Mark's ridicule and the disbelief of the police, I had been *right*.

"Emma!" I whispered into the darkness as I set my foot on the ladder. "Emma, I'm coming!"

There was no answer. Maybe the owner had taken her away—but it didn't matter, now that I had discovered this place, this dungeon, the police would *have* to believe me. They would have to investigate the place properly, put out a search warrant.

I got out my phone, ready to take a photo—evidence, if they thought I had lost it completely—but as I did the rope ladder swayed beneath me and I fumbled the phone, cursing as I heard it fall, and then land with a crack far below. This shaft went a long way—and when I thought about the layout of the house, I realised there must be a space behind the larder in the kitchen, concealing a shaft that led deep, deep below, right down to a cellar not shown on the plans.

"Emma," I whispered.

I began to climb into the darkness.

I was about halfway down the shaft, climbing steadily, the smell of damp earth growing stronger, when I heard something—something that made my heart stutter, with terror.

It was the sound of the door at the top of the shaft moving.

I began to climb, as fast as I could, my shoes slipping on the rungs, the rope tearing at my hands. I was just a few feet from the top when the door shut, plunging me into complete blackness. For a moment I just stood, paralyzed, clinging to the rope ladder, too frightened almost to breathe.

Then I heard the click of the padlock outside.

The sound jolted me out of my frozen state, pure terror flooding through me.

"Stop!" I screamed, banging at the door. "Let me out, I'm trapped in here."

There was no answer, and I banged again, blindly in the inky darkness, thumping until my fists hurt.

"Let me out! My husband knows I'm here! I have a phone!"

The voice that came back through the crack in the door was a sibilant whisper, too hoarse to tell even if it was male or female, but it was one that I was sure I had never heard in my life before.

"Husband?" it whispered. "You have no husband any more. You are Emma now. Welcome home . . ."

THE SALESMAN OF DEATH

KIRA PEIKOFF

I sell death for a living. When I said it the first time you came to my office, you chuckled without a hint of discomfort.

"Then you're in luck," you told me.

We exchanged a dry smile, and I could tell right off the bat that you appreciated morbid humor. That in spite of your reason for seeking me out, you could still make light out of the darkest darkness. You wouldn't believe how rarely I see that.

When you first walked in, with your lithe figure and your silky dark hair, I groaned to myself. You'll have to forgive me for not taking you seriously. I thought you might be one of the hypochondriacs who sometimes comes to my brokerage. Convinced of their approaching deaths, they want to sell their existing life insurance policies for a quick buck. What an annoying bunch. Don't they realize that their medical records speak for themselves? I can never haggle a good deal when my buyers see perfect blood counts and hormone levels and not a single diseased cell, not even a rash. *Go home*, I tell them. *Get a life. Like the one you already have.*

But you didn't have a bone of self-pity, and that was how I knew you were the real deal. Then I noticed the bald spot like a thumbprint when you turned your head, and I felt guilty for thinking your model-thin body was beautiful. For even thinking of you that way. My business depends on my detachment. You came in need of serious cash for your policy. At twenty-five years old, your beneficiaries were your parents, and they didn't need the money—but you did. You wanted to travel the world before your short time was up. We spoke of your desire to snorkel the Great Barrier Reef, and stand next to Winged Victory in the Louvre, and hunker down in an Irish castle, wandering the countryside. I could see the fierce clinging to life in your eyes, the defiance of your onrushing fate. Six months, you told me. That was it.

I tried not to let on that I admired you.

As soon as you left, I called my best customer, a hedge fund in New York City. They'd gotten hit hard with the subprime crash and were looking for much safer bets this time. What else was more predictable than the Dow, more certain than gold, a higher yield than bonds?

"The only guarantees in life are death and taxes," I liked to remind my buyers. "And the former has no loopholes."

So this fund was buying up "lives" to balance their risky portfolio. They took over paying the premiums of the life insurance policies until the person's death, and then became the new beneficiaries. The sicker the person—and thus the more imminent their demise—the higher I could negotiate.

In truth, your deal was an easy one. I got through to Billy Peterson, the fund manager, after one ring. He and I were still on good terms then; I didn't yet realize the kind of man I was dealing with, nor how desperate he might become.

"Happy Monday," I said. "Twenty-five-year-old female, cancer, family history for three generations. You'll get your payout by Christmas."

"Sweet!" he exclaimed. "Just in time for bonuses. Send her records."

By the next morning, we had agreed on $200,000. I did drive him up a bit, because I liked you. I wanted you to take every trip you had planned.

You did. Every damn one. You even sent me postcards, scrawling quick, exuberant messages, always signing off tongue firmly in cheek: "Still kickin' it." I hung each one up on my bulletin board. Sometimes I'd glance up and picture you swimming the glass-blue Australian sea or catching your first glimpse of Paris at night. I wondered if you met anyone.

That was four years ago.

No one expected you to live this long, least of all me.

Billy wasn't very happy when he called me up last week. The economy's still dragging, he said. His fund was drying up. They were in desperate need of capital. They needed cash fast, and you were the easiest "asset" to collect on. Long overdue. I couldn't believe what I was hearing. Call me naïve, but the business of death is usually a gentlemanly one.

He has your records; he knows where you live. Worse still, his hired guns would make your death seem natural. If you happened to go in your sleep, who would do an autopsy? Your family has been expecting this day for ages.

And if I expose the scandal, I'd have to reveal my part as the facilitator of the deal. I can just see my customers galloping away like spooked horses. A whiff of corruption in this industry is enough to squeeze a poor broker out for life. Billy knows it as well as I do.

But even after all the deaths I've seen, I can't sit back and let it happen—not like this.

So, I found you a fall guy. Someone no one would ask about. A sad old schmuck whose time is near. He didn't take good care of himself, physically or otherwise. His ex-wife thinks him depraved, a description he doesn't dispute. He's got no kids to leave behind. Has he lived a good life? Done noble work? Made good use of his time on earth, like you? Doubtful.

But you're still kicking. Last I heard, you had even found a man, gotten engaged. You stopped writing me after that, but I was only a little hurt. Mostly, I was thrilled for you. You must not have much money left, though. You blew through your cash payout years ago; even you thought you'd be long gone by now.

I knew I had to act soon, before Billy made his move. So I called him a few days ago. The deal went down like any other. Except this time, I was proud. For the first time in my life, I was doing right.

"Got you a sure thing," I said. "Huge payday right around the corner. So no funny business, okay? You leave that woman alone."

"Oh yeah?" His voice was like a snarl now. "How sure?"

I reeled off the facts with practiced neutrality, my voice shaking only a little: "Male, sixty-five, history of heart attacks, smokes three packs a day. Never exercises. He recently found out his carotid is 95 percent clogged."

It was the truth. Unlike some of my competitors, I never exaggerate to make my clients look worse than they are.

And it was perfect timing; my doctor broke the news to me this week.

Billy gave a low whistle. "Guy must be dying as we speak."

I swallowed, a cold sweat prickling my skin. "No doubt."

Then I drove a hard bargain, a good salesman to the end. I was determined to get every penny I could out of the jerk; he deserved it.

Rest easy that you're out of the woods—on Billy's account, anyway. Sorry, can't help with the cancer part.

You'll find a check enclosed. Think of it as a wedding gift—no need to send a thank-you.

Just hit me back if we ever meet again.

I hope it won't be soon.

RISK ASSESSMENT

ZOË SHARP

It's her voice that lures him in. Kind of husky, as if she's smiling as she speaks. As if she's happy to be spending part of her Saturday morning on the phone, talking to someone like him.

She tells him her name is Helen. From her date of birth, he calculates she is thirty-two. Seven years his senior, but he doesn't care about a little thing like that. Her postcode puts her in the heart of the Derbyshire Peak District—probably less than a three-hour drive from his office in London.

"Lovely area of the country," he says approvingly. "Except in the winter, I imagine."

"It can be a bit tricky when it snows," she agrees. "But I'm on the edge of a village, and they usually plough the road for the school bus."

"I expect that pleases everyone—except the kids."

She laughs. "Yes . . . I expect it does." Her tone suggests she's never given it much thought.

No kids, then.

She's divorced, she tells him, when he asks her marital status. There's a cheerful note to her voice. If it gave her a bad time, it is now firmly behind her. Maybe she was the instigator?

Can't have come out of it too badly, though. The property has a name rather than a number. And when she gives him the registration, make, and model of her car, it's a mid-range BMW coupé less than two years old. Not cheap, by any stretch. She's never had an accident and her licence is clean.

"Do you use any other vehicles—belonging to another family member, perhaps, someone living at the same address?"

"There's nobody else here, only me. But I have a motorcycle. Does that count?"

"Unfortunately, yes." He's surprised, but not unpleasantly so. "So you're a bit of a biker as well, are you?"

"Oh yes. Nothing quite like it in the summer, especially through the Peak District National Park—you know, over Cat and Fiddle, or across Saddleworth Moor. Wonderful twisty roads."

"Bit isolated, though. Aren't you worried about breaking down on your own in the middle of nowhere?"

"Not really. Modern British bikes are a lot more reliable than they used to be in the bad old days."

"You be careful of the speed traps, then, or that licence of yours won't stay clean much longer."

She laughs again. It plugs straight into his nervous system, zeros in on his groin. He shifts in his chair, uncomfortable, hurries on with his questions.

Both the car and motorcycle are kept in the garage overnight, which is integral to the house.

"And you always put the car away? Only, if you ever leave it out on the driveway, you're better off saying so, just in case."

"No, no," she says. "I have a remote for the up-and-over door, so when I get home from work I drive straight in."

"Very handy."

"It is! Especially if it's raining. Lazy, I know, but useful for unloading shopping or what-have-you."

"Is the garage covered by an alarm of some sort?"

"I've never bothered. It's quiet round here. I don't think there's been a burglary anywhere in the village for years."

"Well, that should help anyway."

"Oh, good."

"Let me just have a little look and see what we can do for you . . ."

He finishes keying in her information, hits "return," and waits until his screen refreshes with quotes from all the major insurance companies. For the coverage she is after, the top quote is competitive. He scrolls down until he finds an alternative, one where the premium is almost double. He reads that out instead, his voice regretful.

"I'm afraid that's not as good as my current insurer," she tells him. "I've had the renewal through, but I always like to check I'm getting a good deal."

"Ah, what a shame. Well, that's the best price coming up on my system, I'm afraid. I hope you'll give us another chance when your bike insurance falls due. Now, is there anything else I can help you with today?"

After she disconnects, he sits for a while, isolated in his cubicle with the hubbub of the office floor going on unheard around him. He is a submerged rock in a sea of choppy waters, unmoving and unmoveable.

He taps on his keyboard, calls up Helen's details again, and takes another look. Remembering. Discreetly, he slides his smartphone from a pocket, photographs the information on the screen. Then he follows protocol, hits the delete key, and watches as every last traceable byte of her disappears into the server's cyber shredder.

He waits a month. Long enough for her to have phoned another half-dozen companies and brokers. Long enough for her to have arranged insurance elsewhere and forgotten the company he works for and his name, which he always takes such care to mumble. Long enough for the mindless sub-routines of her daily life to go on. And long enough for him to research her on social media. She's been cagey with how much she gives out on Facebook and Instagram, but he has her full name, address, and birthday. Helen is easy enough to identify.

He takes the time to study photographs of her in a bikini on the beach in Mauritius, snapshots posted of a holiday with her sister. He locates her house on Google Earth and does a virtual drive-by on Street View to check out the proximity of her neighbours. He even runs a search on local police response times, and is heartened by the lacklustre result. All done, of course, using the Tor browser to cloak his identity for forays into the Dark Web.

Helen is petite and blonde and pretty. Different enough in type from his last selection to confuse the profilers.

He takes the time to plan.

And his anticipation grows into hunger.

When the day arrives, he is more than ready. He drives a nondescript Toyota borrowed from the office pool and signed for with an illegible squiggle. He has already lined the boot of the car with polythene sheeting, available from any builder's yard, double-layered. He has temporarily disabled the boot's internal release handle, too. Not that he expects she will be in any condition to operate it. But best to be sure.

He dresses in clothing bought from charity shops spread around the city, including shoes a size too large that have a wear pattern not his own. If you're going to leave evidence, it may as well work for you as against you.

He will burn everything when he is done.

He drives the motorway miles sedately, baseball cap pulled

down over his forehead, sunglasses covering his eyes. The registration number on the car *is* a match to a Toyota of the same model, year, and colour—just not this one. Instead it belongs to a vehicle currently in long-term parking at Heathrow while its elderly owners enjoy an anniversary cruise. He arranged their travel coverage before the trip.

He has left his smartphone at home, where its GPS chip is dutifully recording its blameless position, should anyone ever feel the need to check.

He parks in a lay-by—another product of his Street View reconnaissance—and heads across the fields, following a footpath he located on a local ramblers' website. It is chilly enough for hat, gloves, and scarf not to raise suspicions. Openly, he carries a lead for a non-existent dog to both justify his presence and make it seem more innocuous.

In his pocket is a knife and a set of plastic zip-ties.

He picks out the rear aspect of her house through the trees, but keeps walking all the way to the road, then turns around and slowly retraces his steps. It is a quarter to five in the afternoon in early March. He waits until lights start to come on in the far village. No lights come on in Helen's house.

He makes his move.

The back door leading into the utility room behind the garage is uPVC with a double-glazed upper panel and a standard euro cylinder lock. He bumps it in less than two minutes, using a custom key he made courtesy of a YouTube "How To."

And he's in.

For a moment, he stands motionless on the doormat, listening to the sounds of an empty house. The cycle of the fridge compressor, the tick of a radiator valve in the hallway.

Nobody home.

He maps out in his mind the route she will take when she gets back from her office job in administration. From garage to utility room and through to the kitchen. The garage has the usual detritus: gardening tools, barbecue, a muddy bicycle . . . there is a car-sized void in the centre of the space, years of oil-stains on the bare concrete floor.

The motorcycle she mentioned sits shrouded against the back wall. He's tempted to take a look, but can't risk her noticing any disturbance of the cover, bright in her headlights as she drives in.

He wonders who will own it next.

He shakes himself, checks the time, and closes the door between garage and utility on his way back into the house. Where to wait for her? Always the question. Deep enough inside that she won't balk from entering. Not so deep that she has a chance to turn and run.

He decides on the kitchen itself. It is shaped so that he will be out of sight of the doorway, and Helen is tidy enough not to leave any possible weapons close to hand on the gleaming countertops.

A shiver of excitement passes through him. The waiting is exquisite torture.

He wishes it were over.

He wishes it would last forever.

Lights swing into the driveway at 5:43. He hears the whirr and clank of the electric garage door slowly rising. The car's engine sounds louder, more boomy, as she pulls inside. Then it dies away to silence.

A car door opens and closes, the bleep of the alarm, together with the solid thunk of the door locks engaging. Footsteps, approaching . . .

He is holding his breath.

She enters the kitchen in a flurry of cold air, heads to the table to deposit her bag and the coat slung over her arm. He is close enough to smell her shampoo, her perfume. She turns away to reach for the kitchen light.

Now.

He steps up, steps in, grabbing her upper body from behind. The knife is out, ready in his hand, the blade at her throat.

Mine!

It is the last thing he remembers.

Awareness returns slowly. And with it, pain.

Pain in his limbs, his head, his gut. He is slumped in an upright chair with his chin propped on his chest. He doesn't know how long he's been there, but when he raises his head his neck clicks stiffly.

The room is stark and bright beyond his slitted eyelids. Cautiously, he rolls his shoulders, finds his hands secured behind him and feet bound at the ankles to the legs of the chair. He thrashes against the constriction in a surge of panic. Almost instantly, he stills from the spike of pain as the bones grate in his right wrist and forearm. He fights back nausea.

Eyes wide now, he realises he is in the dining room. Blood from his nose, his mouth, has splashed onto the front of his shirt.

What the hell happened?

There is a blank space where the memory should be. It terrifies him.

So do the footsteps he hears in the hallway.

The woman who enters is a stranger. Medium height, medium build. Without the long blonde wig, her hair is a choppy bob in shades of red and gold. She is wearing jeans, boots, and a leather jacket. Over her arm, on a hanger, is the business suit she wore in her guise as Helen.

But it is her hands that drag his focus.

She wears black latex gloves and carries a knife.

His knife.

"Wh-who . . . ?"

Carefully, she lays the suit across the dining table, moves to within a few feet of him, and holds up the knife. Something about the practised way she does it sends another shiver through him. It is a long way from excitement this time.

"My name's Fox," she says. "I'd offer to shake hands but . . ." a shrug.

The name means nothing to him. He is certain he's never had *her* details up on his computer screen. She sees his confusion, adds, "At this stage, Drew, all you really need to know is that *I* know exactly who *you* are. And what's more, I know exactly what you're about."

"Where is she?" He can't help blurting out the question. He feels cheated, betrayed.

"Helen? She isn't here," the woman says. "In fact, she was never *going* to be."

His mouth opens, gulps like a drowning fish.

"But—"

The front door slams. The woman calling herself Fox steps sideways, calls over her shoulder, "In here."

Another woman comes in—taller, more elegant, long dark hair, and long bones. Still not Helen. She pauses when she sees him, her expression one of guarded distaste. She also wears gloves, handing over what looks like a set of keys.

"Did you find it?" Fox asks.

The other nods. "Just down the road. Fake plates," she says, which jolts him as much as the knife. She is pale in the artificial light as she adds, "The whole of the back is prepped for a body dump."

"Of course it is," Fox murmurs. She turns to him, inspecting the edge of the blade, the weight and the balance. "So, now I've caught him for you, Madeleine, what do you want to do with him?"

"Hand him over to the police?" the dark-haired woman offers, but there's a dubious note in her voice.

"If that's what you want, but you know as well as I do that you can't prove what he's done. As far as they're aware, it's a first offence. Given a half-decent brief, and a judge with a room-temperature IQ, he might even get away with it."

For the first time since he came round and found himself tied to a chair, he begins to hope that all is not lost.

"And you've broken my bloody arm, you bitch," he blurts, finding both voice and bravado. "I ought to sue."

"You put a knife to my throat." She pins him with a dead eye. "So, *I* ought to have ripped your arm off at the shoulder and beat you to death with the wet end. Sad, isn't it, how we can't always have what we want."

"So, what are we going to do with him?" Madeleine asks.

"How many has he taken, do you think?"

A frown. "Four in the last year—that we know of, anyway. Could be more if he has some secondary method of selection."

He goes hot and then cold as his body primes for flight. There's a hollow feeling beneath his ribs. "You can't prove anything . . ."

"Prove? Maybe not." Fox moves in front of him, forcing his neck to crane as he looks up into her face. "But *know*, that's something else again. Because my friend here is an expert with computers. And *you* are not."

She leans a little closer. He tries not to cringe but he's afraid now. Seriously afraid of what he sees in her eyes. And of what is missing. He sees that same look, that same lack—when he stands in front of the bathroom mirror every morning. He recognises it in others.

There seems no point in further denial. He asks, almost in a whisper, "How did you know?"

She glances across at her companion, a "do you want to tell him or shall I" kind of a look. Madeleine shrugs.

"When you're at work, your phone connects to the company Wi-Fi network. Any photos you take during working hours automatically back up to the cloud. And when I was brought in to run a cyber-security audit, we found those pictures."

He lets his eyes close briefly, rallies his bravado for a last stand. "Fuck you. No one's going to convict me on that. You've got nothing." Even so, he hates how desperate he sounds.

"It would be difficult, but not impossible," Fox allows. "Prosecutors don't like to chance having the 'victim' resurface after a guilty verdict's been handed down. Still, there *have* been murder convictions in the past without a body."

He says nothing, swallows, and knows she registers his fear.

"But somehow I don't think any of *your* victims are going to reappear, are they?"

"What victims? *You* attacked *me* here. It's your word against mine."

"He has a point there, Charlie," Madeleine says. "I just hate to think, after everything . . . there's a chance he might walk."

Her voice holds indecision he doesn't immediately understand. And when he does, the fear starts to tingle across his shins again, to roil in his gut.

Charlie Fox simply regards him, flatly. The knife still balances lightly between her gloved fingers.

"He might," she agrees. "Except . . ."

His eyes swivel from one to the other and back again. He wants to wait her out, but can't stand the tension. "Except *what*?" he demands.

"Look around you, Drew. You're the one tied to a chair. I'm the one with the knife. You've already lined the back of your car with plastic. You even brought your own shovel." She smiles. It is not reassuring. "Do you really think I'd let all that effort go to waste?"

DUE DILIGENCE

CATHERINE AIRD

"I must say I don't like the idea at all myself," said Simon flatly. "Otherwise, I can see that it would be a very good place to live in."

"Quite," said Kenneth Marsden, the estate agent, patently unperturbed. The word was one he was very fond of using with his clients. It implied agreement without actually spelling it out. "Quite."

"Nor me," chimed in Simon's wife, Charlotte, quickly. Too quickly.

"Quite," said the estate agent. Kenneth Marsden had found that this all-purpose word also usefully concealed disagreement by not actually spelling out the fact to prospective purchasers of attractive properties newly on the market in rural Calleshire. "I do understand, naturally. It was all very, very unfortunate."

"I mean," said Simon Cullen, "it's not every day that something like that happens in someone's house."

"Quite so." The man from Messrs. Crombie and Marsden paused and then said judiciously, "On the other hand, it has at the same time to be remembered . . ." Kenneth Marsden was also in the habit of making all unwelcome pronouncements in the impersonal tense, ". . . that there are very few domestic properties in this country—especially genuinely old ones such as the Manor at Cullingoak—in which, over the years, somebody has not died."

"Naturally," agreed Simon, "but this death occurred only the other day, didn't it?"

"Which is why the present owner wishes to dispose of it so quickly," said the estate agent smoothly. He then changed the subject with the skill born of long practice. "By the way, how did you happen to hear about the Manor being up for sale? We shan't be advertising it until the end of the week."

"Somebody at work mentioned it to me." It was Charlotte Cullen who answered him, "and I rang my husband and got him to collect the key when he was in Berebury so we could see over the house while I could still fit it in. I've got to go abroad for the bank tomorrow."

Kenneth Marsden translated her message without difficulty. What she was actually telling him was that there would be no problems with money or mortgages.

"But the lady of the house didn't just die, did she?" persisted Simon.

"My husband means that there was a fatal accident in this house," spelt out Charlotte for him. "Don't you, Simon?"

Simon Cullen did not respond to this.

"I do understand," Kenneth Marsden hastened soothingly. Actually he understood a great deal more. He now knew which half of this couple, metaphorically, wore the trousers. This knowledge was as important to him as it would be to any experienced negotiator.

"The publicity . . ." pointed out Simon.

"Unfavourable," conceded the estate agent immediately. He allowed a little pause to develop before he said obliquely, "You yourselves would, of course, be benefiting from this to the extent that the property has been placed on the market at a substantially lower price than it would have been had the—er—unfortunate accident not occurred." Within the privacy of the partners' room of Messrs. Crombie and Marsden, Estate Agents and Valuers, Kenneth Marsden had described the amount he had shaved off his valuation of the house as "blood money."

"We do appreciate that," murmured Charlotte Cullen. "It is an important factor in our even considering purchasing a property such as this. I must say, though, that I agree with my husband that it is a very nice house . . ."

The vendor of Cullingoak Manor, to his eternal credit, had not demurred at Kenneth Marsden's suggested figure. Indeed, for a money man—he was a stockbroker—Mr. Wetherby had shown very little interest in the prospective sale, only in disposing of the property at the earliest possible moment. Needless to say, Kenneth Marsden did not mention this now. Instead, he nodded his agreement with Charlotte. "Yes, indeed, Mrs. Cullen," he said easily. "It's a very fine example of its period."

Charlotte, who was rising rapidly through the upper-middle echelons of the Bank of Calleshire where she worked, leaned forward and said, "Actually it was the price which first attracted my husband."

"I'm sure," said Kenneth warmly.

Simon said nothing.

"I hesitate to use the word 'bargain' in these particular circumstances," went on Marsden, matching spurious frankness with superficial if seemingly transparent honesty, "but there's no denying that but for the tragic incident, the Manor at Cullingoak would be much more highly priced than it is today."

"My husband," began Charlotte again, ". . . was quite taken with the actual property, too . . ." She turned towards Simon and said, "Weren't you, dear?"

Simon had long ago decided that Charlotte must have read

in a women's magazine that when the wife was the money-earner it was important that she deferred to her husband on each and every occasion where this was at all possible. And that her constant litany should be, "I'll have to ask my husband." He also knew, however, that she did this only when his answer wasn't important.

"The kitchen could do with a bit of work," said Simon spiritedly, "and the larder window needs fixing." He made both statements without any fear of being described as a 'house husband.' Charlotte had never ever brought herself to tell the world that her husband had been made redundant from his job at the metal works in Berebury and that he stayed at home while she made the money. And quite a lot of money it was these days, too, to be sure. He wasn't complaining about that. It was her end-of-the-year bonus, she had told him, that was going to make buying the Manor at Cullingoak possible.

When asked what her husband did Charlotte always replied with perfect truth that he was a bimetallist. Since she moved in the world of corporate banking, this was almost always taken by her office colleagues to mean that Simon was an economist who was concerned with monetary systems in which two metals are used in fixed relative values, not someone trained in the coefficients of expansion of all metals. Charlotte never disabused them of this misapprehension. When the more knowledgeable responded with remarks such as, "Gold and silver, I suppose," she would say uncertainly, "I think so, but I'm afraid it's not really my field . . ." That people did not talk much about their work went without saying in banking circles, and the conversation would move on.

"I daresay that the owner might agree to that sort of repair being taken into account," the estate agent was saying to Simon, without for one moment revealing how very useful it was in a negotiating situation to have a few small bones to chew over. The smaller the bone the better, of course. In the world of the estate agent, work on a larder window was easily conceded, and the cost of an upgraded kitchen something to be wrested from the owner after a nominal struggle.

"Who is the owner, anyway?" asked Charlotte casually. "He wasn't around."

"A Mr. Wetherby," replied Kenneth Marsden. "He's naturally still very shocked at losing his wife, you know, and not too keen on going back to the house."

"I'm not surprised," said Charlotte Cullen. "Poor man."

Simon gave Marsden a hard look. "And I take it that the whole place has been re-wired?"

The estate agent looked pained. "I can assure you that the electrical system was the very first thing that was checked after the accident. It was found to be in good order," he gave a slight cough, "in spite of . . . everything."

"Everything?" queried Simon.

"Mrs. Wetherby's electrocution seemed quite inexplicable. Mr. Wetherby was at work when it happened and so wasn't able to help much with the coroner's enquiries."

"Then there shouldn't be anything for us to worry about, should there?" said Charlotte in the same decisive tones she used to wind up many a meeting at the bank.

"No," said Kenneth Marsden automatically.

Charlotte raised an enquiring eye in her husband's direction and went through her routine. "What do you say, Simon? It's up to you, of course, but I must say I like it . . ."

"Me, too," he said meekly.

"Right." She turned to Kenneth Marsden. "You can tell Peter Wetherby that we'll take it."

"I don't think you'll regret it," said the estate agent heartily, shaking their hands as they left.

Simon Cullen was inclined to agree with him when, six weeks later, he and Charlotte duly moved into the Manor at Cullingoak.

The larder window had been fixed and the men were due to come that Monday morning to improve the kitchen layout. Simon had no hang-ups about doing the cooking, belonging as he did to the very workman-like "if you can read, then you can cook" school of *haute cuisine*, but equally he saw no point in ever working under less than optimum conditions. He brought to the task of cooking the same attention and care that had served his previous employers very well until the advent of the worldwide decline in the heavy metals industry.

"Now, then, Mr. Cullen," said the foreman, "before we get started, can you just check that this plan here is how you want it all done? Measure twice and cut once, as my old boss used to say."

Simon switched the electric kettle on as a gesture of good intent before he joined the man peering over the drawings laid out on the kitchen table. "That's right," he said after duly studying the design. He pointed to the door larder and with his hand sketched an imaginary journey round the kitchen in the direction of the stove via the work surfaces and the kitchen sink. "Store, wash, prepare, cook, serve . . . that's how it should be."

The foreman scratched his head. "I hadn't thought of it like that."

"Only if you're right-handed," said Simon. "The lady who lived here before must have been a south paw."

"Both her hands had burns on them," the man informed him ghoulishly.

"Though they never did find out how she got them," chimed in his mate, Fred.

"Electrocuted in the utility room she was," said the foreman lugubriously. "But don't you let that worry you. They went over that room with a fine-tooth comb after it happened."

"Couldn't find a thing amiss, though," said Fred in his role as Greek chorus.

"They never did find out what went wrong."

"Really?" said Simon, absently moving in the direction of the worktop. The kettle had come to a boil and switched itself off. "Tea?"

"Milk but no sugar for me," said the foreman, undiverted. "Thought it must have been something to do with the ironing board, they did, because that was lying on the floor beside her when her husband found her. There was a pile of nearly dry washing in the laundry basket beside her, too."

"And a television," supplemented his assistant eagerly, "because she always did the ironing while she watched her favourite afternoon programme."

"My wife, too," said the foreman. "Thanks," he added, cradling the mug between his large dirt-ingrained hands. "I don't know which channel, though," he added in the interests of accuracy, "because I'm not home then."

Simon decided this was not the moment for reciting the famous quote, "But what was the play like, Mrs. Lincoln?"

"Two lumps for me," said his mate, stretching his hand out for his tea. "They thought she must have died just before the programme came on at four o'clock . . . and that's what the man who did the post-mortem said, too."

"Pathologist," supplied Simon.

"But they never found out how she came to be electrocuted," said the foreman, addressing himself to his drink. "Never."

"Funny, that," murmured Simon Cullen.

"It said in the paper that her husband was at work at the time it happened," expanded the foreman.

"At a meeting all afternoon," chimed in Fred. "It said that, too. About a dozen people there with him all the time."

"My wife spends a lot of her time at work in meetings," said Simon. "I know because she tells me when not to ring the office."

"If you ask me," opined the foreman, pushing back his chair, "most meetings are a waste of time. Let's get started here, Fred."

Simon swept up the empty mugs and drifted off to take a look at the utility room with new eyes. It was situated off the kitchen and housed the central heating boiler and the washing machine as well as all the impedimenta associated with living in a sizeable house in the country—including Simon's new green wellies. The Wetherbys' ironing board was gone and Simon had stood the Cullens' one in its place but otherwise the room looked very much as it must have done in the days of the previous occupants.

Propped up beside the ironing board and the radiator was the clotheshorse which Simon and Charlotte had brought with them from their old house. In fact, the only relic of the Wetherbys' regime was one of those old-fashioned wooden clothes airers which could be lowered by a thin rope, loaded with damp washing, and then hoisted back up to the ceiling above the boiler to dry.

Simon examined everything in the room with his customary care but was no wiser at the end of his survey. He did not know, in fact, that he had reached the same conclusion as the investigating authorities had—that something must have electrified the metal of the ironing board.

When he gave the men their tea in the afternoon he said, "You might just put a lick of paint on that small scratch on the radiator in there next time one of you has a paintbrush in his hand."

"No problem," said the foreman. "No sugar, thanks."

"Two lumps for me," Fred reminded him. "Worked out how it was done, have you?"

"Done?" said Simon.

Fred gave him a knowing wink. "They said the husband had got a lady love tucked away somewhere."

The foreman set his mug down and said sapiently, "What he had got was an alibi, so you mind what you say here, Fred."

Fred bridled. "There's no smoke without fire. Besides, don't forget that most murderers are widowers."

"Because they've killed their wives," nodded Simon. "I've heard that one before."

"Remember," pronounced the foreman magisterially, "it didn't say anything about that in the newspapers—not even the Sunday ones."

"What *did* it say?" asked Simon, adding in spite of himself, "I suppose it is theoretically possible that the ironing board was live—electrified, that is—a long time before Mrs. Wetherby touched it . . ."

"Not before one o'clock it wasn't," insisted Fred vigorously. "Ivy Middleton was here all that morning. She put the dirty washing in the machine and started it up before she went home like she always did, dinner-time."

"That's right," said the foreman. "I was forgetting about Ivy. She touched that ironing board and she didn't get an electric shock, did she, Fred?"

Simon and Charlotte hadn't kept Mrs. Ivy Middleton on to do the rough housework. As Charlotte had put it so pithily when she ("they") paid for the Manor, "We can afford Cullingoak Manor—just—but not the extras as well." Ivy had rated as an extra and so Simon saw entirely to the running of the house.

"There could have been some cable and a time switch," he said. It was just as well Charlotte was at work. She wouldn't have approved of his wasting the workmen's time, let alone his gossiping with them like this. "You know, an electric wire from the nearest power point to the ironing board, timed to come live after Mrs. Middleton had left."

"Now, if I may say so, that's where you're wrong," said the foreman placidly. "The police thought of that, too." He took a swig from his mug. "It so happens that there wasn't any such timer in the house or garden and believe you me, they searched for it."

"I can quite see that they would have," murmured Simon.

"And," the foreman tapped the table with his forefinger for greater emphasis, "they had a witness that the husband—Peter Wetherby, that is—didn't leave the house before the police arrived so he couldn't have hidden a timer anywhere outside the house."

"Got it in for him, haven't you?" said Simon absently. "This Peter Wetherby." Suddenly something about the name jarred in his mind. He couldn't quite place the memory but it was there, somewhere.

"Ironing boards don't come alive on their own," shrugged the foreman, starting to get to his feet.

"I reckon," said Fred, "it was suicide."

"Suicide?" echoed Simon.

Fred nodded. "I think she connected a wire from the socket to the ironing board herself and her husband came home and found her and removed the evidence pretty quickly. Didn't want anyone to know she'd done it because of this other woman, see?"

The foreman said, "You're a great one for your theories, Fred, but it don't get the work done. Come along now, let's get started here or we'll never be done."

Over the next few weeks Simon had to agree Fred's suicide theory was the most tenable. Something like a kettle flex could have been plugged into the nearest power point and the bare wires at the other end made to touch the metal of the ironing board. Turn the switch on, clasp the ironing board, and Bob's your uncle. A married man becomes a widower in no time at all. And all the husband would have had to do in order to destroy any evidence of a suicide was to put the proper plug back on the appliance before he rang the police—the work of a moment—and no-one would be any the wiser. Oh, and perhaps change the face of the plug in case there were burn marks there, too.

He gave this thought whenever Charlotte was away. She was away for the bank rather a lot these days. At least he thought it was for the bank until they telephoned one weekend needing to speak to her urgently and he referred them to their conference but they said they weren't having one. That was when he remembered what it was about the foreman's use of Peter Wetherby's Christian name that had bothered him. Charlotte had known it even though the estate agent had only given them his surname. When he came to think of it, she had known, too, about Cullingoak Manor being for sale at a low price before it had even been advertised. That still didn't explain how Mrs. Wetherby had died while her husband was well away from the action unless it had been by her own hand. Simon Cullen was rapidly coming to the conclusion that it hadn't been. That was when he laid his plan.

"Darling," he said to Charlotte the next evening, "I think I'm going to have to have a couple of nights away next week. Uncle George wants me to go up to Yorkshire to see him."

"Fine," she said. "Remember me to the old boy. Not that I've seen him since the wedding."

"No more you have," he said. Charlotte didn't much care for his relations. "I'll go on Tuesday and be back Thursday evening . . . that all right?"

"Fine," she said. "By the way, before I forget, I may be back a bit late on Friday. We've got a big meeting at the bank Friday afternoon." She smiled. "Salary review committee—mustn't miss that."

"Not on any account," he agreed gravely.

Simon studiously avoided the utility room when he got back to the Manor on Thursday evening. He and Charlotte had a quiet evening together. "You might switch the washing machine on first thing, Simon," she said as they went upstairs. "I went through my summer clothes while you were away and want to get them ready for storage."

"They'll all be beautifully ironed," he said, "by the time you get home."

"It's getting too chilly to wear them now. I must say I was quite glad of the central heating when I got in yesterday."

"The afternoons are getting cooler," he agreed amiably.

As soon as Charlotte had left for work on Friday morning—the day of her big meeting—Simon entered the utility room very carefully. He didn't switch on the washing machine, though. Instead he examined the room with extreme caution. There was indeed a plug in the power socket and a length of flex tucked away behind the radiator. It ran, almost out of sight at ground level, to the nearest leg of the ironing board. Fred had been right about that, anyway.

But he wasn't into metals and Simon was. Also behind the radiator, firmly taped to it, was what he had been looking for—that which would make the whole thing live. But not just yet. Not until the heating warmed the radiator.

"Clever," he murmured to himself appreciatively. "Very clever." It was a short metal bar which neither the police nor anyone else would have looked at twice had they noticed it lying around. It was half copper and half steel lengthways. It was pressed firmly against the back of the radiator, the copper side set alongside, but not touching, one of the two wires in the flex—which had been scraped bare. He checked the thermostat and found that the central heating was set to come on at three o'clock as usual. Simon thought it would take about an hour for the copper part of the bar to heat up enough to expand to touch the flex and complete the electrical circuit. He went back to the kitchen to wait for something to happen to establish that he was alive and well while Charlotte was away at work.

At twelve o'clock their next door neighbour came to the door. "Your wife has just rung me, Mr. Cullen, to say she thinks she can't have put the telephone back on its hook properly because she keeps getting the engaged signal."

"I'll check," he said, knowing it would be so. "Thanks for letting me know . . . Like a coffee?"

"Some other time, if I may, please . . ."

"I'll look forward to that," he said and meant it. His neighbours really were very agreeable people indeed. Getting to know them in future was going to be a pleasure.

When Charlotte got back at six o'clock he was out of sight behind the utility room door. She went straight there, calling out his name as she did so. He did not answer but when she was right inside the room and standing, puzzled, in front of the ironing board, he stepped out quietly from behind the door and gave her a gentle push towards it. She put out her hands to save herself and screamed as she touched the ironing board.

At his trial, before pronouncing a life sentence on him, the judge described Peter Wetherby as the clever, calculating, and callous killer of the two women in his life.

A SAD MISTAKE

R. L. STINE

When the stranger arrived at Dr. Frankenstein's house, I did my best to send him away. Strangers aren't normally drawn to Giron, our village, so distant from Geneva and unknown but to the farmers who have worked the hills for generations.

The man didn't appear threatening. Far from it, with his slender face, damp straw-colored hair falling over square spectacles, his cheeks pale and pinched, his overcoat open and dust-covered from the journey, and his boots . . . I noted his boots especially—small for a man and caked with dirt.

The horse, a scrawny brown mare bathed in sweat, uttered a cough. Behind her, the canvas tarp over the man's wagon rattled in the strong breeze that never stops blowing through our valley.

He looked down at me from the wagon seat. "My name is Nathaniel Borne. I believe this is the house of Dr. Victor Frankenstein," he said formally. His voice was high, his diction clipped. Like a schoolteacher, I thought.

"You believe incorrectly," I told him. "There is no one by that name in this house."

He grunted. An unpleasant sound. He raised his eyes to the cabin door. "He is in there," he said. "He *must* see me. He will avoid me at his peril."

I saw his gaze and could read his thoughts: *How could Victor Frankenstein be reduced to living in this lower-than-humble cabin?*

A question I asked myself when I first found him. Living in this tin-roofed cabin with the wallboards peeling and splintering and no furniture save his cot, which sat beside the stove. When I found him he was huddled by that stove, shoulders hunched, gripping the knees of his worn trousers with his long bonelike hands murmuring her name—

Elizabeth.

I found the great doctor nearly by accident during one of my travels through the picturesque villages south of Geneva. I like to paint, and the red roofs and white walls of the rustic houses caught my eye. I don't have the skill to capture the billowing greens and browns of the rolling hills, but I have pleased myself with my canvases of stark farmhouses jutting up from flat, green fields.

I think my brush has captured the loneliness of these places.

I wasn't prepared for the loneliness and degradation of Victor Frankenstein when I stumbled upon the cabin during what I thought would be my last day in Giron. I knew immediately that I had a mission here, and so I stayed. I took it upon myself—invited myself, actually—to nurse him back to health . . . to rehabilitate the man.

And he hadn't the strength to send me away. As he realized my good intentions, he began to talk, to relate the tragedies of his life to me, tragedies all self-created, as he put it.

Whenever his guilt subsided, it was replaced by shivering fear. "He's still out there. The monster still walks this earth. I must find him and kill him. I cannot think or work or breathe while my monstrous creation still lives."

The good doctor was obsessed, and this unhealthy obsession had loosened his mind from all rational thought. Tortured he was, by the name Elizabeth, the bride he lost, and tortured he was by the monster, his creation, who murdered her.

As the weeks passed, I could see my caring efforts having a positive effect on the man. The spots of color on his sallow cheeks . . . his full voice restored, no longer a hoarse whisper . . . the eyes occasionally focused on the present and not the past.

I thought I was making progress. But what took place last week told me that perhaps my optimism played me for a fool.

I was returning from market day in Giron, when, from a distance, I saw the white smoke. The sky over the hill was gray, the air heavy, and the smoke, spread by the steady wind, at first appeared to be a cloud descending to earth.

Then as I came closer and the cabin came into view, I could see the flames dancing beside it. The white smoke floating up to the low sky. And Victor standing there, encouraging the fire, adding to it, making the flames leap.

All of his books. His only worldly possessions. His texts of science and history. All of them into the fire. That's how he used his renewed strength. I could see the flames flickering in his wild eyes. He's mad, I thought. He's still mad.

He tossed the last of the volumes into the heart of the flames. Then he saw me. "Why, Victor?" I demanded, shouting over the roar of the fire. "Why?"

He didn't hesitate in his answer. "My search for knowledge destroyed my life." His voice trembled with excitement. "Never again! Never again!"

I grabbed his bone-hard shoulders and held tight. I stopped him from walking into the flames.

Less than a week later, the stranger pulled up in his wagon. I knew Victor was not ready for company. I tried to send the man away. But he made his shrill threat: "He will avoid me at his peril."

Nathaniel Borne, he said he was. He climbed down and pulled a wooden crutch from the wagon. That's when I noticed his withered leg. Leaning heavily on the crutch, he turned his back on me to struggle with the horse's reins. I blinked when I saw why he struggled. Mr. Borne had only one hand. The left sleeve of his overcoat revealed a soft, pinkish stump, cleft like a rabbit's foot.

Once he was satisfied that the animal was tethered to the wagon, Borne lowered his shoulder and used the crutch to brush me out of the way. I started to cry out in protest, but too late. He was already limping inside.

And when I followed him in, I saw Victor jump up from his cot and spill his teacup to the floor, his expression startled, mouth hanging open. The cup clattered on the plank floor but didn't break. Victor raised his hands in the air as if surrendering.

"I tried to send him away," I said. "But he insisted on seeing you."

Victor and the stranger stared at each other for a long moment. I didn't see recognition in either's eyes. Borne was the first to speak. "Dr. Frankenstein, I need your help."

Victor didn't lower his hands. His shirt was ragged with wet tea stains down the front. "I can offer no help to myself or to others," he murmured.

"I know who you are," Borne said. "I know you can help me." He scratched his stump with the fingers of his right hand, his unblinking eyes behind the spectacles fixed on the doctor.

Victor shrugged. "As you can see, I am but a farmer without a farm."

"I know you are the only one who can help me," Borne said. "My need is urgent."

Victor didn't reply. He sank onto his cot with a sigh. His hands dangled near the floor. He shook his head. "Show this man the door," he said to me, voice barely above a whisper.

Borne crossed the arms of his overcoat in front of him. His voice became even more shrill. "I can expose you," he told Victor.

"Do you like it here in this pretty little farm village? Do you like your privacy, Dr. Frankenstein? I can end it. I can tell the farmers who you are. Do you think your quiet life would last for long?"

A pathetic sound escaped Victor's throat. Almost an animal bleat. He couldn't disguise his pain.

"I don't wish to threaten you," Borne said, leaning on his crutch. "But I am desperate. I will stop at nothing to obtain your help." He eyed Victor coldly. "Nothing."

Victor sighed. I could read his face. I could see defeat dull his eyes. Defeat and fear. Would Borne carry out his threat?

Victor rose to his feet. "What is it you wish me to do?" he whispered.

Borne motioned to the door with his good hand. We followed him outside. Pale sunlight had broken through the low clouds. The horse, chewing a clump of brown weeds, raised its head as we approached.

Borne limped to the canvas tarp that covered the flat wagon. He grabbed one corner with his good hand. "Help me," he said to me. He untied the cord that held down the tarp.

I moved to the other side of the wagon. My eyes stopped on the wide mountain of ashes just a few feet from the path. All that was left of Dr. Frankenstein's book collection. I glanced at him, hovering in the cabin doorway, and I knew he was a pile of ashes, too. How could he help this man?

Borne and I took corners of the tarp and slowly pulled it back. The canvas fell from my hand and I staggered back with a gasp as I stared at the corpse lying face-up in the wagon.

Victor didn't move. Didn't make a sound. Borne's jaw clenched and unclenched. He glimpsed the body, then shut his eyes. "My brother," he murmured.

Victor couldn't hide his curiosity. Corpses held no terror for him. He had much experience with them. He stepped to the wagon, gripped the side rail, and leaned over the body to get a closer look.

The corpse was clothed in a loose-fitting, gray suit, wrinkled and stained. He was broad-shouldered, big-chested, powerful looking even in death. His round face was bruised, purple welts on both cheeks. His hair was black and oily, with curly sideburns down his cheeks. The eyes were wide open, only slightly sunken, clear as glass.

Everything about him was big. Even his lips, which were cut and swollen, set in a tight-mouthed scowl.

Victor gripped the corpse's chin in one hand and tilted the head from side to side. He raised his fingers to the eyelids and slid the eyes shut. Then, still silent, he turned inquiringly to Nathaniel Borne.

"My brother," Borne said softly. He lowered his glance to the dirt. "My dear, good brother."

A sweet-sour smell rose up from the corpse. The smell of death. It made my eyes water.

Victor stepped back from the wagon. "Why did you bring him here?" he asked sharply.

Borne raised his eyes. He sucked in a deep, shuddering breath. Were those tears trickling down his pinched cheeks? "My dear brother. He was everything to me."

"What do you want?" Victor demanded.

"I want you to use your talents," Borne said. "I want you to bring my brother back to life."

Victor's eyes flashed, then went dull again. "I can't do that," he said, returning Borne's stare.

"Yes, you can."

"You have made a sad mistake," Victor said. "Someone has misguided you. I am not God. I cannot bring the dead to life."

Borne stared down at the corpse. He patted the bulging chest tenderly with his good hand. "Perhaps you would like to discuss this with the villagers, your neighbors," he said through his teeth.

Victor's eyes flashed again. He uttered a choking sound from deep in his throat. The thought of being exposed held untold terror for him.

"I don't like to threaten," Borne said, scratching his cheek. "I see you are a man who wants to live quietly, away from prying eyes."

"I . . . can't do it," Victor repeated, eyes on the body.

A fly landed on the corpse's broad forehead. Another fly disappeared into the dead man's right nostril.

Borne brushed them away with a wave of his hand. "Bring my poor brother back to life," he said, "and I will let you keep your life of isolation. I will tell no one who you are and what I have found here."

Victor didn't move, but I could see the debate in his eyes. He wasn't a man to respond to threats. Awash in sorrow and guilt, he cared about nothing of this earth. He responded not to sympathy or friendship or caring or encouragement. He felt no peace, even in this desolate outpost away from all society.

But I had worked so hard these weeks to nourish him and bring him back to whatever strength he possessed. I didn't want to see it all end with an attack by frightened, ignorant villagers. And yes, to be completely truthful, I was curious about Victor's unique powers.

I could see Victor falter. His face went pale, his lips colorless, as if his thoughts were draining him. I grabbed his arm and led him to the side of the cabin.

Flies buzzed around our heads. The corpse was drawing a hungry, winged army. Victor swept back his tangled hair and leaned against the cabin wall. "Perhaps I shall attempt it," he said, eyes on the fields behind me.

I held onto his arm. "Yes," I said. "It might be easier than defying this man."

Victor shook his head. "Nothing could be more difficult," he replied. "But perhaps, for once . . . for once . . ." The words caught in his throat. "For once, I can use my knowledge for good."

I turned and saw Borne waiting impatiently at the wagon, leaning on the crutch, shifting his weight from foot to foot . . . those tiny unmanly boots. Who was this little cripple? How did he know where to find Dr. Frankenstein? My questions would have to wait.

"I know it isn't atonement," Victor continued, speaking low for my ears only. Or perhaps as he often did, he was speaking aloud to himself. "But perhaps for once I can *bring back* a life." He shook his head. "I have destroyed so many."

He strode back to Borne at the wagon, his hands balled into tight fists. "I make no guarantees," he said.

A pleased smile spread quickly over Borne's face. Behind the spectacles, his eyes lit up. "My brother deserves to live," he said, patting the fly-ridden corpse again.

Victor sighed. "Does life always hand us what we deserve?"

Not another word was spoken. The two men weren't much help as I hoisted the heavy corpse from the wagon. Again, the sweet-sour odor invaded my nose and watered my eyes. The man's skin felt cold and rubbery. His head bumped the side of the wagon as I attempted to slide him onto my shoulders. It made a soft, unexpected sound, like a ripe tomato hitting the floor.

I half-carried, half-dragged the body into the cabin. It fell heavily onto its stomach on Victor's low cot. A whoosh of air escaped the body as it landed, and the room filled with the odor of death.

By the time I had rolled the corpse onto its back, my muscles throbbed, my heart pounded my chest, and sweat drenched my clothing. The eyes had opened again and stared blankly at the cabin rafters. The purple bruises on the man's cheeks appeared to have darkened. Slender threads of dried blood, like cobwebs, spread from the bruises.

Victor knelt beside the cot and turned the man's big head from side to side. Borne stood in the open doorway, blocking the dying sunlight. "My brother Percy didn't deserve to die," he repeated.

Victor didn't reply. "I shall need to collect a fresh brain," he said, speaking again to himself. "And a throbbing heart."

"NO!" Borne bellowed. Leaning on his crutch, he limped heavily toward the cot. “There is no time, Doctor! The body is fresh enough. The heart is most likely still warm. Percy died only yesterday.”

Victor shook his head unhappily. He poked at the corpse’s chest, reached under the heavy suit jacket and squeezed an arm, again slid the head from side to side.

Borne stared down at his brother. “Frankenstein, you shall know my gratitude,” he said softly. “I hope you will forget my threats. I am a desperate man, as you can see. But I must have my brother back. I must, for he is the last of my family.”

I knew what Victor was thinking. For Victor had no family members still alive. None at all. I had come upon him the *very next day*. The day after his father had died, the last one of his family . . . the last.

“I make no guarantees,” Victor said again. I saw his hands tremble as he unfastened the corpse’s shirt.

I wiped my eyes with my shirtsleeve. The smell in the cabin was heavy and rank. I could feel the odor seeping into my clothing.

Borne dropped onto the edge of the cabin’s only chair, stiff-backed of hard wood. He set his crutch on the floor beside him. He sat upright and tense, and clasped his good hand tightly around his pink stump.

“In what way can I assist you?” I asked Victor.

“You cannot,” he replied tersely. He appeared to be massaging the corpse’s pulpy neck. “The animation of life is mine alone to give.” He raised his eyes to me. “Stand back, my friend, and allow me to work without interruption or conversation. The process is not long, but difficult, and will strain my nerves and body and mind—but do not step in to rescue me, for success requires more than human effort.”

I took a step back, trying to digest Victor’s words. And as I watched him begin to work, I saw a change come over his face. A calmness in his eyes I hadn’t seen. A steadiness in his hand. As if the doctor was replacing the man.

Victor worked over the body, kneading and massaging, prodding certain muscles, murmuring to himself as he worked. He worked the body for nearly an hour, then disappeared into the tiny, cramped storage room in back.

Outside the open doorway, the sun sank behind the farm fields. Blue shadows fell over the cabin. I left my place against the wall to light candles.

In the flickering yellow light, I could see Borne still sitting so stiffly on the edge of the chair, tensely gripping his deformed hand. The candlelight played over his spectacles, but I couldn't see his eyes behind the gleam. So much of him remained a mystery.

Victor returned with bottles and vials, powders and unguents. He lowered himself to his knees again and calmly and deliberately returned to his work on the body. He rubbed thick ointments on the dead man's chest, then began to massage the loose skin over the heart. He powdered the chest, dabbed ointments on the throat, prodded and massaged.

Back in my place against the wall, my stomach growled. But I knew there would be no dinner tonight.

Victor moved in and out of the light, vanishing like an apparition, then reappearing in a flickering, yellow vision. The scene began to take on an unreality, as if I were watching a dream that occurred outside my body, in front of my waking eyes.

"You must live . . . You must live again . . ." Borne's muttered words brought me back to the world. In his agony, the man seemed more shriveled than when he had arrived. His misshapen leg curled beneath him. His slender body shuddered despite the warmth of the room. He had taken a gamble by coming here. The odds favored grave disappointment.

Of course, Victor was taking the biggest gamble. Failure for him would mean sinking back into his pit of sorrow and guilt.

Another hour passed, an hour of shadows and flickering dream. Of muttered words and low grunts of concentration. Victor wrapped the arms and legs of the corpse with heavy cords and tied them securely to the table.

I watched in silence. Victor disappeared once again into the back room.

Flies buzzed in the darkness. A gust of wind made the candle flames bend. In a distant pasture, cows moaned. A cat cried. Life all around.

When Victor stepped back into the light, he held a creature in front of him, clasped tightly in one hand. I couldn't identify it until he raised it high and it rose into bright candlelight. A field mouse, its spindly legs kicking frantically.

Victor raised his other hand to reveal a long syringe. My heart skipped in my chest. Why? Was I fearful for the mouse? No. I realized the ordeal was nearing its climax, for good or bad.

The mouse let out a squeal as the needle sank deep into its belly.

Borne gasped and leaped to his feet.

The mouse's cry faded. Its head sank. As Victor slid the syringe out, the creature died. Victor let it fall to the floor. He spun around—and with a groan, plunged the needle into the dead man's chest.

"Oh! Oh!" Borne staggered, gripped the chair arm to keep himself from collapsing.

Victor kept the syringe in the corpse, pushing the fluid from the mouse deep into the swollen chest.

I couldn't move. I had to struggle for breath.

Finally, Victor slid the syringe from the dead man's chest.

Silence.

Silence. No one moved. A frozen tableau.

Failure, I realized.

The room spun in front of me. My thoughts were on the toll this disappointment would take on Victor's mind. *He won't recover,* I thought. *This will sink him into the deepest morass.*

Then I uttered a cry of shock as one hand of the corpse twitched. I felt my heart skip when I saw the fingers clench.

And then a hoarse groan. From somewhere deep inside the dead man. A groan that quickly rose into a wail. A long animal howl of pain.

So horrifying, I covered my ears. But I couldn't shut out the shrieks and cries. Scream after scream.

Victor jumped to his feet. The dripping syringe fell from his hand and landed on the edge of the cot.

My stomach heaved. If it hadn't been empty, I would have been sick on the cabin floor. The yellow lights danced crazily in front of my eyes, like fiery stars against an unfamiliar sky. Where was I? I felt as if I were floating somewhere far away, perhaps a distant planet.

Floating in a world of the impossible.

And then I returned to earth as the corpse kicked and strained its hands against the cords that held him down. "Noooooo! Noooooo!" He lifted his head off the table, repeating his moan. "Nooooo." How quickly his pain turned to rage.

He thrashed his body, twisting, twitching. His hands and feet strained against the cords until they snapped away. Then he stopped his cries and slowly . . . slowly . . . sat up. He shook his head, blinking groggily. He coughed. Coughed some more. Spit up something from deep in his throat.

Even in the dim light, I could see the wild-eyed excitement on Victor's face. I'd never seen him smile. Never seen him laugh. But he was laughing now, laughing in triumph, in his utter relief.

At last. A moment to celebrate his brilliance.

The corpse fiddled with his open shirt buttons. Scratched his head. Squinted into the dancing lights.

"He's alive! Alive as any man!" Victor cried.

"Alive," the corpse rasped.

"Percy!" Borne cried. "Percy! Do you know me?"

Percy squinted his broad face in confusion. He climbed off the cot. Stood unsteadily, gazing around the small room.

"Percy, do you remember who I am?" Borne demanded.

The huge man didn't answer. He blinked. He took a heavy step toward his brother. One step, then another, hands out at his sides as if walking a circus tightrope. When his eyes stopped on Borne, his mouth curled into a smile of recognition.

"Percy—" Borne leaned on his crutch. "You're alive, man! Alive!"

"Alive," Percy repeated one more time. The smile clung to his face.

I watched them, expecting a hug, a joyful embrace, a celebration of reunion. But Borne's next words were a surprise.

"Do your job!" he cried. He pulled a long-bladed knife from under his jacket and slapped it into Percy's hand. "Do it! Now!"

Did Victor see this? No. He had slumped onto the cot. Exhaustion had quickly replaced his ecstasy. His mouth hung open. His eyes were shut.

With his good hand, Borne gave Percy a shove. "Now," he repeated. "Do your job. I've paid you well. Do what I paid you to do."

"Yes. My job," Percy murmured, wrinkling his broad forehead, thinking hard.

"What are you talking about, Borne?" I demanded. "Are you not overjoyed to have your brother back?"

The candlelight lit up his spectacles. I still couldn't see his eyes. But I could see the shrill look of distaste on his face. "He's not my brother," Borne said. He shoved Percy in the back again. "Kill Frankenstein. Kill him!"

Percy staggered forward, the knife clenched in his big fist.

I threw myself in front of him. "Are you *mad*? Dr. Frankenstein just gave you back your life!"

"Step back," Borne ordered. "I hired this man to assassinate Frankenstein. I paid him every cent I own. And now he shall perform."

On the cot, Victor raised his head and blinked. I could see his slender chest heaving up and down. But he made no attempt to rise.

Borne gestured at his own weak, misshapen body. "Obviously,

I couldn't do the job. So I hired this assassin. And then the fool got himself beaten to death in a drunken fight."

He uttered a bitter laugh as he turned to Victor. "Congratulations, Dr. Frankenstein! You have revived your own murderer!"

Victor uttered a weak cry. Then he managed to force out one word: "Why?"

Percy took another heavy step toward the cot. Borne stood silent for a moment, debating whether or not to answer Victor's question. Finally, he said through gritted teeth, "Look at me!"

The words seemed to hang in the thick cabin air.

Borne held out his stub of a hand. "Do you think I was born like this, Dr. Frankenstein? Your creation—your monster—tore my hand off. He ripped my hand from my arm as I screamed for mercy."

Victor stared at him, as if not understanding.

Borne's chest heaved up and down. He began panting like an animal. The words came out in a breathless rush of anger. "Your monster . . . trod on my leg . . . so it's *useless* to me now. Useless."

He waved the stub frantically in front of him. "Feast your eyes on your sins, Doctor. I'll be the last person you see *before you die*!"

Victor lowered his head and gripped the side of the cot with both hands. He made no attempt to escape. "Kill me," he said softly. "Please. Kill me. You are right. I deserve to die." His eyes watered over with tears.

With a growl, the assassin dove at the cot.

I wasn't paralyzed by emotion. I moved quickly. I grabbed the syringe from the cot . . . raised it high . . . and jabbed it deep into Percy's neck.

He let out a high squeal, like a mouse. Yes, he squealed like a mouse as I emptied the remaining liquid into his body.

The squeal cut off sharply. I whipped the syringe out. Percy's eyes rolled up in his head until I saw only the whites, and he dropped to his knees beside the cot.

He stayed there on his knees, head slumped over his chest,

hands dangling on the floor. He didn't move, but I knew he was dead—for good this time.

I didn't take time to breathe. I spun away from the assassin and dove across the floor toward the startled Borne. He stood gripping the chair back with his one hand. I think he was waiting for Percy to stand up and finish his assignment.

Borne was a helpless runt. I had no fear that he would cause a problem. I grabbed his crutch, held it by the tip, swung it with all my might, and smashed the handle into his face.

It made a cracking sound, and blood spurted up in all directions. I swung the crutch again and saw the skin fly off his face. Yellow bone underneath, and his teeth were revealed from the roots. I smashed his face again. Again. Until my arm muscles ached, and my throat throbbed. I didn't even realize I was screaming.

Borne died an ugly death. His face reminded me of a peeled fruit left out in the sun for days.

I tossed the bloodied crutch onto his body. Then, gasping for breath, I turned to Victor. Poor Victor, blinking at me as if he didn't recognize me. He still hadn't risen from the cot. His face showed no understanding, no recognition, of me or what I had done.

I tucked Victor under the blanket on his cot. I soothed him, made him comfortable, and managed to lull him to sleep.

He was in a state, his mind far away. I knew it would take time to bring him back. But I had time. Plenty of time.

First there was work to do, some necessary but unpleasant tasks.

I had deep holes to dig. Bodies to bury before morning.

Then I could begin with Victor Frankenstein again. Begin all over again.

I want him to be his brilliant self when I reveal that I loved Elizabeth, too. But I loved her more than he ever could, more than anyone.

Elizabeth . . . strangled on the night of her wedding to Victor.

Murdered for his sins. Murdered for his arrogance and pride . . . for his defiance of Nature's laws.

Elizabeth taken from me forever.

And so, I couldn't let this intruder Borne have his way with Victor.

Because I have my own plans for the good doctor.

And plenty of time to carry out my plans.

But there must be no intruders to trouble him. No intruders . . . and no witnesses.

I am a patient man—and a *careful* man.

No witnesses.

I hurried outside to murder the horse.

AN UNLIKELY SERIES OF CONVERSATIONS

WALTER MOSLEY

1.

Laertes Jackson showed up at the human resources office of Martin, Martin, and Moll at 10:37 on a Tuesday morning in May. The mid-size investment firm was located on Maiden Lane in the Wall Street area of Lower Manhattan. There was no ostentatious sign outside and only the initials MMM appeared on the legend at the entrance. Even then, just one floor, the fourteenth, was identified as housing MMM while the firm actually occupied seven contiguous floors. In the past two years MMM had been sued by various individuals and government agencies for multiple civil rights and sexual harassment violations. The CEO and several VPs had been relieved of their positions and the corporation itself had been fined millions of dollars in reparations.

The new CEO, Ms. Winsome Millerton-Pomerantz, had made a public statement vowing that the investment firm, which oversaw more than a dozen multibillion-dollar retirement funds that, either in full or in part, served public employee unions, would make *a supreme effort to right the listing ship of their intentions*.

Taking this intelligence to heart, Laertes decided to apply for an entry position at MMM.

Arriving at the fourteenth floor, Laertes encountered B. Chang, a young Asian woman sitting within a semi-opaque and circular azure desk.

"HR is on the twentieth floor, Mr. Jackson," she said with a lovely red-stained smile. "Take the elevator to the right."

On the 20th floor Clarissa Watson, a woman whose skin was even darker than Laertes's, gave him a confused, turquoise-tinted smile, saying, "But your appointment isn't until 1:40, Mr. Jackson."

"I'm usually early," Laertes said, cocking his head and smiling softly. "My father always told me to get there before your competitor because you can never tell what will be left over later on."

Young Miss Watson smiled and nodded. She said, "We have magazines and bottled water. You can sit in the waiting area and I'll try to get you in early. Ms. Rodriguez is interviewing applicants for the trainee broker position and sometimes the interviews take less time."

Laertes picked up the *Wall Street Journal*, turning pages until his eyes fell upon the phrase "*trying to define the first stock transaction . . .*" It seemed that there was a great deal of disagreement among economic scholars about the age of the idea of stocks, investments, and interest.

"Mr. Jackson?" a woman said so softly that Laertes wondered if indeed he had actually heard the utterance.

He looked up and saw a roundish woman with pale skin, dark locks, and eyes that seemed to see past him into some other realm beyond his comprehension—and maybe hers.

"I'm Jackson," he said.

"My name is Rahlina Rodriguez. I'm supposed to interview you."

"Okay," Laertes said, rising from his perch on the coral-colored couch. "I took the day off from work so I have as much time as you need."

"Where do you work?" Rahlina Rodriguez asked.

"Maritime Merchants Bank over on Twenty-Third."

"Savings and loan," she stated.

"I don't know about that but it's pretty mom and pop. I've been a teller there the past twenty-four years."

"Have you worked with investments?"

"Not really."

"What does that mean?" The expression on Rodriguez's wary face was a leftover from childhood when she was too cute for her parents to punish; at least that's what Laertes supposed.

"I ask new clients opening savings and checking accounts if they want to connect their money in an investment account and, if they do, I check that box on their online form. But whatever it is, I don't understand it nor have I anything to do with where the money goes."

Something about what Laertes said seemed to bother Rahlina.

"We should go to my office," the bank officer said.

"Okay," Laertes replied with a forced smile. He followed her down a gray-tiled hallway toward a bright yellow door. Rahlina moved through the doorway like a dancer, swaying from side to side, creating an aesthetic of walking. Laertes trailed her with his dogged, straight-ahead gait.

The yellow door led to a room that was drained of any color. The white floor, walls, and ceiling sheltered an ivory-colored desk and a whitewashed pine chair where the subject who was there to be interrogated had to sit.

"Have a seat, Mr. Jackson."

He knew where to go. In his mind he'd answered the first question correctly because he didn't need to ask where.

Rahlina Rodriguez settled in the seat behind the smallish pale desk. She placed the fingers of both hands on the ledge before her and smiled, slightly.

"Before we begin," she said. "Do you have any questions?"

"Are you Mexican?"

"Um," Rodriguez said, maybe as a criticism.

Thinking she hadn't understood him Laertes said clearly, "I said, are you Mexican?"

"We don't ask questions like that here at Triple-M."

"If not, then how do you plan to right the listing ship of your intentions?"

"That's a corporate-wide initiative unattached to any particular individual, nationality, race, age, or gender."

"But still you have a black man named Laertes meeting a maybe Hispanic woman named Rodriguez during a hiring period where the cultural tendencies of the company in question are not serving the makeup of the unions that you represent."

"The facts that you are African American and that my name has roots in the Spanish language have no direct bearing on your application for the entry position of trainee investment advisor." Rahlina Rodriguez was not happy with the direction of the interview.

"The letter I got from human resources said that this interview might be recorded," Laertes said. "Is it?"

"It might be."

"Is that the answer you're supposed to give me if the cameras and tape recorders are turned on?"

Rahlina's dark eyes darkened. The locks of her raven hair took on the appearance of razor wire.

"I don't know," she said. "We have both signed away our right to privacy in this conversation and so we may or may not be recorded."

They gazed across the white expanse of the desk, under the pallid ceiling.

"That's the other thing," Laertes said after a minute of this white-wall silence.

"What is?" the interlocutor asked.

"You call me African American but I don't answer to that description. People who come from another country to this one use the hyphenate name. You know, Italians who came over a generation or two back calling themselves Italian-Americans. Maybe they kept up contact with home or followed cultural norms that are particularly Italian. But a man like me, a man whose ancestors were kidnapped, chained, and dragged over here centuries ago is not, cannot be a hyphenate. At least not the kind of hyphenate that you say. You might call me an Abductee-American, an originally Unwilling-American. You might say that I'm a partly Disenfranchised American. But African American? I mean even if my mama was from Guinea, you'd do better to call me a Guinean American than African. Africa's a continent not a country, not a culture. You don't use the term White-American because that has no cultural basis; even saying Euro-Americans makes very little sense."

"We say African Americans because that is the parlance," Rahlina interjected.

"Used to be the parlance was colored, Negro, Afro, nigger, coon, jigaboo. The parlance don't make a word right. And I refuse to be called after a continent that no one in my family remembers."

"Well, Mr. Jackson, if you say that you are not African American, I suppose this interview is over."

"Why is that?"

"The commitment of this firm is to hire and promote peoples from various ethnic backgrounds including African Americans." With that Rahlina Rodriguez stood up and waited.

After a moment or two Laertes realized that he was being asked to leave.

He stood also, raised his eyes to the ceiling, and said, "If this conversation has been recorded I want a copy of it delivered either to the address on my application form or to my business email address thereupon."

After that he exited the white room on the 20th floor of the offices of Martin, Martin, and Moll.

2.

Three Thursdays after Laertes's failed interview he was offered what turned out to be $112.37 in change from Zuri Chin—a seven-year-old child. Her mother, StaceyAnn, had presented the child's canvas bag of coins while little Zuri pulled her head up over the ledge where the money was being passed from StaceyAnn to Laertes.

"You know, Ms. Chin," Laertes said. "We're not supposed to take loose change in these over twenty dollars."

"But that's my money," Zuri called over the banker's counter.

"I know your rules, Mr. Jackson," Zuri's mom said. "But you and I both know that one day, when she has money of her own, Zuri will remember the bank that made an exception for her Christmas savings."

Laertes noticed a short man in a black suit standing at the front of the line for the next free teller. That window, belonging to Ms. Becky Blondell, opened up and the short man offered his place to the petite woman behind him. She smiled, nodded her thanks, and moved ahead.

"So will you take my money?" Zuri Chin asked, hoisting herself up once more.

"Of course," Laertes told the medium-brown child. "Leave it here and we'll count it in the machine overnight."

"Yaaaaaa!" Zuri cried.

"Thank you," said her mother.

"You're from Jamaica, Ms. Chin?" the teller asked.

"Yes I am. How did you know?"

"Your *r*'s."

The next visitor to his window was the short man in the black suit who had let the woman behind go to Becky Blondell's window.

"How can I help you, sir?" Laertes asked.

"Howard Sansome," he replied. "I started a regular checking account at your Fort Green branch a short while ago but now I wish to upgrade it to your investment-plus plan."

The man calling himself Sansome handed Laertes a plastic card designed in metallic gold, red, and blue colors. His name was superimposed in lowercase black lettering across the middle of the card.

"I'll need to see some ID," Laertes told him.

"Of course."

Laertes checked the New York State driver's license and entered the bank number on his computer.

"Changing your account would be easy enough," Laertes advised. "But the order has to be okayed by the manager of the branch where you started the account."

"I moved from Brooklyn to Manhattan since then," Howard Sansome said with something approximating an apology on his wide face. "Can't you just make a note on my file or something like that? It would be inconvenient for me to try to get out to Fort Green at the hours the branch is open."

"You could make the change by mail," Laertes suggested.

"I don't trust the post." Sansome's eyes were searching the teller's face.

"I'd be happy to make the update . . ." Laertes said.

A canny look invaded the bank customer's visage.

". . . if you just talk to the manager here and have her call your branch," the cashier added.

"Can't *you* call him?"

"No phones at the windows."

"I could let you use mine," the customer offered. There was the hint of a smile on his mouth.

"Also against the rules." Laertes shrugged to underscore the apology.

"Well," Howard Sansome said on a sigh, "I guess there's a trip to Brooklyn in my future."

With that he turned and walked away.

Friday was much like Thursday. Eighty-six customers with 216 transactions, a zero balance, and a trip to the vault to install his cashbox.

On Saturday he had lunch with his ex-wife Bonita and their eleven-year-old daughter, Medea. Bonita and Laertes had met at the 23rd Street branch of Maritime Merchants Bank when they were both tellers. Now she was a senior vice president at National Trust Investments and Loan. They divorced because, she claimed and he agreed, he had little ambition in his banking career.

"How's history coming?" Laertes asked his daughter after the first few awkward minutes amongst the three at Jammy's Diner on 18th Street.

"It's great," the child said. She was a deep brown color with big eyes and an infectious smile. "I just read everything three times like you said and then I know it without thinking."

"You always have to think," Bonita corrected.

Fifteen years younger than Laertes, Bonita was slender, tall, and strong. He was still attracted to her even though she'd married Hero Martin, a German-American from Pittsburgh. He had nothing against Martin except for the fact that Medea called him daddy.

"There's nature, second nature, and thought," Laertes said in response to his ex-wife's criticism. "The first is physical, the last of the mind, and the middle is something you know so well that it's just there like a sleeping fish in calm waters."

Medea's big eyes seemed to be fixed on her father's words. At moments like this he liked to think that she saw something worthy in him.

"Are we going to order?" Bonita asked. "Medea promised her father that they'd go to the Met together this afternoon."

On Sunday Laertes took a train to All Saints Rest Home in Nyack to visit Helena Havelock-Jackson, his mother.

"Pompey!" the ninety-one-year-old matriarch exclaimed. For the past five months or so Helena had seen Laertes's father's face when looking at him; another kind of fish in a different depth of water, Laertes thought.

"Hi, Mom."

"You look so tired, honey. I'll make us some marrow soup and we'll go to bed early." She placed four fingers on her son's left hand and a sigh came unbidden from way down in his throat.

"How are you, Mom?"

"You know nothing's wrong with me," was her rote answer. "Are you having trouble at work?"

"No."

"Are you gonna get that promotion soon?"

"They went with somebody else."

Helena's skin was dark like her son's and similar to Pompey's, when Pompey was alive. Her eyes were both furtive and vulnerable.

"What do you mean?" she asked, pain tucked in with the words.

Taking hold of both her hands, Laertes explained about his harebrained scheme to get a job at Triple-M. And though she thought she was talking to her late husband, Laertes knew that she heard and mostly understood his words.

"That's always been your problem," Helena Havelock-Jackson said to her son through the medium of her husband. "You think bigger than the people who believe they already big. That's why you called our children by them Greeks and why your daddy named you for a general to freedom."

On Monday afternoon at 4:21 p.m. Laertes Jackson departed Maritime Merchants Bank. He left behind a zero balance and a cashbox containing $6,627.14. He had completed in excess of four hundred transactions that day.

"Excuse me, sir," someone called. "Mr. Jackson."

Laertes turned and saw a short man in a muted maroon suit trundling toward him. There was something familiar about the man but because he saw people all day long Laertes's mind had learned to discard faces.

But now he was shaking hands with someone who at least knew his name.

"Uh . . ." Laertes said.

"Howard Sansome," the small but powerful man said.

"Um . . ."

"Last Thursday. You told me that I had to go to Fort Green to update my account."

"Either that," the teller said, "or send it by mail."

"Can I buy you a drink?" the man with the wide face asked.

"Excuse me?"

"I know," Sansome said with an air of confidentiality. "It seems kind of odd for someone who just knows you from a single encounter through a window of bulletproof glass to act like we're friends."

"Yeah."

"But we have a lot more in common than that."

"And what is it we have in common?" Laertes asked. In spite of himself he was intrigued by Sansome.

"Martin, Martin, and Moll," the man said with a glimmer of conspiracy in his eye.

"What?" Laertes said. "What do they have to do with you?"

"My title is VP in charge of investigations at Triple-M. Around the seventy-ninth floor they call me 'the VP in charge of trouble.'"

"Your office building doesn't go that high."

"We own other buildings."

"What kinda trouble do you investigate?"

"Right now, you."

"Me how?"

"Can we get that drink? There's a bar down the street called The Dutchy. They serve a great Manhattan all Monday afternoon for half price."

Twenty minutes later the drinks had been served to the short white man and his much taller black friend.

"This *is* very good," Laertes agreed after his second sip.

"They use bourbon instead of rye and the vermouth isn't nearly as sweet as most."

"So," Laertes said hoping to prime the explanation of why they were there.

"You know the cards are stacked against just about everybody in America," Sansome said instead of complying.

"You including all of North and South America or do you just mean the United States?" Laertes couldn't help himself.

"So is that your thing, Jackson?" the pickup host asked. "You need to argue with every word the bosses or their representatives say?"

"No, not at all."

"You told Ms. Rodriguez that you weren't African American," Sansome offered.

"Is she Mexican?" Laertes asked. "Either that or any other kind of new world so-called Hispanic?"

Howard Sansome downed his drink and gestured at the

bartender, a sallow woman of middle age that had the look of having lived hard. He told her to bring two more.

Then the man turned to Laertes and said, "No."

"No to what?"

"Rodriguez is not any kind of new world anything. Her people are French, but her ex-husband was Puerto Rican."

"So it just happens that she's heading up Triple-M's drive for integration?"

"I doubt it."

The drinks came and Howard asked the haggard mixologist to keep them coming.

"So it's like a . . . like a capitalist conspiracy," Laertes said. "They put somebody there who will represent their needs and who gives a fuck about mine."

Sansome sipped and thought. After a minute he almost said something but then decided to drink a little more.

Finally, he said, "I believe that the head of HR thinks that Rahlina really is Puerto Rican. The only thing that matters to Mr. Hawthorne is that all his employees move to the same beat. So it's kind of like a conspiracy but one that nobody is quite aware of."

Laertes felt as if a light had been turned on in his chest, casting a brilliance that traveled everywhere.

"That's what I mean when I say that I'm not arguing with everything the bosses say," Laertes averred. "If you told me that the sky was blue or that this drink was good, I wouldn't argue. But if you tell me that the word American only meant U.S. citizens or that I am in any way the cultural outcome of the continent of Africa, that I'm African American before I'm Slave-American, well then, I'd have to argue."

Two more drinks came.

"So," Sansome said. "You're on a quest for justice and not a job."

"Not justice," Laertes said and then he downed the cocktail in one swallow. "Not justice, no. Uh-uh. The expectation of justice would be for a man like me waiting on the second coming. It would be like thinking I could absolve myself of all the pain that is the true inheritance of my ancestral history."

Laertes could see that his answer was unexpected. Sansome had thought that he understood why Laertes said the things he did. But now he could see that he'd been wrong.

"If not justice then what?" the vice president in charge of trouble asked.

There was yet another Manhattan before Laertes.

"I would just like," Laertes said, "the words people say to have some modicum of truth to them. I'd like for people to see that some folks are named after countries and cultures while others are ill-defined by so-called race and continent. That's all."

Having told his truth about truth, Laertes downed his fourth cocktail.

"Your records say that you only have a high school diploma," Howard Sansome said.

"Education is simply the process of thought being applied to knowledge," the bank teller said. "Thought . . . applied to knowledge. Most people just say things having never thought about what whatever they're saying means. You got presidents do that."

Sansome turned on his barstool so that he was facing Laertes.

He said, "So you're telling me that you bollixed up your interview because the woman was white with a Spanish name and she called you African American."

"I'm saying that the words I hear and the words I speak should make sense. You can't live a life in terms that are wrong—not a good life."

"And are you living a good life?" Howard Sansome asked.

The bank teller felt the full force of the four cocktails upon hearing that question. He blinked and shook his head trying to find an answer that he believed should be second nature.

"I'll be in touch, Mr. Jackson," Sansome said.

Watching the short man in the dark red suit walk from the bar, Laertes felt that the world was tilted to the right. He wondered how that new balance would affect what he believed.

3.

Five weeks later Laertes's life had changed in small ways that promised to be large. *Are you living a good life?* The question resonated at the back of his mind through every activity and even in his sleep. There was certainly goodness in his life. Medea was a beautiful child and she loved him even though she called another man father. Things had been good with Bonita before her ambition cast its gaze on him. He was good at his job, rarely had other than a zero balance.

Other things were less than good. His rent had gone up twelve percent in the last two years and another hike would necessitate a move. He needed more money but didn't want an officer's position because he felt that they misrepresented the value of the accounts and loans they pushed on customers. He hadn't been on a date in nine years—since the divorce.

So now he bought his first computer and started trawling date-sites for companionship. His explanation of who he was and what he wanted was seventeen pages long and his photograph was of a dark-skinned man who wasn't smiling and seemed confused by the camera.

The few responses he had online were tentative but interested.

Agnes327 wrote, "Your profile was so serious, Laertes8, what do you do to have fun?"

"I read the *Times*," Laertes wrote, "and take each story apart imagining how what they say happened could have happened. Then I write responses when I feel that I've struck upon a contradiction."

Lucy!! asked, if he could change the world he found so problematic, how would that look?

Laertes wrote a 62-page response over a three-day period in which he addressed the economic system, the problems of a *standardized education*, medical care, the environment, the misconceptions of race and gender, and the waste of human potential on distractions created to keep human passion tamped down.

Laertes only got sixteen responses to his dating-site profile. After answering all of them he only got one second reply. This reply, written in the third week after Howard Sansome had asked his devastating question, was from Mona_Loa_Love. She asked him where he'd retire when he could.

He replied that the notion of retirement in the animal kingdom was tantamount to exile or death and not something one should pursue. "I believe that when we age, we lose our physical edge but gain wisdom and patience," he wrote. "I'd like to become an advisor to younger members of our nation; that and maybe I'd like to tend a flock of sheep."

Laertes used a facility on the site to allow her, and all other potential suitors, to read his answers. By the fourth week, Mona_Loa_Love had crafted a reply that was both delicate and blunt.

Dear Laertes8,

It intrigues me that you included a photograph of yourself but refused to identify by gender, race, or age. There's something genius in that. I love the long, well thought out answers you gave to the others who responded. And I can understand why they didn't reply. These women are looking for something they've already seen and don't want to be challenged, but rather loved—and cared for in various ways.

I am not interested in dating you. As a matter of fact, I can see no reason in our meeting. But I am deeply moved by your convictions and your resolute inability to compromise. I hope that we can have an epistolary relationship over this medium, or maybe you'd like to send me your email address. I could use your wisdom and, I believe, you might have some use for my understanding.

Mona_Loa_Love

If Howard Sansome's question had been devastating, Mona_Loa_Love's response was worse . . . *your resolute inability to compromise* was the most painful phrase. She saw something in him that he had not seen himself. As a matter of fact, even though he saw the truth of her words, still he did not understand how to leave them or live with them.

Laertes did not go on the dating site for a week after this last response. He went to work, visited his mother and estranged family, read the *Times*, but did not perform his usual exegeses on its articles. On that Saturday, around midnight, he felt very much alone in his studio apartment on the third floor next to a woman whose hound dog howled every evening from six to just about seven. The bank teller felt the urge for a Manhattan cocktail. He took a shower and put on his medium gray suit. He buttoned the white shirt up to the throat but forwent a tie. He took sixty dollars from a twenty-year-old manila envelope in his writing desk, pocketed the house key, and went toward the door.

His hand was not yet on the doorknob when the landline rang. He rubbed his fingers together and the second volley of sound pealed. He turned to look at the phone he had no intention of answering. This would be the third and last ring. After that the automated answering service would take over.

The fourth ring surprised him; as did the fifth, sixth, and seventh. By the eleventh ring Laertes was certain that the world he'd known, and despised, had fallen off its axis.

"Hello?"

"Mr. Jackson? Laertes Jackson?" a woman's soothing voice asked.

"How come my phone didn't send you to voice mail?"

"Our technology sidesteps that process," she said. "Mr. Jackson?"

"Yes. I'm Jackson."

"So pleased to meet you, sir. You have been on my mind for quite a while now."

"And who are you?"

"My name is Winsome Millerton-Pomerantz, CEO of Triple-M."

"It's Saturday night, Ms. Pomerantz. Most people are taking it easy around now."

"Money never sleeps."

"I don't know about that. My little bit of change been nappin' my whole life."

"Exactly."

Laertes felt that there was deep meaning in the words they shared but he still hankered after a well-made, not too sweet Manhattan.

"Ma'am, I was just about to go out. So if you want something, just ask and I will answer."

"Monday morning, 7:45, seventy-ninth floor," she said. "Number 2 Broadway."

"I'll be there."

Laertes didn't remember much about the rest of that Saturday night. There was a bartender and a woman named Briance. He bought quite a few drinks, and someone might have helped him up the stairs. His sixty dollars were gone but that was all. The hangover kept him from seeing his mother the following day. He wondered if Helena Havelock-Jackson would miss her husband's weekly visit.

Laertes arrived at Number 2 Broadway at 6:10 Monday morning. The security guard let him in after verifying his identity and looking up his name on the executive computer file.

Howard Sansome sat at the receptionist's desk on the seventy-ninth floor.

"Hey there, Laertes," the squat, powerful vice president greeted.

"This your job too?"

"Ms. Pomerantz wanted to make sure that it would be you who came."

"Who else could it be?" Laertes asked.

"You got any listening or recording devices on you?"

"No, sir," Laertes said.

The VP in charge of trouble grinned then took a device from his pocket. It looked somewhat like an extra-thick cellphone.

"I'm just gonna run this around you to make sure," Sansome said.

When he was finished, he asked Laertes if he wanted coffee, "or maybe something stronger."

"No. I'll just sit here and compose my thoughts."

"Suit yourself."

Sansome rose from behind the desk and departed through a doorway that had no door.

Laertes expected the man to return but he didn't.

Later, Laertes would see that brief space in time, the moments between Sansome's departure and his interview with Millerton-Pomerantz, as the most important span of his life. He wasn't concerned with a future job. What he thought about was

Mona_Loa_Love and her, if indeed it was a woman, deep understanding in simple language, of the thought processes he'd been swaddled in for so many years that he could no longer separate the bondage from the man.

I am my own prison, he thought. *The truths I've wielded have hidden that fact from me. Whatever I do from this moment on will derive from those unassailable facts.*

"Mr. Jackson," a strong and yet melodious voice announced.

She had soft red hair and eyes the color of pale blue diamonds. Ms. Winsome Millerton-Pomerantz was tall and slender, and like Laertes, in her fifties but much younger looking. There was a smile on her lips as if she had been anticipating this meeting. She wore a blue and white woman's business suit that might have been made from silk or maybe, Laertes thought, some space-age material.

"Yes," Laertes said.

"So happy to meet you," she said, holding out both hands.

He rose and took those hands as he had his mother's on Sundays over the past seven years.

"Would you like to go to my office or meet here at the front desk?" Winsome asked. "I gave everyone but Howard the day off."

"I leave it up to you, ma'am. This is your fief."

The CEO grinned and said, "Follow me."

Laertes remembered walking but not the spaces through which he traveled. His mind was on the topic of his imprisonment and the unlikely meeting with a woman of both beauty and power.

Ultimately they came to an office, the walls of which were a singular pane of glass. From there one could see the entire panorama of Lower Manhattan and beyond.

"Let's sit on the sofa," Ms. Winsome Millerton-Pomerantz said.

It was a yellow divan upholstered in fabric that reminded Laertes of velvet-like pigskin. It seemed to hug him, to pull him in.

Winsome turned toward her guest and said, "Before we begin, do you have any questions?"

"Rahlina Rodriguez asked me that. Is that a prescribed beginning around here?"

The CEO smiled and shook her head, no.

"Then could you tell me how I got here?"

"Would you like me to start with the *Jesus of Lübeck*?"

It was Laertes's turn to grin. He knew about the slave ship from 1564.

"No, ma'am," he said. "I'm just interested in why a major firm like yours would have me followed and questioned and brought to this amazing place. I thought I'd been rejected by Ms. Rodriguez."

"You would have been," Millerton-Pomerantz said simply. "But when you announced to our recording devices that you wanted a copy of what had transpired, our lawyers got nervous."

"Nervous about what?"

"We've spent more than fifty million on suits and settlements, lawyers' fees and golden parachutes. Our legal team has been trying to stem that flow."

"So I'm here because you're worried that I'll sue?"

"No." Her smile was lovely. "I sent Mr. Sansome to talk to you and by the time he'd finished the legal team said that there was nothing we had to worry about."

"Then why am I here?"

"Howard likes to make full reports. He was, in his way, very impressed by your mind. He told me that almost everything you said surprised him and that you might be a valuable asset to our firm."

"I don't know what he means by that. I've been a bank teller for two and a half decades. The only promotions I ever got was from entry teller to senior cashier. Your boy told me how I didn't have but a high school diploma."

"He said that you told him that education was merely the process of applying thought to knowledge."

"He remembered that?" Laertes asked.

"You are a unique individual, Mr. Jackson. You understand a world that most others don't even suspect."

"I can hardly walk a straight line without tripping over my own feet."

"I believe that. Genius, true human genius, has no patience for the mundane."

Laertes was suddenly aware of his heart beating. There was sweat on his hands and his hands had never perspired before.

"Would you like some water, sir?"

"Are you telling me that you don't think I can be a normal person?" he replied.

"Yes."

"How come you know about the first slave ship?"

"I studied world history at Sarah Lawrence. I met a man from a wealthy family named Jared Pomerantz. We married, he died, and I assumed the mantle that he'd left behind. We are cut from similar cloth, Mr. Jackson. The only difference is that I've been lucky with money."

"Not with love?"

"Jared was a pig. It shamed me that I was happy that he died."

"Okay then," Laertes Jackson said.

"Okay what?"

"If you got a job for me, I'll consider it."

4.

Dear Mona_Loa_Love,

I got your email and it nearly broke my heart. I always thought that it was my choice not to compromise but when you said it was my inability, I knew it was true. I was never going to reach out to you again but then something happened . . .

Laertes explained about Triple-M, Howard Sansome the Vice President of Trouble, and the CEO Winsome Millerton-Pomerantz.

. . . they offered me a job, Vice President in Charge of Reeducation. I have a desk on the seventy-fifth floor and an inbox that brings in data (knowledge) and an outbox that reflects my thoughts on that knowledge. They just want me to think about what they should do and they promise to take my ideas into consideration. I asked my ex-wife about it and she invited me out to dinner. I told my manager about it and she laughed in my face.

Dear Laertes8,

I am so happy that you finally decided to answer me. Reading your communications, I felt for the first time in so long that there was finally a kindred out there for me. Not a lover or a husband, not a sugar daddy or father figure. Not even a mentor, not really. You are, at least potentially, a friend.

And as a friend I feel your fear and confusion. The office of that CEO is the heir to the offices that made your people slaves. Would working for them, no matter how good all intentions were, be a betrayal of your truth? Can you make a difference? Probably not. But should you try? That is a question that only you can answer.

Mona_Loa_Love

All that happened six months ago. Laertes still has his job at Maritime Merchants Bank. He still has the most zero balance days of any teller ever. His ex-wife asks him on Saturdays if he's taken the new job. His mother has taken to asking him if he's seen his father anywhere. He and Mona_Loa_Love write to each other every other day. Winsome Millerton-Pomerantz calls on Saturday nights to ask if he has finally made up his mind.

"I figure if I wait long enough you'll find someone else," Laertes tells the CEO.

"There is no one else, Mr. Jackson. It is either you or nothing."

TOMORROW'S NEWS

SAMANTHA LOKAI

Twilight faded into night, its usual tapestry of pink and crimson blotted by fog and grey clouds. As the sky darkened, shadows of neighbouring buildings crept across the room in strips and columns like the bars of a prison door closing shut. The stern, rhythmic tapping of the clock on the wall echoed across the empty newsroom, insisting it was time to go.

Her desk was the smallest, set aside from the others, but someday she would claim her place at the front and write feature stories with a front-page name highlighted in the byline. Late nights as a junior reporter writing obituaries would be a thing of the past and everyone would know her. Thunder grumbled in concurrence with her thoughts and the desk lamp flickered with a soft click.

As fate would have it, everything was about to change that night—and a desire would soon be fulfilled.

Turbulent weather hadn't been forecasted, but it sounded like a storm was moving in. Time to head home. She collected her things, pausing at a folded newspaper on the edge of her desk. She had already thrown it out twice, unread, but here it was again. Someone in the office must've been toying with her before they'd left for the day. Annoyed, she tossed it into the trash, then glanced down at it, wondering if she might want to read it later. The front-page headlines glared at her in bold black captions.

SUNDOWN VALLEY KILLER STRIKES AGAIN
HERO SHOPKEEPER RESCUES CAT FROM FIRE

Hope and despair side by side, the paper's underlying need to sensationalise. She frowned at the cliché. Either pull at the heartstrings or disturb the hell out of the reader. Stories that sell. She should know, every newspaper reporter did. Tomorrow there will be a new hero and a new victim. She left it lying in the trash basket; it was already old news.

Lightning flashed, washing everything of colour, and for a moment, the stark white light projected her into a black and white motion picture. She counted the seconds. One Mississippi, two Mississippi. She was at five when a low rumble bellowed, its harshness muffled by distance and windows. Too late. The storm was close, and she braced herself for the onslaught of wind and rain.

The hall between offices was without the regular hub of frantic activity, and she savoured not having to scramble out of people's way, apologising for every bumped shoulder. Up ahead, the elevator glowed in spectral white, more prominent than usual without a crowd gathered in front of it. The lights overhead flickered and for a second she thought it was lightning, but there were no windows along the corridor of closed office doors.

What was it with the lights tonight?

She would have to mention it to the janitor tomorrow. It could be due to the storm, but it was also an old building, one of the city's historical treasures. Unfortunately, its age meant a lot of the infrastructure had started to deteriorate.

She called the elevator, idling around the lobby till it came. On the reception desk was another copy of the latest edition of the *Sundown Gazette*—but the headlines weren't the ones she'd seen earlier. It didn't make sense. The copy on her desk had to be the most recent; she remembered seeing tomorrow's date on the front page. Before she could get a better look, lightning flared and her attention was diverted.

The door to the last office had been left wide open and its floor to ceiling windows framed the jagged outline of the city against an ominous horizon. It took her breath away. Gathering clouds against a backdrop of glowing purple and red hues looked like a page out of a sci-fi comic. Streaks of silver veined the sky and the room glared in rapid bursts of light, illuminating dark corners and shapes in startling contrast. When it faded, she found herself in complete darkness. The power was out.

You've got to be kidding me.

She pulled her cellphone from her handbag to use the flashlight but the screen before her remained black. When was the last time she'd charged it? As she struggled to remember, the elevator doors chimed open, startling her. She cleared her throat to mask the small gasp that escaped, even though no one was there to notice. Light filtered in weakly from the office window. It couldn't be a blackout—other buildings on the block clearly had electricity.

Dammit.

Darkness swelled, forming a sinister presence. It was also odd that the elevator still worked in the outage. The interior light was out, not a good sign, and she was doubtful whether to risk it. There were the stairs, but being this high up without a flashlight meant a treacherous descent in the dark. She envisioned herself tumbling down and breaking her neck, only to be found days later, bloated beyond recognition, with her limbs mangled from the fall.

Hardly anyone used the staircase, there's no telling when they would find her, and there wasn't anyone waiting at home to notice if she hadn't made it back.

What a pathetic way to die.

She'd take her chances with the elevator. It must work on a backup generator or something. Inside, she felt for the control panel, having used it enough times to estimate the ground floor button. The doors began to slide across and relief washed over her. In a few seconds she would be at the exit. Thunder rolled as the doors thudded closed, sealing out sound and the remaining traces of light. There was an irrational comfort in staying still; safe in her own space. When she was little, she didn't dare move under the covers after the lights went out, restrained by the unknown, afraid of waking the monster in the closet. Closing her eyes, she remained completely still as the elevator made its descent.

Silence. Darkness.

She thought ahead to her cosy night in with old thrillers and Jack Daniels. The stormy weather was the perfect backdrop for the eerie suspense of Hitchcock Hour. Her mouth salivated at the thought of the bottle of Jack waiting for her. She could smell it, smoky and woody, as if it was right there. Until the air carried something else along with it.

Her eyes snapped open and as she turned to look behind her, the elevator juddered to a halt. When the doors failed to slide apart, she tapped what she thought was the "Open" button repeatedly. Nothing. She tried random buttons, panic rising with each one, but the elevator didn't respond.

"No, no, no. This can't be happening!"

She pounded the doors and finally hit upon the emergency button. In all her years working here, there had never been cause to use it.

"H-hello? Is anyone there? I-I'm stuck. I mean, the elevator's stuck."

She hunched closer to the speaker and gave her location. A sharp crackle was followed by a faint voice, interrupted by static, then silence. Their words were barely recognisable, but fragments sounded like help was on the way.

"I'm sorry, can you say that again?" she shouted.

There was no response, not even static, only the hope that someone must have heard her. All she could do was wait.

Silence. Darkness.

An article about a woman who had been buried alive came to mind. When they found her, her fingernails were shredded and bloody from trying to claw her way out. Some of her fingers were worn down to pulpy stubs, and clumps of hair were ripped from her scalp. The dead woman's face was contorted in terror, mouth frozen wide in a silent scream. It was this grisly vision that haunted her the most, surfacing during times she was desperate to be heard too. She was like that woman. Trapped. Stifled. Except hers was an invisible box, one she'd never escape if people didn't take her seriously. Tonight however, confined to the pitch blackness of this airless elevator, the memory was truer to its origin, and she wondered how long it would be before she tore her own hair out.

Stop it. Help is on the way. Maybe.

She shook her head to dislodge horrific thoughts from forming and focused on slow deep breaths. The faint smell of tobacco and musty air teased again, probably from smokers and dirty carpeting. At least that's what she hoped, before realizing the scent was growing more pungent and cloying. Her face flushed hot and her palms chilled with perspiration.

"Hello? Is someone here?"

The elevator was cold, but a warm breath fluttered against her neck, and the second time, it lingered. Her skin prickled and her heart hammered against her chest. She dared not move.

A soft shuffle came from behind her.

It's nothing. Just the air vents.

Then came the breathing, raspy and shallow.

Fear surged like electrical volts. "H-hello?"

She peered into the darkness and listened, thinking of things she could say—that help was on the way or someone was waiting for her at the exit, but they would know these were empty threats. Every swallow and heartbeat amplified, like the room was growing smaller. She hated tight spaces, and here she was, frightened with no way out. The image of the woman's contorted face and gaping mouth taunted her, and she swallowed against the bile rising in her throat. She tried random buttons before hitting the emergency switch again, then banged on the elevator doors until her fists burned and throbbed.

"Help!" The metal doors were cold against her cheek and palms. "Somebody! Please."

No one was coming.

Slowly, she turned around as her panting filled the elevator, echoing and closing in. She stepped forward and there was a sudden shift in the air. She felt it, a presence. Body heat moving closer. She held her breath, and as she did so, she heard someone else exhale.

Jolts of panic coursed through her. She was weightless, free falling, even though the elevator wasn't moving, and she grabbed onto the handrail to steady herself.

"Please," she begged in a hoarse whisper. "Why are you doing this?"

A lungful of sour, humid air settled on her face. Shivers snaked up her spine, fear mostly, but for a fleeting moment there was something else too, an alluring thrill, a brief instant the mundane had been broken. It was better than being alone, stuck in an elevator, without a single soul to notice she was missing, and maybe that was more terrifying. She reached forward with her hand, slowly parting the darkness.

The elevator interrupted with a hum and lurched to a start.

Within seconds it came to a stop. Desperate not to miss her chance, she squeezed through the half-opened doors, tripping over her handbag and falling onto the cold marble of the ground floor lobby. Dazed from a blow to her head, she scrambled to untangle her feet. It was dark and her vision clouded by tears, but she caught sight of a shadowy figure in front of the elevator doors as they slid closed behind. Wide-eyed and terror-stricken, she ran toward the exit, guided by the beam of street light bleeding in through the glass exit.

The door opened into a deluge and violent gusts, and as it closed behind her, sharp metal falling onto marble clinked faintly. She cursed under her breath for not parking nearer to the building. Rain lashed down like ice picks on her skin and she struggled against the strength of the wind. Lightning flashed and the stark white light cast her once again in black and white, the star of a classic movie, a damsel in distress.

Where's Cary Grant when you need him?

Out in the open, thunder drummed louder and brasher. The staccato beat of her high heels echoed along the sidewalk as she hurried to her car. Overhead, the storm thrashed and blared with brutal force, and another bolt of lightning cracked across the sky, illuminating a figure emerging from the shadows . . . and the glint of a blade.

The *Sundown Gazette* was bustling the next day. The serial killer had claimed another victim overnight and the *Gazette* was the first to obtain the inside scoop yet again, much to the dismay of its competitors. Within a few hours, the online story had already gone viral, and a special late edition was about to hit the newsstands. The editor-in-chief leaned back in his chair, basking in his success. His inside reporting on the Sundown Valley Killings had given him the reputation he had longed for. The last victim was one of the *Gazette*'s own, a junior reporter vying for a featured byline, like the rest of them. Instead, she had made the headline, and because of the paper's personal connection to the story, they were now the leading news source in the city.

He had tried to warn her, like he had with all his other victims, by leaving on her desk the newspaper mock-up reporting her death. Luckily for him, none of them ever paid enough attention. Although the last one came pretty close; she had a reporter's eye after all. Taunting them with it was the most thrilling part—their fate was in their own hands—and tomorrow's news depended on it.

A GUID SOLDIER

CHARLES TODD

He remembered when the raw recruit had come up the lines. Dougal Kerr was solidly built, and strong, but not as tall as most men his age. A good soldier. Quiet and dependable. One of too many who would die before the week, the month, or the year was out. Rutledge made a point, as he always did, of speaking to the newcomer that night, asking him where he was from and a little about his family. It was important to know something of each man for when the time came to write the letters to the dead men's families.

Dougal said, "I'm fra' Glasgow. No family. I've been in care ever since I can remember."

An orphan. No mother to grieve, no father to weep in private or boast about his hero lad in public.

"Good luck, son. Come to me if you need help. It's not easy, it never is, to deal with the fighting."

A broad and appealing grin spread across Dougal's face. "Thankee sir, but I doubt I'll have trouble. I've always wanted to be a soldier."

From time to time after that, Rutledge saw Dougal going about his duties with good grace and no complaints. Sergeant MacNabb called him "laddie." Hamish, standing beside Rutledge one night as they watched the German lines across No Man's Land, spoke of Dougal as "a guid man." Others on the line took a fatherly interest in him.

It wasn't until they took the machine gun nest that Rutledge found himself in close company with Dougal. He'd sent most of his men toward the German line as a distraction while he and five others crawled toward the unguarded side of the machine gun emplacement. In a last second rush, they were on their feet and inside before the gunners could turn and protect their flank. The surprise was complete.

Two of his men went down as Rutledge, followed by another soldier, leaped into the nest with his pistol drawn while Dougal stood on the rim of the emplacement, rifle at the ready. The gunner and his crew got slowly to their feet, shock on their young faces, their hands beginning to rise in surrender. But before Rutledge could speak to them, Dougal fired five times at nearly point-blank range, killing the Germans where they stood.

Rutledge wheeled, shouting, "Enough of that!" But it was too late. His eyes met Dougal's, and in those eyes Rutledge saw an expression that for an instant disconcerted him.

He leaned down to disable the machine gun before leading his men, carrying their wounded, back to their own line.

Afterward, he asked Dougal why he'd shot the Germans as they were surrendering.

"They're machine gunners, aren't they? Lower than the low!"

"Yes, that's what's said in the lines," Rutledge retorted angrily. "But it doesn't give you the right to kill them out of hand!"

"No, sir," Dougal answered slowly, his eyes cast down. "I got carried away a bit—the excitement and all."

There was nothing else Rutledge could say. No one else had

seen what he had seen. Others were slapping Dougal on the back and calling him a hero.

But the expression on Dougal's face as he'd shot the enemy down was burned into Rutledge's mind. He had seemed gleeful. He tried to tell himself that the man was young, that he'd only been at the Front for a week. But Rutledge had been a policeman before the war, and what he'd seen had sent the hairs on the back of his neck rising up in alarm.

There was no such thing as a born killer.

When he got a chance, he spoke to Hamish. The Scot shook his head. "I've seen nae sign of trouble," he said skeptically, "but I'll keep an ee oot."

Rutledge had more on his mind than Dougal for the next seventy-two hours, with a push on by the Germans and the men under his command tiring under the onslaught and the heavy shelling. Hamish, reporting on the losses and the wounded, said, "I must tell ye that young Dougal has a guid eye. He found the sniper before I did."

And Corporal Hamish MacLeod had one of the best eyes Rutledge had ever come across.

"Did he shoot the man?" Rutledge asked. "Or did you?"

Hamish grinned. "We tossed for it. He won. Private Chisholm called it a rare shot."

Chisholm was one of their own snipers, a man born to gamekeepers on a Highland estate who was a gamekeeper himself. Rutledge said nothing.

Hamish went on. "Though I must tell you that he took undue pleasure in the shot. I couldna' be sure if it was his pride in the marksmanship or the thrill of bringing doon the man that set him up sae well."

"Yes. He appears to take pleasure in killing."

Hamish shrugged. "It's what a soldier does. Still . . ." He paused for a long moment, then shrugged as if to himself and said, "He doesna' complain. And he's no laggard o'er the top."

In the quiet of the night Rutledge and Hamish stood there, shoulder to shoulder, watching the stars come out as clouds moved on. Rutledge could see Orion clearly now. And the Great Bear.

Hamish said after a moment, "There's something I canna' like in him, for all he's a guid soldier. What's lacking, I canna' say."

Rutledge said, "I've heard the men call him lucky."

"Aye, he is that. He doesna' seem to ken what death is."

Rutledge's fingers went to the tear in the cloth of his sleeve where a shot had just missed him. It had been close, but not close enough. "He's quiet in rotation, back of the lines. He has little to say for himself. I've asked. And there's no mail for him."

"An orphan," Hamish reminded him.

"Yes." Rutledge was silent for a time, then added, "No past."

Hamish chuckled softly. "Ye're no' a policeman, man. No' here. He's verra young. Two days ago I saw him try to shave." He grinned in the darkness, white teeth a flash of brightness in the shadows of the trench wall. "It wasna' successful."

Later in the day Rutledge spoke to Sergeant MacRae about Dougal.

MacRae said, "It's strange. You notice no one calls him by his surname. He's Dougal, like a boy."

"He looks like a boy," Rutledge agreed, "as if his mind hasn't caught up with his body."

MacRae frowned. "He's a guid soldier," he said, echoing Hamish's words, "but somehow I canna' trust him."

Rutledge turned to look at MacRae's lined face, the face of a man who'd been dragged back into the war after retiring from the Army in 1912, and said, "That's an odd thing to say."

"Aye, it is. He charges hell-bent for the Hun lines as if he hears no orders, and tries to get up as close as he can. It's almost as if he wants to see the faces of the ones who lay dying after they've been shot. He's likely to get himself shot being sae stupid, and we'll have to send other men out to bring him back. I do na' care for foolishness." He stopped to listen to the sounds of distant fire, then turned to his men and called to them to be watchful. "But he's a guid soldier," he repeated, as if trying to convince himself of the fact.

When Rutledge spoke to Dougal about his rash charges and the danger they posed to others in the company, the boy only grinned and said, "I hit more that way," as if he were keeping count. "There were sixteen yesterday. I made sure of each kill." Then, with a puzzled look, he added, "I'm not sure why I like it so much, but there's something about fighting that makes me feel good." He looked up at Rutledge as if searching his face for an explanation, for some kind of understanding he couldn't quite reach on his own.

Rutledge found himself shivering. The policeman in him, alert and uneasy, listened for overtones, the voice of someone who killed for sport. But the boy seemed unaware of Rutledge's suspicions. If anything, he seemed surprised by his own admission and eager to examine it further.

There were days when Rutledge watched Dougal and debated with himself about speaking to his commanding officer about the boy. But Dougal had done nothing wrong, nothing that could support Rutledge's concerns. Still, a small voice inside his head asked him how well Dougal would adjust to civilian life again after the war. Would he continue doing what he loved best back home, ultimately ending up being caught and hanged by Scotland Yard? Or would his taste for killing end with the war?

There were no answers for any of his questions. And no time for them.

They were under attack again. The Germans were probing under cover of artillery, testing the British lines to the north of their position. In a strong counterattack, the British took back the yards the Germans had gained, then counted their dead. They had brought back all of their men except one—Maxwell, who hung on the wire.

The two men sent to retrieve him were shot down and had to crawl painfully back to safety. "He's twitching, but for all I can see, he's dead," one of them informed Hamish with a shake of his head.

"We'll wait until after dark to bring him back," Hamish said.

Watching the man hang there, his limbs moving erratically, one hand beckoning as if begging for rescue before it was too late, was having a bad effect on morale in the sector. Maxwell was well liked. Death was one thing. They had grown used to it. But helplessly watching one of their own suffer was another. For the young recruits who had just come to the front, it was appalling. One sat down, head in his hands, and wept. Another cursed steadily, as if damning the man on the wire. That night Sergeant MacRae sent another two men out to attempt to bring him back. Both died in a hail of bullets from behind the German lines.

It was one of the worst days of Rutledge's life. He watched the dying man and prayed to God that it would be over soon.

Finally another soldier volunteered to try and bring him in, but MacRae refused to let him. Hamish, leading the soldier away, said for all to hear, "Sometimes when the brain is shot, the heart keeps beating. He doesna' know he's twitching! He doesna' feel it."

"I wish someone would shoot him and put him out of his misery. Why don't the Germans do it for us?" someone said, his voice tight with anger.

"It's no' in their nature to be merciful," the sergeant snapped.

Hamish said, "As long as he keeps hanging there, they know we'll keep sending more men out to try bringing him in. They've done for four of us already."

And then Dougal stepped up to the trench wall, brought up his rifle, and fired.

The man on the wire sagged and was still.

Dougal said, "It's over." But there was something in his face, a flash of something dark and pitiless, that Rutledge caught before the boy turned away.

He enjoyed it, he thought. *And when the war is over, he'll go on killing.*

MacRae was shouting at Dougal Kerr, threatening to send him off to face court-martial. Others stood staring at him, horrified. But Dougal just walked off down the line, ignoring all of them.

That night, while Rutledge was writing a letter to the matron of the home where Dougal had grown up, in order to request information about him, Private Chisholm came to find him. Chisholm was their best sniper, a man with steady nerves and steadier hands. But the face of the man who stood before him at the moment, asking permission to speak, was twisted with anger and his hands trembled with his efforts to control himself.

"That was my mate on the wire," he said, "and you let that bastard shoot him!"

"I didn't let anyone shoot Private Maxwell," Rutledge replied, keeping his voice level. "It happened before any of us could have prevented it."

"Then why hasn't he been sent for court-martial? That was *murder*!"

"Sergeant MacRae is taking it up with the major. But the general feeling is that it was an act of mercy. The Germans were using Maxwell to draw us out. And he was dead. The two men who came back after the first try said he had been shot in the head and was not responding."

"He was alive! That's what everyone says. He was *alive*. We don't shoot our wounded."

But they had been shot, more than once, Rutledge could have answered. Perhaps not like this case, but men who couldn't be brought back, who lay in the shell craters and screamed for release. *It had been done* . . . But that would have been no comfort to Chisholm.

"What am I to tell his family?" Chisholm demanded. "How am I going to face them?" He was on the point of breaking down, his voice unsteady. "I'm to marry his *sister*, for God's sake! What am I to tell *her*?"

"That he died in battle," Rutledge said. "I've already written to them. I told them nothing that would upset them. And neither will you. What you know you will keep to yourself."

"I can't. You're telling me to condone what Dougal Kerr did!"

"I'm telling you that whatever you may feel about him, you will spare the family of a man who died for his country." Rutledge's voice was cold. "Is that understood?"

Chisholm was silent for a time as if replaying the words in his mind. Then he took a deep breath and said, "Yes, sir. I understand. I won't let them hear of this, I swear."

He was on the point of turning away, when he asked, "What do you think Headquarters will make of this?"

"They're too busy worrying about Verdun," Rutledge said frankly. "The French aren't holding and something has to be done."

"Yes. That makes sense, then," Chisholm answered, nodding. Then he was gone in the darkness.

Rutledge finished his letter concerning Dougal and sent it off by runner. Then he stepped out into the night, looking for Chisholm. But the man was already asleep, his head on his arms.

Would Chisholm get over it? Or would Maxwell's death become a festering sore in this tightly-knit company of men fighting to hold onto inches of land, all the while fully aware that most of them would become cannon fodder if another big push came? Maxwell's body had been brought in after nightfall, and it was clear that he wouldn't have survived even if he'd been retrieved and sent back to hospital. Half of his head had been shot away.

It was plain to see that what Dougal had done, however reprehensible, had also been merciful. It was also cold-blooded—he seemed untouched by it. Something needed to be done about this. For Dougal's sake, Rutledge told himself. But he had a feeling the boy wouldn't understand—or would refuse to understand—a rebuke.

He went in search of Dougal and found him to be enveloped in sleep as well—the sound sleep of a man whose conscience is clear.

The next few days were frenzied, unrelenting hell. Rutledge had no time to think about Dougal or to discuss the situation with anyone.

It was on the last attack of the day that Rutledge found himself making a futile, hopeless charge across No Man's Land toward the German lines with Dougal, Hamish, and another man from the ranks. Chisholm and two other snipers were set on bringing down a German sniper who was so cleverly concealed that no one had yet spotted him, and it was hoped that a direct attack on the German positions would bring him into the open. Additionally, the reports had shown that the German line was weakest at this point, and that it might be possible to take the sector with a determined assault. In a corner of his mind, Rutledge wondered if HQ knew what they were doing.

Dougal was firing his rifle with his usual cold skill, picking off enemy soldiers as their heads popped up over the trench lip. His skill was amazing, his aim relentless. And that look in his eyes was back—pure excitement and blood lust. A killer's face . . .

Then, without warning, Dougal spun around, stumbled, and fell, going down hard. Rutledge, his policeman's brain working behind his soldier's façade, noted the way the boy had spun. Then he was too busy to think about anything but getting his men back alive as reinforcements poured into the German lines and the British attack faltered.

They brought Dougal in with the other dead and wounded. Rutledge went to examine him. Hamish, behind him, looked over his shoulder.

"It couldna' been a Hun bullet," he said softly, for Rutledge's ears only.

"One of our own?" Rutledge asked quietly.

"No' one of the men at our heels. Look you, the angle is wrong."

"I saw that. Yes."

"Chisholm was the sniper on our right. He could ha' brought Dougal down."

The implication behind Hamish's words was clear. Rutledge had already reached the same conclusion. Chisholm could well have exacted his revenge for Maxwell today. And who would have been the wiser?

Sergeant MacRae came to stand with them. "A guid soldier," he said, shaking his head.

It was an epitaph, recognition of one man's usefulness in war.

Rutledge found it fitting, but incomplete. Keeping his thoughts about Dougal to himself, he asked to see Chisholm.

"He's dead," MacRae said with deep regret. "They just brought him in."

So much for getting to the bottom of what had happened.

Rutledge got to his feet and walked away, checking on his men one by one. When that was done, he found himself wondering what he should do. Dougal was dead. Chisholm was dead. It was finished.

But his policeman's mind wasn't satisfied. Had this boy been a born killer who had found his place in a war where killing was face to face and rampant? Or had he been a boy who'd had an extraordinary talent with a rifle and who'd been too young to understand what his skills meant in terms of human life?

There was nothing the policeman could do. Nothing Rutledge the officer could do. It would be unsettled, and he would be uncertain for the rest of his life, whether Dougal deserved to die at Chisholm's hands. And whether Chisholm himself was a murderer, with Dougal's blood at his door . . . or a hangman doing his duty.

Ten days later, at the end of June, a letter came from the home where Dougal had been cared for as a child.

"He is a most unusual boy," the letter said. "A busy and loving child. But there was something about him that frightened me then and still frightens me now. He was a firestarter, you see. He loved to watch things burn. We were quite concerned about that and were secretly glad when he ran away after the barn burned down with all of our horses inside. We tried to trace him, without any luck. Will you be sending him back to us? He's only fourteen, you see, and shouldn't be in the army at all. I've written to the colonel to ask if we could have him back again. But I wish there was somewhere else he could go. I'm so sorry to say that of a child. It means I've failed the boy. But the truth is, I'm more than a little afraid of him . . ."

After some thought, Rutledge showed the letter to Hamish. He read it through and then said, "Puir lad. He was a guid soldier. But he liked to kill more than was natural. She'll be relieved, this matron, to know he's no' coming back after all."

Case closed, Rutledge found himself thinking, his policeman's mind persuading him that there was nothing more that he could do, or should do. He would let the dead sleep in peace.

But in his mind's eye he could see Dougal's wide grin and cheerful face even now. Odd, he thought, how his carefree spirit had so brightly concealed a gradually uncoiling darkness—one that was just beginning to find expression along the sights of a rifle barrel.

THE SUMMER WOMAN

TENNESSEE WILLIAMS

Every summer it was much the same, coming down through the Alpine passes into the blistering long stretch of Italy toward Rome, the sky blanched with a fine white powder that rises from dry countries in prolonged heat, the yellowish-brown fields having a devoured look as though cropped clean by ravenous beasts. Here and there along the tracks were groups of peasants and workmen who accepted the passage of the "Grand Express" from Paris as interval from their labor. They lifted their hard, gentle faces into the white blaze mostly without expression or with the stunned look that is peculiar to the faces of mortally wounded men, shock cases about to expire. But these men were strong and not wounded. Their eyes, staring out of the white powder and scorched knobs of their faces, looked back into his, most of them, without any sign of hostility. That was the way it had been the five past summers. And yet this summer had, after all, an element of change, and it was in those faces along the tracks that the change was visible. They stared at the train as it shot past them, not with a look of resentment, not even wistfully, but with a very ancient and enormous knowledge, stared unblinkingly through a mist of white powder into the windows of the first-class carriages sweeping past them as the fortunate had always swept past them, for ages unnumbered, while they worked in that pulverous blaze of summer.

Yes, it had been like that every summer descending into the plains of Rome from the tall, white city of Genoa where the dry country started, but this summer, no, this summer was, after all, just a little bit different from the five others and it began to disturb him. He was a man easily disturbed by impression, a man with taut nerves and uneasy stomach, and it had seemed to him each summer that the hard, gentle faces of workmen along the tracks were each time just a little bit harder than the time before and a little less gentle. But this time was the first time that, now and then, from an occasional group, a voice was lifted at the passing coaches in a tone that could not be mistaken as friendly. Nobody shouted "Hi, Joe" as they occasionally did in the summer of '48 and '49 and even in '50. They shouted something else, and this thing was shouted several times before he heard it clearly. It was the curious word "*coco*." At first he thought it must be derived from America's national soft drink which was now being promoted vigorously in Europe. It wasn't until he saw it scrawled on the wall of a ruined building close to the tracks as the train pulled into Pisa that it finally dawned upon him what "coco" was. Why, of course, how stupid of him not to have guessed at once. It stood for the so-called *coccobacillus* that his countrymen were charged with having used as a weapon of war in Korea. Then he felt angry. He did not for a moment believe in the accusation. It angered him that these people were so willing to believe such a disgustingly false charge made by enemies of his nation. He sat back in his seat and refused any longer to look out the blazing white window. No, he wasn't angry so much as hurt, for he had loved these people. They had seemed to him somehow sweeter than people of any other country that he had been to, and he came here each summer as someone who has toiled hard in the sun comes into a place of cool shadow, a contradictory thing since this was a country whose summer was hot and glaring, and yet it was quite true, the summers he spent here always had the effect of a retreat into some place restfully cool and tranquil.

He stood up fussily and began to root in his suitcases. He was a short, stocky man; he couldn't quite reach the handle of the suitcase on the rack. He stood on tiptoe to reach it and still couldn't and then he climbed on the seat of his first-class compartment, and then he did reach it. He got hold of the handle of the suitcase on the rack and gave it a forward tug. At the same instant, the train, which had halted, lurched into motion and the suitcase came tumbling down squarely on his head, knocking him almost senseless. He stumbled dizzily to the floor rubbing his head and as he did so he became aware of laughter. A group of workers had been staring in the window at his efforts and had witnessed the mishap and now were laughing about it. The train was halted again, it had only lurched forward a couple of feet, and the workmen were still staring at him. The exertion and perhaps also the blows to cranium and dignity, at the same time, had made him quite breathless. He pushed his window all the way down and leaned out to get more air. Now he could see the group of men distinctly. They had stopped laughing. They were just grinning now, and after a moment he recognized the old, sweet kindliness in them, the gentle, friendly humor which made them always so lovable as a people. One of them, an old one, all white thatch and brown leather, rubbed his head sympathetically and said, "*Fa male?*" He smiled back at the old man and said, "*Non troppo*," and they all nodded to him encouragingly and continued to look into his eyes with simple and friendly interest, just a little amused, until the train began to pull out in earnest, then they all lifted their hands in farewell and a young one called, "So long, Joe!" He felt better. He took out of the suitcase the blank notebook he wanted, but let it rest on his knees, the pencil motionless in his hand, while he looked out the windows again, feeling better, less hurt and uneasy, but the train had not gone far outside the station when he saw again on the wall of the devastated building, of which that was the only wall left standing, the great white chalk inscription of "COCO," then a little farther, "Go Home, Yanks!"

No, he thought, it will not be so good this summer . . .

Nine months of the year, he was intensely occupied as the remarkably young head of the English department at an important southern university, and also at writing. He wrote learned treaties as well as occasional stories and verse, and in the late spring and early autumn he made lecture tours. None of this sort of activity and ambience was at all compatible with the Bohemian sort of existence that he really longed for, that his true nature wanted. He had it only in Europe in the two months of summer he spent there, July and August. There in Europe, mostly in Italy, he had his other life, the existence that his heart longed for, Bohemian, sensual, not at all academic, not in the least reserved. He had not found this other life through any powerful and vast genius for it. It had been handed to him by someone else, a Roman girl named Rosa. She had taken him by his cold, nervous fingers and led him into that country and made him quickly at home there. He had loved her for it, but not enough. He had not loved her for it enough to overlook or forget the fact that he had first met her on the street. That was in the summer of '48, his first summer in Rome. At the end of that summer, she had asked him to marry her. Such an idea had never entered his mind. For a few moments, to do him credit, he had thought it over, given it some moments of serious consideration. But, no, it would hardly do. She had beauty, she had grace, she had style and intelligence, but after all he had met her on the street and was that something that someone in his position could overlook? And so he had told her gently it wouldn't do. He had explained to her about the academic world, and she had said almost eagerly, *"Si, lo so, lo so!"* Romans understood those things even better, oh, in fact much better, than people of the new world understood them. They had understood them for thousands of years, yes, even thousands of years before they had been understood by people of the new world. But still she insisted: "Take me, take me with you!"

There was an arrangement. He didn't take her with him, but he sent her money to keep her off the street. Unfortunately, these remittances had a way of becoming irregular as the year progressed. In September and October and part of November they would reach her each week, then there would be lapses of two, then lapses of a month or two months, because each year, as the year progressed, his recollection of her and of Rome and of that world would dim out, until he almost thought, toward the end of spring, that all of that was now something he ought to gently forget, something wild and unsuitable, belonging to the afternoon of his youth, now too late for. Gone by!

But when summer came, after the close of school and the final lectures before clubs and societies of the big northern cities, then it would suddenly come back on him, incontinently, the longing to go back to her and back to Rome.

Each time he'd wonder if she would still receive him, or would she, now, at last, have hardened her heart against a lover who lost heat like a stone removed from the fireplace? Then wanted it all back again upon the same one-sided terms.

As the train dropped into the long Campana Romana, he felt himself lapsing into a very old anxiety, one that had plagued him since childhood, the fear of not being able to talk to people. He was a man who was keyed to a life of continual pressure, and when that pressure was gone, he was still keyed to it and he found it impossible for a good while to let himself relax into a state of repose. So he sat stiffly in his first-class compartment with that anxiety creeping up about him like a cold rising water. First it tightened his nerves, stiffening his whole body, then it began to sicken his stomach. He had a dry sensation in his mouth, as if a great wad of hot, dry cotton had been stuffed into that cavity and had swabbed out all of its moisture. He felt his tongue sticking to the roof of his mouth, and he thought to himself, *I will not be able to speak to anybody. I will not even be able to give the address to the driver of the cab. God, how awful!* He got up and opened the lustrous, red-varnished doors of the little lavatory in his compartment and he leaned over the basin thinking that he would vomit, but disappointingly, almost, it didn't happen and he sat back down again, sickeningly afraid and quite unable to do anything about it.

He picked up his notebook. He didn't remember writing anything in it, but now he saw something had been written in it in a large, scrawling hand that didn't resemble his own but obviously must be his. There were several words. There was the big silly word "COCO," and after that some sort of doodling nonsense, a sort of drawing of an idiot face with crossed eyes. Then, what was it? What was that long word? God, yes, it was Hiroshima! What did that mean? Did it mean that unconsciously he was wondering if they had *really* done it? Done what he had refused to believe they could do? After that: what else?

He picked the notebook up to see it more closely, and finally made out, from its uneven and closely voluted scrawl, the word "WAR." After "WAR," was an arrow, a long twisting arrow that ran down to the bottom of the page. He turned that page and on the next page was also the word "WAR," also followed by a long, spiral arrow that ran down to the bottom of the page. He turned another page and another page and still another, and on each page was the same great scrawling word to the very end of the notebook, and he had done this all the while his mouth was going dry and his tongue sticking to the roof of it and while he was thinking ostensibly only of whether or not he'd be able to speak to people.

God, how crazy can you get in summer!

No, it would be better, yes, perhaps it would be more sensible not even to leave the station but turn on his frightened heels and take the next train north, go back to Paris, away from this white sky quivering with heat and these lost people who had hoped for something and been disappointed again as always before. The girl? Rosa? When they met, what would he find to say, and would he be able to say it if he did think of something? His tongue would surely cleave to the roof of his mouth in that sick, dry way, he would have to drink a great deal to be able to touch her again, knowing how false he'd been to her. Each time she had not betrayed him. She had been faithful to what he had each time so unfairly expected. She had endured and waited: not gone back to the street . . .

This time when they met, if they did once again, it would not be a reunion. It would be two people helplessly facing together the death of something between them.

He reached Rome at four in the afternoon. She was not at the station to meet him although he had wired her, as usual, that he was coming. He had his old apartment, the one he had every summer: two large thick-walled rooms that kept the heat out all day and breathed in coolness at night, good rooms to work in and also to rest in, especially to rest in as he came to Italy every summer feeling tired, for America was the country of effort and exhaustion and for him Italy was a land of retreat and rest.

But she was not waiting for him at the apartment and there was no definite word of her there. The woman who kept the apartment, Mariella, greeted him with her usual slightly mechanical but nevertheless warm-hearted effusiveness, shouting his name as he got out of the cab, running to open the two pairs of doors for him, and he was embarrassed as usual, and stiff and awkward as he always was, asking the same polite, indifferent questions: How is your mother? Is her eyesight better? How is the water-heater, does it work? Do you have any ice? I want a drink. Yes, I am tired, very tired. No, I haven't lost weight but my face is thinner. Are there many tourists? *Multi Americani? Come siempre?*

(His Italian, even after five summers, was disgracefully bad, almost no conjugation of verbs.)

At last he asked Mariella: *"Avete vista Rosa?"*

Not in a long time, she told him.

He felt that she was lying.

"Is she in Rome?" he asked.

"Non so, non so . . ."

Usually he was glad to be done with Mariella, but this time he urged her to stay and have a drink with him. After a measured interval he turned the difficult talk back to Rosa, and this time Mariella admitted that she had seen her, oh, maybe two weeks ago, coming out of the Excelsior hotel one night.

"Solo?"

No, not alone. She was with some American tourists.

"Men?"

Mariella jerked her head in the slightest of nods.

They sat together for a few moments as stiff as a pair of shop-window dummies, and then, without looking at his landlady, he asked her the dreaded question:

"Has she gone back to *la vita*?"

La vita was the popular euphemism for working the street.

Suddenly Mariella gave up her evasive tactics and looked at him directly and he was astonished to see in her face the eyes of those scorched workmen along the tracks, passionless and yet burning.

"Forget her, Signor Roberto. In this country they don't escape from the street."

He didn't sleep that night, although as usual the walls breathed in a coolness after midnight. In the early morning, while he was lying sleepless, about to get up and close the shutters against the beginning of light, he heard a voice calling him at the gates of the building. The voice was hardly louder than waking bird-voices. He did not even stop to put on trousers or slippers, he rushed in his shorts to open the two pairs of doors to let her in. She stood waiting, short and dark, by the outer gates. There was no cry of greeting, no words at all between them. He let her in the iron gates and then stood back till she passed silently in front of him through the great wooden doors. He couldn't see well, for he hadn't put on his glasses. Perhaps she didn't even glance at him as she stalked before him into the building. He was trembling. His tongue was sticking to the roof of his mouth, he muttered a few senseless things, and the little that she said in response was said so quickly, so hoarsely, that he could not understand it. She took her clothes off roughly and flung them at a chair the way that a boy undresses. He stood so stiffly. His body seemed to be made of unjointed metal. He picked up his glasses but didn't put them on and he held them in his fist so tightly that he heard them crack like a nutshell.

"Shall I close the shutters?" she asked.

"*Si, prega*," he muttered.

She closed the shutters but didn't move toward the bed.

Then she spoke.

"Roberto," she whispered, "I have gone back to *la vita*."

He reached out and fumbled for her in the pitch darkness until he had found her motionless, moist body, so unbelievably warm and yielding to his hands and arms, giving itself so completely to the year's starvation that he had brought back with him to this summer country.

This time, he whispered, "Come back to America with me. *Questa volta*, please, *partiremo insieme*?"

THE GREAT MAN

JAMES S. DORR

"You have come from the execution, Monsieur?" a voice next to me asked.

"Eh, what?" I said, turning to gaze at an elderly man who had just sat beside me at the long table, a *pensionnaire* by the still soldierly look to his clothing.

"The guillotining, my friend," he said. "The man who, this morning, 'kissed the Widow'—you went to see it?"

I shook my head, no. I had in fact been at pains to avoid it, no lover of capital punishment I, though I had seen the stark silhouette of the two upright poles—the gleam of dawn on the triangle between them—when I had hurried past the crowded town square that morning. I hastened to explain that it was business which had brought me from England to this small town in the south of France and that it was no more than the thirst of my journey that had brought me here to this dimly-lit cafe for a quick glass of wine, adding only that at least the poor wretch on the scaffold had felt no pain.

"Ah," the old man said. "Yes, that is the theory. When Dr. Guillotine first proposed it to the Assembly in autumn of 1789, soon after the storming of *la Bastille*, his hope was that the blade would be so swift its victim would have no time to suffer. When Dr. Louis designed the first model it had a curved blade, you know—more like that of an axe-head—and it was constructed by a German, Tobias Schmidt. Yet even then there were some who doubted, who said that the knife's quick descent would only suppress the *shock* of the cutting, while the trunk and head would both live on for some moments. You know the story of Charlotte Corday?"

I nodded. I knew, at least, who she had been. "The one who killed Marat?"

The old man nodded. "The murderess of Jean-Paul Marat, yes. I was there when she was executed on 17 July, 1793, only just old enough at the time to be one of the soldiers who stood guard below *la machine fatale*. A very young man, you see, not as I am now." He shook his head ruefully. He'd moved his left arm and I saw, for the first time, that his coat-sleeve hung empty from a point just below the elbow.

He smiled. "Not like now." He raised his arm higher to make sure I saw it, even as he went on. "Not yet with the 'souvenir' your Viscount Wellington left me with in Spain—in 1813, outside of Vitoria. Although, it may have saved my life later on, this old wound. I was a corporal then, and the lieutenant who had commanded us in Paris in '93 had become a captain—Captain Sarbeau—who I'll speak more of later. Yes, there was pain enough with this wound—when that best portion of my arm departed my body, and there was nothing of its surviving after *its* 'good-bye.' But I spoke of Corday . . ."

"Yes," I said, finding myself fascinated by what he was saying, despite what I felt was my better judgment. I called to the *serveuse* to bring us a bottle as I bade the old man go on.

"One of the assistants to the executioner Charles-Henri

Sanson, was a carpenter named Le Gros (who was at the time, of Marat's faction). After the blade fell—it falls with a double crash, you know, the second being the sound of it bouncing back up from the hole the neck had been thrust through—it was he who held Corday's head up, gripping her hair in the fingers of his left hand, for everyone in the crowd to see. But still not content, his anger was so great, he opened the fingers of his other hand and slapped her in the face. Hard, with a 'crack'!

"And everyone saw it. Even I saw it. The blood rushed to the cheek—to both of her cheeks, Monsieur—turning them crimson even as her features twisted into a scowl, such was the indignity she was still able to feel at such treatment! And, as for Le Gros, he was punished for this, for showing disrespect for the dead no matter how or why she came to be that way. But do you know what he said in his defense? That she had not been dead. That death does not come so soon. That even certain doctors have claimed it, among them the learned Pierre Gautier, as early as 1767—before the guillotine's time. That a head might live on, maintaining consciousness for as long as fifteen more seconds, provided blood still flows through the brain."

"Well, yes," I said, "but you do say yourself that that's only opinion, no matter how learned the doctors who've held it. As for the grimace you say people saw, well that could be put down to the excitement of the crowd, could it not? People do fool themselves, thinking they've seen things they haven't really. And as for the crimson you saw on her cheeks, it could have just been blood from this Le Gros's fingers, which I dare say must have been stained with plenty."

The old man nodded. "Yes, it could have been that," he agreed, "or just superstition. Do you know that in the years right after, during the time of the Directory, there were priests who wandered the countryside with thin red lines painted around their necks, claiming that they, too, were the guillotine's victims? They did this in support of the Royalist cause, to show that, through God's grace, they had been resurrected. And many believed it. You see, we were all naive in those days.

"But after Napoleon came home from Egypt to become First Consul and order returned to France, well, it has been science since then. Science, with experiments that can be proven. That's the answer these days, eh? Tell me, my friend, have you heard of Lavoisier?"

Once more I nodded. I was no scientist, but I did know of Antoine Lavoisier, claimed by some to be the inventor of modern chemistry. "It was he, was it not," I replied, "who disproved the phlogiston theory—that there is some substance within combustible matter that disappears from it when it is set afire? Was it not he who—with our own English scientist Priestley, of course—showed that, instead, something is added to things when they are burned, namely oxygen? As I recall, he arrived at this theory by studying the behavior of animals in various mixtures of air, showing the heat their bodies produced to be similar to that of fire."

"Yes," the old man said. "He had his own theory, that there is an element of heat—he called it 'caloric'—that, when added (with air) to any material, will cause that material to burn, whether rapidly as in flame, or more slowly as in rusting or decay. Or, as you say, in the motion of life itself. What I wish to tell you will touch again upon this theory and prove that which you seem not yet ready to accept. But, for now, you know, do you not, that Lavoisier, as well, was a victim of *Sainte Guillotine*? That less than a year after Charlotte Corday, he, too, mounted the scaffold?"

"An abomination," I said. "Yes, I knew that. That such a man should be killed . . ."

"Yes, an abomination indeed, though there were what people then considered to be good reasons. But, as I say, we were all mad then—in our ways—naive and easily diverted from the truth.

Lavoisier, though, was one who sought truth. As was another I shall mention shortly, a great man, too, in his way, one who was, some say, Lavoisier's student, who in time became a general who died at Waterloo, and whose body was never recovered. One who, some say, still lives—which is why I shall not mention his name to you, lest he still uses it, though it is more likely he would have changed it.

"But, as for Lavoisier," he continued, finally getting back to what he had been saying, "did you know that he, when he knew he had no hope of preventing his execution, proposed an experiment? By then, Lieutenant Sarbeau and I had been mustered to war, to aid in retaking Belgium and Holland from the alliance—including your Britain—that had earlier in 1793 risen against us. Therefore, I did not witness what I am about to relate. But I did hear of it.

"This is what Lavoisier proposed—that as soon as the blade fell, he would begin blinking. He would blink his eyes as many times as he could—even as his head was lifted to show the crowd—while one of Sanson's assistants would count the blinks. The assistant was bribed, yes, to carry out his part, but—and this I know well—there was no reason to doubt his honesty. And what he reported afterward was that the severed head of Lavoisier blinked no less than eleven times."

The old man paused then while I called for more wine. "This is still no more than hearsay," I protested, yet, as I say, I found I could not suppress a desire to hear more of this *pensionnaire*'s gruesome theory. And so I prompted, "But, if you have more proof . . ."

The old man nodded. "Yes," he said. "You know those were troubled times for France, and many things went on behind the scenes. Many machinations, some of which affected us in the army. In September 1795, the Directory was formed to replace the Committee of Public Safety, and so we marched back to Paris under a new command—that of Napoleon—to assure the fairness of the new elections. Then we went back to war, this time in Egypt.

However, our commander, having heard that chaos had once more taken over in France, was forced to return to become First Consul. And still later, Emperor.

"And as for us . . . Lieutenant Sarbeau, like I young and hale, became a captain and I, who had had some education, later received my own rating and a post as adjutant to Sarbeau. Thus, together we fought under the Emperor—first at Naples, then Saxony, then in the invasion of Portugal and, finally, the grinding series of battles later called the Peninsular War . . ."

"Where you met Wellington," I interrupted, "who you would meet again."

"Yes," the old man said. "Where we fought your Arthur Wellesley, still just Viscount Wellington then, and where, in time, I lost my arm, thus precluding me from meeting him again. As for Captain Sarbeau, well, while what I have to say of him ends before Waterloo, I will leave you to draw your own conclusions."

The old man paused then, sipping his wine slowly. Finally he went on. "Now the time comes to tell you of the man I will not name—I'll simply call him the 'Great Man.' He was not then of the army, nor a politician, nor of the nobility either, I think, yet behind the scenes, as we were to discover, he wielded much power. He knew Napoleon, that much is sure, and may well have been one who had a hand in that man's rise to power.

"Be that as it may, it was after I lost my arm in the Peninsular War—and after France had been driven from Spain—that I and my captain went to a village not far from here, I to recuperate from my wound, and Sarbeau because there was no other place to send him. France had fallen. The Emperor had been defeated in Russia. Paris was occupied, Louis XVIII had been placed on the throne, and the Emperor had been exiled to Elba.

"And yet there were rumors. Rumors flew in all directions that January of 1815, some that the Great Man himself had been killed—perhaps as early as twenty years before—some that the

Emperor had plans to rise once again. And it was during this time of chaos that we indeed met the Great Man.

"It was January as I say, nearly the end of the month, when Captain Sarbeau and I received a summons to present ourselves at a certain château, one that had been abandoned, or so we thought, since the earlier chaos of the Directory. Even for the south it was cold, with ice in the rivers, so we bundled ourselves in our winter clothing and rode that night to where we had been told, and presented ourselves as requested. At the gate we were met by servants with torches—as if we were still in the days of the *ancien régime*—and helped with our outer coats, then ushered into a room so heated that even had we been clothed in our summer uniforms from Spain we still would have felt some amount of discomfort.

"And then we were left there, alone, in a room filled with apparatuses of all description—great casks and boilers and a steam engine of some kind, retorts and pipes from which one could hear bubbling noises. And, sitting before us in a huge throne-like chair, covered from chin to toe with a thick blanket, was a figure we both recognized as the Great Man.

"We didn't know what to do. First the captain, then I, saluted, although, as I said, the Great Man was no soldier—at least to our knowledge. Nor did he return the salutes we offered but simply bade us, in a harsh rasping voice, to turn around several times, and then to remove our jackets and waistcoats and stand at ease. We stood there—I, with my one arm, and Captain Sarbeau, who was built like an ox then—in our shirtsleeves and breeches while he explained why he had summoned us.

"And then he spoke to us of *la guillotine*."

I must have looked puzzled then, because the old man paused. "Yes," he finally went on, "as I said, my tale will prove what I maintained before. Oh, the Great Man spoke of other things too, of France, of the Emperor, and of how the rumors one heard were correct—that the Emperor and others, with the Great Man manipulating affairs behind the scenes, planned an escape from the prison of Elba in scarcely more than a month's time. But always he returned to that other rumor—that he had been executed himself during the confusion that swept the countryside at the time the Directory had ruled. He had fled Paris by then—you see, there were factions against him—to the southern part of France, anticipating his own guillotining were he to stay longer. And yet, even here . . .

"Well, he told us that even here he took precautions. He had studied the theories of Lavoisier and, having money, had bought the château in which we were standing, and started the rumor that it was deserted. He had brought in apparatuses—some of which we saw now—secretly at night. He had hired assistants, bribing them for their silence, and had bribed officials too—including the town's executioners. Or so he told us.

"You see, we were skeptics. Oh, we had seen Charlotte Corday with our own eyes, and heard of Lavoisier's proof as well—of the instant of life that still remained after one had been beheaded—but to carry it as far as he planned to, well, we were convinced that what he then told us could not have been true. We thought that perhaps his reversals of fortune had driven him mad. The Great Man did not begrudge us our whisperings during his pauses in the conversation. In fact there were many gaps of several minutes or more while the pipes behind him bubbled and others hissed softly, as if he must catch his breath before he went on.

"But he did go on, telling of how the baskets into which the heads fell were later found with their bottoms chewed, by the gnashings of the victims' teeth. And he told of other theories, of Gautier's and others later, including that of the German anatomist Sommering, who theorized that if only some artificial lung could be attached quickly enough to it, the guillotined head would even speak of how it endured. And that of our own country's Dr. Jean-Joseph Sue that the body, too—its limbs and organs—must still feel sensation, at least for an instant.

"And after *that instant*, well, then it came back to Lavoisier—the Great Man told us—and to his theory of caloric, the element of heat which maintained life, but also, when life ceased, engendered decay. And so the Great Man began to take precautions. He had, as I said, bribed the town's executioners so that, at last, when the moment he had so feared had come upon him, when he took the walk up the steps of the scaffold, his hands bound behind him, when he felt his body lashed to the trestle, his head thrust through the hole—'*mounting Madame*,' as we called it in those days—he looked down to see not the red-painted wicker basket sprinkled with bran to soak up the gore, as would have been usual, but an apparatus of his own devising. It was a bucket already filled to the brim with fresh blood—never mind where it came from—to keep his brain nourished. The bucket in turn was placed within a barrel of ice and salt to draw the caloric out from his severed head and cool it until it was nearly frozen, thus slowing the process of death itself until the head could be returned to the château where another apparatus was waiting.

"Then, once more, he paused to take more breath while Captain Sarbeau and I whispered between ourselves that even if such a thing could be, surely it would drive one insane. Imagine the horror—even if one has assured one's survival—of having one's head *cut off*! And knowing when it was—feeling its separation from one's body. Feeling so helpless, knowing your body was dying while you still lived . . .

"That's when the blanket slipped, and we felt powerful hands laid upon us—those of the Great Man's silently returning servants—holding us immobile as we saw, not a body appear as the cloth fell, but rather a framework of tubing and uprights supporting a collar that held the head in place. And, as I say, from the head we saw pipes, some branching off to a steam-powered pump to force fresh air through the artificial lung of Sommering providing not just speech but oxygenation! Others to huge flasks of thick, red liquids—again from we knew not where—still others to the chamber's four walls, tapping the chimneys above its fireplaces to draw in caloric to keep the brain heated to the level at which living blood would have kept it. Inward, outward, fresh air, stale air, fresh blood, and spent blood continually cycling for these nearly twenty years while all around it nations were tumbling, battles were being won and lost, empires were rising and falling. And then, again, rising.

"The Great Man called a halt to our whispered babbling while, within that grim head, his eyes rolled and swept about in their sockets, measuring us one last time as we stood there. Then as other servants wheeled in a great tub packed with ice and salt—the size of a coffin—I saw out the window as the sun rose the shadow of a guillotine in the courtyard. With a scowl the Great Man signaled for my dismissal, as I was not needed. I would be free to go, anywhere that I wished. No one, you understand, had I related at that time what I had seen there, would have believed me.

"But, as for my captain, I saw—as the servants were ushering me from that dreadful chamber—the Great Man's gaze once again come to rest on his tall, strong form. I saw the Great Man smile then for the first time—a ghastly, mad smile—as he spoke again of his plans for Napoléon's reinstatement, adding only this: that if he were now to aid France and her Emperor to the fullest, the time had come when he would require a body."

RUMPOLE AND THE OLD FAMILIAR FACES

JOHN MORTIMER

In the varied ups and downs, the thrills and spills in the life of an Old Bailey hack, one thing stands as stone. Your ex-customers will never want to see you again. Even if you've steered them through the rocks of the prosecution case and brought them out to the calm waters of a not guilty verdict, they won't plan further meetings, host reunion dinners, or even send you a card on your birthday. If they catch a glimpse of you on the Underground, or across a crowded wine bar, they will bury their faces in their newspapers or look studiously in the opposite direction. This is understandable. Days in Court probably represent a period of time they'd rather forget and, as a rule, I'm not especially keen to renew an old acquaintance when a face I once saw in the Old Bailey dock reappears at a "Scales of Justice" dinner or at the Inns of Court garden party. Reminiscences of the past are best avoided, and what is required is a quick look and a quiet turn away. There have been times, however, when recognizing a face seen in trouble has greatly assisted me in the solution of some legal problem and carried me to triumph in a difficult case. Such occasions have been rare but, like number thirteen buses, two of them turned up in short order round a Christmas which I remember as being one of the oddest, but certainly the most rewarding, I ever spent.

"A traditional British pantomime. There's nothing to beat it!"

"You go to the pantomime, Rumpole?" Claude asked with unexpected interest.

"I did when I was a boy. It made a lasting impression on me."

"Pantomime?" The American judge who was our fellow guest round the Erskine-Brown dinner table was clearly a stranger to such delights. "Is that some kind of mime show? Lots of feeling imaginary walls and no one saying anything?"

"Not at all. You take some good old story, like *Robin Hood* . . ."

"Robin Hood's the star?"

"Well, yes. He's played by some strapping girl who slaps her thighs and says lines like 'Cheer up, Babes in the Wood, Robin's not far away.'"

"You mean there's cross-dressing?" The American visitor was puzzled.

"Well, if you want to call it that. And Robin's mother is played by a red-nosed comic."

"A female comic?"

"No. A male one."

"That sounds interesting," he said in a tone that suggested he had the wrong idea. "We have clubs for that sort of thing in Pittsburgh."

"It's not what you're thinking," I assured him. "The Dame's a comic character who gets the audience singing."

"Singing?"

"The words come down on a sort of giant song sheet," I explained, "and she, who is really a he, gets the audience to sing along."

Emboldened by Erskine-Brown's claret (smoother on the tongue but with less of a kick than Château Thames Embankment), I broke into a stanza of the song I was introduced to by Robin Hood's masculine mother.

"I may be just a nipper,
But I've always loved a kipper . . .
And so does my loving wife.
If you've got a girl, just slip her
A loving golden kipper
And she'll be yours for life."

"Is that all?" The transatlantic judge still seemed puzzled.

"All I can remember."

"I think you're wrong, Mr. Rumpole."

"What?"

"I think you're wrong and those lines do indeed have some significance along the lines I suggested." And the Judge fell silent, contemplating the unusual acts suggested.

"I see they're doing *Aladdin* at the Tufnell Park Empire. Do you think the twins might enjoy it, Rumpole?"

The speaker was Mrs. Justice Erskine-Brown (Phillida Trant as she was in happier days when I called her the Portia of our Chambers), still possessed of a beauty that would break the hearts of the toughest prosecutors and make old lags swoon with lust even as she passed a stiff custodial sentence. The twins she spoke of were Tristan and Isolde, so named by her opera-loving husband Claude, who was now bending Hilda's ear on the subject of Covent Garden's latest *Ring* cycle.

"I think the twins would adore it. Just the thing to cure the Wagnerian death-wish and bring them into a world of sanity."

"Sanity?" The visiting judge sounded doubtful. "With old guys dressed up as mothers?"

"I promise you, they'll love every minute of it." And then I made another promise that sounded rash even as I spoke the words. "I know I would. I'll take them myself."

"Thank you, Rumpole." Phillida spoke in her gentlest judicial voice, but I knew my fate was sealed. "We'll keep you to that."

"It'll have to be after Christmas," Hilda said. "We've been invited up to Norfolk for the holiday."

As she said the word "Norfolk" a cold, sweeping wind seemed to cut through the central heating of the Erskine-Browns' Islington dining room and I felt a warning shiver.

I have no rooted objection to Christmas Day, but I must say it's an occasion when time tends to hang particularly heavily on the hands. From the early morning alarm call of carols piping on Radio Four to the closing headlines and a restless, liverish sleep, the day can seem as long as a fraud on the post office tried before Mr. Injustice Graves.

It takes less than no time for me to unwrap the tie which I will seldom wear, and for Hilda to receive the annual bottle of lavender water which she lays down rather than puts to immediate use. The highlights after that are the Queen's speech, when I lay bets with myself as to whether Hilda will stand to attention when the television plays the National Anthem, and the thawed-out Safeway bird followed by port (an annual gift from my faithful solicitor Bonny Bernard) and pudding. I suppose what I have against Christmas Day is that the Courts are all shut and no one is being tried for anything.

That Christmas, Hilda had decided on a complete change of routine. She announced it in a circuitous fashion by saying, one late November evening, "I was at school with Poppy Longstaff."

"What's that got to do with it?" I knew the answer to this question, of course. Hilda's old school has this in common with polar expeditions, natural disasters, and the last war; those who have lived through it are bound together for life and can always call on each other for mutual assistance.

"Poppy's Eric is Rector of Coldsands. And for some reason or other he seems to want to meet you, Rumpole."

"Meet me?"

"That's what she said."

"So does that mean I have to spend Christmas in the Arctic Circle and miss our festivities?"

"It's not the Arctic Circle. It's Norfolk, Rumpole. And our festivities aren't all that festive. So, yes. You have to go." It was a judgement for which there was no possible appeal.

My first impression of Coldsands was a gaunt church tower, presumably of great age, pointing an accusing finger to heaven from a cluster of houses on the edge of a sullen, gunmetal sea. My second was one of intense cold. As soon as we got out of the taxi, we were slapped around the face by a wind which must have started in freezing Siberia and gained nothing in the way of warmth on its journey across the plains of Europe.

"*In the bleak mid-winter / Frosty wind made moan* . . ." wrote that sad old darling, Christina Rossetti. Frosty winds made considerable moan round the rectory at Coldsands, owing to the doors that stopped about an inch short of the stone floors and the windows which never shut properly, causing the curtains to billow like the sails of a ship at sea.

We were greeted cheerfully by Poppy. Hilda's friend had one of those round, childishly pretty faces often seen on seriously fat women. She seemed to keep going on incessant cups of hot, sweet tea and a number of cardigans. If she moved like an enormous tent, her husband Eric was a slender wraith of a man with a high aquiline nose, two flapping wings of grey hair on each side of his face, and a vague air of perpetual anxiety broken, now and then, by high and unexpected laughter. He made cruciform gestures, as though remembering the rubric "spectacles, testicles, wallet, and watch" and forgetting where these important articles were kept.

"Eric," his wife explained, "is having terrible trouble with the church tower."

"Oh dear." Hilda shot me a look of stern disapproval, which I knew meant that it would be more polite if I abandoned my overcoat while tea was being served. "How worrying for you, Eric."

The Rev. Eric went into a long, excited, and high-pitched speech. The gist of it was that the tower, although of rare beauty, had not been much restored since the Saxons built it and the Normans added the finishing touches. Fifty thousand pounds was needed for essential repairs, and the thermometer, erected outside the church for the appeal, was stuck at one hundred and twenty pounds—the proceeds from an emergency jumble sale.

"You particularly wanted Horace to come this Christmas?" Hilda asked the Man of God with the air of someone anxious to solve a baffling mystery. "I wonder why that was?"

"Yes. I wonder!" Eric looked startled. "I wonder why on earth I wanted to ask Horace. I don't believe he's got fifty thousand smackers in his back pocket!" At this, he shook with laughter.

"There," I told him, "your lack of faith is entirely justified." I wasn't exactly enjoying Coldsands Rectory, so I was a little miffed that the Reverend couldn't remember why he'd asked me there in the first place.

"We had hoped that Donald Compton would help us out," Poppy told us. "I mean, he wouldn't notice fifty thousand. But he took exception to what Eric said at the Remembrance Day service."

"Armistice Day in the village." Eric's grey wings of hair trembled as he nodded in delighted affirmation. "And I prayed for dead German soldiers. It seemed only fair."

"Fair perhaps, darling. But hardly tactful," his wife told him. "Donald Compton thought it was distinctly unpatriotic. He's bought the Old Manor House," she explained to Hilda. From then on the conversation turned exclusively to this Compton and was carried on in the tones of awe and muted wonder with which people always talk about the very rich. Compton, it seemed, after a difficult start in England, had gone to Canada where, during a ten-year stay, he had laid the foundations of his fortune. His much younger wife was quite charming, probably Canadian, and not in the least standoffish. He had built the village hall, the cricket pavilion, and a tennis court for the school. Only Eric's unfortunate sympathy for the German dead had caused Compton's bounty to stop short at the church tower.

"I've done hours of hard knee-work," the rector told us, "begging the Lord to soften Mr. Compton's heart towards our tower. No result so far, I fear."

Apart from this one lapse, the charming Donald Compton seemed to be the perfect English squire and country gent. I would see him in church on Christmas morning, and we had also been invited for drinks before lunch at the manor. The Reverend Eric and the smiling Poppy made it sound as though the Pope and the Archbishop of Canterbury would be out with the carol singers and we'd been invited to drop in for high tea at Windsor Castle. I prayed for a Yule log blazing at the manor so that I could, in the true spirit of Christmas, thaw out gradually.

"Now, as a sign of Christmas fellowship, will you all stand and shake hands with those in front of and behind you?" Eric, in full canonicals, standing on the steps in front of the altar, made this suggestion as though he had just thought of the idea. I stood reluctantly. I had found myself a place in the church near a huge, friendly, gently humming, occasionally belching radiator and I was clinging to it and stroking it as though it were a newfound mistress (not that I have much experience of new- or even old-found mistresses). The man who turned to me from the front row seemed to be equally reluctant. He was, as Hilda had pointed out excitedly, the great Donald Compton in person—a man of middle height with silver hair, dressed in a tweed suit, and with a tan which it must have been expensive to preserve during winter. He had soft brown eyes which looked almost at once away from me as, with a touch of dry fingers, he was gone and I was left, for the rest of the service, with no more than a well tailored back and the sound of an uncertain tenor voice joining in the hymns.

I turned to the row behind to shake hands with an elderly woman who had madness in her eyes and whispered conspiratorially to me, "You cold, dear? Like to borrow my gloves? We're used to a bit of chill weather round these parts." I declined politely and went back to hugging the radiator, and as I did so a sort of happiness stole over me. To start with, the church was beautiful, with a high timbered roof and walls of weathered stone, peppered with marble tributes to dead inhabitants of the manor. It was decorated with holly and mistletoe. A tree glowed and there were candles over a crib. I thought how many generations of Coldsands villagers, their eyes bright and faces flushed with the wind, had belted out these hymns. I also thought how depressed the great Donald Compton—who had put on little gold half-glasses to read the prophecy from Isaiah: "For unto us a child is born, unto us a son is given: and the government shall be upon his shoulder: and his name shall be called Wonderful"—would feel if Jesus's instruction to sell all and give it to the poor should ever be taken literally.

And then I wondered why it was that, as he had touched my fingers and turned away, I had felt that I had lived through that precise moment before.

There was, as it turned out, a huge log fire crackling at the manor, throwing a dancing light on the marble floor of the circular entrance hall with its great staircase leading up into private shadows. The cream of Coldsands was being entertained with champagne and *canapés* by the new Lord of the Manor. The decibels rose as the champagne went down and the little group began to sound like an army of tourists in the Sistine Chapel—noisy, excited, and wonderstruck.

"They must all be his ancestors." Hilda was looking at the pictures on the walls and, in particular, at a general in a scarlet coat, on a horse prancing at the front of some distant battle.

My mouth was full of cream cheese enveloped in smoked salmon. I swallowed it and said, "Oh, I shouldn't think so. After all, he only bought the house recently."

"But I expect he brought his family portraits here from somewhere else."

"You mean, he had them under the bed in his old bachelor flat in Wimbledon and now he's hung them round an acre or two of walls?"

"Do try and be serious, Rumpole. You're not nearly as funny as you think you are. Just look at the family resemblance. I'm absolutely certain that all of these are old Comptons." And it was when she said this that I remembered everything perfectly clearly.

He was with his wife. She was wearing a black velvet dress and had long, golden hair that sparkled in the firelight. They were talking to a bald, pink-faced man and his short and overdressed wife, and they were all laughing. Compton's laughter stopped as he saw me coming towards him. He said, "I don't think we've met."

"Yes," I replied. "We shook hands briefly in church this morning. But didn't we meet somewhere else? My name's Rumpole. I'm staying with the Longstaffs."

"Good old Eric! We have our differences, of course, but he's a saintly man. This is my wife Lorelei, and Colonel and Maudy Jacobs. I expect you'd like to see the library, wouldn't you, Rumpole? I'm sure you're interested in ancient history. Will you all excuse us?"

It was two words from Hilda that had done it—"old" and "Compton." I knew then what I should have remembered when we had touched hands in the pews, that Old Compton is a street in Soho, and that this was perhaps why Riccardo (known as Dicko) Perducci had adopted the name. I had received that very same handshake—a slight touch and a quick turn away—when I had said good-bye to him in the cells under the Old Bailey and left him to start seven years for blackmail. The trial had ended, I now remembered, just before a long-distant Christmas.

The Perducci territory had been, in those days, not rolling Norfolk acres but a number of Soho strip clubs and clip joints. Girls would stand in front of these last-named resorts and lure the lonely, the desperate, and the unwary in. Sometimes they would escape after paying twenty pounds for a watery cocktail. Unlucky, affluent, and important customers might get even more, carefully recorded by microphones and cameras to produce material which was used for systematic and highly profitable blackmail. The victim in Dicko's case was an obscure and not much loved Circuit Judge, so it was regarded as particularly serious by the prosecuting authority.

When I mitigated for Dicko, I stressed the lack of direct evidence against him. He was a shadowy figure who kept himself well in the background and was known as a legend rather than a familiar face round Soho. "That only shows what a big wheel he is," Judge Bullingham, who was unfortunately trying the case, bellowed unsympathetically. In desperation I tried the Christmas approach on him. "Crimes forgiven, sins remitted, mercy triumphant, such was the message of the story that began in Bethlehem," I told the Court, at which the Mad Bull snorted that, as far as he could remember, that story had ended in a criminal trial and a stiff sentence for at least one thief.

"I suppose something like this was going to happen sooner or later." We were standing in the library in front of a comforting fire, among leather-bound books which I strongly suspected had been bought by the yard. The new, like the old, Dicko was soft-eyed, quietly spoken, almost unnaturally calm—the perfect man behind the scenes of a blackmailing operation or a country estate.

"Not necessarily," I told him. "It's just that my wife has many old school friends and Poppy Longstaff is one of them. Well now, you seem to have done pretty well for yourself. Solid citizens still misconducting themselves round Old Compton Street, are they?"

"I wouldn't know. I gave all that up and went into the property business."

"Really? Where did you do that? Canada?"

"I never saw Canada." He shook his head. "Garwick Prison. Up-and-coming area in the Home Counties. The screws there were ready and willing to do the deals on the outside. I paid them embarrassingly small commissions."

"How long were you there?"

"Four years. By the time I came out I'd got my first million."

"Well, then I did you a good turn, losing your case. A bit of luck His Honour Judge Bullingham didn't believe in the remission of sins."

"You think I got what I deserved?"

I stretched my hands to the fire. I could hear the cocktail chatter from the marble hall of the eighteenth-century manor. "Use every man after his desert, and who shall 'scape whipping?" I quoted *Hamlet* at him.

"Then I can trust you, Rumpole? The Lord Chancellor's going to put me on the local Bench."

"The Lord Chancellor lives in a world of his own."

"You don't think I'd do well as a magistrate?"

"I suppose you'd speak from personal experience of crime. And have some respect for the quality of mercy."

"I've got no time for that, Rumpole." His voice became quieter but harder. The brown eyes lost their softness. That, I thought, was how he must have looked when one of his clip joint girls was caught with the punters' cash stuffed in her tights. "It's about time we cracked down on crime. Well now, I can trust you not to go out there and spread the word about the last time we met?"

"That depends."

"On what?"

"How well you have understood the Christmas message."

"Which is?"

"Perhaps, generosity."

"I see. So you want your bung?"

"Oh, not me, Dicko. I've been paid, inadequately, by Legal Aid. But there's an impoverished church tower in urgent need of resuscitation."

"That Eric Longstaff, our rector—he's not a patriot!"

"And are you?"

"I do a good deal of work locally for the British Legion."

"And I'm sure, next Poppy Day, they'll appreciate what you've done for the church tower."

He looked at me for a long minute in silence, and I thought that if this scene had been taking place in a back room in Soho there might, quite soon, have been the flash of a knife. Instead, his hand went to an inside pocket and produced nothing more lethal than a chequebook.

"While you're in a giving mood," I said, "the rectory's in desperate need of central heating."

"This is bloody blackmail!" Dicko Perducci, now known as Donald Compton, said.

"Well," I told him, "you should know."

Christmas was over. The year turned, stirred itself, and opened its eyes on a bleak January. Crimes were committed, arrests were made, and the courtrooms were filled, once again, with the sounds of argument. I went down to the Old Bailey on a trifling matter of fixing the date of a trial before Mrs. Justice Erskine-Brown. As I was leaving, the usher came and told me that the judge wanted to see me in her private room on a matter of urgency.

Such summonses always fill me with apprehension and a vague feeling of guilt. What had I done? Got the date of the trial hopelessly muddled? Addressed the Court with my trousers carelessly unzipped? I was relieved when the learned Phillida greeted me warmly and even offered me a glass of sherry, poured from her own personal decanter. "It was so kind of you to offer, Rumpole," she said unexpectedly.

"Offer what?" I was puzzled.

"You told us how much you adored the traditional British pantomime."

"So I did." For a happy moment I imagined Her Ladyship as Principal Boy, her shapely legs encased in black tights, her neat little wig slightly askew, slapping her thigh and calling out, in bell-like tones, 'Cheer up, Rumpole, Portia's not far away.'"

"The twins are looking forward to it enormously."

"Looking forward to what?"

"*Aladdin* at the Tufnell Park Empire. I've got tickets for the nineteenth of January. You do remember promising to take them, don't you?"

"Well, of course." What else might I have said after the fifth glass of Erskine-Brown Saint-Émilion? "I'd love to be of the party. And will old Claude be buying us a dinner afterwards?"

"I really don't think you should go round calling people 'old,' Rumpole." Phillida now looked miffed, and I downed the sherry before she took it into her head to deprive me of it. "Claude's got us tickets for Pavarotti—*L'Elisir d'Amore*. You might buy the children a burger after the show. Oh, and it's not far from us on the Tube. It really was sweet of you to invite them." At which she smiled at me and refilled my glass in a way which made it clear she was not prepared to hear further argument.

It all turned out better than I could have hoped. Tristan and Isolde, unlike their Wagnerian namesakes, were cheerful, reasonably polite, and only seemed anxious to disassociate themselves, as far as possible, from the old fart who was escorting them. At every available opportunity they would touch me for cash and then scamper off to buy ice cream, chocolates, sandwiches, or Sprite. I was left in reasonable peace to enjoy the performance.

And enjoy it I did. Aladdin was a personable young woman with an upturned nose, a voice which could have been used to wake up patients coming round from their anaesthesia, and memorable thighs. Uncle Abanazer was played, Isolde told me, by an actor who portrayed a social worker with domestic problems in a long-running television series. Wishy and Washy did sing to electric guitars (deafeningly amplified) but Widow Twankey, played by a certain Jim Diamond, was all a Dame should be—a nimble little cockney, fitted up with a sizeable false bosom, a flaming red wig, sweeping eyelashes, and scarlet lips. Never have I heard the immortal line, "Where's that naughty boy Aladdin got to?" better delivered. I joined in loudly (Tristan and Isolde sat silent and embarrassed) when the Widow and Aladdin conducted us in the singing of "Please Don't Pinch My Tomatoes." It was, in fact and in fairness, all a traditional pantomime should be, and yet I had a vague feeling that something was wrong, that an element was missing. But, as the cast came down a white staircase in glittering costumes to enthusiastic applause, it seemed the sort of pantomime I'd grown up with and which Tristan and Isolde should be content to inherit.

After so much excitement I felt in need of a stiff brandy and soda, but the eatery the children had selected for their evening's entertainment had apparently gone teetotal and alcohol was not on the menu. Once they were confronted by their mammoth burgers and fries I made my excuses, said I'd be back in a moment, and slipped into a nearby pub which was, I noticed, opposite the stage door of the Empire.

As the life-giving draught was being poured I found myself standing next to Washy and Uncle Abanazer, now out of costume, who were discussing Jim the Dame. "Very unfriendly tonight," Washy said. "Locked himself in his dressing room before the show and wouldn't join us for a drink."

"Perhaps he's had a bust-up with Molly?"

"Unlikely. Molly and Jim never have a cross word."

"Lucky she's never found out he's been polishing Aladdin's wonderful lamp," Abanazer said, and they both laughed.

As I asked the girl behind the bar to refill my glass, in which the tide had sunk to a dangerous low, I heard them laugh again about the Widow Twankey's voluminous bosom. "Strapped-on polystyrene," Abanazer was saying. "Almost bruises me when I dance with her. Funny thing, tonight it was quite soft."

"Perhaps she borrowed one from a blow-up woman?" Washy was laughing as I gulped my brandy and legged it back to the hamburgers. In the dark passage outside the stage door I saw a small, nimble figure in hurried retreat—Jim Diamond, who for some reason hadn't wanted to join the boys at the bar.

After I had restored the children to the Erskine-Browns' au pair I sat in the Tube on my way back to Gloucester Road and read the programme. Jim Diamond, it seemed, had started his life in industry before taking up show business. He had a busy career in clubs and turned down appearances on television. "I only enjoy the living show," Jim says. "I want to have the audience where I can see them." His photograph, without the exaggerated female makeup, showed a pale, thin-nosed, in some way disagreeable little man with a lip curled either in scorn or triumph. I wondered how such an unfriendly-looking character could become an ebullient and warm-hearted widow. Stripped of his makeup, there was something about this comic's unsmiling face which brought back memories of another meeting in totally different circumstances. It was the second time within a few weeks that I had found an old familiar face cast in a new and unexpected part.

The memory I couldn't quite grasp preyed on my mind until I was tucked up in bed. Then, as Hilda's latest historical romance dropped from her weary fingers and she turned her back on me and switched out the light, I saw the face again quite clearly but in a different setting. Not Diamond. Sparker? No, Sparksman. A logical progression. Widow Twankey had been played by Harry Sparksman, a man who had trained as a professional entertainer, if my memory was correct, not in clubs, but in Her Majesty's prisons. It was, it seemed, an interesting career change, but I thought no more of it at the time and once satisfied with my identification I fell asleep.

"The boy couldn't have done it, Mr. Rumpole. Not a complicated bloody great job to that extent. His only way of getting at a safe was to dig it out of the wall and remove it bodily. He did that in a Barkingside boutique and what he found in it hardly covered the petrol. Young Denis couldn't have got into the Croydon supermarket peter. No one in our family could have."

Uncle Fred, the experienced and cautious head of the Timson clan, had no regard for the safe-breaking talents of Denis, his nephew, and, on the whole, an unskilled recruit in the Timson enterprise. The Croydon supermarket job had been highly complicated and expertly carried out and had yielded, for its perpetrators, thousands of pounds. Peanuts Molloy was arrested as one of the lookouts after falling and twisting an ankle when chased by a night watchman during the getaway. He said he didn't know any of the skilled operators who had engaged him except Denis Timson who, he alleged, was in general charge of the operation. Denis alone, he said, had silenced the burglar alarm and deftly penetrated the lock on the safe with an oxyacetylene blowtorch.

It has to be remembered though, that the clan Molloy had been sworn enemies of the Timson family from time immemorial. Peanuts's story sounded implausible when I met Denis Timson in the Brixton Prison interview room. A puzzled twenty-five-year-old with a shaven head and a poor attempt at a moustache, he seemed more upset by his Uncle Fred's low opinion of him than the danger of a conviction and subsequent prolonged absence from the family.

Denis's case was to come up for committal at the South London Magistrates' Court before "Skimpy" Simpson, whose lack of success at the Bar had driven him to a job as a stipendiary beak. His nickname had been earned by the fact that he had not, within living memory, been known to splash out on a round of drinks at Pommeroy's Wine Bar.

In the usual course of events, there is no future in fighting proceedings which are only there to commit the customer to trial. I had resolved to attend solely to pour a little well-deserved contempt on the testimony of Peanuts Molloy. As I started to prepare the case, I made a note of the date of the Croydon supermarket break-in. As soon as I had done so, I consulted my diary. I turned the virgin pages, as yet unstained by notes of trials, ideas for cross-examinations, splodges of tea, or spilled glasses of Pommeroy's Very Ordinary. It was as I had thought. While some virtuoso had been at work on the Croydon safe, I had been enjoying *Aladdin* in the company of Tristan and Isolde.

"Detective Inspector Grimble, would you agree that whoever blew the safe in the Croydon supermarket did an extraordinarily skillful job?"

"Mr. Rumpole, are we meant to congratulate your client on his professional skill?"

God moves in mysterious ways, and it wasn't Skimpy Simpson's fault that he was born with thin lips and a voice which sounded like the rusty hinge of a rusty gate swinging in the wind. I decided to ignore him and concentrate on a friendly chat with D.I. Grimble, a large, comfortable, ginger-haired officer. We had lived together, over the years, with the clan Timson and their misdoings. He was known to them as a decent and fair-minded cop, as disapproving of the younger, Panda-racing, evidence-massaging intake to the Force as they were of the lack of discretion and criminal skills which marked the younger Timsons.

"I mean the thieves were well informed. They knew that there would be a week's money in the safe."

"They knew that, yes."

"And was there a complex burglar alarm system? You couldn't put it out of action simply by cutting wires, could you?"

"Cutting the wires would have set it off."

"So putting the burglar alarm out of action would have required special skills?"

"It would have done."

"Putting it out of action also stopped a clock in the office. So we know that occurred at 8:45?"

"We know that. Yes."

"And at 9:20 young Molloy was caught as he fell while running to a getaway car."

"That is so."

"So this heavy safe was burnt open in a little over half an hour?"

"I fail to see the relevance of this, Mr. Rumpole." Skimpy was getting restless.

"I'm sure the officer does. That shows a very high degree of technical skill, doesn't it, Detective Inspector?"

"I'd agree with that."

"Exercised by a highly experienced peterman?"

"Who is this Mr. Peterman?" Skimpy was puzzled. "We haven't heard of him before."

"Not *Mr.* Peterman." I marvelled at the ignorance of the basic facts of life displayed by the magistrate. "A man expert at blowing safes, known to the trade as a 'peter,'" I told him and turned back to D.I. Grimble. "So we're agreed that this was a highly expert piece of work?"

"It must have been done by someone who knew his job pretty well. Yes."

"Denis Timson's record shows convictions for shoplifting,

bag-snatching, and stealing a radio from an unlocked car. In all of these simple enterprises, he managed to get caught."

"Your client's criminal record!" Skimpy looked happy for the first time. "You're allowing that to go into evidence, are you, Mr. Rumpole?"

"Certainly, Sir." I explained the obvious point. "Because there's absolutely no indication that he was capable of blowing a safe in record time, or silencing a complicated burglar alarm, is there, Detective Inspector?"

"No. There's nothing to show anything like that in his record . . ."

"Mr. Rumpole." Skimpy was looking at the clock; was he in danger of missing his usual train back home to Haywards Heath? "Where's all this heading?"

"Back a good many years," I told him, "to the Sweet-Home Building Society job at Carshalton, when Harry Sparksman blew a safe so quietly that even the dogs slept through it."

"You were in on that case, weren't you, Mr. Rumpole?" Inspector Grimble was pleased to remember. "Sparksman got five years."

"Not one of your great successes." Skimpy was also delighted. "Perhaps you wasted the Court's time with unnecessary questions. Have you anything else to ask this officer?"

"Not till the Old Bailey, Sir. I may have thought of a few more by then." With great satisfaction, Skimpy committed Denis Timson, a minor villain who would have had difficulty changing a fuse, let alone blowing a safe, for trial at the Central Criminal Court.

"Funny you mentioned Harry Sparksman. Do you know, the same thought occurred to me. An expert like him could've done that job in the time."

"Great minds think alike," I assured D.I. Grimble. We were washing away the memory of an hour or two before Skimpy with two pints of nourishing stout in the pub opposite the beak's Court.

"You know Harry took up a new career?" I needn't have asked the question. D.I. Grimble had a groupie's encyclopaedic knowledge of the criminal stars.

"Oh yes. Now a comic called Jim Diamond. Got up a concert party in the nick. Apparently gave him a taste for show business."

"I did hear," I took Grimble into my confidence, "that he made a comeback for the Croydon job." It had been a throwaway line from Uncle Fred Timson—"I heard talk they got Harry back out of retirement"—but it was a thought worth examining.

"I heard the same. So we did a bit of checking. But Sparksman, known as Diamond, has got a cast-iron alibi."

"Are you sure?"

"At the time when the Croydon job was done, he was performing in a pantomime. On stage nearly all the evening, it seems, playing the Dame."

"*Aladdin*," I said, "at the Tufnell Park Empire. It might be just worth your while to go into that alibi a little more thoroughly. I'd suggest you have a private word with Mrs. Molly Diamond. It's just possible she may have noticed his attraction to Aladdin's lamp."

"Now then, Mr. Rumpole." Grimble was wiping the froth from his lips with a neatly folded handkerchief. "You mustn't tell me how to do my job."

"I'm only trying to serve," I managed to look pained, "the interests of justice!"

"You mean, the interests of your client?"

"Sometimes they're the same thing," I told him, but I had to admit it wasn't often.

As it happened, the truth emerged without Detective Inspector Grimble having to do much of a job. Harry had, in fact, fallen victim to a tip-tilted nose and memorable thighs; he'd left home and moved into Aladdin's Kensal Rise flat. Molly, taking a terrible revenge, blew his alibi wide open.

She had watched many rehearsals and knew every word, every gag, every nudge, wink, and shrill complaint of the Dame's part. She had played it to perfection to give her husband an alibi while he went back to his old job in Croydon. It all went perfectly, even though Uncle Abanazer, dancing with her, had felt an unexpected softness.

I had known, instinctively, that something was very wrong. It had, however, taken some time for me to realize what I had really seen that night at the Tufnell Park Empire. It was nothing less than an outrage to a Great British Tradition. The Widow Twankey was a woman.

D.I. Grimble made his arrest and the case against Denis Timson was dropped by the Crown Prosecution Service. As spring came to the Temple gardens, Hilda opened a letter in the other case which had turned on the recognition of old, familiar faces and read it out to me.

"The repointing's going well on the tower and we hope to have it finished by Easter," Poppy Longstaff had written. "And I have to tell you, Hilda, the oil-fired heating has changed our lives. Eric says it's like living in the tropics. Cooking supper last night I had to peel off one of my cardigans." She Who Must Be Obeyed put down the letter from her old school friend and said, thoughtfully, "Noblesse oblige."

"What was that, Hilda?"

"I could tell at once that Donald Compton was a true gentleman. The sort that does good by stealth. Of course, poor old Eric thought he'd never get the tower mended, but I somehow felt that Donald wouldn't fail him. It was noblesse."

"Perhaps it was," I conceded, "but in this case the noblesse was Rumpole's."

"Rumpole! What on earth do you mean? You hardly paid to have the church tower repointed, did you?"

"In one sense, yes."

"I can't believe that. After all the years it took you to have the bathroom decorated. What on earth do you mean about your noblesse?"

"It'd take too long to explain, old darling. Besides, I've got a conference in Chambers. Tricky case of receiving stolen surgical appliances. I suppose," I added doubtfully, "it may lead, at some time in the distant future, to an act of charity."

Easter came, the work on the tower was successfully completed, and I was walking back to Chambers after a gruelling day down at the Bailey when I saw, wafting through the Temple cloisters, the unlikely apparition of the Rev. Eric Longstaff. He chirruped a greeting and said he'd come up to consult some legal brains on the proper investment of what remained of the Church Restoration Fund.

"I'm so profoundly grateful," he told me, "that I decided to invite you down to the rectory last Christmas."

"*You* decided?"

"Of course I did."

"I thought your wife Poppy extended the invitation to She . . . ."

"Oh yes. But I thought of the idea. It was the result of a good deal of hard knee-work and guidance from above. I knew you were the right man for the job."

"What job?"

"The Compton job."

What was this? The rector was speaking like an old con. The Coldsands caper? "What *can* you mean?"

"I just mean that I knew you'd defended Donald Compton. In a previous existence."

"How on earth did you know that?"

Eric drew himself up to his full, willowy height. "I'm not a prison visitor for nothing," he said proudly. "I thought you were just the chap to put the fear of God into him. You were the very person to put the squeeze on the Lord of the Manor."

"Put the squeeze on him?" Words were beginning to fail me.

"That was the idea. It came to me as a result of knee-work."

"So you brought us down to that freezing rectory just so I could blackmail the local benefactor?"

"Didn't it turn out well!"

"May the Lord forgive you."

"He's very forgiving."

"Next time," I spoke to the Man of God severely, "the Church can do its blackmailing for itself."

"Oh, we're quite used to that." The rector smiled at me in what I thought was a lofty manner. "Particularly around Christmas."

THE MURDERER AT THE FALLS

MICHAEL MALLORY

The continuous terrible roar of the Alpine falls sounded like a thousand angry lions trying to shout down a violent thunderstorm. With the noise came the incessant, swirling white mist, which penetrated the heaviest cloth and made one's flesh damp and clammy no matter how many layers were worn. But in spite of the deafening roar, in spite of the moist chill that caused him to secretly shiver, Sherlock Holmes remained motionless as a statue, stoically accepting the damp cold, completely still except for his darting eyes which took in the scene around him. Holmes was waiting, waiting for the solution to the final problem. Alone now—his companion having been summoned back down the mountain to the village of Meiringen through one of the most transparent hoaxes he had ever encountered—Holmes felt no fear; rather, a pulsating excitement.

His long and dangerous dance with the Napoleon of Crime was going to come to an end this very day, if not this very hour. Whether he would survive the final deadly tarantella was of secondary concern to him. More important was his determination to rid the world for once and all of the nefarious Professor James Moriarty.

In an instant, Holmes's thoughts were suddenly shattered by a new sound, one which cut through the din of the falls like a stiletto, a sound that Holmes recognized immediately as the scream of a man. A figure in black flashed past his field of vision. Whirling around, he was barely able to make out the form of a man, plummeting to the bottom of the hellish falls, where it was devoured by the white roiling water. In spite of himself, and against all logic, Holmes cried out, but the black-garbed apparition was gone.

Holmes's mind raced: Who was it that had fallen? Had it been Moriarty? Had he been robbed by fate of the ultimate conclusion? Then a terror even more fearsome than the infernal power of the Reichenbach Falls gripped him: how would he ever know for certain whether the falling man had indeed been Moriarty?

A rare cry of rage escaped from Holmes's lips, and he turned to start the descent back down the mountain. He had taken no more than three steps when he saw another figure a distance away, blocking his path. At first glance, Holmes believed it was his archenemy, awaiting him for the final battle. But when his keen eye fully recognized the man, he stopped cold, his mouth gaping in astonishment. "*You?*" Holmes cried.

"I've surprised you at last, eh, Holmes?" the other said, casually, wiping the moisture off of his moustache with a grey gloved hand.

"I had rather expected Professor Moriarty," the detective replied, raising his voice to be heard over the din of the waterfall.

"Oh, make no mistake, Moriarty was here, waiting for you. But I dispatched him."

"Then it was his body I witnessed being consumed by the water?"

The other nodded.

"It appears that you have accomplished what I came here to do," Holmes said, a tone of bitterness colouring his voice. "You have usurped not only my role in this drama but my destiny as well. You will forgive my rudeness if I do not thank you."

"I have become quite accustomed to your rudeness. Forgiveness, on the other hand, is another matter."

"Whatever do you mean?"

The man took a step towards Holmes. "I have completed only half of my task today."

Holmes's eyes narrowed. "By that I presume you mean that I am to join the Professor in that white hell below?"

"It is the only way," the other replied.

"The only way for what?"

"For my survival."

Holmes stared at the man then began to laugh, mirthlessly. "What threat do I pose to you?" he demanded. "I have done nothing to you except offer my hand in friendship, and perhaps bring you a taste of fame that would otherwise have been denied an undistinguished man of medicine."

The man with the moustache let that barb wash off of him in the spray of the falls. "Indeed you have brought me a measure of fame, but at a cost far greater than I ever wished to pay."

"Your personal problems are of little interest to me at the moment," Holmes sneered, starting to walk towards the other man. "Kindly step out of my way and disappear."

"I will not!" the other shouted, rushing the surprised detective and knocking him to the wet, rocky ground. The two powerful men grappled, tumbling dangerously close to the precipice.

"Do you not see, Holmes?" the other cried. "For years I have stood in the shadow of your singular genius, to the point where I have ceased to be my own man. It is a situation I can no longer put up with. I long to stand and run on my own two feet, not ride on the coat-tails of another. The time has come, Holmes. It is either you or I. It must end here."

"I suppose you feel no remorse for what you are attempting to perpetrate," Holmes spat, struggling against his opponent's unsuspected strength.

"None whatsoever," the other replied.

"And what of your oath as a healer?"

"To hell with it!"

A strained smile crossed the detective's thin lips. "Do not expect the world to forgive you, doctor."

Having pinned Holmes to the ground, the larger man sighed. "Conceited to the very last," he observed. "With all your cool, rational intelligence, you never realized that it was your own ego that would condemn you. This is the way it must be. I now bid you good-bye forever, Mr. Sherlock Holmes!"

With a sudden, powerful movement the man with the moustache clutched the detective to his breast, then rolled to the very edge of the precipice, where he let him go. Holmes's body slid over the edge, but he did not fall. Tightly clutching a jutting rock with one bloodied hand, Holmes kept himself suspended in air, in defiance of the terrible death that beckoned below. Holmes looked into the face of his killer and grimaced. "We are not yet finished, you and I," he cried.

"God, but you die hard!" the doctor shouted, trying to peel Holmes's thin fingers from the rock. At last he was successful, and for a moment the detective appeared to hang in the heavy, sodden air, exhibiting no more weight than an idea. Then at once he plummeted down, cartwheeling helplessly into the cloudy abyss. But a moment before he disappeared into the vicious, churning waters of Reichenbach Falls, the voice of Sherlock Holmes echoed back, *"I shall return!"*

The doctor shook his head. That damnable ego, that volcanic force of personality, which had all but overwhelmed his own. It had been that personality, and its refusal to stay contained, that had truly been the detective's undoing. "Nothing can bring you back now, Holmes," the doctor panted, "nothing."

He sat to catch his breath, then peered one last time down into the boiling white cauldron of water. Then, after rising and brushing the mud off his tweed suit as best he could and once more wiping the moisture from his waxed moustache, Dr. A. Conan Doyle started the trek down to the village of Meiringen, whistling as he went.

ACKNOWLEDGMENTS

A book like this—and truly, any book—is the product of many minds and many hands, all working together to ensure it sees the light of day. To say it took over twenty-five years to publish this collection is no exaggeration. This book would not have been possible without the help of our publishers and so many friends, family members, agents, editors, colleagues, and, of course, the hundreds of contributors who, over the last two and a half decades, have entrusted their work to *The Strand Magazine*.

We'd like to thank everyone at Blackstone Publishing for making this such a positive experience, especially Rick Bleiweiss; Anthony Goff; Stephanie Stanton; Josie Woodbridge; our cover designer, Larissa Ezell; Ananda Finwall; Riam Griswold; Rachel Sanders; Rebecca Malzahn; and the proofreaders, the typesetters, and everyone behind the scenes. It was Rick who came up with the idea that *The Strand*'s twenty-fifth anniversary should be marked by a collection of our best short stories; it was Anthony who, with unwavering support, gave that idea vision; and it was Ananda, Stephanie, and Larissa who helped make it a reality. Thanks also to Josh Stanton, CEO of Blackstone, who has fostered a culture focused on publishing exceptional books and prioritizing quality above all.

Our heartfelt thanks to all the authors, their agents, and their estates. Many thanks to the incomparable Alexander McCall Smith for the numerous stories he has contributed to *The Strand* and for writing the excellent foreword to this collection, and to master short story craftsman John Floyd for his loyalty, his friendship, and all the fantastic stories he has written for us over the last two and a half decades. A very big thank-you also to Ruth Ware, Michael Mallory, and Jeffery Deaver for their support and encouragement over the years. Ruth has consistently championed both *The Strand* and this book. Michael has been with us from the beginning and is always a source of insight and great stories. And Jeffery Deaver has never hesitated to say yes to any of our ideas, generously and wholeheartedly jumping in on every project we've proposed—including the 2011 quixotic collaborative novel *No Rest for the Dead*, which raised funds for the Leukemia & Lymphoma Society.

While Michael Bond, John Mortimer, Catherine Aird, Caroline Todd, and Ray Bradbury are sadly no longer with us, we have nothing but warm memories of their generosity, humor, and kindness. It's been a pleasure to highlight their wonderful work and versatility with this book. Their literary estates were kind and forthcoming, and we are so grateful to Karen Jankel of the Michael Bond estate; Penny Mortimer; Charles Todd; and Cristina Concepcion, who represents the estate of Ray Bradbury. We are also indebted to Valerie Borchardt, who represents the estate of Tennessee Williams.

Illustrators give life to great stories, and we're proud to have featured the work of many talented artists in *The Strand* over the years. But we would be remiss if we did not specifically thank Jeffrey B. McKeever, who, for most of the magazine's life, has been our own Sidney Paget—only in full color. Jeffrey's illustrations are not only striking but also deeply in tune with the stories they accompany. While we would typically highlight key plot points for our illustrators to capture, with Jeffrey, that only lasted for one issue. His intuitive grasp of narrative and his ability to pinpoint the most pivotal moment in any piece of fiction is so perfect, we learned to simply send him the full story and eagerly await the brilliant oil painting he'd deliver.

Thank you to our agent, Alec Shane of Writers House, for his faith in *The Strand*, his commitment to this book, and his unwavering guidance throughout the process. Many thanks also to Lukas Ortiz of the Philip G. Spitzer Literary Agency for his support and advice over the years and for securing permission to feature in this book the short stories by James Lee Burke and Michael Connelly. Our thanks as well to Heather Rizzo for her help with the Connelly permissions, and to Lorenzo Carcaterra, who for years has encouraged us to publish a collection of *The Strand*'s short stories. A special thank-you also to Anne Schluender and Christian Lewis, whose meticulous copyediting—at different stages in *The Strand*'s history—sharpened and strengthened its stories.

And finally, to our readers: Thank you for reading, subscribing, writing to us, and keeping *The Strand Magazine* alive. This book is for you.

—Andrew F. Gulli
and Lamia J. Gulli

ABOUT THE AUTHORS

MICHAEL CONNELLY was born in Philadelphia, PA, and is the bestselling author of forty novels and one work of nonfiction. With over eighty-nine million copies of his books sold worldwide and translations into forty-five languages, he is one of the most successful writers working today.

His debut novel, *The Black Echo*, won the prestigious Best First Novel Award from the Mystery Writers of America in 1992. Over the course of his career, his work has been honored with the Diamond Dagger from the CWA in 2018 and the Outstanding Contribution to Crime Writing Award from Theakston's Old Peculier Crime Writing Festival in Harrogate, England, in 2022. He was also named a Grand Master by the Mystery Writers of America in 2023.

Two of Connelly's novels have been adapted for the screen: *Blood Work* (2002), directed by and starring Clint Eastwood, and *The Lincoln Lawyer* (2011), with Matthew McConaughey as Mickey Haller. Connelly serves as executive producer of *Bosch* and *Bosch: Legacy*—Amazon Studios original drama series based on his bestselling character Harry Bosch. He is also executive producer of *The Lincoln Lawyer* on Netflix, starring Manuel Garcia-Rulfo as Mickey Haller, as well as the documentary films *Sound of Redemption: The Frank Morgan Story* and *Tales of the American*. He created and hosts the podcasts *Murder Book* and *The Wonderland Murders & The Secret History of Hollywood*.

His recent *New York Times* bestsellers include *The Waiting*, *Resurrection Walk*, *Desert Star*, *The Dark Hours*, *The Law of Innocence*, *The Night Fire*, and *Dark Sacred Night*. He divides his time between California and Florida.

JEFFERY DEAVER is an international number one bestselling author whose novels have appeared on bestseller lists around the world. His books are sold in 150 countries and have been translated into twenty-five languages. A two-term president of Mystery Writers of America, he was recently named a Grand Master by the organization, joining the ranks of Agatha Christie, Ellery Queen, Mary Higgins Clark, and Walter Mosley.

The author of fifty novels, more than one hundred short stories, a nonfiction book on the law, and the lyrics of a country-western album, Deaver has received—or been short-listed for—dozens of awards. *The Bodies Left Behind* was named Novel of the Year by the International Thriller Writers, while *The Broken Window* and *Edge* were also finalists. He won the CWA's Steel Dagger for *The Garden of Beasts* and its Short Story Dagger for his short fiction, with another story short-listed for the same prize. He has been nominated eight times for an Edgar Award by Mystery Writers of America.

Deaver has received numerous lifetime achievement honors, including those from the Bouchercon World Mystery Convention, *The Strand Magazine*, and the Raymond Chandler Award in Italy.

Several of his works have been adapted for the screen: *A Maiden's Grave* was made into an HBO movie starring James Garner and Marlee Matlin; *The Bone Collector* was turned into a feature film starring Denzel Washington and Angelina Jolie; and an adaptation of *The Devil's Teardrop* aired on Lifetime. His Lincoln Rhyme series was adapted into the NBC drama *Lincoln Rhyme: Hunt for the Bone Collector*. More recently, *The Never Game*—featuring his character Colter Shaw—was adapted as the CBS series *Tracker*.

JAMES LEE BURKE is an American author best known for his mysteries, particularly the Dave Robicheaux series. He has twice received the Edgar Award for Best Novel, for *Black Cherry Blues* in 1990 and *Cimarron Rose* in 1998.

Burke was born in Houston, Texas, but grew up on the Texas–Louisiana Gulf Coast. He attended the University of Louisiana at Lafayette and the University of Missouri, receiving a BA and MA from the latter. He has worked at a wide variety of jobs over the years, including as an oil lease negotiator, a reporter, and a social worker. He was writer in residence at the University of Louisiana at Lafayette, succeeding his good friend and posthumous Pulitzer Prize winner John Kennedy Toole, and preceding Ernest Gaines in the position. Shortly before his move to Montana, he taught for several years in the creative writing program at Wichita State University in the 1980s.

Burke and his wife, Pearl, split their time between Lolo, Montana, and New Iberia, Louisiana.

SIR ALEXANDER MCCALL SMITH is the author of over 120 books that have been published throughout the world. His best-known series is the *No. 1 Ladies' Detective Agency* series, of which twenty-five volumes have been published to date. Translated into over forty languages, these books became a successful television series and film under the direction of the late Anthony Minghella. His many other works of fiction include the world's longest-running serial novel, the *44 Scotland Street* series. The *44 Scotland Street* books are published on a daily basis in *The Scotsman* and then appear in book form. There are seventeen volumes to date.

He has received numerous awards for his writing, including the American Academy of Arts Medal for Literature, the Lifetime Award of the Scottish cultural organization the Saltire Society, the

UK Author of the Year Award, and honorary degrees from thirteen universities in Europe and North America.

JOHN M. FLOYD is the author of more than a thousand short stories in publications like *Strand Magazine*, *Alfred Hitchcock's Mystery Magazine*, *Ellery Queen's Mystery Magazine*, *The Saturday Evening Post*, *Best American Mystery Stories* (2015, 2018, and 2020), and *Best Mystery Stories of the Year* (2021 and 2024). A former Air Force captain and IBM systems engineer, John is also an Edgar nominee, a Shamus Award winner, a six-time Derringer Award winner, a past recipient of the Edward D. Hoch Memorial Golden Derringer for Lifetime Achievement, and the author of nine books. He and his wife, Carolyn, live in Mississippi.

JOYCE CAROL OATES is a recipient of a National Humanities Medal awarded by President Barack Obama, the National Book Critics Circle's Ivan Sandrof Lifetime Achievement Award, the National Book Award for Fiction, the Jerusalem Prize, the Prix Femina, and the Cino Del Duca World Prize, and is a five-time finalist for the Pulitzer Prize. She has written some of the most enduring fiction of our time, including the bestsellers *Blonde* and *We Were the Mulvaneys*. She is the Roger S. Berlind '52 Distinguished Professor of the Humanities Emerita at Princeton University and a member of the American Academy of Arts and Letters. In 2024 she won the Raymond Chandler lifetime achievement award given to "a master of the thriller and noir literary genre."

JONATHAN RABB is the author of the novels *Among the Living* (a finalist for the 2018 Townsend Prize for Fiction), *The Second Son*, *Shadow and Light*, *Rosa* (winner of the Director's Prize at Semana Negra, 2006), *The Book of Q*, and *The Overseer*. He has published short fiction and nonfiction in a number of magazines and journals, including the *Oxford American*, *Lit Hub*, *Huffington Post*, *Opera News*, and the *Journal of Interdisciplinary History*. He originated the role of Fermat in the off-Broadway production of *Fermat's Last Tango* and has soloed with the New York Pops at Carnegie Hall, the Albany Symphony, and the Harrisburg Symphony, among others. He has taught at NYU and Columbia and is currently a professor of writing at the Savannah College of Art and Design (SCAD).

ANDREW CROWLEY lives in Toronto with his wife and daughters. His short fiction has appeared most recently in *The Magazine of Fantasy & Science Fiction*, and "Peephole" was his first published story. The idea for it came during a bout of insomnia: "I wanted to capture the feeling of a waking nightmare. I thought if I could commit it to paper, maybe I could finally get to sleep, so I wrote 'Peephole' without any plans to get it published. It did help, and I did get to sleep, and some months later I sent it in to *The Strand* and was very pleased to have it published under one of those great, dark *Strand* covers that captured that middle-of-night atmosphere so well. It's an honor to have 'Peephole' appear in *The Strand*'s twenty-fifth-anniversary collection."

MICHAEL BOND, CBE, was born in Newbury, Berkshire, on January 13, 1926. He started writing while serving in the British Army and stationed in Cairo at the end of World War II, but it was over a decade later, while working as a television cameraman for the BBC, that he was inspired to start writing stories about a small bear found on a London railway platform.

Although best known for his books about Paddington Bear, Michael Bond wrote many other stories for children, including a number of books about his daughter's guinea pig, Olga da Polga, and two television series: *The Herbs* and *The Adventures of Parsley*.

In 1983, he turned his hand to adult fiction and published the first in a series of eighteen humorous detective novels about Monsieur Pamplemousse, an ex-member of the French Sûreté turned food guide inspector, and his faithful bloodhound, Pommes Frites.

In 2007, despite having left school at the age of fourteen without a single academic qualification to his name, Michael Bond was granted an honorary degree of Doctor of Letters by Reading University. Eight years later, he was awarded a CBE in the Queen's Birthday Honours list for his services to children's literature.

Michael Bond continued to write every day of his life until he died at his home in London on June 27, 2017. He was honored with a memorial service in Saint Paul's Cathedral and is laid to rest, very appropriately, in Paddington Old Cemetery.

JO NESBØ is a musician, songwriter, screenwriter, and economist, as well as one of the leading crime writers in the world. He is recognized for having widened the scope of the thriller with his unusual literary qualities and ambitions, his psychological insights, and his in-depth knowledge of life in a modern, globalized world. His books have garnered countless international awards, sold more than sixty million copies, and been translated into fifty-one languages. In addition to the Harry Hole series and the *Kingdom* diptych, Nesbø is the author of several stand-alone novels as well as the children's books in the *Doctor Proctor's Fart Powder* series.

H. G. WELLS (1866–1946) earned a reputation as "a prophet of his time," thanks to groundbreaking classics such as *The Time Machine*, *The Invisible Man*, and *The War of the Worlds*. Born into humble beginnings in Kent, England, Wells rose to become one of the most widely read and influential authors of the twentieth century. A true polymath, he wrote across genres—from speculative fiction to political commentary—and found enormous success with his nonfiction work *The Outline of History*. His works have been adapted numerous times, including the 2005 blockbuster

War of the Worlds directed by Steven Spielberg, the 2020 horror reimagining of *The Invisible Man*, and various BBC and streaming adaptations of *The Time Machine*. In addition to his many short stories, Wells's visionary themes continue to resonate, securing his legacy as a pioneer of science fiction and modern thought.

LAURA BENEDICT is the Edgar and ITW Thriller Award–nominated author of eight novels of mystery and suspense, including *The Stranger Inside* and the *Bliss House* gothic series. In addition to *The Strand Magazine*, Benedict's short fiction has appeared in publications such as *Ellery Queen's Mystery Magazine*, *Mystery Tribune*, and numerous anthologies. When she's not writing, Laura teaches writing workshops and edits fiction for emerging writers from her home in the Midwest.

SHIRLEY JACKSON was born in San Francisco on December 14, 1916. She first received wide critical acclaim for "The Lottery," which was published in *The New Yorker* in 1948 and went on to become one of the most anthologized stories in American literature. She is the author of six novels, including *The Haunting of Hill House* and *We Have Always Lived in the Castle*; two bestselling family memoirs, *Life Among the Savages* and *Raising Demons*; hundreds of short stories, many published in five collections; several children's books; and two plays. An extraordinary compilation of her personal correspondence was recently published as *The Letters of Shirley Jackson*. For many years she lived in North Bennington, Vermont, with her husband, the renowned literary critic Stanley Edgar Hyman, and their four children. She died on August 8, 1965.

MARK MOWER is a crime writer and historian whose fascination with Sherlock Holmes and Dr. Watson began at the age of twelve, after watching an early black-and-white film featuring the iconic screen duo of Basil Rathbone and Nigel Bruce. Mark quickly sought out the original stories by Sir Arthur Conan Doyle and tracked down every film and television adaptation he could find, and his interest soon became a lifelong passion.

A member of the Crime Writers' Association, the Sherlock Holmes Society of London, and the Solar Pons Society of London, Mark has written numerous crime books and contributed to over twenty Holmes anthologies, including *The MX Book of New Sherlock Holmes Stories* (MX Publishing), *The Book of Extraordinary New Sherlock Holmes Stories* (Conari Press), and *Sherlock Holmes: Before Baker Street* (Belanger Books). His own Holmes titles include *A Farewell to Baker Street*, *Sherlock Holmes: The Baker Street Case-Files*, *Sherlock Holmes: The Baker Street Legacy*, and *Sherlock Holmes: The Baker Street Epilogue* (all published by MX Publishing).

Mark is also the author of several nonfiction works, such as *Zeppelin over Suffolk: The Final Raid of the L48* (Pen & Sword Books), *Bloody British History: Norwich* (the History Press), and *Foul Deeds and Suspicious Deaths in Suffolk* (Wharncliffe Books). His essays have appeared in over thirty publications, including *Mobile Holmes: Transportation in the Sherlockian Canon* (Baker Street Irregulars) and *Truly Criminal: A Crime Writers' Association Anthology of True Crime* (the History Press).

LORENZO CARCATERRA is the author of fifteen books—*A Safe Place*, *Sleepers*, *Apaches*, *Gangster*, *Street Boys*, *Paradise City*, *Chasers*, *Midnight Angels*, *The Wolf*, *Three Dreamers*, and the Nonna Maria cozy trilogy. He was the managing editor for the five-season run of the CBS series *Top Cops* and was a writer/producer for *Law & Order*. He has contributed short stories to a number of anthologies and has published articles in *National Geographic Traveler*, *The New York Times Magazine*, and *Reader's Digest*.

He lives in New York City with his English bulldog Rocco, travels to Italy as often as he can, spends fun times with his two grandsons, and works out every day—allowing him to drink more wine than he should in the evenings. He is currently at work on his next novel—*The Collectors*.

RAY BRADBURY (1920–2012) was the author of more than three dozen books, including such classics as *Fahrenheit 451*, *The Martian Chronicles*, *The Illustrated Man*, *Dandelion Wine*, and *Something Wicked This Way Comes*, as well as hundreds of short stories. He wrote for theater, cinema, and TV, including the screenplay for John Huston's *Moby Dick* and the Emmy Award–winning teleplay *The Halloween Tree*, and adapted for television sixty-five of his stories for *The Ray Bradbury Theater*. He was the recipient of the 2000 National Book Foundation's Medal for Distinguished Contribution to American Letters, the 2007 Pulitzer Prize Special Citation, and numerous other honors.

P. G. WODEHOUSE was an expert humorist and master of light verse. He was born in Guildford, Surrey, in 1881 and educated at Dulwich College in south London. After a spell in a bank, he then spent some years freelancing as a journalist. During a literary career spanning over seventy years, he wrote more than ninety books and twenty film scripts and collaborated on more than thirty plays and musical comedies. The first of many visits to the US took place in 1904, and he moved there permanently in 1947, settling in Southampton, NY, gaining citizenship in 1955. Sir Pelham Wodehouse died on Saint Valentine's Day, 1975, at the age of ninety-three.

RUTH WARE lives with her family in Sussex, on the south coast of England. She is the number one *New York Times* and *Globe and Mail* (Toronto) bestselling author of *In a Dark, Dark Wood*; *The Lying Game*; *The Death of Mrs. Westaway*; *The Turn of the Key*; *One by One*; *The It Girl*; *Zero Days*; *One Perfect Couple*; and *The Woman in Cabin 10*, which comes to Netflix as a movie starring Keira Knightley in the fall of 2025. Ruth's sequel, *The Woman in Suite 11*, will be published in July 2025. Visit her at RuthWare.com and follow her on socials @RuthWareWriter.

KIRA PEIKOFF is the author of *Baby X*, *Mother Knows Best*, *Living Proof*, *No Time to Die*, and *Die Again Tomorrow*. She has a degree in journalism from New York University and a master's in bioethics from Columbia. Her articles have appeared in *The New York Times*, *Newsweek*, *Popular Mechanics*, and other outlets.

ZOË SHARP is a neurodiverse autodidact who opted out of mainstream education at the age of twelve and wrote her first novel at fifteen. She created her award-winning crime thrillers featuring ex–Special Forces trainee turned bodyguard Charlotte "Charlie" Fox after receiving death threats in the course of her work as a photojournalist. She began making a living from writing in 1988, and since 2001 has penned various novels: the long-running Charlie Fox series, including a prequel novella; the Blake & Byron mystery series; the McColl & Weston psychological thrillers set in the English Lake District; stand-alone crime novels; and collaborations with espionage thriller author John Lawton, as well as numerous highly acclaimed short stories. Her work has been used in school textbooks in Denmark, inspired an original song and music video, and been optioned for TV and film. www.ZoeSharp.com

CATHERINE AIRD (1930–2024) was the acclaimed author of more than twenty detective novels and three short story collections, most of which feature the quietly brilliant Detective Inspector C. D. Sloan and his earnest foil, Detective Constable W. E. Crosby. Aird held an honorary master's degree from the University of Kent and was appointed an MBE in 1998. In recognition of her significant contribution to crime writing she was awarded the Crime Writers' Association Diamond Dagger in 2015.

R. L. STINE is one of the best-selling children's authors in history. Goosebumps, which recently celebrated its thirtieth anniversary, has more than four hundred million books in print in thirty-two languages. The Goosebumps series made R. L. Stine a worldwide publishing celebrity (and frequent *Jeopardy!* and crossword answer) and has inspired two hit television series and two feature films starring Jack Black. His other popular children's book series include Fear Street (the inspiration for four feature films on Netflix), Mostly Ghostly, the Nightmare Room, and Rotten School. In 2024, Stine received a Grand Master lifetime achievement award from the Mystery Writers of America. R. L. Stine lives in New York City with his wife, Jane, a former editor and publisher.

WALTER MOSLEY is the author of over sixty novels, nonfiction books, memoirs, and plays. His work has been translated into twenty-five languages. He is the winner of numerous awards, including an O. Henry Award, the Mystery Writers of America's Grand Master Award, a Grammy, several Edgars, several NAACP Image Awards, and PEN America's Lifetime Achievement Award. In 2020 he was named the recipient of the Robert Kirsch Award for lifetime achievement from the Los Angeles Times Festival of Books and was awarded the Distinguished Contribution to American Letters Award from the National Book Foundation. He divides his time between New York and California.

SAMANTHA LOKAI is originally from the Caribbean and is now based in England. She writes dark fiction, incorporating elements of neo-noir, suspense, gothic, and horror. Her work has appeared in *Strand Magazine* and various anthologies, including *Dangerous Waters: Deadly Women of the Sea*, *Crimson Bones*, and *The Horror That Represents You*. As a lover of the strange and unusual and an enthusiast of all things retro and vintage, she has a deep appreciation for the charm of bygone eras, and this often influences her work.

You can connect with her on Twitter @samanthaslk1 and Instagram @samanthaslwrites for updates on future publications, or email samanthaslkmail@gmail.com.

CHARLES TODD is the *New York Times* bestselling author of the Inspector Ian Rutledge series and the Bess Crawford series. *A Christmas Witness* (Ian Rutledge Mystery) is due October 21, 2025, followed by *A Day of Judgment* (Ian Rutledge Mystery) in spring 2026 and a new Bess Crawford mystery. He has published over forty titles, including two stand-alone novels, an anthology, and twenty short stories appearing in mystery magazines and anthologies worldwide. His works have received the Mary Higgins Clark, Agatha, and Barry Awards and nominations for other major awards. He was a guest of honor at Killer Nashville, Malice Domestic, and Bouchercon in 2025.

TENNESSEE WILLIAMS (1911–1983), one of the twentieth century's most superb writers, was also one of its most successful and prolific. His classic works include *Cat on a Hot Tin Roof, A Streetcar Named Desire, The Glass Menagerie, Summer and Smoke, Camino Real, Sweet Bird of Youth, Night of the Iguana, Orpheus Descending*, and *The Rose Tattoo*.

JAMES DORR's *Avoid Seeing a Mouse and Other Tales of The Real and Surreal* was published in January 2024 by Alien Buddha Press. His previous works include *The Tears of Isis* (a 2013 Bram Stoker Award nominee for fiction collection), *Tombs: A Chronicle of Latter-Day Times of Earth*, and *Vamps (A Retrospective)*, an all-poetry volume. Specializing in dark fantasy and horror, with forays into mystery and science fiction, Dorr has been a technical writer, an editor on a regional magazine, a full-time nonfiction freelancer, and a semiprofessional musician. He currently harbors a goth cat named Triana and counts among his major influences Ray Bradbury, Edgar Allan Poe, Allen Ginsberg, and Bertolt Brecht.

SIR JOHN MORTIMER was a novelist, playwright, and barrister. The first book featuring his most famous character, Horace Rumpole, was published by Penguin in 1980, and Mortimer went on to publish a dozen collections of Rumpole stories as well as a handful of novels, culminating in 2007 in *Rumpole Misbehaves*. He was knighted in 1998 for his services to the arts and died in January 2009.

MICHAEL MALLORY is the author of the Amelia Watson ("The Second Mrs. Watson") and Dave Beauchamp mystery series, and the stand-alone novels *The Mural*, *Death Walks Skid Row*, *Ebeneezer Scrooge and the Battle for Christmas*, and *The Ambulance*. His short stories—some two hundred to date—have been published everywhere from *Ellery Queen's Mystery Magazine* to *Fox Kids Magazine*. His story "What the Cat Dragged In," first published in *The Strand Magazine*, was selected for inclusion in *The Mysterious Bookshop Presents the Best Mystery Stories of the Year 2023*.

In the realm of nonfiction, Mike has authored eleven books on popular culture subjects, including the bestselling *Universal Studios Monsters: A Legacy of Horror*, and more than six hundred articles for scores of publications including *Variety*, the *Los Angeles Times*, *Animation Magazine*, *The Hollywood Reporter*, and *Mystery Scene*. A former actor whose credits include the television shows *Mad Men*, *Parks and Recreation*, *Vegas*, *Mob City*, and *Angie Tribeca*, Mike lives in the Greater Los Angeles area.

ABOUT THE EDITORS

ANDREW F. GULLI is managing editor of *The Strand Magazine*. He is also the coeditor of *No Rest for the Dead*, a thriller written by twenty-six internationally bestselling authors, including David Baldacci, Tess Gerritsen, Jeffery Deaver, Kathy Reichs, and Alexander McCall Smith.

LAMIA J. GULLI is fiction editor at *The Strand Magazine*. Along with her brother Andrew, she is the coeditor of *No Rest for the Dead*. She lives in Detroit, Michigan.